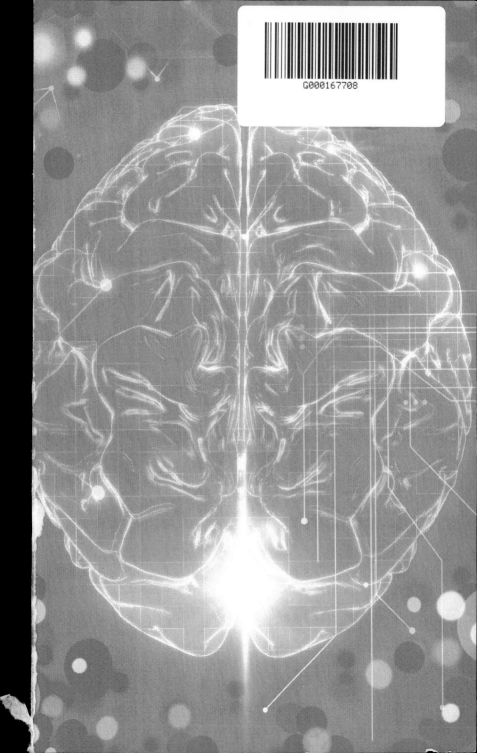

LYNN
WATSON

SECRETS
OF
BLUE
AND
GOLD

Matador
9 Priory Business Park,
Wistow Road, Kibworth Beauchamp,
Leicestershire. LE8 0RX
Tel: 0116 279 2299
Email: books@troubador.co.uk
Web: www.troubador.co.uk/matador
Twitter: @matadorbooks

ISBN 978 1789013 498

British Library Cataloguing in Publication Data.
A catalogue record for this book is available from the British Library.

Printed and Bound in the UK by 4Edge Limited
Typeset in 11pt Minion Pro by Troubador Publishing Ltd, Leicester, UK

Matador is an imprint of Troubador Publishing Ltd

For Rob, Jay and Lani
and with sincere thanks to all my curious early readers

Chapter 1

She stirred the mottled froth of her coffee until the perfect leaf pattern dissolved into a long swirl and vanished. As she looked around before surreptitiously licking the spoon, the man at the next table leaned towards her. She took in his smart navy jacket and thick but well-tended grey eyebrows.

'Would you mind keeping an eye on my things while I step outside for a quick call?'

'No, that's fine. I'm in no rush.'

He left his leather man bag lying on the table beside an open laptop, a wire-bound notepad covered in squiggles and a stylish fountain pen. There was something half-jutting out of the bag – a wallet or card holder, was it?

Looking again at the sleek black pen, she felt a familiar shiver. Bad idea; she jolted her head to shake it off. The dark-haired woman sitting near the window, the only person she had noticed when she entered the café, was staring at her. Their eyes met and blood rushed to Fran's cheeks. Had she behaved oddly or acted suspicious? No, it was a passing thought, nothing more. She was dutifully looking after someone else's property. The woman let her gaze wander before she glanced across again, offering a cryptic smile, almost playful, while the man with the eyebrows returned to his table and mouthed a quick 'Thank you.'

She had to get a grip, once and for all. She couldn't afford to blow it, screw up her new life in London. The impulse was weaker now, thankfully. She had never seen a therapist but had long assumed that the snatching – stealing, let's face it – was linked to her first memory: the screeching of tyres or brakes and the figure of a man in a helmet flying through the air, limbs outstretched; a motorbike on its side by the wall; her dad sweeping her up and passing her to a stranger, toddler legs kicking wildly in protest. And before that indelible sequence, in the lost and critical opening scene scattered in pieces on the cutting-room floor of her mind, the proof that it was all her fault.

There were some things you couldn't just chuck out or hand in at the charity shop when you moved home, whether it was your fault or not. And some unbidden thoughts that tended to bubble up at exactly the wrong moment. She was here now though, in a small café in a part of London in a corner of the universe where no one knew her – except perhaps Ned, a little.

She looked over to the window table and then through the glass door to the visible stretch of pavement. The dark-haired woman had disappeared, slipped away without her noticing. It was time to go, anyway; she could sit here all day but she had set out on a circular walk, to see if she could find a new route back along the river.

The quaint row of shops made her think of a stage set or a children's model village – the French patisserie café, an old-style butcher, fishmonger and greengrocer, a bijou dress shop called Frocks and Chocs and a fancy jeweller's

2

dealing in beautiful new and second-hand pieces. There were also the ubiquitous estate agents and charity shops, plus a hair salon and a tattoo parlour, but in this setting even they managed to project a kind of traditional charm.

Once again, the striking window display in the dress boutique made her stop and look. Two mannequins modelled red and purple frocks, while scarves and lingerie items were draped across a mirrored dressing table, a chest of drawers and carved wooden chairs. In between the clothes, there were white boxes of chocolates arranged across the furniture and floor space, some with lids open and others closed, wrapped with purple or red ribbons. She wondered if they changed the ribbon colours to match the dresses in the window. It was a funky name, Frocks and Chocs; she liked it. Now all she needed was a special occasion to justify splashing out on a new outfit.

***

Lying on her side, one knee resting on the other, she yielded to the silkiness of the pillows, which insisted on curling up around her head instead of staying firm and flat like her less plush ones at home. She rolled onto her back and stretched her arms towards the high blue ceiling, fingers and thumbs splayed wide and peach nails gleaming in the shaft of light that fell through the half-open door into Ned's bedroom.

Along the length of one wall, there was a high black shelf displaying a row of hats. Fran brought her hands down together, gently deflating the duvet under its striped cover, while her eyes scanned the shelf and she named each hat in a near-silent whisper: fedora, trilby, top, bowler, panama, sombrero, homburg, cowboy, deerstalker, military beret, fez, porkpie, Cossack, tricorn, boater, wizard and finally, in the near corner, a pirate hat with red feather and glow-painted skull and crossbones.

Did Ned wear any of these hats, and did he have a special favourite? The brown fedora, perhaps, together with the stone-coloured trench coat he had on the first time she saw him, waiting at the door to the pub with his collar turned up against the teeming rain. The image of the long coat and fedora fitted with her idea that there was something more secret agent than estate agent about Ned, although he said he owned and rented out properties – flats, houses and industrial units spread across South London – and she had no good reason to doubt it.

She felt for her phone on the unfamiliar bedside table. It was almost nine, time for dinner. Turning towards the middle of the bed, she contemplated the rounded muscles of Ned's exposed upper arm and shoulder, the prominent ridge of his spine and the well-defined hairline across the back of his neck. Was it just her who found this part of a man so alluring, wanting to run her fingers along the edge of his hair or ruffle it up if possible, twirling any relic of a duck's tail? She would ask Judi about it, if they still had time left to talk. Judi was fading fast. And as for long-haired men, the seriously long-haired ones, that was a while ago now.

Her hand reached out and touched Ned's hair, first at the nape of his neck and then the light downy growths beneath his ears that had escaped or been spared the razor. It was a rich brown, with scattered flecks of grey. How old was he – mid forties, a little younger, older? He murmured at her fingertip caress, stirring and smiling sleepily, she imagined, although she couldn't see his face. Propping herself up on her elbows and looking across the duvet to the end of the bed, she saw that his feet were suspended over the edge, even though his knees were bent.

When he surfaced, it would be quick showers and dressing for dinner in the velvety twin bathrobes. This already felt like an established ritual, although she had only been to the flat four times, including tonight. Ned would have the ingredients laid out on the granite kitchen counter or chilling in his up-to-the-minute smart fridge, so he could just spin them together and serve up the meal in half an hour.

'It's the fridge that decides what to make. It's got all the ideas and recipes and I don't argue. I'm in love with it.'

His bedroom was blue and manly, decorated by a stained-glass lamp with a stem of twisted snakes, and a wooden hatstand with assorted umbrellas, walking sticks and squash racquets propped around it. An open wardrobe took up an entire wall and held a large collection of clothes and shoes, arranged by colour and season. There were two guitars on hooks, black-and-white photos of a semi-naked couple above the bed, and the obligatory bachelor-pad dumbbells, two pairs, stacked in the corner.

'Hey you, still here? Are you ready to eat?'

He had finally come to and was looking up at her from the sea of pillows. His eyes were light brown, with a fan of deep creases at each side.

'Yes, that'd be wonderful.' She sat up properly. 'I'm ravenous, now you mention it; I can't think why.'

He gave her a butterfly kiss on the forearm, his long eyelashes fluttering on her skin. 'You're a very sexy woman, do you know that?'

She stretched up her arms again and nestled further under the duvet. 'You're quite cute yourself, Mr Hat Man. You'll have to give me a fashion show one evening – just the hats, nothing else.'

'Sounds like fun – I'll speak to my agent and see what we can offer.'

She watched as he swivelled his legs to sit on the side of the bed, then leant down to gather up the crimson robes that lay spreadeagled on the floor. Handing her the smaller one, he stood up, being careful to allow her a few glimpses as he fumbled to find the sleeves of the robe, shook his shoulders into it, straightened the collar, pulled the sides firmly across and tied the belt. She dismissed the lingering thought that they might come back to bed after dinner. The pattern and tone of their evenings was set now and she wasn't inclined to disturb the rhythm.

It was pasta tonight, linguini with thinly sliced beef and a colourful mix of vegetables, all beautifully chopped. She sat on a high bar stool with a bowl of cashew nuts cradled in her lap. It was pretty good so far, living in London, totally different from before and a far more positive start than she had dared to imagine.

'You chop like a proper chef,' she said, pointing with salty fingers towards the tightly packed rows of onion and the red and green pepper slices waiting to slide gracefully into the frying pan with the sizzling beef.

'Well, it was my first thing, catering, when I dropped out of school at seventeen and came to the city to seek my fortune. I found a live-in job at a hotel; not one of the well-known ones and it closed down years ago and was turned into flats. Funnily enough, I now own three of them.'

'Three of the flats, you own them, really? It must have worked for you, then.'

'Yep, you could say that. My peppers are always perfectly chopped, that's for sure, and I'd challenge anyone to beat me in a race to slice the perfect carrot without ending up with half a finger.'

She raised her wine glass. 'I'll lay a bet on it. You're the first super-chopper I've met. You must give me a masterclass one day and I'll return the favour.'

He turned and laid down the stirring spoon to clink glasses with her, right arms intertwined to bring their faces together. In the bright yet warm light of the ultra-modern kitchen, she noticed for the first time the specks of wildcat-yellow in his hazel irises.

'What's *your* hidden talent then, Fran? What do you want to teach me?'

'Hold on, I'm not sure, thinking about it. It'll have to be good, to match your prowess with the carrots. Maybe I won't say just yet, keep you guessing.'

'Okay, as long as I have the option of refusing. I won't leap from a great height, for a start, or explore an underwater cave, even if the fish are fabulously beautiful.'

'God, no way; nothing would induce me to jump out of a plane or dive off a cliff. It's hard enough avoiding free fall in everyday life. The deep-sea cave idea, though, I like that.'

They moved through to the sitting room with its two large bay windows. The flat looked down on a tree-lined

7

street, where a middle-aged couple walked arm in arm and a passing group of young men ranged loosely across the pavement and into the middle of the road. The trees were heavy with white blossom and spring-green foliage, which obscured the view sufficiently for Ned to leave the curtains half-open. Fran sat down, closed her eyes and took in the aromas of garlic, basil and superior red wine. A fun, self-indulgent evening – nothing complicated, just as she wanted it.

After dinner, while they were loading the dishwasher, Ned began to talk about his teenage daughters, who lived in Paris with their mother and whom he saw very infrequently because his ex-wife did whatever she could to sabotage his visits. The older daughter was keen to have more contact but the younger one was resistant and avoided communication as far as possible.

Fran turned on the tap and squeezed washing-up liquid into the sink to soak the pans, while watching her reflection in the dark glass of the window. Ignoring the yellow plastic gloves, she made her hands disappear in the soapy water and gazed downwards, as if entranced by the suds and exposed pan handles. Ned's ex would tell the same story very differently, of course; or an entirely different story, and one that would inevitably change shape over time.

The evening ended, as usual, with coffee in delicate china cups, broken-off pieces of dark chocolate and background jazz music, sitting one each end of the enormous U-shaped sofa. He drove her home and they stayed quiet, wrapped in their thoughts throughout the ten-minute journey. She fiddled with her phone in the top pocket of her bag, thinking there might be an upbeat message from one of her children, Max and Chaddy, or that Judi might have called again, which she guiltily half-dreaded.

Ned had shown an odd lack of curiosity about her family and previous life, or about what she might be doing now for work. He had skipped all the usual introductory questions. But then again, it didn't feel that odd. It followed the unspoken terms of their relationship and she was happy with it, happy to play in the shallows. She hadn't invited him into her home yet and, for whatever reason, she preferred them to meet on his territory. The arrangement was for him to drive over and pick her up around seven, sending a ten-minute alert to her phone. When he arrived, she was waiting inside her front door with a bottle of wine and bar of chocolate – orange, mint or ginger for preference – intrigued and excited at the prospect of their next four hours together, each hour lightly spiced, amusing and delicious.

***

It was early on a Monday morning, with office workers streaming towards the tube station and shop staff reeling out the striped awnings and organising their trays of fresh produce, flowers in metal buckets and stands full of postcards or long silken scarves. One or two were also dousing and brushing the pavement, as far as they could manage in the midst of the procession of commuters. Fran walked slowly, taking her time to arrive at the parade of shops and enjoying the sense of having no commitments for the rest of the day. The paving stones along her street were broken up at intervals by twisting tree roots breaking free from their subterranean domains and creating hazardous uneven hummocks. The elegant semi-detached homes opposite were also outgrowing their allotted spaces, extending upwards and down with new lofts and basements. Scaffolding was speedily erected and dismantled, rubbish skips were filled to overflowing and builders' vans arrived promptly at eight o'clock, six days a week.

On this side of the street, her side, the houses were not so grand. They were late-Victorian terraced properties with an archway between each row of four and a roughly paved path leading to the grassy lane running behind the back fences. Some of the small front gardens were beautifully kept, with tiled paths laid out in the original style, spreading flowers and evergreen shrubs in terracotta pots. Others were neglected, concreted over or packed with an assortment of domestic debris, bicycles and out-of-control weeds.

Catching a powerful scent of rosemary, she paused to inhale and to sweep the palm of her hand discreetly across the overhanging bush. A tortoiseshell cat, hardly more than a kitten, padded behind her as far as the corner, where it jumped up and crouched low on the wall. After less than three months living here, such familiar smells and everyday incidents still felt novel and somehow remarkable.

The shops were beyond the triangular area of grass that would have been the old village green before it was swallowed up by the encroaching city. There was the medieval stone church with its squat tower and small, crowded cemetery, while two traditional-style pubs bordered the green, their hanging baskets, flower tubs and benches waiting to welcome the late-morning customers after opening time. There was even a village pond in the centre of the grass, with waterweeds, lilies and noisy ducks.

Gazing into the patisserie window at its enticing display of cakes and fruit flans, she felt the presence of someone standing close to her, too close. She stepped sideways to create a more comfortable space, trying not to make it obvious. The woman didn't look directly at her, but she was watching Fran's reflection as she spoke.

'Spare some change, lady? I need money to get me to the hostel, for the bus. It's urgent.'

Fran turned her head reluctantly. The woman, a girl really, had a bloodshot eye and a purple bruise, starting to turn black, across her cheek. Her streaky hair was messily twisted and tied on top of her head and she wore a dirty-green parka that was too big for her. Her expression was openly imploring and she reached out both hands to show that they were also cut and bruised. Fran flinched and stepped back, fearing the girl was going to touch her on the arm, but she simply stood there, hands outstretched.

'Yes, of course, you must get there right now. Wait a moment.'

She unzipped her shoulder bag, taking care to keep it well to the side, away from the girl. 'How much is it, the ticket?'

'Five quid, it's a long way. The near one's got no space; they won't take me anyway.'

Fran suspected that five quid was over the top for a single bus fare, but she just wanted the wretched-looking girl to go away and leave her alone. Panicking in case she didn't have a five-pound note and might have to pay her off with a tenner, she scrabbled unseeing in the depths of her bag to avoid bringing out her coin-heavy purse. Thankfully, her fingers soon found a fiver.

The girl half-grabbed the note out of her hand and mumbled, 'Cheers, lady' before taking off at a lolloping run, weaving through the morning traffic and disappearing towards the green. Her pink canvas trainers were coming apart and gaping at the heels. A lorry driver hooted as she darted across in front of his cab. Fran felt rattled, disturbed by the intrusion into her tranquil space more than by the girl's predicament.

She decided to have a coffee and one of the mini fruit flans. Pushing the café door open, she was immediately seduced by the smell of fresh bread and bought a tuna baguette as well, to have later for lunch. *Nothing much has changed*, she mused as she waited for her order. In the days of the old village there would have been beggars, together with a ducking stool for the witches, the stocks on the green and a pile of rotten vegetables for respectable folk and local kids to throw at the miscreants and misfits. It wasn't all that long ago.

The morning crowd had thinned to a trickle by the time she emerged. Making sure the girl was nowhere in sight, she paused at the dress shop, Frocks and Chocs, to note the small changes in the window display. Walking on past the door, two large black words on a printed poster caught her eye: *Sales Vacancy*. It was for a sales assistant with substantial retail experience and a strong interest in fashion – part-time hours to suit, good rate of pay, apply within. She studied the poster to memorise the details and continued on down the pavement, thinking hard. Her retail experience was back in the mists of time, and rudimentary at that. After art school, she had spent most of her career as a secretary and director's PA and, when that went pear-shaped, as a marketing manager in an international home furniture company. Still, these various jobs had depended on being persuasive and personable and she shouldn't find it difficult to sell nice clothes and fancy chocolates.

She made a mental list of the plus points as she carried on with her walk, no longer looking into the shop windows as she passed. It was local, it could help her get to know people, the clothes looked lovely and she would probably get a decent discount, not to mention the occasional free box of chocs. And then the minus points – the 'good rate of pay' would be less than she was used to, it could get boring if sales were slow and she may have lost the patience or inclination to deal with disgruntled customers. Against which, both the shop and the local area were definitely classy.

Too distracted to continue exploring, she walked back to the green and stood watching at the edge of the pond. A single female duck was swimming round in circles, while two drakes competed for her attention with various aerial and diving antics. Fran turned and retraced her steps. She was meant to be reinventing herself and this was a good way to begin, close to home and without a twice-daily battle to elbow her way on and off a tube train. Even so, it was nerve-racking having to present herself in a certain way, judge it right and quite possibly end up being rejected.

Standing at an angle to the shop window so she wasn't obviously visible from inside, she inspected the cleverly laid-out display in more detail, then walked home and changed into a tailored skirt and cream blouse, summer jacket and black patent, low-heeled shoes. It was probably too conventional a look, but after some dithering she had decided it was better to play safe and feel comfortable. When she got back and entered the shop, a bell tinkled in the background and she heard rapid, light footsteps coming down the stairs behind the sales counter.

She would not forget her first sight of Daniela framed in the doorway, the tripping footsteps belying the figure of a large, shapely woman with a thick mane of highlighted golden hair, dark eyes and a pretty face. Her yellow-and-black dress was patterned in bold, abstract shapes, and the belt with its extravagant silver buckle emphasised her generous curves. It was hard to tell her age, but she was probably mid fifties, maybe sixty. She strode round the counter with a dimpling smile and a wide, welcoming gesture.

'Good morning, madam. Please excuse me for keeping you waiting. I was packing up some items for collection.' There was just the hint of an accent, possibly Spanish.

The job interview was held in the shop, as there was no one else to look after customers. Daniela didn't offer Fran a seat but took her on a whirlwind tour around the four walls of the boutique, sweeping her left hand along the clothes rails and picking out special items to swish about on their hangers.

Fran explained that she had recently moved to London and gave a somewhat embellished account of her retail experience and knowledge of fashion and style trends. Daniela nodded encouragingly throughout this spiel but showed most interest in her marketing experience at the home furniture business. Fran pretended she had enjoyed the job, although in fact her manager had turned into a bully after being over-promoted and she had considered herself constructively dismissed following several heated run-ins and a final dramatic bust-up in the office. In her jaded and no doubt old-fashioned opinion, such incompetent bozos with their ridiculous marketing-speak and half-baked 'creative' ideas had taken over the world, with disastrous effect.

After almost an hour, with brief interruptions to check on browsing customers, Daniela concluded the interview, putting her hands together as if in prayer and contemplating Fran over her winged, purple-framed glasses. Fran fixed her gaze on a pink feather boa hanging on a hook behind Daniela's head. She would return to buy that feather boa whatever happened, either as a reward or a consolation.

'It's good, Fran. I want to offer you the position on a trial for six months. It will be four half-days a week and alternate full days on Saturday, with the usual staff discounts. Do you need time to consider?'

'No, that's great, thank you, and I'm happy to accept right now. I'm going away to see friends and want to finish sorting a few things, but I can start a week on Monday, if that suits you.'

As she was about to leave, a woman walked past the window and turned to enter the shop. Daniela beckoned her across and touched Fran lightly on the elbow to guide her forward. It was the dark-haired woman from the café, the one who had appeared to scrutinise her so closely and almost catch her out.

'You have great timing, Vicky! This is Fran, who will be joining us as our new sales assistant. Vicky is our IT consultant and tech wizard. She keeps me up to date and makes sure the online operation runs smoothly. And on the chocs side, we're setting up a new venture together, selling a distinctive brand of chocolate truffles.'

This time, Vicky gave Fran a full sweeping glance, instantly taking her in from head to toe as Fran did the same in return. It was more than the usual casual exchange of looks, rather that rare experience of instinctual, clocking recognition. Vicky was petite, especially next to the statuesque Daniela, with smooth olive skin, blue-green eyes and black hair cut in a long bob with a full fringe touching her eyebrows. A neo-'60s look, very chic.

Fran was eager to find out more about the online business and their new joint venture, the special chocolates. However, Daniela was ushering her out and it would have to wait.

As she walked past the pond, where the female duck now swam round happily on her own, she wanted to tell someone the news. Max and Chaddy were studying and working in San Francisco and Hong Kong and it wasn't the right time of day to call them. It would have to be Judi then, her fondest and oldest friend who was inescapably dying and was still waiting for her to call back and confirm her visit this weekend. She would do it today, now, as soon as she got home.

Chapter 2

Fran's first best friend, Wendy, had fallen ill and died when the two girls were just six. Her mother said that Wendy had moved away, but then Fran overheard her telling a relative that it was 'terribly tragic, losing little Wendy like that, and to think she was dressing up here with Francesca just two or three weeks before.'

Little Francesca knew then, from the tone of voice as much as the words, that Wendy was gone forever and wouldn't come to visit, as she had been half-promised. She remembered creeping forward on tiptoe to the sitting-room door, not showing herself but staying hidden in the hall, her fingers picking at a crack in the paint of the door frame and her bare knees shaking uncontrollably. She realised straight away that this was going to be another of those big and somehow shameful secrets that she must never mention and that would remain unexplained.

Some years later, when she knew a little more about childhood diseases, she concluded that Wendy had died of leukaemia. However, this was simply to bring an end to the story, rather than being based on actual knowledge. Wendy herself, a chubby girl with red cheeks and a blue plastic hair slide, was replaced by another girl as Fran's best friend and gradually faded out of her imagination and longing.

Reliving this ancient episode, she was finally on her way to see Judi, speeding by train out of London and through the lush countryside of full-blown spring. She glimpsed a fox picking its way across a field, and then a whole family of rabbits darting about on the steep railway embankment. Towards the end of primary school, Judi had invited her to make a solemn declaration of 'best friends forever'. Over the following years, turning into decades, their friendship had ebbed and flowed through successive phases of education, work and family lives. Now, and especially since the onset of Judi's illness, they were closely bonded again.

It was Andy, Judi's partner, who had answered when Fran phoned to say she was coming. He told her that Judi only wanted to be with her, Fran, this weekend and they had put off other friends. This made her even more ashamed of her reluctance, her conflicted feelings about seeing Judi in this final and protracted stage of her decline. She had used moving house and settling in London as an excuse for not going to the coast over the past weeks and months. Judi had gone along with it and said she wanted to visit Fran's new place, but they both knew it was too late. It wasn't going to happen.

The boy hunched in the opposite window seat wasn't at all thrilled by her sightings of foxes and rabbits, and barely nodded when she called, 'Look, there's a…', sweeping her pointing finger backwards as the train rushed past whatever she had spotted. She was intermittently trying to entertain him, as his mother had asked if he could sit there and implicitly assumed Fran would keep a watch on him. The boy was about eleven and obviously travelling back to boarding school after the half-term holiday. He was in uniform and had a battered old suitcase, probably his father's handed down, and a thick coat that was too heavy for the time of year. His mother said he had plenty of games and things to do, but throughout the journey he had left the case unopened and kept remarkably still, staring fixedly out the window.

Fran now noticed that his eyes were welling up and he was rubbing the backs of his fingers across his eyelids to stem the tears. She thought of her own son, Max, at about this age, and the bouts of breakfast-time sickness during his first term at secondary school. From this distance in time, she felt she had been too harsh on him, making light of the problem and not trying to find out what was really troubling him. She managed to catch the boy's eye and offer a sympathetic smile.

'Are you okay? Worried about going back to school?'

He nodded miserably. 'I hate it, all of it. I want to blow it up – boom, like that!'

'You've got a best friend, maybe – someone you like?'

He looked blank and shrugged his shoulders. She decided not to venture further, and anyway, he was standing up now. As the train slowed, she saw a group of schoolboys on the platform, all in the same uniform and herded by two tweedy teachers. She craned her neck against the window to watch her boy take a flying leap, his case thrown out first and his feet landing squarely on the ground, no wobble. Several boys saw him jump and ran forward, yelling and tugging on each other's blazers to reach him before the others. The last she saw of them, a smaller boy was struggling to carry the unwieldy suitcase, while her boy strolled confidently at the head of the group to the station exit and the teachers shouted and waved their arms ineffectually at the rear.

Twenty minutes later, she was in a taxi approaching the small village where Judi and Andy had lived since they got together ten years before. It was little more than a narrow main street with a number of lanes branching off in the direction of the chalk cliffs, which dropped precipitously to the beach about half a mile away. Fran walked the last little stretch along the rutted lane, past the row of stone cottages and the field where Judi's daughter's grey pony was grazing next to the fence. She stopped to stroke her muzzle and hold out a swatch of long grass, reminded as always of Judi's frisky childhood pony Jambo and the yellow wooden trap they had been allowed to drive on the family farm and along the criss-crossing, high-hedged lanes, all those years ago.

As she passed the second row of cottages and came to the one at the far end, she could see Andy's top half framed in the kitchen window. He smiled and raised his soapy hands in welcome, then disappeared to open the front door. Fran stopped at the gate and drew three or four long breaths to slow her heart. She knew Judi would look physically worse, even thinner if possible than she was on her last visit, but she had no idea what her mood would be like, or if she would be as confused and incoherent as in some of their recent phone calls. She and Andy had a brief, tightly clasping embrace in the front porch and he gestured her in towards the sitting room.

Judi's voice was surprisingly strong and her tone imperious. 'Frankie, come here, right away! I'm in here, let's see you!'

Judi was the only one to call her Frankie, she and Andy, since her dad died.

A bed was now set up near the window and positioned to give the best view across the wide sloping fields towards the sea, which was out of sight from this level. Judi was propped up among brightly patterned cushions, her expression strangely altered by the changing shape of her face, almost spectral. When Fran leaned over to hold her, she tried not to exert pressure on the fragile shoulders under the white cotton pyjamas. Judi grasped her hands and laughed in that irresistibly infectious way she always had; still had even now.

'Just don't tell me I'm looking great, 'cause I know I'm a living skeleton.'

'You'd be good on the catwalk, girl, that's what I'm thinking.'

Fran produced the box of miniature cakes she had selected in the patisserie on her way to the station. Somehow she had managed not to squash them on the journey.

'Beautiful, Frankie, they look much too gorgeous to eat. And I'll need to have all of them to myself, if you and Andy are so determined to fatten me up.'

Andy sat with them at first while they continued the light chat. He owned a small building company and was in great shape for his fifty-two years, his toned muscles and flat stomach accentuated by a close-fitting black T-shirt. Although they didn't know each other that well, he and Fran had developed a shy, half-acknowledged attraction to one another, which Judi appeared to enjoy and had never done anything to dispel, confident in her love of them both and her easy assumption that she, Judi, was and would remain in charge. It was only in the last year or so, when she became unable to travel and Fran began to visit her at home, that Andy had stopped being a background figure and come clearly into focus. Even now, he tended to hover watchfully in the corner or find some reason to make himself scarce. This afternoon he seemed more ill at ease than usual and soon left to walk the dog on the beach.

As he shut the front door behind him, Judi touched Fran on the wrist.

'Will Andy be okay, do you think, on his own?'

'I think he'll be fine. He's got plenty of mates and there'll soon be women in hot pursuit. Like bees round a honeypot, I suspect.'

She could say this kind of thing to Judi; anyway, it was just a new variation on an old theme.

'Yes, but he's so shy. He'll hide out in the pub with all the old sailor boys.'

'It's hardly a hideout, Judi. It's not just men going to pubs! And from what you've told me, some of those old sailor boys aren't exactly leading boring and blameless lives.'

Judi winced with pain and held her side for a few moments, then relaxed.

'Andy fancies you, you know – he always has. He likes super-intelligent women, finds them sexy; that's you and me both, Frankie. And let's admit it – we both go for his lovely bum.'

Fran laughed and then leaned forward to whisper in Judi's ear. 'You're dead right we do.'

Whoops, wrong word, 'dead', but Judi just gave a rueful smile. Fran wanted to ask about her memories of the yellow pony trap and the high drama of a particular episode, a summer picnic by the river.

'Did you ever tell Andy about the games we got up to on your farm, me coming to stay with you when we were kids?'

Judi grimaced and held her side again before breathing out gradually, as she'd been trained to do.

'Not especially, just that you and I were inseparable back then, before I was sent off to boarding school.'

That was right; it was that last summer, when they were eleven. Fran longed to go to boarding school with Judi, having devoured endless children's stories of midnight feasts, pillow fights and escape plans, but she never mentioned her desire and her mother had not concealed her satisfaction at Judi's departure.

'Judi, do you remember that time we went for a picnic by the river and we were swimming naked and Jambo bolted, careering off with the pony trap clattering behind him? You said he'd be happy grazing, but he just took off like the grass was on fire. You scrambled out of the water and raced after him, no thought of putting on any clothes.'

The scene was exceptionally vivid in her mind. The bumpy field of rough, spiky grasses and little Judi like a gazelle racing for its life, darting from side to side and leaping high in the air to avoid the thistles, while Fran watched shivering in her scratchy towel, bewitched by her wild and fearless friend. It was Fran who always did well in class, captained the sports teams and generally managed school life with ease, but underneath all that, she knew

23

she would rather have what Judi had so effortlessly – her daring, her natural grace, her dark eyes and her devil-may-care attitude.

Judi frowned with deep concentration, but only momentarily. Her eyes were noticeably dimmer now, less vibrant.

'No, I don't remember. Or maybe I do, vaguely; I'm not sure but it sounds right. He was one crazy little horse, that Jambo, temperamental as they come. It was only me that could handle him and even then, he broke away from me a few times. I always thought he should have been a wild pony.'

Judi had drifted off to sleep by the time Andy came back and began to prepare dinner. The small kitchen was cluttered and friendly, with a rustic feel heightened by large baskets of vegetables, a battered pine table dating back to the '70s and an unravelling wicker rocking chair. Fran attempted various lines of conversation but Andy was notably subdued, responding only minimally and not picking up any thread until she moved towards him, patted his wrist and asked him how he was *really* coping. He was at the sink and turned to face her, holding the potato peeler in mid-air.

'It's a funny thing but it's easier in a way, now she's weaker and unable to go into battle every time I make a tiny suggestion or the nurses want to do something different. Mentally, she's very up and down, depending on the drug dosage and the pain. Today's a good day because you're here.' He paused and turned back to the sink to pick up the next potato. 'We both wanted you here, this weekend. It's not going to be long. She knows that... we all know that.'

Fran put her arm loosely around his shoulders. He turned the peeler in his hand so it faced downwards like a dagger and slammed it with full force into the potato, splitting it jaggedly in half and jabbing repeatedly until it lay in small, uneven pieces across the bottom of the plastic bowl.

Later in the evening, Judi was sitting up again and they played a game of cards and passed round a couple of joints. Fran only smoked occasionally and she inhaled so lightly that the cannabis had little effect, but she was beginning to feel the high now; that mix of animation and blissed-out calm. Andy selected a compilation of country, blues and late-night jazz, including the long-time favourite tracks that were always going to remind her of Judi. The music took over and the talk became sporadic and more zany, spurred on by the fact that Andy and Judi also shared an ecstasy tablet. For once, Fran was tempted to try it, but she had always instructed her children not to dabble in synthetic drugs and she felt duty-bound not to take them herself, for fear of letting them down or, perhaps more to the point, being found out by them. Not that Max and Chaddy were kids any more, being twenty-six and twenty-four, or even living in the UK right now, but the self-prohibition persisted.

Around midnight, Judi wanted to dance. They supported her to climb painfully out of bed and Andy lifted her slight body as the two of them began to waltz and whirl across the rugs and wood floor. Judi's peals of laughter spread to Fran and Andy as she spun round and insisted that Fran take photos and then video clips, until the manic outburst of energy was suddenly over and she had to lie flat and completely still to recover. Andy turned the music down low to signify the change of mood and Fran was acutely aware of her need to treasure the moment, to hold on to this precious intimacy with them.

It was Judi who broke the silence, her eyes closed and her voice dreamy and faraway. 'I hope you two will go on holiday together.'

The words hung between them, slowly expanding like droplets of water about to fall.

'And I don't want to be a ghost. I want to be a spirit.'

Fran took her hand and brushed it with a kiss. 'You will be, Judi. You'll always be our dancing spirit. That's a promise.'

She slept fitfully in the spare room that night, disturbed by the squawking and squabbling seagulls on the roof and Andy's constant padding up and down the stairs. The whole point about Judi was her readiness and desire to cross boundaries, take a risk and let others think what they liked. It was there in the picnic episode, which Judi didn't even remember, and in their imaginary games among the sloping stack of hay bales in the barn, the dead-rat-throwing contests, the scary dares and the store of squirrelled-away goodies under the big double bed in the draughty spare room of the old farmhouse.

At age fifteen or so, when Judi was at boarding school and Fran was involved with her own circle of school friends, she heard and was inclined to believe the whispered rumours about Judi and her younger brother Jeremy, who must have been thirteen by then. She was also well aware that her own parents regarded Judi's pretty, indulgent mother and handsome, gentleman-farmer father as scandalous people to be avoided, although they never said why this was and naturally she couldn't ask. It was only years later that the two girls, now young women, reignited their friendship, after Fran was married and Judi had separated from her first husband and was a single parent looking after Zoe.

The nurse came and went before eight the next morning. When Fran came downstairs, Judi was in an agitated state.

'Did my present arrive, Frankie? I sent it by special delivery. I rode Jambo to the post office and tied him up so he wouldn't run off again.'

Fran played along. 'What kind of present is it?'

'It's a housewarming present and I think you'll love it.' Then, barely missing a beat: 'Am I talking rubbish? You will tell me, won't you? I'm relying on you and Andy not to let me go crazy.'

'It's the medication. It's not a problem, don't worry.'

'Tell you something, Frankie, just between us. I've got the heebie-jeebies.'

Her confusion increased over the next hour, the odd ramblings punctuated by short lucid interludes when she made a big effort to get back in control. Fran sat close to the bed and watched out the window as Andy walked home across the near field, stooping every now and then to throw a stick for the dog. He was wearing shorts, sandals and the light, tight T-shirt despite the fresh feel of the morning, the calves of his legs brown and muscled and his curly dark hair tousled in the breeze.

Judi was asleep again by the time Fran had to go and meet her taxi at the end of the lane. She kissed her lightly on the forehead and, as she had hoped, her friend didn't stir or make a sound. Outside the front door, she and Andy said goodbye with another tight hug which took her beyond where she wanted to be. He spoke quietly into her ear.

'What did you think of that, last night, what she said to us?'

She leant back to look into his eyes, which were glistening with tears.

'It was amazing. I'm not sure what to think, how to respond. It's too…'

He was still standing on the path when she reached the bend in the lane and swung round to give a final wave. The small grey pony was waiting beside the fence, her wide nostrils twitching with expectation.

***

The pigeons often perched on her chimney pots and she could hear them now, their excited cooing carried down the chimney and into the room. She looked up from her Sunday paper and listened as it got louder and more frenzied. Then there was a thump and frantically beating wings, accompanied by a volley of squawking. Immobilised by an irrational fear, she raised the newspaper to hide behind it while she waited to find out if the bird was going to land on the hearth and whether it would be alive or dead. She went through the various scenarios in her mind, not knowing which would be the least awful – a crazed pigeon flying round her living room, an injured bird requiring veterinary attention, or a sad pile of feathers and broken wings lying on the cracked stone. Her dreadful conclusion was that she hoped it would be unambiguously dead, so she could simply shovel it up and put it in the bin after dark.

None of this speculation was helping her decide what to do right now, how to deal with the situation. The flapping continued but with less urgency, and the squawking, presumably from a second bird on the roof, had died down. Maybe the fallen bird had found refuge on a ledge. This presented yet another scenario – a doomed pigeon slowly starving to death in her chimney while she waited in trepidation for it to drop.

She decided to go into the street and assess what was going on from there. The trapped bird might be up on the roof again and she could watch the pair of them fly off, one a little sooty and humiliated perhaps, but happily free. If not, she needed a board or other barrier to cover the hearth opening and stop it from getting into the room.

Standing on the opposite pavement, she saw a single forlorn bird on the edge of her largest chimney pot, its head cocked to catch any sounds from below. They had probably been copulating in a precarious position and the other one had lost its balance and toppled in. Focused as she was on the rooftop drama and her racy thoughts on what had caused it, she didn't notice a young girl who was speeding along the pavement on a scooter until she had to stop abruptly to avoid a collision, jolting over the handlebars but recovering quickly. She followed Fran's upward gaze and then looked directly at her, wanting an explanation.

'Excuse me, what are you looking at?'

She was about ten or eleven, skinny and wearing a pair of baggy, faded blue cotton shorts. She put one foot back on the red scooter, ready to whizz off again if this turned out to be nothing interesting.

'Hello, are you okay, not hurt?' The girl shook her head. 'It's just the pigeons. You see that one on top there? Well, its friend has fallen down my chimney and it's stuck. I'm trying to decide what to do.'

The girl looked thoughtful. 'I'm Lily. What's your name?'

'I'm Fran. I live in that house there, with the bird on the chimney pot.'

'That's near to mine. My house is Number 32, the one with the green door.'

Fran looked across the street, not wanting to dismiss the child but preoccupied with her immediate concern. It was three doors down the terrace, the other end of her row of four. A flowering purple wisteria trailed untidily around the door and the front bay window.

Lily, meanwhile, seemed to be engaging with the issue as a shared problem.

'Why don't we light a fire so it smells the smoke and flies away? Or I can climb out of your window and go up on the roof and reach in for it. I'm not scared of heights; ask my mum.'

At this point, Fran's next-door neighbour emerged from his house and nodded across to her as he stopped by his wall to rearrange the contents of his rucksack. They had not yet had a proper conversation, but he had briefly introduced himself as Marcus Trim on the day she moved in. Dr Trim, she knew from a letter mistakenly posted through her door.

'Marcus, Dr Trim, do you have a moment? We've got a bit of a problem; a bird's got stuck down my chimney.'

She walked across the road, Lily scooting at her heels, and explained what was going on.

'So we need some kind of board to block off its escape route into the room.'

'And I can climb out the window and up the roof, it's easy,' said Lily, clearly trying to gather support for a heroic exploit.

Marcus seemed disconcerted, although Fran couldn't see his eyes behind his shades. He was a slim black guy with fairly short, uneven dreadlocks, prominent cheekbones and a narrow face with the shadow of a beard.

'Okay, I've got a few minutes.'

He glanced down the street and pointed out an overflowing skip with a piece of what looked like chipboard jutting out of the top. The three of them went to investigate and managed to pull the board away from the tangled debris and carry it back into Fran's house, Lily parking her scooter decisively in the space under the stairs as if she were a regular visitor. Fran was relieved to see there was no sign of the pigeon, dead or alive.

They stood in a silent triangle round the fireplace, listening intently for any movement. After a minute or two, there was a light flutter and then another, followed by an ominous bump that suggested the bird was continuing its inexorable fall to earth. The board covered the chimney opening nicely and they secured it in place with the large Greek vase and her grandmother's tapestry-covered oak footstool. Marcus stepped back to check its position.

'You mustn't look behind it, whatever you do, and

don't move it when the bird drops, if it does. They'll fly instantly towards the smallest chink of light.'

'Thank you so much, both of you. It was starting to freak me out,' said Fran.

Lily pulled herself up straight and beamed as if she had won a prize, while Marcus walked over to the back fireplace.

'It can't get through this way, the grate's firmly shut. It's a shame we can't solve it now, but I think it's a job for a professional.'

'Yes, I'll get someone out to deal with it, poor creature.'

She hoped he didn't feel she had imposed on him, drawing him into this mad situation. His next words reassured her, however.

'At least it wasn't a spider. I won't go anywhere near spiders and if I find one in my bath, I'll probably call you in far more of a panic. Any kind of creepy-crawly gets to me. I can't cope with them. That's why you won't catch me visiting the Caribbean very often.'

Lily's eyes widened at this frank admission. 'I like all kinds of spiders, especially big ones. I'm good at catching them and I know how to let them go safely. I've held a poisonous furry one and had a whole snake coiled round me. You can ask me, both of you. I can come over any time, except I have to be home at five on school days.'

This reminded Fran that Lily was a child and, if she was going to start coming round, she ought to meet her parents. She picked up the scooter from under the stairs and saw them out the door, promising Lily she would let her know how it turned out.

She spent the rest of the day on the internet, exploring

bird rescue options. Having quickly established that local councils, pest control companies and the RSPCA had zero interest in the welfare of a solitary stranded pigeon, she appealed to the world at large, going onto various website forums and tapping in the words: *Help, please! There's a bird stuck in my chimney!* This produced a barrage of individual stories and similar questions, plus the inevitable raunchy and obscene responses. Eventually, in amongst all the dross, she hit on the answer. The person for the job was a traditional chimney sweep. She would call the local sweeps tomorrow.

At 2.30 in the morning, she was sitting up in bed with a mug of tea, staring at the chimney breast where the bedroom fireplace had been bricked up decades ago. Every now and then, tilting her head like the pigeon on the roof, she detected faint scraping and scrabbling sounds that indicated the trapped bird was still alive. She pictured it shivering in its confinement, incapable of vertical take-off and trying to maintain an insecure perch on a tiny ledge.

Her dawn sleep, when it came, was taken over by a frightening dream. She was driving a car, battling to keep it on the road while swerving crazily to avoid spiders, red crabs and other beasts that were crossing in front of her. Then something flew up and hit the windscreen, a pheasant, and she braked hard and pulled to a stop, surrounded by floating red feathers. Her front-seat passenger, a child, was unhurt and still asleep. On the other side of the road, Judi and her little brother Jeremy played with a ball, ignoring her or oblivious to her presence. Fran called to Judi, but her view was obscured by a convoy of menacing nannies, each pushing a gigantic, old-style pram with its hood up, and all in silhouette like cardboard cut-outs.

Rooted with terror, she realised it was a dream and that she had to wake up quickly before she attracted the hostile attention of the nannies. She dashed up some steps into a derelict house and up a central staircase to the attic, where she flung open a window and looked down. The procession of nannies was in the garden now, moving silently along the gravel path that bordered the square lawn. The prams didn't carry babies but birds, millions of them, flying out from under the black hoods and filling the expanse of the sky. She inhaled deeply and tried to scream.

It worked. She was back in her bedroom but her relief was short-lived, as she heard insistent tapping and loud bumping at the window and knew they were still coming for her. It was that nasty trick, the false awakening. Then, in a nanosecond, she really was awake, her breathing shallow and her whole body shaking like jelly. Lucid dreams were not uncommon for her and they could go either way, into a blissful paradise or a vicious hellhole, depending on whether her supposed control of the dream was real or illusory.

As she relaxed and slowed her breathing, she became aware that the tapping and bumping sounds were real. The invisible pigeon was dropping in front of her and she could track its descent down the chimney from bedroom ceiling to floor. Then it went quiet. She checked the time, got up and crept downstairs, fearful of what she would find. In the living room, there was an eerie silence and she noted with relief that the barrier board was still in place. She made herself tea and toast and perched on the end of the sofa, her hands clasped childishly around her bent knees. There was still no sound, but she could feel the presence of the live bird behind the board, poised for flight and waiting for its chance.

The moment didn't come until late afternoon, when the sweep arrived at the door. He was dressed in the regalia of a Victorian chimney sweep, complete with traditional spiky brush and his cheeks cheerfully blacked with mock soot. Apparently, he always wore this uniform 'to bring people good luck', and he and his wife were in the habit of adopting injured victims of chimney accidents. Fran stood in the far corner of the room to follow his method of capture, which was simple and effective. He made a soft, five-note cooing sound, then tipped the chipboard out a few inches and instantaneously grabbed the bird in his cupped hands as it made its streaking bid for freedom. When Fran came close, the pigeon stared sideways at her with its marble black eye, definitely more resentful than grateful. She stepped back quickly, afraid of its malevolent gaze.

She turned to the bay window and watched as the sweep strode into the middle of the road and, with a melodramatic flourish, brought his hands down to his knees three times and then released his captive to gain its balance and soar into the sky, leaving a stream of soot and feathers in its wake. When she moved nearer the window to get a better angle, she saw Lily sitting on the opposite kerb, knees together, scooter up against the wall and hands shielding her eyes from the sun as she twisted round to follow the flight until the bird wheeled over the roofs behind her and disappeared from view.

Chapter 3

It was a warm, sunny day and the ducks were in a playful mood, swooshing down and doing underwater headstands as Fran walked past the pond to the shop. She was settling into the job as smoothly as she had predicted and now, a month in, she was getting ideas about how the frocks side of the business could be developed. If she could attract Daniela's attention today, she would suggest a few possibilities, just to sow the seeds.

The customers were more varied than she had expected. She had imagined most would be women over forty-five, but there were plenty of twenty- and thirty-somethings, even some teenagers coming in to browse or buy individual items. This reflected the demographics of inner London, of course; the streets, parks, cafés, shops, pubs, cinemas and restaurants, all were thronging with young people of every nationality. Chaddy, who had helped her move and stayed on for a few days before leaving for Hong Kong, had commented on it when they explored the neighbourhood.

'Look, Mum, there's an old person over there, two of them even. They must be lost!'

As she passed the café and came to the shop window, she paused to check the display that she and Daniela had created the day before. The mannequins were now in green and silver dresses and Fran had chosen the scarves and lingerie items to drape across the furniture. Daniela liked her idea of having matching ribbons on the chocolate boxes, so these were now light green and silver. The effect was pretty satisfying, for a first attempt.

Inside the boutique, elegant evening gowns hung alongside flamboyant frocks, practical daywear and mildly offbeat outfits for the office, lunch date or festival picnic. It was a clever blend of contemporary and vintage, although there were gaps in the accessories, an unmet demand for items that people could buy along with their main purchase – belts, for instance, and small evening bags.

The chocolates, which Fran had first assumed to be part of the display, actually sold well and were priced on a sliding scale, so the more a customer splashed out on clothes, the higher the discount on a box of truffles. They had an established reputation too, with people saying they had been recommended by a friend, or that their last box had been devoured in no time. Fran initially found it counter-intuitive to link chocolates with shopping for clothes, but she could now see that in this context, with a luxury tag and a slightly bohemian feel, it was positively good for business.

There were the awkward individuals, of course; the ones who were stressed out because they had left it late to get a wedding gift, or who returned their purchases with a bad grace and no receipt. Daniela had warned her about two or three particularly grumpy regulars and reminded her to stay polite and not take it personally. Although she had much more limited retail experience than she had implied at the interview, she didn't find any of this tricky and felt she had negotiated far more difficult situations with unreasonable office colleagues.

As for unwanted purchases, an ex-lover had once asked her to return an unsuitable shower curtain. He sought the favour because she was 'the kind of person who can take things back', while he would likely be arrested or escorted off the premises. The idea of being someone who could take things back had become a standing joke between her and Judi, who was one of the very few people who knew about her kleptomaniac streak. The story also had a serious point in reminding her, as part of her resolve to get on in London, that she should continually check her preconceptions.

There were plenty of characters passing by and a few who stopped to gaze at the display or wandered in to look around. They included an extremely old woman, one of the vanishing few of the older-old generation who were still living locally. She was tiny and stooped, wearing a wide straw hat and pushing a wheelbarrow full of bulging plastic bags, which she parked in front of the kerbside bike rack. She would pull out a dress and hang it across the rail so she could inspect it in detail from every low angle, then replace it neatly and move on down the rail to select another. She was especially fond of velvet and silk, although she rarely touched the material.

Then there was a cross-dressing customer, a man called Alex who was always on the lookout for an evening frock or day dress to fit his angular frame. He would sometimes come in as a woman, also called Alex, and he'd been careful to tell Fran early on that this would happen from time to time. Like many other customers, he seemed to value her opinion and she always tried to be honest, while having a keen eye to making a sale. After putting a foot wrong once or twice by suggesting an alternative option when what the customer wanted was confirmation of their initial selection, she realised it was a delicate art and she needed more practice to perfect it.

On this particular morning when she was hoping to get Daniela's attention, her opportunity came when Daniela returned from the café with coffee and a vanilla pastry for them both and asked how things were going, any sales?

'One so far; a white scarf. Something I wanted to say, Daniela, is that customers are enquiring about belts and evening bags, which they're looking to match with their new dress. I was thinking, maybe we should consider extending the range to include some of these. There's a man on the leather market making gorgeous belts and leather bags, and someone else there appears to be doing a good trade in embroidered silk bags, but the leather market is miles away and I haven't seen anyone selling quality pieces like that in this area. I know you take things from local craftspeople, jewellery for example, so we could see if they want to bring in samples.' She paused. 'Sorry, it turned into a bit of a long speech.'

Daniela looked thoughtful. 'No, you're right that the customer doesn't always like the belt that comes with the frock, or they want a belt when there isn't one. It's an excellent idea, well done. Are you happy to ask them?'

A few days later, before Daniela had a chance to view the belts and bags, she invited Fran to have dinner with her and Vicky at a local restaurant. Fran accepted straight away and took advantage of a quiet period in the shop to try on dresses, finally choosing a royal blue one that she felt would suit the occasion, without quite knowing what the occasion was. Daniela had said they would be 'going over a few things and getting to know each other better' and, as a humble sales assistant, Fran felt pleased and flattered. She was also mindful of the new online venture that Daniela had only elaborated on by saying it involved a special brand of chocolates that would be marketed separately. Maybe they would reveal more after a glass or two of wine.

When the evening came, she was ready in good time but then took a video call from Max, who was doing a postgraduate degree in California. He had just given a presentation to his colleagues and it had gone well, so he was in an expansive mood.

'You should come over for a visit, Mum, do the big West Coast trip and we could drive up to Yellowstone or wherever – there are loads of places I haven't seen yet.'

'Yes, I really want to, Max. I will sometime, but you're there for three years and I'm settling into London and spending on things for the house, so I don't think there'll be a big trip yet. Miss you lots though, and Chaddy too.'

'Yeah, cool, how's she doing in Hong Kong? I must give her a call.'

'She's fine, just arrived and still finding her way around. Look, Max, I'm sorry but I'm going to have to cut short our chat because I'm invited out to dinner by my boss and mustn't be late. Let's talk at the weekend.'

After this delay, she changed into low-heeled shoes and walked briskly to the restaurant, which was down a narrow alley beyond the café and the shop. Daniela and Vicky were in the bar area waiting to be shown to their table and both greeted her with a double kiss. Daniela was in a striking deep-purple frock and lilac jacket, while Vicky wore a low-cut, lacy top and a black pencil skirt. Her suede jacket was a light tan colour with a long diagonal zip and went perfectly with her brown ankle boots.

Fran took in all this detail as she followed the waitress and her two colleagues to the corner alcove. From the back, she noted again the contrast in their size and body shape, Vicky having a slim, boyish figure next to Daniela's shapely curves. Fran was pleased she had chosen the slinky-fitting blue dress, which Daniela quickly recognised and complimented her on.

Once they were settled, Daniela said she had reserved the alcove so they could talk freely without risk of being overheard. The wine arrived and as they ordered from the extensive menu, Fran warned herself to eat and drink slowly, so she could listen properly and ask intelligent questions. The gist of it, as she had hoped from the snippets picked up so far, was that Daniela wanted her to increase her hours and lead on the promotion and marketing of the new chocolate enterprise. They were expanding the Frocks and Chocs website and the sales there were growing nicely. The new online business was highly commercially sensitive, due to what Daniela called the 'secret ingredient'.

'It enhances the health-boosting qualities of dark chocolate, which are being studied by scientists around the world. We have a trial website running and plan to launch the main website in the autumn. There's been a positive response but we face fierce competition globally, so we have to be light-footed to stay ahead of the game.'

Fran's head was buzzing with questions. 'What does…, I mean, where do they come from, the chocolates? Are they made in the UK?'

'No, but that may change. I'll give you a little more information now, so you can make a decision. If you want to join us, I'll give you my "chocolate briefing" when you have signed the contract and the confidentiality agreement.'

Fran nodded, her curiosity piqued. Vicky gave her a knowing wink while Daniela continued.

'The cocoa beans are grown in South America and the chocolate is produced there. It was my cousin Osvaldo who started it. He asked me to go into partnership with him, as I was in the chocolate business already and he wanted access to export markets in the UK and continental Europe. I go to South America regularly to see him – it is safest that way. You will probably never meet him.'

'You mentioned a secret ingredient, Daniela…'

'Yes, please be patient, I'm getting to that. Our cocoa beans make extremely rich chocolate. The secret element is a natural plant product found in the rainforest, which is added to the cocoa beans at an early stage in the preparation process. The effects of this mix are to heighten the imagination, set it free and harness it at the same time. It makes people more curious and inventive, so they can see things differently, discover or reawaken their talents and be inspired to pursue their passions.'

Daniela was becoming passionate herself, hands gesticulating perilously close to her wine glass and the half-full bottle of red on the table. She had a chunky gold ring on both little fingers. At this point, she stopped and looked at Vicky, inviting her to take over.

'This is where you come in, Fran,' said Vicky. 'We need your skills to refine the message and hit the right note for the type of customers we aim to attract. It's a fine line because we want to create a buzz without drawing too much attention or making the headlines. Not yet anyway; that will come later, but only when we're ready for it. We believe you're right for this role – your personality and your skill set, it all fits.'

So much for Neil, her bozo furniture boss, and his disparaging comments about playing too safe, always rehashing old arguments and failing to come up with any creative ideas or innovative solutions. What a complete dork. Fran wanted to whoop out loud and hug these two amazing women, but instead she sat up straight, as Daniela was keeping it formal.

'We rely on you to be totally discreet. We can expect that our business competitors will try to get hold of the formula and make a profit at our expense.'

Fran looked from one to the other, astonished at their decision to place so much trust in her and revelling in a rush of excitement. She thanked them for their confidence and said she would sleep on it, but she knew she wasn't going to let this opportunity slip past. And when she woke at four in the morning and had a predictable dawn wobble, thinking how little she knew about either Daniela or Vicky, she pushed the anxiety away and drifted back to sleep.

***

The chocolate briefing took place the next day in the office above the shop. Daniela strode back and forth in front of her large office desk, bringing her hands together and then opening her arms in a swaying, rhythmic motion as she moved. *A woman on a mission*, Fran thought when she signed the confidentiality agreement, *someone who truly believes in what she is doing.*

The secret ingredient was the seed of a blueberry-like fruit growing in a remote area of the rainforest. The seeds had been discovered by a team of university ornithologists studying the adaptive behaviour of birds. They had observed that bird species living near the fruit bushes had introduced an unusual variety to their nesting materials and the shape of their nests. These birds continued to make adaptations, while birds of the same or very similar types in otherwise similar localities followed their established nesting habits. There were also emerging signs of changes in feeding and mating behaviour among the 'berry birds', although those effects were less clear at this point.

The discovery had not been reported in the news media or published in a scientific journal, as the academics wanted to gather more evidence and rule out other possible causes. They were also considering whether the berry seeds might have an effect on human behaviour. They didn't want to win round one with birds, only to hand the ultimate prize, finding out and proving the effects on human ingenuity, to their better-funded international competitors.

'It's important to understand that research like this involves all kinds of regulatory hoops, ethics committees and so on. Our scientist colleagues aim to circumvent this, in the short term, by teaming up with Osvaldo and his logging company and with us and our chocolate-loving customers.'

Fran listened while her mind conjured up a sunny glade in the South American rainforest, where a group of earnest scientists and rugged loggers sat on fallen tree trunks drinking beer and eating handfuls of berries. According to Daniela, testing it on themselves had convinced the group that the seeds did indeed have an effect on the human imagination and it wasn't only hallucinogenic.

'And now, finally, I can show you our fabulous chocolate.' Daniela held up her ample arms for dramatic effect. 'Let me introduce you to Junoco.'

She walked across the office and opened the twin doors to a tall metal filing cabinet. Rows of royal blue boxes were piled neatly to the top of every shelf. Daniela picked up one of the boxes, opened the lid and handed it to Fran. It was hexagonal in shape and inside, arranged in a circle, there were twelve chocolates with alternate light blue and shiny gold wrappers. Daniela watched as Fran studied the contents and then ran her fingers over the raised gold letters on the box lid: *Junoco Truffles*. She looked up quizzically, trying to make a connection.

'The name Junoco – where's it from? It sounds good, and definitely chocolatey.'

'Yes, that's the idea. "Junoco" rhymes with "cocoa", but it actually comes from "Juno". I decided to elevate the Roman goddess Juno, Queen of the Gods. Her father Saturn and her husband Jupiter were given major planets, while Juno only had a minor planet named after her and then it was later downgraded to an asteroid. So she's with *us* now, with Junoco, promoting an awe-inspiring and planet-altering chocolate!

'The truffles work in pairs, a blue and a gold one each time. For the best effect, we advise having the blue-wrapped one first and the gold one an hour later. The timing is not critical, but they seem to be most effective taken like that. It's what we're recommending.'

'How often do you take them? Does it matter?'

'We're not certain yet, but we're saying maximum once a week, to be cautious. The effect can last for twenty-four hours but it varies, according to our initial reports. We are all part of the ongoing trial and we urge everyone to keep a diary.'

'Yes, I can do that. I can't wait to try them!'

'Good, that's agreed. Ideally, we recommend you involve a partner, close friend or family member, someone who's a little adventurous and you can trust to be discreet. That way, you can talk about it while you're experiencing the effects, observe each other and create a more in-depth record. There is only one condition – you must not pass on to your Junoco buddy any intelligence about the constituents or origin of the chocolate, apart from saying it has a secret ingredient and this is a wholly natural plant product. That gives them the same details as our customers. Do you accept the condition?'

'Yes, of course. I'll say exactly that: there's a secret ingredient and it's a wholly natural plant product.'

Fran felt uncertain whom she would ask to be her Junoco partner, but said she had a friend who was perfect for it – thinking of Judi, who was indeed perfect but was far too unwell. Daniela invited her to take two more boxes of truffles from the filing cabinet and the briefing was over. Fran had taken notes on her laptop while Daniela was talking and she now headed along the pavement to the patisserie, to reflect on what she had heard and carry out some research of her own.

The café was quiet, as she expected on a Friday morning. She had a friendly word with the manager, Jean-Claude, chose her usual spot and settled down to search key words on the internet. She immediately struck lucky with 'brain foods', finding out from one source that attention had shifted from the benefits of the omega-3 foods, such as oily fish, walnuts and green vegetables, to another group of chemicals, the flavonoids, found in fruits such as blueberries and blackcurrants and also in cocoa, green tea and red wine. She copied down a few sentences, just to capture the main points for rereading and decoding later.

Flavonoids have been found to improve attention. They activate biochemical pathways that increase the expression of genes linked to memory. They can raise the level of proteins that are important for learning... They also increase the elasticity of blood vessels. This increases blood flow to the brain, which is good for mental performance.

Then a quote from a scientist:

'Blueberries appear to have almost drug-like effects. It's possible that these food-derived components may be used in the future as precursors for mind-enhancing drugs.'

Blueberries and cocoa – both brain foods. There it was, quick validation for the main selling point of Junoco, although the emphasis was on the potential to prevent or treat age-related conditions and the article made no reference to imagination or curiosity. There were words of caution too. Not all the scientists agreed on the potential benefits of flavonoids, but that was to be expected at the early experimental stage. Anyway, the unique make-up of Junoco, as Fran understood it, was taking brain enhancement to another level, where the wild imagination and the focused mind were boosted alongside each other.

There was plenty more stuff on how chocolate was good for the brain. One study indicated that *high-flavonoid cocoa helps to rejuvenate specific brain activity through increased blood flow*, while another reported that research participants given cocoa with high flavonoid levels scored better on cognitive tests than those who were given cocoa with moderate amounts. Also, to get enough flavonoids from chocolate, it had to be dark chocolate with an extremely high percentage of cocoa solids, higher than in most of the chocolate currently on sale and too bitter for accustomed tastes.

During her search, she also turned up lots of references to 'smart drugs' and 'legal highs'. This information was so extensive and sprawling that she would have to investigate its relevance another time. In their discussions so far, she had registered Daniela's insistence that Junoco was a legitimate enterprise with no connection to banned drugs.

After over an hour of this immersion, she was lured out of the café by the sunshine and decided to take a long walk along the river to Central London and back. She had promised herself this walk for weeks and now would be a good day to do it, when she had so much to ponder. And as she had just read, flowing water was good for thinking.

She stopped for lunch at a riverside pub and arrived home at four in the afternoon, feeling invigorated. As she was putting the kettle on, the doorbell rang. It was Lily from three doors away, without her scooter this time but with her hands clasped around a small furry creature. Fran sensed she had been waiting and watching for her to come home.

'Hello, Fran. I've come to show you Sahara, my hamster. She's six months old.'

She carefully adjusted her hands to reveal more of the twitching little nose and impressive whiskers.

'Hello, Lily. Do you want to come in? She's lovely, looks very inquisitive. Did you tell your mum and dad you were coming?'

'Mum's at work. She doesn't get back till about five. I've told her about you, that we're friends. Dad's not living here now. He's in Germany, and so is Ferdi.'

Fran beckoned her in and found an empty cardboard box for Sahara to nuzzle around in safely. She was about to open a packet of chocolate biscuits when Lily asked if she could have a cheese sandwich and a glass of milk – and a small piece of carrot or celery for Sahara.

It was still warm outside and Lily was wearing her baggy shorts again, with a stripy T-shirt and red trainers. Her hair was pulled back into an untidy long plait, her skin pale with light freckles.

'I'm going to be a vet, I've decided.'

'That would be excellent, very ambitious. A vet is a great thing to aim for.'

'Are you going to be something… else?'

'Me?' Fran laughed, taken aback by the question. 'Actually yes, I've got a new job selling chocolates and fancy clothes.'

'That's good, except I don't like chocolate. And I always put on my old clothes when I get home. I'm glad you like Sahara. Do you want to be friends?'

'Do I want to be friends with you or with Sahara? Yes, we can all be friends, but I'd have to meet your mum first.'

'She won't mind. She wants me to have more friends now that Ferdi isn't here.'

'Who's Ferdi? Is he your brother?'

'Yes, he's nearly ten and I'm eleven and a half. Ferdi went to live with Dad and I stayed with Mum and we moved here. Mum says it's a lot more peaceful now, but I'd like them to still be here, Dad and specially Ferdi. We had the same bedroom in our last house and we talked about animals and planets and robots and stuff like that before we went to sleep.'

'Oh, Lily, that's sad for you. I hope you can see him often? I had a little sister and I miss her.'

This was true, although she had hardly ever expressed it; she missed Marina, even now, after all this time. The sadness in Lily's family would cast a shadow long into the future, far longer than her parents imagined in their attempts to set up a workable arrangement for the kids. Fran had moved to the window and was staring at the patch of sky over the roofs, the pristine white clouds. In her mind's eye, she was reliving that first memory once again – the flying man in a helmet, the spinning wheels of the motorbike, the screaming and the struggle not to be carried away by a stranger.

As she lowered her gaze, she saw Marcus, her next-door neighbour, swinging into his front path. She didn't know what kind of work he did, but he usually arrived home early on a Friday. She turned round and watched Lily for a full two minutes as she played teasingly with Sahara on her knees.

'It's after five now, Lily. Do you want to check if your mum's home? I need to get on with making my tea.'

At that moment, the doorbell rang. It was Lily's mother, a tall, slim woman with her hair pinned back in a neat chignon. She smiled and introduced herself as Petra, then looked past Fran down the hallway.

'Yes, Lily's here with Sahara. I hope that's okay? I think she's taken a fancy to my cream cheese sandwiches!'

She was aware of Petra's unconscious appraisal, the rapid lowering and raising of the eyes to complete the body scan.

'That's good with me, it's not a problem. I hope she is not disturbing you. She has a vivid imagination and she is in her own world, on her own little planet.'

Fran called Lily, who appeared with Sahara cushioned between her hands and held close to her chest. As the visitors left, Fran glanced across the street and saw a young woman with long hair and a big sports bag coming along the pavement. Absorbed by her mobile phone, she tripped on the exposed roots of the chestnut tree opposite and almost fell.

***

After dinner, Fran signed in to her favourite online dating site to check for any messages or prospects. Her preferred time for this was later at night, between twelve and one, when the mood was more relaxed and the conversation often amusing. Many of the guys on the site, or those she exchanged messages with, were not serious. They enjoyed the virtual flirting and the sense of possibility, sometimes going as far as a phone call or even venturing out on a real date, but then finding a reason, genuine or confected, why it wouldn't work. On the rare occasions when she decided she wanted to see someone more than twice, they almost invariably went silent, had a dramatic family disaster or discovered they were still in love with their ex. This kind of nonsense was only acceptable because she behaved in much the same way with some of the men who showed an interest in her.

She clicked on Ned's profile. Yes, it was still there, and he had put up a new photo of himself in a dinner jacket and bow tie, which made him look even more handsome and debonair. He had to be attracting loads of attention. Did she care? Yes, in the moment she felt uneasy and discomforted, but it was the deal, what worked for them both right now. They were in a bubble of their own creation, and bubbles were by definition fragile and fleeting.

She continued web-surfing for a while, then turned off the computer and curled up on the sofa with a pile of magazines. She was just dozing off when someone slammed a door and she heard raised voices. She uncurled her legs and sat forward, straining to hear the words and trying to detect where the noise came from. It was next door, Marcus' house, although whoever was shouting was on the street.

Fran dimmed the lamp and tiptoed to the bay window. Crouching low, she used her thumb and fingers to open a crack in the venetian blind on the small side window. The person was very close, but not in her line of sight. She closed the blind for a moment and stepped back, but then gingerly opened the slats again, slightly wider this time. It was midsummer and the sky wasn't completely dark, plus the street light was nearby so she could make out the figure in some detail. It was the young woman she had noticed across the road by the tree; medium height, with braided black hair reaching halfway down her back. She was wearing tight jeans with a short pink or white jacket and her sports bag was on the ground beside her.

'Please, Marcus! Let me in! I just want to talk to you.'

There was a muffled reply from the house and Fran shifted her angle of vision slightly, still keeping the opening in the blind narrow so she wouldn't be seen. Marcus was in his front room and talking through the slightly open top half of the window. He had a deep and naturally soft voice and was attempting to calm things down, but to no effect.

'It's late. There's nothing to talk about. There's no point, Kirsty. Please go.'

He shut the window with a firm click and closed the curtains.

'Fuck you, Marcus! You're a useless shit. I'm back now and I've come halfway around the world to see you again. I've just got off the plane today, for fuck's sake.'

She sat down on his low front wall and put her head in her hands. At this point, Fran heard another front door opening and a new voice, angry and indignant. It was the neighbour on the other side of Marcus, the sour-faced woman with the grumpy husband. Fran had had the misfortune to encounter them on the day she moved in, when they emerged from their house and, instead of welcoming her to the street, complained about her removal lorry being parked partly in front of their property. Although she couldn't see them from her position at the window, she could imagine the grim couple standing side by side in their doorway.

'What's going on, young lady? What makes you think you can come here and disturb the peace? This is a respectable neighbourhood, or used to be.'

The young woman stood up and turned defiantly towards the speaker, happy to continue the tirade with a new antagonist.

'Fuck off, you moany old slapper. And you too, you grizzled old fart. Mind your own fucking business.'

There was a moment's silence. Fran pictured Marcus cowering under his windowsill. She suppressed a giggle, although no one was close enough to hear.

The husband took over now, all self-righteous. 'Right, little madam, that's quite enough of your lip. I'm giving you ten seconds to clear off and I don't want to see you here again, understood? Ten seconds and I'm calling the police. I'll have you arrested for breach of the peace. Now off you go, skedaddle!'

The young woman flicked her head contemptuously and hesitated for several seconds before deciding to take off at speed. Fran altered the angle of the blind again to get a better view and saw her turn and continue to run backwards for several steps, hurling a final and inaudible insult before she swung round with her bouncing bag and disappeared into the night.

Fran heard the neighbour couple closing their front door and then, a minute or two later, Marcus emerged and crept towards the pavement, peering down the street to make sure the young woman, Kirsty, really had left. Emboldened by the theatrical nature of the scene she had witnessed, Fran went quickly to her own door and out onto the path.

'Marcus, are you okay? I couldn't help overhearing...'

'No, I'm sure the whole street must have heard it. I'm sorry to disturb you so late. It was my ex-girlfriend, as you probably gathered. She must have waited for me outside the office and followed me home. She was working abroad for two years and I never told her this address.'

'Well, she gave the neighbours something to think about, anyway! Those two have been off with me ever since I moved in – most unfriendly.'

This was delivered in a kind of stage whisper, as she had mixed feelings about whether or not she wanted the couple to overhear. Marcus returned to his door and replied in a similar tone.

'Yes, that's Eric and Delia for you. Friendly isn't their style. They'll issue me with a stern warning tomorrow, you can bet your bottom dollar. I swear they sit in silence looking at each other across the room and waiting for a pin to drop, so they can complain about it. They knock on the wall every time they hear me so much as pick up my saxophone – not that I'm much good at it, I have to admit. Look, Fran, rather than stand out here with them trying to spy on us, why don't you come in for a quick drink or a coffee?'

'Oh, thank you but I have to... no, okay then I will, just for half an hour.'

Although they hadn't spoken since the incident with Lily and the falling bird a few weeks earlier, she had found him pleasantly unassuming, very likeable, and despite the late hour, she felt comfortable accepting the invitation.

Entering the house, she was surprised to see that the original Victorian layout had all but disappeared and the ground floor was now open-plan. There was a wrought-iron spiral staircase in the centre and a spacious kitchen and dining area extending out into the garden. The main pieces of furniture were modern and there were several large paintings on the walls, as well as a beautiful lamp and wall lights in stained glass.

'Wow, what a lovely place.'

'Thank you, yes. I didn't do any of the structural changes. That was all done when I bought it and that's why I decided to go for it – plenty of light and space.'

She looked around and pointed towards one of the pictures, a tropical beach scene with fishing boats moored up to a jetty and two young children sitting on the wooden structure, dangling their legs over the edge.

'What about the paintings and the stained-glass pieces? Are they originals?'

'Yes, they're all mine, actually. I'm still doing the day job but I rent a studio not far away and I sometimes work in my summer house at the end of the garden. It needs a proper tidy out, which is why I haven't been using it yet this summer. And it's another bone of contention with Eric and Delia, the noise when I get going on cutting glass. I'm glad you've moved in on the other side, anyway.'

They chatted over a glass of wine and Fran discovered that in the day job Marcus was a civil servant at the

Department of Health. She told him about her sales position in the shop, leaving out the Junoco marketing offer and her meteoric promotion, if that was what it was. They kept off the topic of the ex-girlfriend too; another one for another day, if she got to know him better.

Chapter 4

There was an empty space on the high black shelf, where a hat was missing; the brown fedora, naturally. Maybe Ned was a secret agent, after all. Fran smiled and reached her hands towards the ceiling, her nails shimmering pink this time in the scattered light of the glass lamp with its twisted blue and orange snakes.

'Are you awake, Ned?' she whispered.

He made a husky sound, very dreamy, and lifted his head under the duvet, facing away from her. 'No... yes, sort of – I'm coming to.'

She stroked his shoulder and lightly fingered the back of his neck.

'It's after nine – dinner time.'

He turned round with fake grumpiness and they wound their bodies together for another couple of minutes until he started tickling the soles of her feet with his toes. Her legs retracted in a reflex action, making her knees press against his stomach.

'Stop it, Ned, that's not allowed; too ticklish. It's time to pass me my robe. And after dinner, I've got a special treat for you.'

'What is it? Not too energetic, I hope?'

'No – at least, I don't think so. I'll tell you later.'

She went quiet for a few moments and then spoke again. 'Ned?'

He murmured to let her know he was still awake.

'How long will this last, do you think?'

He turned over and lightly kissed her forehead. 'Who knows – maybe until someone decides to jump on our sandcastle?'

Dinner was a green Thai curry and coconut rice, flavoured with lemongrass and cardamom. As usual, the ingredients were lined up on the counter and she watched from her perch on the high bar stool as Ned shredded, blended, stirred, seasoned, simmered and fluffed them up to transform them into a new creation, garnished with coriander. Fran breathed in to capture the exotic smells as he carried the serving dishes past her and into the sitting room.

'I love coconut – delicious. Did your clever fridge decide we'd have this for dinner?'

'Yes, as always.'

'But how does it know what else…?'

'It doesn't. It only knows what's in the fridge – it's not psychic, yet. If I serve up a beautiful Bolognese without any spaghetti one night, you'll know why.'

The white blossom was gone now and the trees lining the wide street wore the deep green leaves of summer. The thick foliage still ensured that no one could see in and they weren't in a hurry to move away from the window and onto the sofa, engrossed as they were in their conversation.

She had put two pairs of Junoco truffles on the table and instructed Ned not to touch them. He peered closely at them.

'So, what's so special? Where do they come from? When can I try one?'

'Hold on, not yet. There's a lot I don't know myself, but I'll give you some of the background and then you can decide if you want a taste.'

Ned laughed and marched his fingers towards the nearest chocolate, as if making to snatch it away. 'Yes, I do want a taste, most definitely – but go on, tell me.'

Fran explained how she had met Daniela and Vicky and been invited to join them in the new business. As she had anticipated, he was intrigued from the beginning and didn't need much information, beyond the fact that there was a secret ingredient and the combined effect of that and the ultra-dark chocolate was to make you more curious and imaginative. He was a natural risk-taker; that much was obvious. It probably explained how he had achieved such success in life.

'It sounds thoroughly shady already, nicely dubious! Carry on, I'm enjoying this but I want my truffles soon, please.'

She refilled their wine glasses and helped herself to a satsuma from the fruit bowl. Shady and dubious – the term 'pillow talk' came to mind and she imagined him in his long trench coat with its upturned collar and the fedora at a rakish angle. It was a shame that their arrangement didn't involve going back to bed after dinner. He was leaning forward and gazing pleadingly at her across the table.

'Can I open a chocolate now, please? I'm beginning to feel like a little kid with a surprise birthday present.'

'Okay, okay, very soon. It's 10.30, so we can have the first one now and the second one in an hour's time. I know it's extending our usual evening but I guess that's okay, for a special occasion. It's good to sleep afterwards, so the timing is just right. I'll take a cab home tonight and tomorrow we can send each other messages on how it's going. I'd like you to take notes, if you will – key points about how it feels.'

'What – homework to spoil the fun?'

She had considered asking if she could stay the night with him, but it wasn't what she wanted and it would upset their rhythm. The thought of having her first experience with Junoco at least partly in solitude was also appealing.

His fingers were now hovering above the truffles.

'Okay, are you ready?'

'Here we come, ready or not!'

They both picked up and opened the blue-wrapped chocolates. They were spherical with a wavy surface and very dark; the darkest chocolates she had seen in her life. She popped the whole truffle into her mouth, while Ned bit his in half. As she sucked on the chocolate and tried to speak at the same time, her voice was muffled by the melting lump.

'Ooh, that's super strong and bitter, more so than I imagined. I'll have to get used to it. It won't take effect straight away, remember. And there's a second one.'

They finished eating the first chocolates, pulled frightened faces at each other and laughed nervously. Fran moved her tongue around her lips, making sure she had consumed all of it and relishing the aftertaste.

'Wow, I can see what they mean by intense. Nobody's going to want to scoff too many of these at once. The advice is for only one pair of truffles a week.'

'One pair a week? Sounds like socks!' He suddenly raised his right hand and pointed his forefinger to the ceiling in a mock gesture of exclamation. 'I've had my first brilliant thought! Your magic dust might be working already. Let's try out some new ideas, just for practice.'

He leant back, tipping his chair and lifting both hands triumphantly. 'Okay then, here goes. We could set up a new type of male escort agency, with me as the number-one hunk and a few other sexy guys. We'd be co-directors – you'd wear big, black-rimmed specs and all the clients would adore you. That's the brilliance of it: its appeal to women that are tempted to get involved but wouldn't use a purely online escort service, most of which don't actually exist anyway. The fraudsters see it as the perfect opportunity to fleece naive guys for upfront fees and then run off with the dosh. We'd pride ourselves on managing it properly.'

Fran was almost sure he was teasing her, although he seemed to know a fair bit about the world he was describing. She adopted a stern expression and pretended to take off her black-rimmed specs.

'Be careful what you wish for, boy. It sounds beguiling to me. We'd need to be picky about recruitment; the guys naturally, but also the female clients – definitely high-end, that's where the market is at the moment, I imagine. Let's see – American businesswomen in town for a few days, lawyers and so on, people who are expected to attend formal social events, the odd hen party perhaps, and women who want a luxury break with extras, as it were.'

'Yes, exactly – we're on the same page. Let's hold that one there, fantastic idea. What about you? Have you got one?'

She frowned and put her fist under her chin in the classic 'thinker' pose. 'Well, okay. One off the top of my head is to set up distraction robberies. Say we go into a café separately, a crowded place, lots happening. You order cooked breakfast, and when it arrives you pick up the bottle of ketchup, take the lid off and shake it wildly from side to side, so a stream of ketchup erupts in blobs and goes all over the customers sitting at the nearby tables and across their books, laptops or coffee cups. In the ensuing chaos, with staff and customers preoccupied or going over to help, I do a flash sweep of tables as I leave the café and we split the booty.'

It was his turn to laugh. 'It sounds so precise. Come on, have you actually done this?'

'No, but I've seen the ketchup episode and thought afterwards that was what I should have done, instead of giggling helplessly into my mug of tea.'

'Well, what do you think, Fran? Has the chocolate had any effect yet?'

'I'm not sure. It's too soon. Are we being imaginative or just plain silly?'

They continued in this vein until it was time to sample the second, gold-wrapped chocolate. This was also round and dark, but with a smooth surface. The taste was similar to the blue, but with the hint of a flavour that neither of them could name. Once it had fully melted in her mouth, Fran suddenly felt ready to leave and they agreed they would get some sleep and report back the next day. She called a cab and they had a lingering goodnight kiss, in breach of normal protocol.

***

The house was in semi-darkness when she got back, the street light lending a low white glow to the front room. She lit two long candles and sat on the sofa to check for any early effects, mentally noting that she needed to get a diary organised. A paper notepad would be easiest for getting the initial notes down and then she would write a weekly report on her computer. The candlelight was playing on the wall of the chimney breast and she began to recognise geometric shapes, in outline at first but growing brighter and more colourful as she watched; a red circle, a yellow triangle, squares, cubes and pyramids.

She looked around the room and back to the hearth, where Guacamole sat on an animal-skin drum that her uncle in Africa had sent to her as a child. Guacamole was a soft toy about ten inches high, a furry mole dressed in a white cable-knit jumper and peering over a pair of round, gold-rimmed spectacles, which perched lopsidedly halfway down his nose. She had bought him on impulse at a country Christmas market because he looked like her dad, and she called him Guacamole because it was suitably pretentious for a mole of his type and demeanour and Dad would have found it amusing.

Guacamole returned her gaze, his expression no longer static but apparently full of emotion – what was it – sad, affectionate? She held his stare for a short while and started to feel spooked, so reached to switch on the table lamp. In the brighter electric light, he still looked different but had regained his fixed expression, which she now interpreted as one of gentle amusement. It was her father's habitual expression, she realised now. It wasn't only the trademark jumper and the gold-rimmed specs that made them alike. She walked over to Guacamole, picked him up and kissed him on the top of his soft head.

'Goodnight, Guacamole. Sweet dreams. See you in the morning.'

It was late by this time and she lay in bed, letting her mind wander, turning on the radio to catch the last haunting notes of *Sailing By* and the late shipping forecast while she continued to monitor her mood and physical state – relaxed and calm, toes and fingers tingling, blinking at the passing colours and shapes, pentagons and hexagons, floating...

She woke soon after dawn in a dreamlike state. In front of her was a vast lake and she was sitting on a rock looking over a beach of coloured pebbles, which ranged from deep brown through red to orange and sandy yellow. A flotilla of small craft, boats and rafts, was coming towards her and as they got near to the beach, she stretched out her legs and gave them a gentle push with her bare feet to send them back into the water. She wasn't frightened and treated it as a game, seeing how many she could keep at bay as the numbers increased and they kept bobbing back towards her.

There were people on all the boats but the only ones she recognised were her father, Lawrence, and her little sister, Marina. Dad stood beside the tiller to steer them in, while Marina, who was about two years old, waved at Fran over the side of the boat as they approached. She allowed them to land and then they were standing in a line at the edge of the water, throwing or skimming pebbles into the now-deserted lake. Marina had light blue eyes, elfin features and a mass of curls. Lawrence was wearing a navy cable-knit jumper and sunglasses instead of his gold-rimmed specs, but the gentle amusement was there, as well as his evident joy in playing with his two children.

The scene faded away. What type of dream was it, how different, how to describe it? Firstly, Fran felt certain she had been awake throughout. It was like a lucid dream turned inside out – as if she were bodily awake and experiencing a daydream, yet with the bizarre happenings and accepted irrationality of a full-on sleep dream. It was time to begin her Junoco diary.

At the kitchen table, she focused first on recalling the sequence of events in the dream and the magical setting by the lake. She went to the oak chest to find her notebook and lying beside the notebook was a big sketch pad, which she had left untouched for years, and a tin full of old pencils and crayons. She sharpened three pencils, thick, medium and fine, and spent the next hour drawing a picture of Marina, with her blue eyes and untidy mop of curls. When she had finished, she wrote in the bottom left-hand corner of the page: *Marina with Francesca and Dad by the lake.*

Her father was more difficult to draw, because she was trying to achieve a likeness to the person she had known and loved for so long and who filled her memories down the years. She started on the sketch several times, tearing out each page after a few minutes and crumpling it into a ball before shooting it at the wastepaper basket. She put it aside temporarily and went back to Marina, conjuring up an image of how she would have looked at twenty-one and drawing her easily and confidently. The fair curls were still there, but longer now, more wavy, and her face was open and reassuring, just as Fran's was always said to be.

Looking up at the kitchen clock, she saw it was only just after seven. She wasn't due at the shop until the afternoon, so she could keep going on this for a while longer. She was immersed, finding the flow of her sketching for the first time in years and believing, with her depictions of Marina, that she was producing a near-perfect likeness to her sister, although there was no photo or actual memory to go on.

Her phone vibrated beside her and she turned towards it, not wanting to break her concentration but attuned, like everyone now was, to respond to its demand for attention. It was Judi calling, too early in the day but probably just to confirm that Fran was still going to visit them on Saturday.

'Frankie, is that you?'

It was Andy's voice, distinctly shaky. This was it. Her stomach contracted.

'Hi, Andy – what's happened?'

'She's gone, an hour ago. The nurse was here. We've lost her.'

Fran shifted the phone to her left ear, automatically picked up her pencil and continued with her drawing of Marina through their short conversation and long silences, her eyes pricking and her right hand shaking as she added shading and tried to get the nose and chin exactly right.

She carried on sketching through the morning, having set herself a project to draw Marina at different ages. She didn't want to think about Judi, losing her. To gain inspiration, she put Marina in some of her strongest memories, reimagining her as an indulged little sister making dens in the hay bales, a favourite auntie playing with Fran's children in the garden and an attentive grown-up daughter standing beside her at Dad's funeral.

She could have persevered with this all day, but forced herself to stop in good time to get dressed and ready for work. On the short journey there, she noticed that everything was brighter and she was picking out details that she hadn't seen before: the black centres and deep orange of the tall poppies that had sprung up in her front garden, the shape and fall of the rosemary sprigs, and the unusual markings on the tortoiseshell cat that appeared from nowhere and followed her a short distance but never beyond the corner.

Luckily, it was school holidays and they had a young girl, Amy, working in the shop, so Fran was able to stay in the background more than usual as customers came and went. She could hear that Vicky was upstairs in the office with Daniela and she wasn't surprised when they asked her to join them.

She described her lakeside dream scene and her conviction that she was awake and letting her imagination flow, rather than asleep and having an ordinary dream.

'I was aware of being in both places. I was lying in bed and at the same time I was beside the lake. When it faded out, I felt compelled to go downstairs and draw sketches of my little sister and my dad. I became immersed in it right up until… I was immersed in it for hours, which was odd and must have been down to Junoco as I haven't done any sketching for years; hardly at all since I left art school when I was twenty.'

Vicky was taking notes and she looked up sharply at this point, while Daniela clapped her hands in triumph.

'This is exactly what we want! All the signs are that we've got the mix right, just enough of an effect and so far the reports are almost all enjoyable and positive. Well done, Fran, an excellent report.'

'I'm not saying the sketches are any good, mind you, but I was moved to pick up the sketch pad and pencil, which was extraordinary. Oh, and I forgot to say that the evening before, about an hour after having the chocolates, I started seeing radiantly coloured shapes, triangles and hexagons and so on, tumbling through space.'

She also mentioned that she had shared the Junoco truffles with a friend and would feed back on his experience. The one piece of information she withheld was the Guacamole moment, her feeling of emotional connection with him. It was too surreal, too personal and difficult to talk about.

She returned to the shop and was happy to be distracted by Alex, the friendly cross-dressing customer, who was looking for something special to wear at her god-daughter's christening; something gorgeous but 'not so gorgeous that it upstages the baby'. They had just decided on the dress when Vicky came downstairs. She waited until both Alex and Amy had left.

'Are you okay, Fran? You looked tired earlier and sounded a bit flat, even though what you told us was so exciting. Is there anything else to say about the chocolates? Did they make you feel down, change your mood at all? We're trying to assess all the evidence as best we can, so we can report back to the scientists in South America and ensure the optimal beneficial effect.'

Fran felt herself finally giving way and her tears erupted in a flood, sudden and unstoppable. Vicky clasped her forearm, tightening and then loosening her grip rhythmically as if to instil courage. Without asking any questions, she suggested they went for a drink at the Green Duck pub by the pond when the shop closed. Fran just nodded, relieved that she didn't have to offer an apology or immediate explanation.

***

They found a quiet table beside a tree in the far corner of the pub garden. The landlord welcomed them as he prepared the oven and spit for the Friday night summer hog roast. It was hard to say that Judi had died, passed away; to speak it out loud and confirm the stark reality. She told Vicky about their long history and her friend's illness, the remissions and relapses, the way Judi was dismissive of pain and full of plans for the future when offered any vestige of hope by the medical teams or the many alternative practitioners she came to believe in. She had searched online and bought heaps of potions and pills from India, Cambodia, China and other countries, saying she had nothing to lose but often feeling too ill to try them if and when they arrived.

'And Vicky, she had such a wild streak, she always did. I loved her for it at ten years old and I still love her for it now; a crazy girl from beginning to end, beautiful, rebellious and always a bit over the edge. One time, we had taken the pony and trap – she lived on the most incredible farm, and we took the trap, it was painted yellow – and we went off on our own for a picnic and a swim in the river, and while we were swimming, the pony, Jambo, he...'

By mid-evening, the oven was spitting its final embers and the two women were swapping stories about their love lives. Vicky was single too, having broken off a fraught relationship with her long-term partner some two years earlier. She had one son, who was eighteen and living with his dad in Manchester while doing an apprenticeship.

As they stood up and walked towards the pub's garden gate to exit onto the side path, Vicky returned to the topic of Judi.

'Can I suggest something, Fran? You don't have to say yes, but I mean it. Shall I come with you to the funeral, as you said you'd be going on your own? Only to support you and be there and I wouldn't have to come to the actual service, unless you wanted me to. It's a beautiful part of the coast and we could find a B&B and stay over the night before, or after, whatever. I can sort out looking after the shop and Daniela can always contact me if there's a problem.'

In the course of their conversation, Fran had talked about Ned, her new lover, and Marcus, her neighbour and potential friend, but she hadn't mentioned Andy by name, referring to him only as Judi's partner. As soon as the news had sunk in, she had wanted to be there but when she suggested visiting on Saturday as already planned, Andy put her off, saying the house would be full of their local friends. She knew she would feel awkward, an outsider. No, she had to focus on choosing a poem to read, as Judi had requested.

'That's really kind of you, Vicky. I feel overwhelmed at the moment. Can you give me a bit of time to think about it?'

Vicky took hold of her hand and stroked it.

That night, Fran lay in bed listening to the silence –

no passing cars, no rumble of trains in the distance, no cat fights, no pigeons, no builders and no tipsy late-night revellers. It was the dark and empty silence of loss, the silence of someone never coming back.

Eventually, she slept and dreamt she was in a hotel room, trying to pack her case in time to catch the bus to the airport. She knew she was going to miss it and felt rising panic as she started unpacking again when she couldn't find her passport or her purse. Then she was walking across a field towards the sea, switching the suitcase from one hand to the other and hoping to hail a taxi so she could get to Judi and Andy's place before they left home. She lost the path and a cyclist was wheeling unsteadily towards her through prickly thistles and long grass. It was someone she knew well, except they didn't speak or acknowledge her as they brushed past, seemingly unaware of her presence. She dropped her suitcase and turned to call out, but the figure was already a microscopic dot in the far distance and she was forced to look away, dazzled by the sun.

Chapter 5

Fran booked them into a guest house beyond the headland and close to the Beach Plaice, a restaurant and art gallery where the mourners were invited to gather after the service for a late lunch of fish and chips. The funeral itself was to be held in the village hall, with a small number of family and friends going to the crematorium for the committal. They drove down in Vicky's car, arriving too late to do anything other than settle into their attic bedroom, which looked out to the dark shapes and moving lights of ships on the horizon. The night was clear and they left the dormer window open to the sky, so that when she gave up on sleep and gazed over the bay, Fran was reminded of the times when she and Judi camped out in a little green tent, leaving the door tied back so they could watch the stars. Vicky was a quiet sleeping companion and lay on her side near the edge of the bed, her arm falling towards the floor and her face lovely in repose.

In the morning, they took a circuitous route to the village hall, walking along the beach, up the cliff steps and back along the coastal path until it met the grassy track leading into the village, past Judi and Andy's cottage and the pony paddock. Vicky was silent, leaving Fran to talk or dwell in her thoughts. They stopped for her to stroke the nuzzling pony and offer a handful of the lusher grass growing on the track side of the fence. Reaching the hall, they weaved through the milling crowd and took their seats in the second row from the front, as Fran was among the inner circle going on to the crematorium. Vicky studied the two photos of Judi on the order of service: on the back, as a child with a mischievous grin; and on the front, a picture taken in one of the good phases during her illness, when she still somehow managed to look stunning.

Fran felt tense but was looking forward to her poetry reading. When the time came and she was introduced by the humanist celebrant as Judi's oldest friend, she walked confidently to the lectern and scanned the strained, serious or politely sombre faces in front of her. She had planned a short speech, and in the event she made it even shorter.

'Judi was mesmerising, a dazzling free spirit. She inspired me and led me astray. I've chosen a poem that reminds me of her mystery and the wild little pony she loved as a child.'

She took it slowly, her voice unwavering and her eyes lifting at the end of each verse to glance at the family mourners in the front row. Andy's eyes were unnaturally bright and glittering.

As she skirted the stone pillar to return to her seat, there was a quick darting movement across her path and she glimpsed the back end of a mouse vanishing down a hole in the skirting board. She sat down, exchanged a sad smile with Vicky and watched the mouse hole while the celebrant prepared the guests for a short interlude of music and silent reflection. Sure enough, the little mouse reappeared, sniffing the air before scampering along the edge of the wall and stopping to pick up a crumb or some other object of interest. Wary and quivering, it held her attention as Guacamole had done on the night she had eaten the Junoco truffles. It was there to alert her, to remind her or to console her; in any event, it felt like more than coincidence.

She concentrated on recalling something she had read in her recent online research, about laboratory mice becoming more timid and risk-averse when given the kind of brain-enhancing drugs that improve alertness, focus and mental performance in humans. She couldn't remember the precise theory behind this, but it had something to do with the smart mice becoming more conscious of danger and consequently more cautious.

Her train of thought was broken as the funeral guests began to shift and gather their things. The mouse swivelled round and scuttled to safety in a flash. *Goodbye*, Fran mouthed silently, aware that Vicky was putting a comforting arm around her shoulders to guide her out, and that her cheeks were burning hot and streaming with tears.

An hour later, with everyone socialising in the restaurant, Andy came up and hugged her in his sudden, edgy way. She took his hands and squeezed them hard before stepping back and introducing him to Vicky. Then she saw Judi's brother waving in recognition, and he came across to join them. Annoying little Jeremy had grown into a ruddy-faced and solid middle-aged man, every inch the English gentleman farmer, as his father had been. Andy moved away to talk to his other guests and Jeremy began to reminisce about how he would try to sneak up on Fran and Judi to get in on their picnics and invented games.

'I was banned on the grounds of age and sex, needless to say. It was a select club – girls over ten only, no exceptions!'

'I'm sorry, Jeremy. We probably were very mean to you, but rules are rules.'

Soon after this, Fran and Vicky slipped out to the car and had a lively conversation on the journey back to London, ranging from the state of global politics to embarrassing incidents in their personal lives. Fran had rather more silly anecdotes than Vicky, having spent a lot of time on internet dating over the past few years. And as if on cue, a text message came in from Ned asking if she was free for dinner on Friday. She had managed a brief call with him to find out how he had been affected by their Junoco experiment, but she hadn't mentioned anything to him about going to Judi's funeral.

As they approached London and were slowed down by traffic, she turned the conversation back to the day's events.

'I'm glad I said that about Judi leading me astray. People turn into saints, don't they, the moment they die, and it's so dull and uninspiring just to hear about all their good works and generosity. In fact, the other speakers went a bit off-track today, as far as my truth about Judi is concerned. I wanted to say what a gift she had for shoplifting, but it was probably good that I didn't, in the circumstances.'

'I think you got it about right, and I guess the oldest friend can take a few liberties, if anyone can. I wanted to ask, what did Judi call you? I heard Andy calling you Frankie.'

'Yes, that was Judi's name for me, ever since we were kids. My mother called me Francesca, but I was Frankie to my dad too; it was his pet name for me.'

'It suits you, it really does.'

Fran realised Vicky wanted to call her Frankie, but she wasn't ready for that. It felt good, all the same. It had made a difference, having Vicky there.

***

She had to travel back down to Sussex on the following Friday, in response to an agitated phone call from her mother.

'George is being difficult again, Francesca. I won't go into details on the phone. Cerise and I can't get through to him and we thought maybe you can persuade him to see sense. He has listened to you in the past, although he's a lot worse now.'

It was true that Fran had persuaded Uncle George to let them throw out some of his stuff and restore a semblance of normality to his part of the house. This had happened several times, and each time the unbelievable clutter and junk became even more unbelievable. In his tiny flat on the top floor, hoarded items had overflowed onto the narrow landing, so the path to his bedroom was nearly impassable. On her last visit, he had insisted that nobody touch an armchair draped in a heap of crumpled shirts and socks because there was a hedgehog nesting underneath it, despite it being pointed out that the bedroom was two floors up and it would be a strange and inexplicable feat for a hedgehog to get to it.

George and Cerise were brother and sister, now aged eighty-two and eighty. Fran's father Lawrence had married Cerise some twenty-five years previously, when Fran was in her late twenties and married herself. Her mother, Eleanor, had left her father and abandoned the family home, although the lure or provocation behind this move was never made clear. Fran was introduced to Cerise a few months after her parents split up, and within a year Cerise had moved in with Lawrence. The twist in this so far unremarkable story was that, after Lawrence died suddenly in his seventies, Eleanor moved back in to live with Cerise and they were joined a couple of years later by George. The other notable fact was that Fran got on far better with Cerise than with her mother, finding her amusing, warm and generous to the world. Eleanor, by contrast, had always maintained a distance between herself and her only daughter, and she was getting progressively more querulous and intolerant as she got older.

Walking from the station towards the large red-brick house, which was conveniently located close to the town centre, Fran saw teenagers from her old school in practically the same uniform, hanging round the bus stops and sitting on the low walls. She was eight when they moved here, her father having been offered a consultant surgeon post in the county hospital. In the few years until the end of primary school, Judi had regularly come round to play at her house, but Fran couldn't remember these visits nearly as vividly as the times she spent with Judi on the farm. She did recall them sneaking downstairs at night to raid the pantry, and also that her mother was distinctly frosty towards Judi's mother whenever she arrived to pick her up.

It was Cerise who opened the front door to welcome her. She was dressed, as ever, in flowing silky garments, including loose white trousers and a scarf covered in boldly drawn birds and butterflies. Fran's immediate thought was that Cerise would just adore Frocks and Chocs and she should invite her up to London soon. Also, that Cerise was a bit like Daniela, or how she imagined Daniela might be in another twenty years.

The parrot, Pansy, made her customary weird screeching noise as Fran entered the house. It was hardly a welcome but she felt sympathetic, knowing that the bird had once talked a lot but had said almost nothing in the years since Lawrence died. She approached the cage, which extended from floor to ceiling and took up an entire corner of the front hall. Pansy cocked her head to one side, fixing her with a beady eye, rather like the ungrateful sooty pigeon from the chimney episode, but less hostile and with an added streak of curiosity. She was a magnificent bird, a blue-and-gold macaw that had been acquired by Cerise's mother in the 1970s and was now well over forty years old. Cerise was ambivalent towards her as she thought she should be living in the wild, but Lawrence had struck up a relationship with Pansy over time and had enjoyed and encouraged her clever mimicry.

Her mother was upstairs in her sitting room and Cerise suggested she went up quickly, as Eleanor kept asking when she was going to arrive. Once she got there, the conversation was as guarded as usual, with Eleanor showing initial interest in her move to London but soon looking at her watch when Fran started describing her new job, which she had decided to refer to vaguely as being 'in the fashion business'. Her mother was thinner now and her liver-spotted hands were those of an old woman, but her eyes were bright and she retained an aloof kind of elegance. She soon moved the conversation on to George's latest exploits. His flat upstairs was more chaotically bursting than ever and he was bringing home anything that might be useful to his current project of building a computer that was so advanced it was going to revolutionise future space travel.

'It's something like that, anyway. I probably haven't described it right but it's all very silly and it will just lead to more and more junk and dirty plates. The problem now, what I want to tell you, is there's a man called Tom Harrison who has attached himself to George over the past few weeks. He's a homeless type and he's not been in the area long, but somehow he has sniffed George out at the café or somewhere and George has told us that he is asking for money, and we suspect George is giving it to him. I don't know how much.'

At this point, Cerise called them down for tea, which was a home-made fish pie followed by raspberries from the garden with double cream. Cerise had arranged a vase of sweet peas on the kitchen table and opened the window to let in the late-afternoon sun. George made his way in slow stages down the two flights of stairs and was pleased to see Fran. He began to tell her about his space computer but was quickly interrupted by Eleanor.

'Francesca doesn't want to hear all that, George. How many crackpot projects have you started and never finished? She wants to know why you have let your flat get so messy again, after all her hard work clearing it out last time.'

'Be nice to George, please, Eleanor. Let's not have an argument now, when it's so sunny and Francesca's come down to see us.' Cerise was playing her self-appointed role of peacemaker, which sometimes had a positive effect. Not today, however.

'Well then, I've told Francesca that George is giving money to that man Tom and she thinks it's all wrong, don't you, dear?'

Before Fran could reply, George abruptly stood up, toppling his chair sideways, and stomped red-faced out of the kitchen and back upstairs, breathing heavily as he went. The three women looked at each other, Eleanor rolled her eyes and Cerise put George's barely touched fish pie back in the oven to keep warm.

In the circumstances, Fran decided she couldn't ask her mother about what had happened to Marina, as she had fantasised about doing ever since she had seen her little sister in her lakeside dream and sketched her imagined likeness at different ages. She had even brought the initial Junoco-inspired toddler drawing with her, in the hope of perhaps showing it to Eleanor, but the time, as ever, was not right.

On the way home on the train, she realised she also hadn't told her mother, or even wanted to tell her, that Judi had passed away. For her part, Eleanor had presumably forgotten that Judi was seriously ill – or perhaps she just thought it too insignificant to mention.

***

By early August, preparations for launching the online chocolate business were progressing rapidly and Fran had devoted time to thinking about the marketing and promotion, so she could impress Daniela and Vicky with her ideas and insights. Her further experiences with the Junoco truffles had contained similar elements to the first: the desire to draw sketches, the heightening of her senses without any feeling of disorientation or loss of control, the powerful waking dream and the connection with Guacamole as he sat on his drum.

On the day of her next meeting with Daniela and Vicky, the flow of commuters towards the tube station was relatively light, as it was the school holidays. Fran was now adept at avoiding the exposed tree roots and she clicked along nicely in the red shoes with uncharacteristically high heels that she had bought on impulse the day before.

As she approached the triangle of the green, she noticed a dark mound on the grass. Her instinct was to swerve off and cross the road, so that she wouldn't pass close to it. Something made her keep to her path, however; whether it was the fixed obliviousness of the passers-by or her resolution to toughen up and handle these things, she wasn't sure. Perhaps she realised, without being fully aware of it, that the bundle on the grass was the injured and desperate girl who had accosted her outside the café and begged money for the bus. She had seen her once or twice in the intervening weeks but had been far enough away to avoid the risk of another direct encounter.

When she drew level with the curled figure, she slowed and looked over to it. The young woman's arms were clutched around her knees, and she lay sideways like a high diver about to hit the water. Her bleached hair fell across her forehead and her face, what little could be seen of it, was unnaturally pale, with brighter patches that were probably fading bruises. Her eyes were closed and she was quite still.

'Just leave her. She's sleeping it off and she'll come round, unfortunately.'

The smartly dressed man marched past Fran without slowing down. His voice was confident and dismissive, oozing superiority. Fran consulted her watch. She had twelve minutes before her meeting and it would take three or four minutes to get to the office without arriving flustered. She thought of Max and Chaddy. What if the girl's mother were to see this on video; what if it were shared around on the internet? Every last incident was recorded by someone these days, every indignity, every tragedy. What if the mum watched the stream of people hurrying by, so they didn't arrive too late to pick up a coffee and croissant before heading into work? Would she even care a jot, if she did watch it? Max and Chaddy would expect their mum to act, or at least to call for help. It wasn't that difficult.

She picked her way carefully across the green, afraid that her heels might sink in although the mown grass was bone dry. She stepped behind the girl and leant over her snail-like body to look closely, taking care not to touch her. She was wearing so many layers of clothing that Fran couldn't immediately tell if she was even breathing. She dialled for an ambulance, ignoring the small cluster of people that had gathered on the pavement now that there was some action.

'Is she unconscious?' asked the call operator.

'I don't know. She could be unconscious, or asleep. Maybe she's okay. Maybe she's taken something and is sleeping it off. Shall I just leave her?'

'Can you put your hand under her nose, just to see if you can feel her breath?'

Fran bent down again and tentatively reached out her hand. Without warning, the girl's arm lunged up and she grabbed the air with her fist, almost succeeding in getting hold of Fran's fast-retreating fingers. Fran backed off and, hot with embarrassment and fear, regained the refuge of the pavement, where a larger group had now assembled. The call operator was trying to get her attention back, while Fran's only wish was to bring this drama to an end.

'She's woken up. She's okay, I think. I must have made a mistake.'

The girl was still lying on the ground in the same position.

'No problem. From your description, I think she's known to us. We'll send a car round to check it out, just in case. Can you wait for a few minutes, to give us an update if necessary or let us know if she runs off?'

Fran was risking being late now, and it was crucial to be punctual and completely reliable. Her voice rose almost to a shriek. 'No, I can't wait. I have to be somewhere in a minute. Can I leave her, please? There are other people here.'

She felt a light tap on her shoulder and turned to see a round-faced man smiling at her. His voice was calm and measured; a deep African voice.

'Don't worry. I have the time and I am a doctor. I can stay here and wait with her.'

She took a long breath and reached out to touch the man's arm. He was the only one among the watching group who had not slipped away.

84

'Oh, thank you, yes please. I'd really appreciate it, and if you're a doctor, well, you'll know what to do much better than me.'

They shook hands as if to seal the pact and she let the call operator know. The man inclined his head and spoke quite formally.

'My name is Dr Kwesi – my first name, it is easier.'

'I'm Fran – nice to meet you.'

He gestured ahead, towards the corner café and the shops. 'Go then, quickly, Fran, you are a busy person. I have the whole day.'

Walking on towards Frocks and Chocs, she took several deep breaths and switched back to rehearsing her key points for the meeting. She managed to arrive on time and found Vicky and Daniela making coffee. Vicky was in light blue jeans, teamed with a long white shirt and high-heeled open sandals. Her hairstyle was different, a bit shorter and more shaped around her face, which accentuated the neo-'60s look and showed off her striking green-and-black earrings. As for Daniela, she had to own a large number of boldly patterned and flowery dresses, as so far she had never worn the same one twice.

Daniela began by saying she aimed to have the new website operational in two months. She stressed again that everything was to be discussed or exchanged on a strictly need-to-know basis and that Vicky and Fran wouldn't meet the people involved in other stages of the production and distribution chain, unless she felt it necessary.

'We are operating in an immature and largely unregulated market. That has positives and negatives. Interest in brain enhancement and ways of making humans smarter and more intelligent is growing all the time and it will soon be very big business, as well as a major scientific phenomenon. There is also much ignorance and misinformation around it, so the public and consumers can be easily confused or misled. The opportunities have to be seized now.'

Fran presumed from this that the confusion and misinformation were among the negatives, although it sounded ambiguous. Daniela turned to the big whiteboard behind her desk and brought up a multicoloured graphic headed *The Chemical Secrets of Chocolate*. She stood aside to let them read through the list of beneficial ingredients.

Flavonoids were top of the list, with the claim that they *maintain the elasticity of blood vessels and help to ward off heart disease, as well as stroke and other diseases of old age*. Fran remembered that these were also found in blueberry-type fruits, as well as green tea and red wine. Next was caffeine, *the well-known stimulant that acts on the central nervous system*. After this were four near-unpronounceable chemicals that Fran had never heard of, each with a short description: theobromine, *a mild stimulant with mood-elevating effects*; tryptophan, *which helps the brain make serotonin, promoting feelings of well-being*; anandamide, *a messenger molecule associated with natural highs similar to the effects of cannabis*; and lastly the whopping phenyl ethylamine, *a substance that is popularly dubbed the 'love chemical', associated with feelings of attraction and excitement*.

'Wow, that's mind-blowing,' said Fran. 'Is it all true?'

She was wondering if there was a need for any additional special ingredient, but she decided not to make a joke of it, in case it was misunderstood or taken badly. Daniela thumped the palm of her hand with the laser pointer as she replied, giving extra emphasis to particularly significant words.

'I don't have the direct evidence to hand, but this is about chocolate, remember. People will believe practically anything about the benefits of wine or chocolate. And this graphic comes from an authoritative published source. The problem is that to get real benefit it has to be consumed in concentrated form, at least eighty-five per cent cocoa mass. There are well-funded research programmes going on around the world and it may soon become available as a pill, which will make it even more concentrated and more palatable to most tastes.'

'Well, yes,' said Fran, 'but then the chocolate loses all its sensuality, surely, if it's in a pill?'

Vicky was still staring at the board, checking out what she was about to say. 'The interesting thing for us, for Junoco, is what's missing from the effects. It's mostly about physical health and mood. There's nothing about freeing the imagination, stimulating creativity and being inspired to work on your talents.'

'Yes, that's right. Junoco is the missing piece,' said Daniela. 'What we have to decide is how much we play on the magic formula, as opposed to highlighting the strength and purity of our cocoa beans. On the one hand, the secret element could draw unwelcome attention, but it will also be irresistibly enticing to that section of the public who crave more mystery and adventure in their lives.'

While Fran was considering this, Vicky talked about the need to operate at least two parallel websites, so they could pop up and if necessary disappear at a moment's notice, using a planned exit strategy. She was also keen to generate a 'viral buzz' to draw in a high volume of customers through social media channels. All of this was new territory for Fran and she listened intently.

When Vicky finally paused, Daniela turned to Fran and smiled encouragingly.

'Fran, you're deep in thought – tell us.'

They spent the next hour discussing the agenda items that she had prepared: brand identity and design, current and potential competitors, target customer groups, distinctive selling points, promotional partners and so on. At the end, Daniela and Vicky seemed satisfied and Fran had accumulated a long list of new tasks.

The agreed strategy was to begin by attracting individuals who were already using or exploring mind-enhancing products, or who were naturally keen to increase their curiosity and improve their mental performance. The curiosity seekers, Fran branded this group in her mind. Once a certain volume of sales was achieved and they had created the viral buzz, the second stage was to branch out and target large institutions or companies that aspired to be cutting-edge and would appreciate the value of selling the Junoco truffles or offering them gratis to customers, clients, guests, employees, members, students and so on. Ultimately, the ambition was to make the Junoco brand part of an upmarket and highly enviable culture, with a streak of counterculture, that appealed in particular to the creative, intellectual and business elite.

'And we'll do it by stealth,' added Vicky. 'No traditional publicity campaign or contact with the press. Everyone involved will have a vested interest in discretion. That way, we can hope to reap our success quickly and quietly, without interference. Isn't that right, Daniela?'

'That's exactly right. And it's imperative that we are disciplined and watchful and support each other. There will be problems and unknown risks. Don't expect a picnic, as you say.'

On that note, Daniela dismissed them by saying she was going to make a phone call to her cousin Osvaldo. This gave Fran the chance to invite Vicky back to her house for lunch, although she didn't feel ready to talk about what they had just heard. It was so ambitious and there were huge implications. She couldn't get her head round it yet, and she didn't want to come across as less than wholly enthusiastic and committed.

'I have to admit, Vicky, I've got an ulterior motive, as well as wanting to show you my place. There are glitches with my IT, probably something wrong with how it was set up when I moved in. The different parts of the system aren't communicating properly.'

On the way home there was no sign of the crumpled girl on the grass, or the kind Dr Kwesi. As they turned the corner, chatting about moving house and the obvious pitfalls you fail to anticipate, Fran saw Lily sitting on the front wall with her scooter beside her and Sahara the hamster nestling in her hands. She stood up and walked towards them.

'Hello, Fran. I wanted to tell you I am going to Germany on holiday tomorrow and I won't see you for two weeks.'

'Ah, okay Lily, thanks. Have a great time and I'll see you when you get back.'

Lily stood in their path, clearly not wanting to be dismissed so lightly. 'Can I come in for a minute? My mum's popped out to the shops and she'll be back soon. She's happy for me to come round to yours. I've told her that you're scared of birds getting inside the house, and Marcus is scared of spiders and creepy-crawlies.'

Fran sent a questioning glance over Lily's head to Vicky, who nodded and appeared relaxed about it.

'Okay then, just for a short while because my friend Vicky here needs to sort out my computer and then we're having lunch together.'

Lily turned to Vicky and gave her a deeply suspicious look before stretching out her hands to introduce her to Sahara, who was busy fiddling with her whiskers.

'Hello, Vicky. I'm Fran's friend too, and this is Sahara, she's a girl hamster.'

Once inside the house, and with the scooter parked under the stairs, Vicky set to work on the computer. Lily sat back in the big armchair and took the opportunity to start a conversation with Fran about the cosmos.

'Did you know there are 100 billion stars in the Milky Way, at least, probably lots more, and that's just in our galaxy? There are billions and billions of stars in the whole universe.'

'Yes, I know that – and did you know that there are also 100 billion neurons or nerve cells in our brain? It's amazing, isn't it? The stars and the brain cells are alike, in a way, and both are still mysterious, there's so much more to discover.'

Lily was quiet for a few seconds, struck by this coincidence and how you could play with it. 'What if, instead of the 100 billion nerve cells, I had the 100 billion stars in the Milky Way inside my brain – like they got mixed up somehow?'

Fran laughed. 'Your head would be all lit up at night and it would twinkle more and more as the stars came out. But I'm not sure what would happen if your brain cells were spread out across the sky. They might get taken off by aliens and used for good or evil. It's a fantastical thought, Lily.'

'You're clever, Fran; that's one reason I like you.'

'You're even cleverer, because you're only eleven and you know so much.'

Lily pondered this for a moment. 'I am clever but I'm not cool. It's okay. I don't want to be cool and I don't want a new phone either, though nearly everyone has one. Sahara is much better, more fun.'

'Well, I think you're great, Lily, and I'm glad we're friends. I wanted to ask, does your mum come from Germany?'

'Yes, she's from East Germany, when she was a child. Now it's all one country, Germany.'

'Are you going to see your brother when you're there – Ferdi, isn't it?'

'Yes. I'll stay with my dad and Ferdi lives with him. Do you see your little sister, the one you said you missed?'

Fran flinched, taken aback by the direct question. She had started this line of conversation by mentioning Marina previously. It wasn't fair to shut it down now.

'I did see her recently, but not in real life; more in a dream or a memory.'

This was hopeless; she was acting like her parents. You

had to talk honestly to children. Lily in particular was well able to handle it, and she would probably be more curious than upset.

'Actually, Lily, I'm sorry to tell you that my sister, who was called Marina, died when she was only two years old. It happened a long time ago.'

She looked up and saw that Vicky had stopped work on the computer and was listening too. The sense of release, the relief at knowing that her new friends had heard and taken in this simple statement of fact, was immense.

Chapter 6

She had just finished wrapping items for a customer when Vicky called. Daniela wanted to see them urgently and another sales assistant was coming in to look after the shop. When Vicky arrived and they went up to the office, Daniela was on the phone talking in Spanish, her tone of voice indicating barely suppressed frustration. Ending the call curtly, she threaded her fingers through her hair and stared down at the desk for a full minute. Then she looked up at them, regaining her composure and apologising for bringing them in at such short notice. She had to warn them that someone had approached her, not through the temporary website but at her local jive class the previous evening. Whoever it was, they had quite unnerved her.

'Who on earth was it, Daniela? What did they want?' asked Vicky.

'Did you know them?' added Fran.

'It was a man in his forties, smartly dressed and quite a talented dancer, I have to say. It's a class where you change partners every few minutes and in the short time we were going through the standard moves, he informed me that we were involved in the same line of business. He didn't mention Junoco or chocolates, but I knew immediately it wasn't Frocks and Chocs he was interested in.' She paused for dramatic effect.

'What happened after that? Did he reveal anything else?' Vicky prodded.

'He said his boss was interested in coming to a business arrangement with me and there would be mutual benefit in working together, each bringing different things to the party, as he put it.'

'What kind of business is it? What are they proposing?' asked Fran.

Daniela shot her a withering look. She shouldn't have spoken up; should have just listened and digested, instead of wading in like that.

'I didn't ask him. It's a veiled threat, don't you see, it's not a serious business proposition. I've got something the boss wants, that's the point, and he is sending a message to show he intends to get it, one way or another. The middleman wasn't going to tell me anything more – who the boss is or what he does – and I didn't tell him anything about Junoco either.'

Fran sat back and sighed inwardly, cursing her naivety. Vicky spoke next, very deliberately as she was still absorbing the information. She would hit the right note, unlike Fran with her brainless questions.

'He knows about Junoco's unique formula, not the fact there is one because that's already public knowledge on the website. Either he knows what our added ingredient is or, more likely, he wants to find out and thinks he can intimidate or con you into telling him. It's odd, though, approaching you at a dance class, don't you think? It's generally a furtive, park bench type of thing.'

'That's why I was speaking to Osvaldo when you came in. He swears it has nothing to do with him. Have either of you told anyone or dropped any hints about the forest berries or the birds?'

Fran felt confident that she had stuck to the official 'natural product' description and not given away too much when she made Ned her Junoco partner. She also realised that because of Judi's death happening when it did, she hadn't reported back to Daniela and Vicky on Ned's Junoco experience. This was well worth recording, as he had found himself writing fluent and expressive letters to his daughters in French, which over the years he had allowed to become rusty from disuse.

'No, we haven't told anyone, but it wouldn't take much to find out,' said Vicky. 'If you were curious enough and had access to the right lab equipment, you could get the truffles analysed, although the test wouldn't identify the exact type of berries if they are still unknown to the outside world.'

'Right then, thank you both,' said Daniela, standing up abruptly and speaking with an air of authority intended to discourage any speculation. 'We operate with high vigilance – report to me if anyone approaches you, online or in person, or if you have a suspicion or bad feeling about any of your contacts. Also, no one must find out that Junoco is managed from above the shop. This building is Frocks and Chocs, nothing else.'

They had another half-hour before Fran had to relieve the sales assistant in the shop, so she and Vicky slipped out to the café.

'To be honest with you, Vicky, I feel quite shaken by this latest development. Is it okay, do you think – above board, I mean, and safe, or at least not wildly risky? Am I being a wimp, worrying about it? Do tell me I am because I love Junoco already, we're having fun and who knows, we might even make a fortune out of it.'

Vicky smiled fondly. 'Oh, Fran, that's so typical – it's like I've known you for years! If it does start making big money, we have to make sure we're in the right place to profit from it. Daniela's a tough cookie, never forget that, and smart. She has to pass information on to us, but she won't divulge any more than is strictly necessary. As for the risks, I think of them as fairly standard business perils, with a little extra pizzazz to keep us on our toes.'

She smiled at Fran, tipping her face sideways and cheekily raising her beautifully groomed eyebrows to make them disappear under the full fringe. 'If you have a magic formula, your most ruthless competitors will always want to get hold of it and believe me, they will be devious. Ask any number of top companies.'

'You're right, Vicky; it's just a different world. I haven't been involved in anything remotely like this before and I'm only now realising what a sheltered life I've led. I'm truly glad I've moved on from it before it was too late – and the best thing is, I no longer have a bozo for a boss! No, actually, that's not right. The best thing about it, among a load of good things, is that I've met you.' She blew some stray grains of sugar across the table in Vicky's direction to cover her slight embarrassment. 'So there!'

When she stepped out of the café a few minutes later, leaving Vicky to linger over a second coffee before heading off home, she almost bumped into Dr Kwesi. He greeted her warmly.

'Good afternoon, Fran. Are you shopping today?'

'Hello, Kwesi. No, I work in the dress shop along here. It's one of my two jobs.'

He was smiling and stroking his chin thoughtfully, clearly indicating that he hoped for more of a conversation.

'Have you seen the girl again, Kwesi, the street girl? Was she okay?'

'Yes, she stood up before the ambulance car arrived and she ran away when I tried to talk to her. She is a very sad and sick person, an addict. It is common in my country, everywhere.'

She knew she could easily excuse herself again as being in a rush but she felt she owed this man something, because of the way he had come forward and got her out of a tight spot.

'Have you got time for a quick coffee later, after I finish work? I think you may like this little French café here, with all its delicious cakes. Say 5.30?'

'Thank you Fran, I would like it very much. I have the whole day free.'

He had used similar words last time and she wondered where he worked; in which hospital or GP surgery.

When she arrived later at the café, Kwesi was one of a handful of customers sitting inside, as most people were gravitating to the pubs on the green for after-work drinks in the late sunshine. She went to the counter to order coffee and carrot cake for herself and a cherry tart topped with cream for Kwesi. He picked up the spoon, gave her a half-guilty look and felt his stomach through his loose shirt.

'I enjoy the English cakes, they taste special. I will buy a cake for you next time, but I have no money today.'

She asked where he worked and he told her how he had been forced to leave his country – he didn't want to identify it – as he treated a lot of patients with AIDS and was persecuted for it. He was gay, although this was known only to a few trusted friends at home. He had been harassed out of his job and eventually out of his town. Deciding to seek refuge and a new life in the UK, where he had once studied on a university scholarship programme, he had expected to find work as a hospital doctor but it turned out he didn't have the right papers. Now he was involved in a lengthy process of appealing against a decision to refuse him refugee status.

'Are you working at all, then? What's your position now?'

'Yes, I also have two jobs, like you, but they are not good jobs. I worked as an office cleaner in the City, but my company was shut down by the police. I have a new cleaning job but it is part-time, a few hours a week. And in my other job I work at night, packing in a warehouse for a delivery company. It is not secure until I have my papers; then I hope to be a doctor again.'

'Where do you stay? Have you got somewhere, a room, near here?

He hesitated for a long moment and gave her a serious look. 'I will trust you, Fran. You are a good person, I know. I sleep in the library. I stay there in the day as well when it rains and I have a way to get into the building in the evening, after it has closed.'

She knew where the library was, although she hadn't yet visited it. It had been reinvented as a multi-purpose 'discovery centre', but it still had the words *Public Library* engraved in stone above the imposing main door.

'That's terrible, Kwesi.'

'Not always terrible. The library staff, some of them know I am sleeping there. One day I will repay them for their kindness. I have a suitcase with many gifts.'

'Gifts – you brought gifts with you, presents? Who are they for?'

'Yes, presents from Africa, from my country. I filled a suitcase with presents for my new friends in London, when they invite me as a guest into their homes. That is an important custom with us.'

Fran stared at his wide, gently smiling face over her half-eaten and abandoned carrot cake. It was dead right, what she had said to Vicky earlier. She had led a very sheltered life.

***

She was sitting in a shaft of sunlight, her mind swinging between itemising her next tasks in setting up the Junoco business, speculating on the identity of the rival who had made the veiled threat, and deciding what she was going to make for dinner. The children were coming home and there was Lily walking on her own, looking small in her new school uniform and peering in the window as she passed. Fran returned her eager wave, remembering her comment about being clever but not cool. Had Lily ever had a best friend?

An hour later, she surfaced from her doze and saw Marcus from next door running past the window at full pelt. She blinked to wake herself up completely and the doorbell rang. There he was, breathing heavily, in his stylish office suit and pointed brown shoes, leather bag on his shoulder.

'Can I come in please, not for long? I'll explain. I'm sorry to disturb you.'

She stepped back so he could enter and then closed the door behind him. He stood in the hallway, his eyes shut while he regained his breath.

'Come through to the kitchen, Marcus. I was about to boil the kettle for tea – unless you need something stronger?'

'I could do with a cold beer, if you have one, thanks.'

As Fran had already surmised, it was about Kirsty, the ex-girlfriend. She had left him alone for a couple of weeks because she had gone to visit relatives, but she was back now and had accosted him outside his office at lunchtime, saying she had taken a job locally as a nursery teacher and was going to move in with him.

'It's like I've got no option. She's made a decision that we're soulmates for life, those are her actual words, and we're going to have several children and it's all fated to happen, even though she knows I've had a vasectomy. It's not an issue apparently, I can have it reversed.'

'Wow, easy as that. Did you live together before you moved here?'

'Yes, for a while, but it ended two years ago. We fell out and she got jealous – well, I guess we both did. She went to Australia on a work visa and I don't know what's happened since but now she's got this fantasy scenario of happily-ever-after with me and a troop of kids.'

'How old are you, Marcus?' It wasn't immediately relevant to the story, but she was curious to know.

'I'm forty-four, for God's sake, well past it. I had my kids young, they're grown up now. I'm too old to deal with this, it's ridiculous.' He paused and moved to the kitchen window, so he was no longer looking directly at her. 'The worst of it is that I did something idiotic, which makes it partly my own fault. I let her stay here for two nights, a couple of weekends ago. It was stupid of me, weak. After she'd left, I realised she'd gone off with my spare key. I've been meaning to change the lock, but I haven't got round to it yet.'

Fran hesitated before responding to this frank admission, aware that their friendship was still new and untested. 'Perhaps you kind of wanted her to come back, to get in – not consciously, but at some level?'

'It's a thought, but no, I don't think that's right. I am sorry for her; she's not got a place at the moment and yes, she's attractive but she's a total nightmare and out of control. I got all paranoid about it this afternoon and rightly so, because I was convinced she was following me home just now. I sensed her behind me and that's why I ended up running: to get ahead and hide out here to see what she does. I just hoped you were in. It's not the best idea, me running along the street, especially not at that pace.'

'Well, I'm glad you thought you could hide here, so don't worry about that.'

As they entered the living room, Marcus suddenly ducked and squatted down low, pointing out the window. Kirsty was on the other side of the road, leaning on the big chestnut tree and, like last time, busy with her phone. Fran closed the lower window blinds so they could still see out over them and Marcus half-stood up and moved, in full stealth mode, to the armchair nearest to the window. He checked his phone, signalling with his fingers that he had received seven voicemail messages and three texts.

Kirsty stayed under the tree for half an hour, then picked up her sports bag and sauntered across the road towards Marcus' house. The wrought-iron gate whined as it swung open, the bell rang twice, and they heard her swearing as she struggled to turn the key in the lock before the door slammed shut. Marcus was bolt upright now, like a startled animal frozen in the critical instant of indecision. Next to him, on the animal-skin drum, Guacamole peered over his wire-rimmed spectacles with an air of benign interest.

Marcus leant forward, putting his hands on his knees and shaking his head. 'Oh no, she's in now!'

'Will she damage anything, do you think? Is she destructive?' Fran was thinking back to Kirsty's aggressive encounter with Eric and Delia; the force of her anger and self-righteousness.

'I can't be sure, but I don't think she'd create havoc in that way. She's more sad than angry. I think she'll just sit and wait for me to arrive home – at least, I imagine that's the plan. She won't want to alienate me, not yet. We are soulmates for life, after all.'

'Do you think you should go round now and talk to her, try and sort it out?'

'If you want me to leave then I will, but quite frankly, I can't face it. I'm talked out and the conversation just goes round in circles. She might snoop about but she doesn't know any of my device passwords, thankfully, and I've got my work tablet and phone here with me. But as I say, I'll only hide out here if it's no trouble to you.'

Fran reassured him and said she had no plans for the evening. She set about cooking a supper of stir-fry chicken and vegetables and put a bottle of wine to chill in the fridge. After a brief discussion on the best place to eat, they carried their plates through to the front room, where the side window was open at the top, so they would know if Kirsty gave up and left.

As time went on and after they had talked about the Kirsty issue at some length, it seemed okay to broach a different subject.

'Can I ask you about something else, Marcus, unconnected to this?'

'Yes, go ahead, I'm all ears.' He had calmed down and seemed to be quite enjoying himself, with the aid of two large glasses of wine following the beer.

'I'm going to ask because you work in the Department of Health and you may be able to tell me something, or find out for me.'

'Okay, it's a big place with lots happening and I may not be able to help, but what is it?'

She told him what she had revealed to Ned about the Junoco venture, again omitting the part about its origin in berry seeds from the rainforest. She spoke carefully, aware that she hadn't yet got a properly refined promotional pitch, and that they were still debating how to promote the benefits of the truffles.

'The effect of the secret ingredient, when combined with the rich chocolate, is to enhance curiosity and creativity. That's what makes it exciting and potentially important. We're not making a big noise about it because we don't want to draw the wrong kind of attention.'

Marcus was sitting forward in his chair now, clearly fascinated by what he was hearing and the unwelcome guest in his house temporarily forgotten. 'It sounds amazing and I've got a million questions, but first off, have you tried the chocolate yourself? And if you have, what happened?'

She told him about the lakeside dream and the pencil sketches of Marina, her father and her late friend Judi, which as a set she considered better than anything she had ever drawn. She had more sketches now, of Marina at different ages and of Judi as a free-spirited child on the farm, plus several of wild animals, especially the large cats and zebras, hippos and different types of antelope. She drew them all from her memory and imagination, as they came to her.

'Wow, Fran, this is awesome. I thought you worked in a local dress shop; that's what you were telling me.'

She laughed and replied in a low, husky whisper. 'That was last month. Now I'm in a global chocolate racket.' She paused. 'No, actually I'm still working as a sales assistant in the dress shop round the corner. That's my day job.'

She followed Daniela's strict instruction and didn't tell him the two businesses were linked and Junoco was located above Frocks and Chocs. She also left out the strange connection she was experiencing with Guacamole and other creatures, real and pretend. It was still too weird and difficult to mention.

'Okay, I'll hold off on the rest of my million questions for now, but I hope you'll show me your drawings one day. What was it you wanted to know from me?'

Fran hesitated, thinking about Daniela's repeated words of caution. 'Before I say anything more, I have to stress the need to keep it strictly confidential; not to talk openly to your colleagues or anyone about what I've asked.'

'I'll be discreet, don't worry. You wouldn't believe the amount of confidential stuff I've got in my head – most of it worthless rubbish, mind you.'

'Well, okay then. I've been doing market research for our promotional strategy and it seems there's a large grey area, legally. First, there are the mind-enhancing or smart drugs, used by students and others, which claim to improve focus and mental performance. Then we have the former "legal highs", which mimic the effects of illegal drugs and are cheap substitutes. They contain nobody knows what, often a cocktail of toxic substances. The Psychoactive Substances Act has banned legal highs, although I don't know how successfully – but that's not the point. What I want to find out is whether the Act covers mind-enhancing substances like Junoco. They are clearly psychoactive, but very different from legal highs or known hallucinogenic drugs. Is it illegal to supply them, or borderline legal? My boss says you can get away with just about anything if you're operating online and as long as we're light-footed, there's no problem.'

Marcus stared into the middle distance, elbows on his knees. He had slim, muscled thighs. 'You're right, it is hugely complex and your chocolates may well fall into a grey area, as you say. The legal aspect is more for the Home Office than the Department of Health, but I know who's likely to be involved from our side and he's a friendly guy, very approachable. I'll talk to him in general terms and get back to you on which way the wind's blowing.'

'That'll be fantastic, and I hope you don't mind me asking. Hey, would you like to try Junoco now, or take a pair of blue and gold truffles home with you?'

'Thank you, but no, I won't. I put too much crazy stuff into my body in the past and decided to draw the line when I hit thirty-five. I'd love to find a creative solution to the Kirsty problem and I'm certainly curious about how her mind works, but I think I'm best coming up with that on my own.'

It was late by now, almost midnight, and Kirsty still hadn't left. Marcus gratefully accepted Fran's offer to stay over and asked if he could sleep on the sofa, as her second bedroom adjoined his own back room and he didn't want Kirsty hearing sounds through the wall and possibly 'putting two and two together and making four – or even five'.

They were up early the next morning and observed Kirsty leaving the house to join the commuters heading for the underground. Fran couldn't make out her facial expression, but she noticed that she didn't have her sports bag and was carrying only a small shoulder bag. Marcus left at a quarter to eight, looking devious himself as he crept down Fran's front path and round their dividing wall to his own door. Within a few minutes, she received a text thanking her for shielding him and saying that all looked as usual, no visible damage. His priority task for the day, as he put it, was to change the locks.

**

She paid the taxi driver and walked up the lane to the end cottage, wondering if she should have come. It was so soon after the funeral. She stopped to lean over the paddock fence, but there was no snort of welcome and no sign of the pony, either in the field or sheltering from the sun under the trees on the ridge. She and Andy had never spent any time together, just the two of them, and the attraction between them had always been cleverly mediated by Judi. It could all be illusory. The butterflies in her stomach were fluttering like crazy, as they invariably did in the final approach to meeting a new date in a pub or café, when she just wanted to turn around and run for home. This was a much bigger thing, complicated by history and fraught with risk, although she hadn't fully considered what the risks were. That she – or they – would let Judi down, betray her memory? That she would look like an utter fool to anyone – and that was everyone – who didn't know what had passed between them and had no knowledge of the history? That they would keep it going too long and for all the wrong reasons?

Stop it, Frankie, lighten up. Judi had simply said that she hoped they would go on holiday together. She had indicated by her deliberate phrasing that it should be short and sweet. This was the spirit in which to keep walking along the lane, although the clear intention of Judi's wish was already compromised by Andy saying he wasn't ready for a holiday yet and it would be more relaxed if she came to the cottage.

As she approached and opened the rickety wooden gate, she didn't look up to see if he was at the kitchen window. The front garden was overgrown and the sweet-smelling lavender bush swarming with bees. She broke off a small twig to sniff it, knocked and waited, unsure what to expect and experiencing a confused mix of sadness, trepidation and excitement.

Andy opened the door instantly; he must have been standing right behind it. They exchanged one of those long, meaningful looks, breaking it with an edgy laugh.

'Are you going to invite me in, then?'

He moved backwards to make space for her to enter, tripping over a shoe or other stray object lying in the porch and almost losing his footing.

Everything looked the same, back to the way it was before they set up the bed in the sitting room, except for the sympathy cards arranged along the shelves, with photos of Judi propped in between. The pine table was covered with freshly picked garden produce in the woven baskets and Andy had laid out a lunch of bread and cheese in the sitting room, with salad, a bowl of deep red tomatoes and fresh orange juice. Another difference from before, she noted, was that Winnie the dog was friendlier, no longer aloof and keeping her distance.

Over lunch, he told her their local friends had been fantastic and he'd had lots of visitors. She listened for any mention of a special friend but he didn't single anyone out, apart from one of his mates who had helped with keeping his building business on track.

'What would you like to do this afternoon? We could take Winnie for a walk to the beach, later perhaps, after you've had a bit of a rest?'

'Yes, later, that would be nice.' Later – would that be before or after?

She followed him into the kitchen and watched as he stacked the dishwasher. His hair was longer, the dark curls at the end twisting and falling in different directions across his neck. As he leant forward and crouched to rearrange the crockery, the smooth brown skin on his lower back was exposed and then hidden again as he stood up and started to run the taps. She couldn't tell if he was shy and playing for time or just carrying out a normal, everyday task in his normal, systematic way. Maybe it was wise to wait until the evening; use the day to relax more with each other.

She waited another minute, feeling the rise in tension as the silence continued and he didn't turn round, busy at the sink. She looked up at the clock; still early afternoon. He started to turn and she made an impulsive move, aiming to seize him round the waist but instead pulling his shorts halfway down his bum. He yanked them up again with a cry of mock indignation and grabbed her hand.

Giggling like teenagers, they raced upstairs, kicked off their shoes and kneeled up face-to-face on the bed, taking off each other's clothes one item at a time. This took Andy longer to accomplish, as Fran only had three items to take off him – shorts, T-shirt and tight black briefs. Naked and aroused, he was every bit as sexy and desirable as she had envisaged; even more so, if that were possible.

When they finally rolled away from each other and lay back to back, just their heels still touching, she reached to feel the small glass perfume bottles on the chest of drawers. Picking out Judi's favourite fragrance, she sprayed a little on the inside of her wrists, twisting her forearms up to her face to catch the haunting scent. Andy turned over to make spoons and they stayed like that, comfortable and deeply relaxed. Fran heard Winnie climbing up the stairs and she soon padded into the room, her tail wagging with pleasure at finding them and then thumping hard against the side of the bed. She jumped up, did a one-and-a-half-circle turn and plonked herself down on top of their entwined legs and feet, which had long kicked off the duvet. When Fran lifted her head and leaned up on her elbows to look at the dog, her wet nose resting between her paws, it felt as if she were staring into Judi's luminous brown eyes.

It was early evening when they set off to the beach, and they had fun throwing sticks for Winnie and watching her leaping about at the water's edge. On the way back, they met a couple on the path who were strangers to Fran. The woman spoke in a personal way to Andy, clearly wanting to show that she was a close confidante with privileged information. She made no effort to acknowledge Fran and Andy didn't think to introduce them. She felt like a spare part, an interloper even. The woman's companion, presumably her partner, was uncivil to both Fran and Andy, striding ahead and waiting, with obvious impatience, fifty yards down the track. Fran's doubts came flooding back. She could have stayed in London and accepted Ned's invitation for dinner this evening. She didn't belong here; it felt all wrong. It could even affect her relationship with Judi, or the spirit of it, which was not to be played around with.

For the rest of the day, she felt conflicted. The chance encounter reminded her of how little she understood Andy. And her position was odd, to say the least; discreditable to others who didn't know her and maybe even to herself, given the overtly lustful nature of her thoughts. It was a tussle, half of her taking this moralistic line and half hanging on to the extraordinary experience that had drawn them all together, the volatile bundle of emotions.

They went to sleep late in their separate bedrooms and she was woken by the brawling of the seagulls, which were noisier and more aggressive than ever, now that the youngsters were growing and battling for perches and air space. She tried to remember her final dream. It wasn't a good dream; she knew that from her uneasy mood on waking. *Concentrate, let it through...* yes, it was a party, she was at a party with Judi and Andy's friends, but Judi wasn't there and she couldn't find Andy in the crowd. Then there was sudden panic, a fire with leaping flames and smoke. Everyone was running to escape from the house and she had to reach Andy and rescue him. It was a promise to Judi, to save him. As she shouted his name, a woman stopped beside her, a local friend but not the one they had met on the path. The woman spoke in a breezy way, saying that Andy was fine. He had got bored and left the party hours ago.

Fran swung her legs over the side of the bed, digging her toes into the deep pile of the rug as she pushed the dream to the back of her mind. Her toes were tingling and she suddenly smiled as she wiggled them about, remembering the fabulous high of the previous afternoon. As she crept along the landing and down the steep, creaking stairs, she managed to avoid treading on the watchful Winnie, who was on guard outside Andy's bedroom and dutifully followed her down.

'Be careful, Frankie,' she said to herself in a half-audible whisper. 'It's only meant to be a holiday. That's all you're covered for, remember. Don't push it.'

Chapter 7

Despite her growing apprehension, she couldn't help admiring Ned's style as he weaved between the tables, stepping back politely to let the tray-wielding waitresses pass. It was the first time she had seen him in a proper suit and it looked beautiful on him. The cut of the trousers accentuated his long legs and the open-neck shirt was just the right shade of pink. Fran glanced sideways to decipher the expression on Daniela's face as Ned signalled to show that he had spotted them.

'Is this him coming over now, Fran? Ah yes, it must be.'

Daniela had no clue that this man was Fran's lover, and Fran had no intention of telling her. Daniela stood up to offer him a businesslike handshake, while Fran attracted the attention of a waitress standing at the other end of the bar, with a bored expression and hands folded in at-ease mode. They were in a Central London hotel, where retired people meeting for lunch mingled with business types briefing colleagues or making deals and freelancers focused on their electronic devices. Today, there was also a sprinkling of hotel guests and foreign tourists deciding how best to enjoy the city in the rain.

The meeting was happening because Daniela had had another approach from the shadowy stranger at the dancing class, this time as she was turning into her own front path after an evening out with friends. She had told Fran and Vicky about it a couple of days ago, commenting that he was turning up the heat, showing he knew where she lived. She had demanded to know the name of his boss and he said he couldn't reveal his identity yet, as he had various business interests and needed to keep them separate. Then he had added, 'We'll use a code name for now. His code name is Infrared.'

The middleman then repeated and expanded on his line that this Infrared character traded in similar products and was interested in coming to an agreement with Daniela, so they could both run their enterprises successfully and wouldn't get in each other's way. Code name Infrared – it sounded both sinister and ludicrous, but this time Fran knew better than to make any rash comment.

Daniela had told them that she might agree to an exploratory meeting, as these guys weren't going to go away and she had to know what kind of threat they posed. She was discussing tactics with Osvaldo but as a cautionary measure, she had decided to close the Junoco distribution centre and set it up again in a new location. Fran had immediately thought of Ned and his portfolio of properties in South London, telling Daniela and Vicky that he was her Junoco partner, had a great head for business and would be reliably discreet.

She felt guilty that she couldn't give Ned the whole picture, as Daniela wanted such strict control over what was said and when. She had simply mentioned the need for a new distribution centre in London, as the Junoco business was starting to take off and they expected a large proportion of their expanding market to be in the capital. As for the uncertain legality of the venture, Ned had shown zero interest in that aspect when she introduced him to the Junoco truffles and she didn't know if he would pursue it now with Daniela. It would probably depend on how attractive an offer she was willing to make. Fran was still astonished by her own involvement in all this and, although alarmed by the rather menacing aspect that had crept in, she was carried along by the thrill of it.

When Ned sat down, Daniela was her normal friendly and expansive self and the initial wariness that Fran caught in her eyes and gestures soon eased off. This allowed Fran herself to relax and start enjoying her role in bringing them together. Ned was attentive, leaning forward and stroking his chin thoughtfully until Daniela came to a natural pause and waited for his response. He spoke confidently and authoritatively, setting out his offer.

'I have an empty warehouse unit, it should be big enough. I'll need to check the dimensions and let you know. It's on an industrial estate and there's decent parking and plenty of delivery vehicles, so your vans shouldn't stand out in any way. The unit has been empty for a few months and I was thinking of selling it, but I'd be happy to give you an initial six- or twelve-month lease.'

He paused and looked round the lounge, as if to check that no one was listening in. A young woman at a nearby table smiled impulsively over her laptop and then quickly averted her gaze, embarrassed that he had caught her admiring him.

'It's relatively high-risk, of course. I'd have to add a

premium to allow for the extra security, care and discretion you require.'

Daniela turned sharply to Fran as he said this, and Fran shook her head almost imperceptibly to indicate that she hadn't breached any confidentiality.

'I explained to Ned that Junoco has a wholly natural secret ingredient, and that our competitors are bound to be interested in trying to identify and get hold of it.'

'That's good. I understand and appreciate your concern over security, Ned, and I'd be happy to come to an agreement, once I've visited and checked out the unit and site. We'll get the details sorted, so we can move in as soon as possible. I have one more thing to settle, before we go any further. Nobody else is to know the location of the distribution centre, not even Fran, okay?'

She then deftly turned the conversation to Ned's wider business interests and, just as she had done in her initial meeting with Fran, zoned in on a particular aspect; in this case, his dealings in expensive apartments overlooking the Thames. Did he own these apartments or manage them? The answer was both. Who were the buyers? They were mainly overseas investors, many of whom had no intention of living in them or letting them out. Fran thought of Ned's charming mansion flat and was glad he had stayed on his quiet, tree-lined street, rather than moving, as he obviously could have done, to a high-spec glass pad with a prestigious view of the river and wealthy, absent neighbours.

'It's interesting that you have a stake in the two hotels, as well,' Daniela was saying. 'I'm beginning to wonder if we should reshape our strategy and bring forward the second stage, when we aim to target institutional clients – hotels, clubs and so on. If you have these contacts, Ned, maybe we could find a way to bring you in? It's just a thought, off the top of my head.'

'Well, it hadn't occurred to me that you were going in that direction, but yes, I am attracted to the business concept and what you're planning to do. Oh, and by the way, my French has improved dramatically since I tasted the Junoco truffles. Even my teenage daughters are impressed, which is saying something.'

What about Daniela's family, *her* personal life? Apart from her cousin Osvaldo, whom she spoke of as a business associate, she hadn't mentioned anyone; a partner or children. Now she stood up and sailed out of the lounge in her billowing way, squeezing herself between two nearby tables and apologising for a tipped-over jug of milk as she went. Fran looked quizzically at Ned, who nodded back while stroking his forehead with his fingers.

'Yes, it was much as I expected, apart from the final suggestion about using my contacts. It appeared to go well, and I like Daniela's business style and directness – quite refreshing. I haven't got the measure of her yet and she was a little guarded, but that's natural in the context and I think we can work together. Thanks for the introduction, Fran, much appreciated. I'm off to France to visit my girls, but what about Friday next week? Are you free for dinner?'

She stirred her coffee and let the froth drop in slow motion off the edge of the spoon. The prospect of dinner with him at the end of next week suited her perfectly, as she was hoping Andy would come to visit her sometime in the next few days.

'I'd love to. You look very fanciable today, I have to say; hunky in pink. Maybe we could have the promised hat show then, entrance by ticket only?'

'I'll ask my agent. It will be expensive for an exclusive show, naturally.'

***

'What are you doing with yourself, Francesca, now you have gone off to London? I have forgotten – fashion, is it?'

Her mother's heavy emphasis on the words 'gone off to London' left her in no doubt as to her gist: *Now you have abandoned me.* It was ridiculous, as Fran could reach the family house from London almost as quickly as when she was living in the countryside. She was beginning to realise that Eleanor had persuaded her to change her weekend plans and come down to Sussex because she felt neglected and needed someone to complain to.

'I've taken a part-time job working in a shop, a boutique place called Frocks and Chocs. It's just five minutes' walk from my house.'

'A shop, that's odd, isn't it, for you? Why would you want to work in a shop?'

She really was a crabby, snobbish old woman.

'It's very nice, actually. It's interesting and fun; I'm enjoying it. The clothes are beautiful and original and some of the customers are colourful characters.'

Eleanor sniffed, tilted her chin and peered at her daughter over her glasses. If only she could understand how boringly predictable she was, how stuck in a rut of her own making. It was unfair, perhaps, to think like this about someone in her eighties, but there it was; Fran wasn't prepared to take the blame any more.

'Well, I've had about enough of colourful characters, myself,' Eleanor said. She was truly spiteful; she always had been.

An episode floated up from the distant past, when Fran was five or six. She had told a visitor she was going to be an actress when she grew up, and her mother had laughed and remarked in her no-nonsense voice, 'My dear, you have neither the looks nor the talent to be an actress.'

Sitting opposite her now, Fran felt the red heat of humiliation all over again and had to fight the urge to talk back, to deliver some belated home truths: *I don't even know what to call you, how to address you. Have you not noticed that I haven't called you anything for forty-odd years? Mum, Mother, Mummy, Eleanor – none of them are right. I don't know who you are to me. You have never talked to me, confided in me, believed in me, rooted for me, not once, ever.*

'Are you listening to me, Francesca? You look like you're gazing out the window.'

Fran plucked a couple of key words from her recall of what her mother had just been saying, filling in the gaps from her wider grasp of the situation.

'I'm listening. You and George aren't getting on and you think Cerise is always taking his side.'

'It's not that we're not getting on, it's that he's impossible. He disappears off down to the café and he forgets to put out his dirty clothes for Mrs Beatty, and she won't go in his room, so he's wearing the same smelly old things every day. On top of which, he can't manage the top stairs any more; he's too wobbly on his feet and he keeps slipping. I can hear him falling about up there.'

Fran sighed to herself. This was going to topple over and land on her, sooner or later. She was an only child and neither Cerise nor George had any children. They were all in their eighties and their home would become unmanageable, being on three floors and with those awkward, old-fashioned bathrooms and toilets. Her father had left his estate in equal shares to his wife and ex-wife, Cerise and Eleanor, no doubt imagining they would sell the house, not set up a ménage à trois with George. As a housemate, but also as George's sister, Cerise was always going to be more tolerant of his eccentric habits and passions than Eleanor, so there was massive scope for friction over what to do about him.

Eleanor was still in full flow, and Fran tuned herself back in.

'He needs to go into a home, I'm afraid to say. He can't look after himself any more, if he ever could. He's buying piles of new stuff and second-hand rubbish all the time, and that parasite of a tramp, Tom Harrison, is still hanging around. Cerise saw him on the corner the other day, where our road turns into Main Street. We're worried he's going to turn up on the doorstep one of these days.'

'What would you like me to do? Talk to George and Cerise?'

'Yes, but first can you phone round the local care homes, find out if they've got a vacancy and go and look at them; see if they'll take George and be prepared to manage him? Don't tell them too much about what he's like or they won't have him.'

Fran had long ago stopped doing what she was instructed to do by her mother. 'No, it has to be the other way round. I have to talk to George first, and Cerise, to see what they want and what ideas they may have.'

Eleanor gave another of her disapproving sniffs. 'You know George's barmy ideas. He's not in the least sensible, never has been, and I don't think you'd like to live with him either, if you're honest about it.'

'Well, if you want me involved, that's how I'm going to do it. I saw George go out and so I'm going to go round to the café now and see if he's there.'

She knew the café well, as in her day the 'in kids' had congregated there on wet afternoons after school to flirt and chat with their friends. It looked run-down now, a victim of the mushrooming growth in coffee bars, chichi tea rooms and smart pubs with all-day food. She could see Uncle George through the front window, sitting with another man, presumably Tom Harrison. George didn't recognise her until she was right beside him.

'Hello, Uncle George. I was passing the café and I saw you in here.'

'Francesca, that's a nice surprise! Have you been here long?'

She laughed. 'I talked to you over lunch at the house. Don't you remember?'

The other man had been watching the exchange, seeing how it was going to unfold. He was shabbily dressed, as she had imagined, but no more so than George himself. Things were going downhill, it was true. The man added another heaped spoonful of sugar to his tea and continued stirring as he spoke.

'I'm not being funny or anything, but is this your girlfriend, George? You never told me about no girlfriend, you cheeky old sod.'

George looked nonplussed.

'No, I'm his niece, if you want to know.' Then, turning to George: 'Let's go back home now, Uncle George. Cerise will have dinner ready soon.'

'Ooh-er, listen to her! It's frigging din-dins time, Uncle George!'

The man had most of his front teeth missing. He was rough and unpleasant; her mother was right about that too. George was struggling to stand up and Fran reached out her hand to steady him as she spoke.

'Come on, then. I suppose you've already paid for the tea and scones for both you and Tom?'

He nodded miserably and they left without saying goodbye to his companion. On the way back to the house, she asked if he was giving money to Tom or if Tom was demanding money off him, but George did his familiar trick of feigning deafness and refused to answer.

Dinner was uneventful because George said he felt unwell and wanted to go to bed. Cerise was in her usual good spirits and Eleanor was more relaxed without George around. Fran told them about her encounter with Tom and the three of them discussed possible tactics to discourage him or scare him off. Even Cerise was happy with the idea, compassionate as she was, because nobody was going to get away with being mean to her brother.

When she stayed overnight now, Fran slept on the sofa bed in Cerise's study, although Eleanor had a spare bedroom on the first floor. Fran's childhood bedroom on the top floor, in George's flat, was packed high with objects and equipment, to the point that neither the furniture nor the floor was visible. The downstairs sleeping arrangement worked better for her anyway, because she liked to spend the late evening with Cerise over a brandy or glass of wine.

She had brought a small sample of the Junoco chocolates with her, thinking she might offer them to Cerise. She was the obvious choice, although it would also be interesting, in different ways, to see the effects of tapping into George's or Eleanor's imagination. Fran was wavering over whether to tell Cerise about the magic formula in advance. She definitely ought to, but here was a tempting opportunity to test whether it would work without the taster having any prior expectations. Cerise was an ideal candidate because she was open-minded and unconventional, whereas George had an untamed imagination to start off with and Eleanor was narrow-minded, judgemental and neurotic.

Cerise was delighted to accept the first chocolate with her Cointreau, so much so that she immediately overplayed the experiment by taking the second one while Fran was in the kitchen refilling her glass of wine. Fran was only mildly concerned about this, as Daniela had said the timing and sequence didn't matter, although it might diminish the efficacy of the truffles. She had planned not to take any herself tonight, so she could keep a good watch on Cerise, but after the second glass of wine she changed her mind and decided to go ahead anyway.

They spent half an hour discussing the problem of George's suspect friendship with Tom. Cerise felt George got something positive from it, but agreed he was being exploited and it would only get worse if Tom continued hanging around. She was considering approaching Tom herself, but Fran cautioned against it, having experienced his vicious attitude at first hand. They then moved on to lighter topics, with Cerise telling her about the various summer music events she had attended and her plans to bake her traditional chocolate cake for the WI stall at the country fete. When they eventually went to bed, Fran left her door slightly ajar, so she would hear any movement or sounds from Cerise.

At dawn, she woke to a Junoco dream, identifiable by its nearness to the surface of her consciousness and her certainty that she was awake and on the sofa bed. She was in a futuristic scene with a city skyline as backdrop and countless people moving in all directions across rocky ground, some quick and purposeful, others slow and seemingly aimless. They were constantly bumping against each other, creating fiery red and blue sparks and bright white flashes. It became apparent that each person was a nerve cell, making up billions of neurons, and the geodesic dome overhead was the top of a vast, universal brain. All this was routine and unremarkable, and Fran was in the midst of the action, unable to avoid colliding with strangers. She looked for someone she knew, but the faces were vaguely drawn and indistinguishable.

She rose to the surface gently, as always with Junoco dreams; more like snorkelling than diving. She could hear Cerise flapping down the hall in her slippers and eliciting a shrill vocalisation from Pansy the parrot, despite the drawn curtain around the cage. Fran lay still for two or three minutes before getting up and creeping out to follow Cerise.

As she approached the sitting room, she heard the piano lid being opened and the stool scraping on the floor as it was repositioned. Looking round the edge of the door into the lighted room, she registered Cerise's set profile and something odd in her pose and the tilt of her head as she raised her hands, fingers poised, and started to play a classical piece. It took a few seconds for Fran to realise that Cerise was actually asleep and unaware of her presence. She entered the room on tiptoe and sat on the arm of a chair, marvelling at the way Cerise played so perfectly from memory, especially as she had never seen her at the piano before. It was George who played ragtime tunes and what they called his 'crooners and divas repertoire', which they all sang along to at their increasingly rare music evenings.

After fifteen minutes, during which time Cerise performed several pieces in quick succession, she stopped playing and carefully closed the lid. Fran watched and followed as she walked back to her bedroom. Fran returned to the sofa bed and took out the sketch pad she had brought with her. She drew a lioness and a half-grown cub at the edge of a watering hole, with the protruding eyes and log head of a crocodile visible above the water, too close for comfort.

Waking from a final light sleep after 7.30, she heard Cerise heading to the kitchen to make their morning tea and followed her again. As they sat down at the table, she told Cerise what she had witnessed and how beautifully she had played. Cerise was incredulous and said she hadn't played anything on the piano, apart from the occasional Christmas tune and *Happy Birthday*, for a good twenty years.

'You were sleepwalking, Cerise. I've heard about people doing extraordinary things in their sleep, even driving cars or going fishing, so it does happen.'

Cerise was frowning with concentration and looking into the distance. 'I did used to sleepwalk, ages ago when I was little. My father once found me in the orchard. I was picking the apples and putting them in a bucket.'

'There you are, then! It was amazing, the quality of your performance.'

She promised herself she would tell Cerise more about Junoco, but not yet. Cerise was so thrilled that Fran feared it would spoil it for her if she knew what had brought it on. Cerise had disappeared to fetch Pansy from her cage, and she returned now with the parrot on her shoulder.

'I was just thinking, maybe it was those delicious chocolates you gave me last night. They were ever so rich.'

'You may be right. These are the truffles that I'm going to be selling in my new job, so you'd better watch out, world!'

Cerise laughed and encouraged Pansy down to her wrist so she could look closely into her strangely pale eyes.

'Now listen, Pansy. Say, "Box of chocs, box of chocs."'

***

She had booked a table for lunch at the hotel where she had introduced Ned to Daniela two weeks earlier. Marcus wanted to meet well away from both his office and home, as he suspected Kirsty was still on his tail and he was trying to throw her off the scent. While she waited, Fran looked around the large room and wondered how many others were taking advantage of the anonymous surroundings, maybe embarking on an affair or negotiating a shady deal. On the surface, it seemed ordinary and respectable, but she was becoming more attuned to the parallel, blurred worlds of the legitimate and the illicit. She also recognised that being single and living alone gave her extra exposure and insight, as she didn't have to account to anyone else and could spend her time like this, sitting quietly in a public place, observing or exchanging a smile, listening in to a snatch of conversation or perhaps initiating one, if she felt inclined.

She had read an article recently on how to pick up a man in ten different European cities. For Paris, the advice went something like this: *Wear black. Find an outside table. Order an expensive wine. Wait.* She tried to remember what it had recommended for any other city, London for instance, or Berlin, but Paris was the only one that had stuck.

'Hi, Fran, so sorry I'm late. My meeting dragged on.' Marcus sat down, a little ruffled as usual and fiddling to neaten up his wayward dreads.

Once they had ordered lunch, she asked if the situation with Kirsty had calmed down, as they had only met in passing since that time he had taken refuge with her. He groaned and made a 'so-so' face.

'She didn't try to get back in, as I said I'd meet her to hand over her bag. She thought she could get round me again – weakness of men and all that – but I stood my ground this time and told her I'd changed the locks and that was it. There were lots of tears, accusations and apologies, but we parted on more or less reasonable terms and I haven't heard anything since. She said she was going to travel again, visit her relatives in Jamaica, but I imagine she needs to earn money first. I'm still worried, frankly, because she's volatile and deluded. She believes I promised her a rose garden.'

At that point, their meals arrived and Fran moved them on to the topic they had come to discuss: the legality of the Junoco enterprise. Marcus had made notes on his tablet, which he set up on the table between them.

'I talked to that colleague I mentioned, the one who works on ageing and dementia, so he has links into some of the broader issues. The first thing is that all governments and political parties want to keep off the subject of illegal drugs and substance abuse, because there are too many grey areas and even where it's not a grey area, the police and border control can't keep up with what's happening and simply don't have the resources, skills or technology to make a real impression. It's an incredibly fast-moving target, with the growth in the online black market and the use of mobile phones to arrange deals and handovers. And the big picture is that terrorism took over from traditional organised crime as enemy number one many years ago.'

'Good grief! It sounds a bit more exciting than I imagined, working in ageing and dementia!'

Marcus smiled briefly but stayed on his serious track, intent on conveying the information he had in front of him. 'The point is that drugs regulation is disease-centred, but in practice people take drugs for a whole host of reasons, apart from treating or trying to cure an illness. With any drug that affects the brain, there's always interest in whether it can improve intelligence, memory or mental performance, even if it's only officially available on prescription to treat a particular condition, such as attention deficit disorder or narcolepsy. The mind-enhancing drugs you're interested in, nootropics they're called, are in various categories. This is confusing, so keep listening. Nootropics can be illegal to sell or possess for any non-prescribed purpose, they can be illegal to sell or supply but not illegal to buy or possess, or they may have no legal status as they haven't been officially tested or regulated. Your Junoco chocolate is in the last category: it's unregulated and with no legal status. In summary, it's a morass.'

'Doesn't the Psychoactive Substances Act set out what's legal and illegal?'

'Okay, it's here in my notes. The Act is designed to ban legal highs. They were being sold in so-called head shops as plant food or bath salts and often had labels saying *Not for human consumption*, but believe it or not there was – and is – a market for them because they're much cheaper and easier to get hold of than traditional hard drugs and there are more than enough self-destructive or gullible people who will take anything to get out of their heads. Now they buy them in more underhand ways on the street or over the internet.

'There are two problems in drafting an effective law. Firstly, the chemical mix can be easily tweaked, so there's a continual stream of new and unregulated substances that manage to bypass the legislation. And secondly, plenty of our foods and drinks are also psychoactive, in the sense of mind-altering, but are socially approved of and regularly used in the mainstream – caffeine, alcohol, cocoa, blueberries and so on.'

Fran was startled at his listing of cocoa and blueberries next to each other, as she had been careful not to reveal more about the secret ingredient than was permitted. It was logical, however, and didn't signify anything. The point to take away was that Junoco wouldn't be classed as illegal because the secret ingredient was berry seeds, not a synthetic and 'tweakable' drug. Wild berries could be highly poisonous, but that was a different issue and anyway, surely they would know by now if there was any danger of poisoning by Junoco? She returned to what Marcus was saying; he had really done his homework on this.

'And to add to the confusion, there's a separate online market in counterfeit food and drink, wine for example, where they put all kinds of stuff in it but people are willing to take the risk to get it at a lower price, or else they think they're buying the genuine product, even if the label is on upside down or the words are spelt wrongly.'

'God, this is a revelation to me, Marcus. I never imagined it was so widespread. But hey, talking of food, yours is going cold. You've told me everything I want to know for now, but I may be cheeky and come back with more questions later on, if that's okay?'

They chatted about other things and she was enjoying her fancy chocolate ice cream when Marcus looked at her fixedly for several seconds, as if weighing up how or whether to proceed. She felt suddenly self-conscious and shifted in her seat. He was very attractive, but patently too young and much too close to home.

'Hey, what is it, Marcus? Have I got chocolate all round my mouth?'

'No, sorry, I was just thinking. There was something else my colleague referred to that may interest you, but I can only give a broad outline as I don't know the status of it or any details. It might be irrelevant.'

'Go on then and let's see. I'm intrigued.'

He said that the government was funding a new research project, as part of a programme in schools called Bright Minds. The aim was to foster more creative thinking in children by assessing the effectiveness of different approaches, including brain-training exercises, intensive music lessons, mindfulness and the use of 'natural brain supplements, vitamins and nutrients'. His colleague had implied that there might be more to it, a hidden element.

'He just mentioned the brain supplements part in a conspiratorial kind of way. That's what I picked up on. He didn't offer any evidence, so it may be nothing.'

'A hidden element – do you mean something suspicious?'

'Yes, possibly; I don't know. He hinted that it could be a drug, presumably a cognitive drug of some kind, to boost creativity.'

'And that might be the main purpose of the research, are you saying?'

'No, I'm not saying that; I don't want to set any hares running. I'll keep my ear to the ground and see if anything develops out of it, but please don't talk to anyone else, will you? It could get me into a whole heap of trouble.'

'I won't, I promise – and the same applies to my Junoco story, okay?'

It was astounding. In the space of a few months she had gone from being asked to look after a stranger's belongings for five minutes to being trusted with a coveted secret formula and now being in on a confidential government experiment. Her mother might not be the least interested in what she was up to, thankfully, but Judi would surely have been impressed.

***

When she arrived home later in the afternoon, Lily was there on the front wall, still wearing her school uniform and holding a bunch of printed leaflets. Fran could tell she had been crying.

'Hey, Lily, what's up? Why are you upset? And what's that you've got in your hand?'

She was unlatching the gate and getting out her door keys as she spoke. Lily followed her into the house and Fran handed her a tissue.

'I'm upset because Marmalade, she's the cat living across from us, has gone missing and the horrible people next door were nasty to me. They told me they don't get involved with anyone and I had no right to ring their doorbell, and if I do it once more they'll report me. And they don't like cats. I hate them.'

It was Eric and Delia again, saying they didn't get involved with anyone. That was a joke. They were always looking for an opportunity to get involved, as long as they could do it with maximum self-righteousness and distress to others.

Lily handed her one of the leaflets, which had a large headline, *Missing*, and a photo and description of Marmalade. Fran immediately recognised the moggy with the distinctive markings who followed her to the corner, and tried to think of the last time she had seen her; a week ago, maybe. Lily said she always came to meet her when she got home from school, but she had been missing for five days. Lily was going round to ask if anyone had seen her and if they would put up a poster in their window.

'Sometimes cats just go off, Lily, and reappear as if nothing has happened, or they decide to go and live with another family who've started to feed them titbits, or else they've got through the cat flap and stolen the other cat's food, so they move in and the other cat moves out.'

'Or she might have been run over by a car. She might be squashed at the side of the road and nobody can recognise her,' replied Lily, unwilling to be lulled by Fran's bright suggestions. 'Or a fox has got her and torn off her head and left her all bloody on the ground, like that Siamese cat where we lived before.'

As they were putting the *Missing* poster up in the front window, Lily's mother, Petra, drove slowly past the house looking for a vacant parking space.

'Hey, there's your mum coming home now. Why don't you run and ask if she wants to come in for a quick cup of tea?'

Lily ran out to the street and Petra met her with a quick cuddle. Fran waved from her front door and they walked towards her, Petra with her arm hung loosely around Lily's shoulder.

'Hello again, and thank you for looking after Lily—'
'Fran's my friend. She's not looking after me.'
'I know, sweetie. You love talking to Fran.'
Lily ran into the front room to finish the job of

displaying the poster and the two women moved into the kitchen.

'Thank you, white with no sugar. Lily prefers adults, doesn't feel comfortable with kids, except her brother Ferdi. He is staying with his dad for now, not with us. I hope she isn't coming round too often and causing a nuisance. She can be a little strange.'

'She is different from a lot of other children, but I don't think she's strange,' replied Fran. 'She has a passion for the things she's interested in and she wants to explore and find things out. She must be clever at school, is she?'

'Yes, although they don't understand the way her mind works. I am a teacher myself and I can appreciate how different she is. One of her more perceptive teachers suggested she might be neuro-diverse and I tend to agree with that.'

Fran hadn't heard the term 'neuro-diverse' before, but she understood what it might mean in relation to Lily. Making links to Junoco, she realised that the striking thing about Lily was her intact early curiosity and her refusal to be lured or distracted by eleven-year-old fashions and obsessions. She wondered if Petra, as a teacher, knew anything about Bright Minds, the schools research project that Marcus had mentioned. She had to tread cautiously, as she had promised to be discreet.

'Do they do anything special? I mean, if they recognise she's different, and to my mind she's exceptionally curious and perhaps creative...'

'Well, she loves to play the piano at home, but she prefers to improvise and she was no good with formal music lessons after the first two or three years. As for school, the education authorities say they want to encourage curiosity and creativity, that's the trend, but do they really? I mean, it can make things harder for the teacher if the kids are questioning everything all the time. I have experienced it myself and it's the opposite of how I was taught, growing up in East Germany. You were told what to think, which isn't good either.'

Lily wandered into the kitchen at that moment and the conversation turned to Eric and Delia, who had lived in the street for over twenty years, longer than all the close neighbours, and had managed to insult, hound or offend every one of them. The stories about their behaviour were so absurd that even Lily ended up laughing.

Chapter 8

She pulled her heavy wheelie bin out of the side gate and yanked it down the path to the pavement. It was early October and there was a distinct chill in the air. She was thinking about Lily and why she, Fran, was content and even keen to spend time with her. Okay, she was missing Max and Chaddy more than she liked to admit, but they were in their twenties now and it wasn't to do with that, she was sure.

'Hi, have you seen Marcus today? Do you know if he's at home?'

It was Kirsty, who had crept up from nowhere. Frosty was the best attitude, as the main thing was to get rid of her as fast as possible.

'Marcus? No, I don't. I haven't seen him and I don't follow his movements.'

'Okay, I was only asking. I'm his girlfriend you see, and I've got something for him but he's not answering the door.'

'Well, he must be out then, or asleep, don't you think? It's getting late.'

The young woman looked tired and anxious, unsure what to do next. Fran felt a pang of sympathy. If she was obsessed with Marcus and couldn't let go, it had to be stopped, but at the same time it must be awful for her.

'Look, it's cold out tonight and you haven't got a jacket or anything. Don't you think you should go home?'

This touched a nerve, and not in the positive way that she intended.

'What do you fucking know about it? Don't you patronise me. I'm not cold, and maybe I don't have a home to go to, for all you fucking know about it. You can tell Marcus I hope he likes his present.'

With that parting shot, she began to walk away and then, apparently changing her mind, she crossed the road and took up position against the big tree. Fran didn't want anything more to do with her or the evolving situation, but decided she would have to text Marcus to warn him of Kirsty's presence.

She had just closed the front door behind her and entered the living room when there was a loud crash of breaking glass. She shut her eyes and put her hand up to her chest. Feeling vulnerable, although the blinds and curtains were fully closed, she ran into the kitchen, knowing she had to call Marcus but anxious where it might lead. In the event, the decision was made for her, as he had leapt over the garden fence and was knocking quietly but insistently on her back door. She opened it and ushered him in, then turned the key sharply to lock it.

'Did you hear that, Fran? A bloody great brick just came through my front window. Excuse my language. It was such a shock; it landed on the floor quite close to my feet. It's Kirsty returned with a vengeance, it has to be.'

'Yes, I saw her out there; she spoke to me. You have to confront her, Marcus, either confront her or call the police, one or the other. It's getting dangerous and she needs help.'

'She'll have scarpered by now. She wouldn't hang around after that and I don't know where she's staying. I can't call the police either. It will have to get worse before I resort to that. They'd probably arrest me, for a start, instead of seeing me as the victim. I'll call in sick tomorrow morning and get a couple of guys in to replace the window. It's turning into a bloody nightmare, this. Maybe I deserve it, but that doesn't make it any better.'

Fran got out two squat glasses and poured generous shots of neat whisky to help them get over the shock. Eric and Delia would either be lying quaking in their beds or waiting for the police to respond to their emergency call. Whichever it was, they were sure to have a field day with this one.

**

The Junoco launch date was set for a Thursday in early November and Daniela was planning an evening drinks party to mark the event. It would be a select group of about sixty, she told Fran and Vicky, taken from the priority list of corporate clients she was aiming to attract to the business. Since first talking to Ned, she had fully embraced the aim of going for the 'high-end' market from the start, in addition to individual customers who would find out about Junoco through chat on other websites or on social media generally. Although Ned wasn't willing to talk to Fran about his involvement in the launch event as he was sworn to secrecy, she assumed he had been instrumental in drawing up the invitation list.

She had confided in Vicky about her relationship with

Ned, trusting that she wouldn't find anything strange about it. She and Vicky now frequented the café and the Green Duck pub quite regularly on the days that Vicky came to work in the office.

'We are lovers, Vicky, and yet I know hardly anything about him. It's not what I would have dreamt of doing before coming to London, but we met through a dating site and it seemed so natural, no need for discussion. He's gorgeous, you'll see. I feel genuinely fond of him, but somehow I don't think I'd ever get jealous over him, I'm fairly sure about that.'

'Sounds perfect to me; I'm looking forward to meeting him. And returning to the subject of parties, there's one happening next weekend near Covent Garden. It's a singles party that they hold once a month in different venues, always private flats that are well furnished but don't appear to be lived in. I've been to one or two of them before and met the couple who run them, and they're aiming at our age group, forty- and fifty-somethings, although a few older and younger ones slip in. It'll be great fun, going with you.'

'Oh, I don't know, Vicky. I'm not sure…'

'Just give it a try, please, it'll be good. We can wander around Leicester Square first and have a drink and something to eat and then go on to the party. If we're not enjoying it, or when we've had enough, we'll leave and go on to a jazz club in Soho. I know one you'll like. It'll be a great night out, whatever happens.'

Fran knew she was caught. She couldn't possibly refuse the offer of an evening out with Vicky, even if she felt intimidated by the suggestion of a singles party.

'Okay, you've got me. I'll give it a go. But we must have a pact that we'll leave as soon as one of us wants to.'

'Agreed; it'll be a quick tap on the shoulder and time for one final snog.'

***

Leicester Square was teeming on the Saturday evening and there was clearly an important film premiere at one of the cinemas, with photographers setting up their equipment around a cordoned-off section with a red-carpet entrance. Fran had been a bundle of nerves all day, reminding her of how she had felt in the run-up to parties when she was fourteen or fifteen and, more often than not, had her eye on a special boy who might or might not be showing interest in her. It must have been Vicky's jokey reference to snogging that brought all that back. Now they were here, she was swept up in the buzz of anticipation as Vicky took her by the hand and they pushed forward towards the metal barriers edging the pavement, where the film stars, the celebrities and the well heeled and well connected would emerge from their purring cars.

As the guests began to arrive, cameras flashed all round and a swirling mass of mobile phones rose above the heads of the jostling crowd. Many of the frocks were sensational and Fran automatically took note of all the dress styles and accessories, so she could suggest new items and ranges for the shop, at rather lower prices obviously. Vicky was clasping her arm now and looking fantastic, her olive skin glowing, her lips a perfect caramel colour and her eyes as beautiful as those of any of the women stepping delicately out of the cars.

Then Fran glimpsed Ned. Of course, it wasn't actually Ned but a man who looked uncannily like him. All the major stars and famous people had already arrived, so he would probably be a wealthy supporter or somebody's friend or relation. He was positioned at the side of a car with his hand held out to the woman who was climbing out and rearranging her dress as discreetly as was possible, with so many eyes and cameras focused on her arrival. They made a striking couple and Fran watched with special interest as they drew level with her on the red carpet.

The man's face was in profile and she peered between the heads of the people in front, who were pushed right up against the barrier. It was Ned, it absolutely was him. His chin, his nose and then his hairline above the sharp white collar were all unmistakable.

'It's Ned, Vicky, that man who just went past! I'm convinced of it.'

Vicky swung round to grasp both Fran's arms, responding to her amazement. 'Where's Ned? Which one is he? Show me!'

'He's gone in now. He got out of one of the cars with a woman. I didn't believe it was him at first, but it was. I knew he mixed with some swish types but I never thought to see him at an event like this, swanning in as if he did it every day of the week.'

'Come on, let's go. It's too busy here. We need to find a quiet place to talk.'

They slipped out of the crowd and started to walk towards the residential side street where the party was being held. After a couple of failed attempts, they managed to grab seats in a pub as people got up to leave, although it was still far from being a quiet place. Fran was astounded, but also keen to talk about Ned.

'He's a mystery man, that's one of the things I like about him. A spy, I thought, when we first met. He has so many hats, literally, a long row of them up on his shelf. It seems obvious now: a hat for each persona.'

'Well, that can be theory number one: an agent or private bodyguard.'

'Or maybe she's his girlfriend, wife even. Maybe he keeps the flat for spending time with me… or with women he meets online…'

'Eek, don't say that! What else, let's think. It could be his double or an identical twin. Or the woman in the car is his sister, his friend maybe, or his friend's sister's friend. I don't know – they're all possibilities.'

While Vicky was casting around for answers, it came to Fran in a flash.

'He's an escort, Vicky, that's what! He's talked about it with me. We discussed it the first time we shared the Junoco truffles. He came up with the crazy idea of setting up a male escort agency together and I said at the time that he seemed to know a lot about it. This is why. He knows all about it because he is one.'

'Well, that's a turn-up for the books. It's the best theory yet. Are you upset?'

'Upset? I don't think so. More shocked, in the sense of surprised. It all fits and… I don't know what I feel, to be honest. I need time to think about it.'

Then she stood up and, in a sweeping gesture,

presented Vicky with her hand. 'Tell you what, we'll think about it later. Because now, Cinderella, you shall go to the ball.'

'Me, go to the ball, in these rags? What chance two handsome princes, one for each of us?'

The party venue turned out to be a basement apartment reached by narrow steps spiralling down from the street. The door was on the latch, so they let themselves in when no one responded to their knocking. The small kitchen was full of guests, while the catering staff were refilling silver trays with finger food and rinsing wine glasses.

They wound their way through the crowd, saying 'hi' or 'hello' to everyone as they passed. There was a row of coat hooks in the hall but they were overloaded, so they folded their coats on their arms and followed the music into the main room, which was larger than Fran was expecting and had a long table on one side and a few scattered chairs in each corner. She noted that there were similar numbers of men and women and most were the right kind of age, as Vicky had promised. They helped themselves to a glass of wine from the table and picked up a handful of nibbles. Vicky indicated towards a cluster of four women surrounding a tall, good-looking man, all making an effort to catch his attention.

'It's invariably like that, in my experience. And now, you won't have done it yet, look around the edges of the room. This is the pattern.'

Fran looked all round, trying to be discreet about it, and saw a number of men standing on their own, not in pairs or groups, either resigned to watching from the sidelines or lying in the undergrowth, waiting to pounce.

Vicky put up her fist, ready to charge. 'Come on then, deep breath and dive in.'

'Yeah, just hope I don't hit my head on the bottom.'

She followed Vicky to join a mixed group and get in on the conversation. She was disturbed by the unexpected sighting of Ned and warned herself not to react by having too much to drink. Vicky was immediately attracting attention and a couple of the women looked her up and down and drifted away from the group, leaving her talking exclusively with a bearded guy in a black sweater.

Fran became aware that she was being watched by one of the men at the edge of the room and, in a bold bid not to seem a wallflower, she beckoned to him with her eyes and a slight movement of her head. It was, she presumed, the only way to enjoy this sort of party. The man cocked his head in return and dutifully came across, much to her relief. He turned out to be an army officer and they had an easy and flirtatious conversation, although afterwards she couldn't remember a single word of it.

After a while, Vicky signalled to her that she was going to the ladies' and Fran excused herself, in time-honoured style, to join her friend for a quick debriefing. After checking that they were both still having a good time, they went back in and Fran found her army officer was deep in conversation with someone else. Feeling confident now and getting the measure of the event, she started to work the room in a way she felt Judi would have admired, introducing herself as Fran, Frankie or Francesca as the whim took her and moving on before she found herself stuck with anyone. Vicky was also moving, and within an hour was having an animated conversation with the tall man who had been the centre of female attention when they first entered the room. There was still one other woman hanging in there, but she finally gave up when Vicky put her arm around the man's neck and gave him a cheeky kiss.

It was all fairly tame and tasteful, considering. At least, this was what Fran thought until she walked through into an adjoining room, which was dark and full of couples writhing around on sofas, some of their phone cameras flashing. She felt a tap on the shoulder and turned to Vicky. Like Fran, she looked a little tipsy but not too far gone. They would find out soon enough when they hit the fresh air, anyway.

'We've reached the snog room and it's time to go, don't you think – game over for tonight? Are you ready?'

They went into the hall to retrieve their coats and remembered they had taken them into the main room.

'Oh, hell's bells, I've forgotten where I put mine. It must be on a chair or a radiator; I don't know.'

'I know where they are. Wait here, I'll get them.' Vicky ran back into the room and returned with her own coat, but not Fran's. Meanwhile, Fran had rustled through the coats in the hall and picked out a long jacket in a sleek leopard print, which fitted her fine.

'Never mind – I'll take this one. Come on, let's go.'

She had registered earlier that the internal front door to the flat opened onto the stairwell, so they could escape the house by that route rather than pushing through the crowded kitchen. Once out on the street, she felt a huge rush, but it wasn't so much the effect of the alcohol on hitting the fresh air. It was the familiar wild head rush of nicking something, following the old compulsion she had suppressed for so long. She had to chase after Vicky, who was urging her to hurry, but she was finding it hard to breathe. Vicky stopped to wait and she got through the dangerous moment, put her head down and took several deep breaths. They giggled and ran hand in hand in the direction of the tube station, slowing to a brisk and not entirely straight stride once they had turned the street corner.

At the tube station, they were held back at the ticket barrier because Vicky tried to use the business card of one of the partygoers, instead of her travel card. She called to Fran waiting on the other side, much too loudly.

'Well, he's no bloody use – his business card doesn't even work!'

Neither of them had noticed the two police officers, who stopped them at the escalator and said they had just been notified of a stolen ladies' jacket that closely matched the description of the one Fran was wearing. When she eventually woke up the next day, it was impossible to remember exactly what happened in the following few minutes, but she knew she was bundled into a police car without Vicky and that she was scared, as well as shivering with cold because they had taken the leopard-print jacket away from her.

When they got to the police station and she stumbled out of the car and into the starkly lit reception area, the aggressive mood seemed to shift and she was offered a mug of strong tea and a sweet biscuit. The weary but kindly officer at the desk checked she had enough money for a taxi home and ordered one, releasing her with the words,

'You're let off this time, honey. It's your lucky night.'

On the way back, a message arrived from Vicky saying she'd been *read the riot act* and sent home with a slap on the wrist. Despite her drunken wooziness and her losing battle to stay awake and upright in the back of the taxi, Fran recognised that it was indeed her lucky night. It was unfortunate that they'd walked right into the local coppers, but she had got away with it and not been charged or thrown in a cell. Someone was watching over her.

The following afternoon when she finally rolled out of bed, she discovered two things. Seventy pounds in cash had been stolen from her purse and she had a message written in black ink on her wrist: *Ring Paul*, and a phone number. She sat down and tried to clear the dense fog in her brain. *Paul...* As she couldn't conjure up any image or memory of him, she went into the bathroom and, after some fierce scrubbing, managed to erase his name and number. Then she took herself back to bed and pulled the pillows over her head.

Chapter 9

What to wear? She had never been to an event like this and the rejected items of clothing were piling up on the bed as she dressed and posed in front of the mirror, squinting critically at her reflection. Some of these things were years old now but were experiencing a revival thanks to the vintage style glamorised by boutiques like Frocks and Chocs, as well as the high-street fashion chains. So far, she had only tried on one pencil skirt that was too tight to zip up, which didn't seem bad going.

She finally settled on jeans, a white top and an oversized jacket. She didn't actually have to go out at all. She hadn't told anyone about the lecture, so there was nothing to explain or justify, except to herself. This was another underrated plus of living on your own, permission for inaction, although admittedly it was often useful to have someone give you that little push. She went downstairs and picked up the free newspaper to look again at the advert:

Esther Simmons Memorial Lecture
Brainpower: Can We Handle It?
Professor Fred Henson-Morris and Dr Alice Stevens
University of London
Public lecture and drinks reception

She was annoyed at her last-minute dithering, given the clear relevance of the topic to her experience with Junoco, both the business side and the truffles. Yet here she was, tempted by the thought of curling up on her sofa with a simple supper, not having to make small talk with strangers or take the tube across London on a chilly autumn evening. Was that all? Was there anything else in the way, some part of her that didn't want to find out too much, risk being scared off?

Go on, Fran, you have to go. You know you'll regret it if you don't.

She turned and looked at Guacamole, who seemed to stir slightly. She stared and thought she saw him move again, back to his original position. He hadn't actually spoken, but she felt she had picked up his thought.

'Okay, you're right, Guacamole. It'll be interesting, fun even. See you later, Mr Mole – and don't you dare drop off. I'll want to discuss it all with you when I get home.'

It was a fair distance but she had time to walk to the university, crossing the river at London Bridge and enjoying a pause to gaze at the lights playing on the water and the changing skyline, where a new super-high-rise tower of glass and concrete seemed to pop up out of thin air every time she walked across.

The lecture theatre was half full and people were streaming in when she got there with fifteen minutes to spare. She found an aisle seat close to the back, so she could make a quick escape if she wanted. This left a single empty seat beside her, which was taken by an old man in a scruffy coat who gave off a pungent, fishy smell. At this point, the presenters were walking onto the stage and the theatre was almost full, plus Fran was too polite to move away from him. He could be a retired professor whose natural eccentricities had become magnified, as had happened with her own set of elderly relatives, or else a street character following the crowd or looking for somewhere warm to sit down – or both, as even professors might conceivably fall on hard times. She tried to turn her attention from his stinking breath and the closeness of his arm and shoulder.

The two speakers were introduced as Professor Fred Henson-Morris from the university's department of neuroscience and Dr Alice Stevens from the department of psychology. As the close-up appeared on the large screen, Fran saw that the professor was about sixty, with a tidy moustache and long, wispy sideburns. He wore a striped shirt, a slack red tie and a conventional navy suit that was at least one size too small. Dr Stevens was more interesting in her honey-coloured skirt, black polo neck and knee-high boots, together with her large, red-framed glasses. Her hair was a soft flaxen colour, wavy and artfully messy, with what looked like delicate streaks of pink running through it. It was difficult to guess her age, but perhaps mid thirties. The old man beside Fran slumped further into his seat and she hoped he wasn't going to do anything more embarrassing than exude his mustiness, like starting to snore.

The professor spoke first, and more engagingly than she had expected on the flimsy basis of her first impression. Yes, he was rather full of himself, but he knew his stuff and how to put it across. In his allotted forty-five minutes, he cantered through the current state of scientific knowledge on human intelligence, the approaches to cognitive enhancement now being researched or applied, and the evidence on their potential and effectiveness.

As he explained, the academic field of brain research was vast and multi-stranded, taking in widely varying approaches, disciplines and scientific methods: electromagnetic stimulation, digital-neural connections, bio-robotics, nootropic drugs, genetic modification, optogenetics, dietary supplements and nutrition, and brain training through puzzles, games and exercises.

Regarding the most recent experimental approaches, he raised the question of how far they would overtake, compete or combine with each other. They were all funded and researched with the primary aim of preventing, diagnosing and treating diseases and medical conditions, but the methods could potentially be applied, or were already being applied, to sharpen mental faculties and enable healthy individuals to gain an intellectual advantage.

Fran was disappointed that he skimmed over the evidence on cognitive-enhancing food and drink, but as a neuroscientist, he was bound to be more interested in cutting-edge and potentially breakthrough experimental research and high-tech advances. He spent several minutes on nootropic drugs, noting that the term 'smart drugs' was misleading, as 'smart' now primarily referred to a new type of drug that could identify and zero in on diseased cells. The nootropics, from the Greek for 'mind' and 'bend', worked by changing the flow of neurotransmitters, natural chemicals in the brain, especially dopamine, serotonin and noradrenaline.

There was evidence that the nootropics, or so-called smart drugs, being taken to boost mental performance had discernible effects, including improvements in working memory and visual pattern recognition, enhanced focus and decision-making, extended wakefulness and a reduction in risky behaviour. With regard to creativity, however, they had shown no positive results and might, like caffeine, actually inhibit it. The expectation among most scientists was that drug-based advances in the near future would continue to result in making our brains more productive and efficient, rather than more creative.

On the side effects of nootropics, the research was inconclusive. Some studies reported a risk of dependence, cardiovascular problems and psychosis, while others found no such effects. The interaction of nootropics with other drugs was still unknown, leading to a game of neuro-roulette for those taking other prescribed medicines or drug cocktails. The professor believed it could take another twenty years to produce a genuine pill for cognitive enhancement, taking into account the necessity of a wide safety margin. In addition to safety, there were many complex ethical issues to be resolved around unfair advantage or unequal access, social pressure or coercion, and questions of personal identity.

It was impressive stuff. Daniela and her associates in South America could really be on to something with Junoco, given that its formulation was designed to stimulate creativity at the same time as improving focus and concentration. Following the talk, there were fifteen minutes for questions, during which Fran let her mind wander while remaining semi-attentive. The old man next to her put his hand up but wasn't selected to ask his question. His smell seemed less pervasive now, almost familiar, and mixed with the warm exhaled breath of the rest of the audience. Sitting in front of her was a youngish man with a soft and neatly tapered hairline that would normally have attracted her attention, but she looked straight past him to watch Alice Stevens walking across to the lectern.

This presentation was also fascinating, and the psychologist peppered her talk with memorable quotations and amusing stories. Her theme was the human desire and motivation to alter or expand the mind – and where this desire could lead in our high-tech era of quicksilver scientific and medical advances, globalisation and rapid social change. Historically, it was seen in the widespread use of psychoactive plant substances, the first evidence of which dated back eleven thousand years and which, according to legend, was documented by the Emperor of China in 2700 BC. The lecturer was very assured, enjoying herself:

'Mind-altering substances, both natural and synthetic, have been a source of inspiration for artists, writers and inventors over the centuries, but often they have been too unstable to be useful. In some cases, the uses have been primarily medicinal, but the craving to get high and have an experience of transcendence can be enough in itself, and this explains the long history of recreational use and the willingness to accept or even revel in the known and unknown risks.

'Human intelligence is far from being understood, and it is too complex to be affected by a single intervention.

Genetically, we are 98.5 per cent the same as chimps, but humans have developed much greater brain capacity since we separated from the chimps around six million years ago.

'Our curiosity takes different forms and goes to different depths. We might be impulsively chasing the latest novelty or popular story; we might be driven by a strong wish to learn and acquire knowledge; we might be provoked by an interest in other people's thoughts and feelings.

'Curiosity can be convergent – in line with the thinking and wisdom of the day – or it can be divergent – out of line, radical and subversive in its implications. It has been famously described as a pure form of insubordination.'

By this time, Fran's head was buzzing with spin-off connections. She tried to formulate a specific question to ask but got tied up with nervousness, as the whole occasion was foreign to her and she was afraid of looking foolish. If she got the chance, she would talk to Alice Stevens at the post-lecture drinks.

She had to wait almost an hour into the reception before there was a sudden break in the crowd and Dr Stevens emerged from a huddled group and moved towards the drinks table to exchange her empty glass for a full one. Fran had rightly judged that standing at the front corner of the table would be a good position for getting into conversation, and she had already had brief exchanges with several other members of the audience.

'Hello, I'm Fran. I wanted to say that I found your talk enthralling and I'm glad I came. I saw it advertised in the free paper.'

'Thank you. I hope I pitched it about right. I'm Alice, as you know. What brings you here tonight, then?'

Close up, Alice was older than she had appeared at a distance, which was no surprise as Fran had registered that her low-pitched voice was that of a mature woman, maybe into her forties. She had a fair, English rose kind of prettiness, and it wasn't a trick of the light; there were pink and silver streaks, rays of colour, in her hair. Her blue-grey eyes were friendly and interested.

'Oh, I've just moved to the big city and I'm keen to find out what's going on. I was taken by what you said about curiosity being subversive. Do you think it's still as true now as it used to be?'

'Well, it's a big question. I think authorities and leaders do wish to promote certain kinds of curiosity but it's worrying to them, even in liberal societies, especially if they want particular rules and views to go unchallenged. There's an example from Texas, only about five years ago, where the state Republican Party announced it was opposed to the teaching of critical thinking skills in schools because, in its view, such programmes were aimed at challenging the students' fixed beliefs and undermining parental authority.'

'Wow, I'd no idea, that's quite shocking, but then, perhaps not surprising when you put it like that.'

'I didn't have time to bring it into my lecture, but governments of many colours have carried out all kinds of mind-control experiments. I don't want to pick on the Americans too much as they are terrific pioneers, but the CIA had a sizeable mind-control programme from the 1950s to the 1970s. One of the things they were trying to discover was whether psychoactive drugs could be effective against an enemy, Fidel Castro for example. In the end, they were too volatile – the drugs, I mean. The programme was abandoned for this and other reasons.'

Fran could have stayed talking to Alice all evening, but the room was emptying and she didn't want to make her feel trapped. It was like how she had felt when she met Vicky: instantly drawn in and captivated, almost mesmerised. That was the word she had chosen at Judi's funeral, as well. What was it she had said in her little speech? 'Judi was mesmerising, a dazzling free spirit. She inspired me and led me astray.'

Professor Henson-Morris was coming towards them now, waving his half-full wine glass in the air. 'Ah, here you are. Just time for one last drinkie before they shoo us out, don't you think?'

Alice introduced him simply as Fred and he gave Fran an abrupt, piercing look that verged on rudeness. She decided it wasn't the moment to take offence and that the man was just drunk and uninhibited, although when he leaned across the table for the last wine bottle, Alice quickly rolled her eyes, suggesting this might be normal behaviour – or maybe she wished they could have carried on talking on their own, or she was just ready to go home.

'We were just discussing the dodgy activities of governments, Fred. Mind-control experiments and suppressing curiosity and things like that.'

'Fascinating, and as scientists we always have to pull the policymakers along with us – but hey, it's late. Let's have a toast to our resounding success this evening, and to more dodgy activities all round!'

He winked at his raised glass, and Fran and Alice smiled at each other. Fran was already plotting how she was going to engineer another meeting with Alice.

When she got home, Guacamole was sitting square on his drum, betraying no sign of vitality. She spoke to him anyway as she dropped her handbag on the floor, flung her jacket onto the sofa and unzipped her boots.

'Well, guess what I found out. There's evidence of humans using mind-bending plant substances as far back as eleven thousand years ago. And curiosity can be a real threat to established wisdom, a form of insubordination. That's your lecture for tonight, Mr Mole. Now I'm going to enjoy a nice hot mug of cocoa before bed. Are you asleep or would you care to join me?'

***

It was the week of Halloween and Daniela had given Fran fifty pounds to buy decorations for the shop window display. She had chosen four witches on broomsticks, which she planned to hang from the ceiling so they were flying in formation but at different heights. As they were relatively high-quality, there wasn't much left in the budget after this, but she put in an extra ten pounds and bought a mobile of a moon and stars to hang in front of the witches. She had positioned the stepladder and placed the tools on top to start fixing the decorations when she heard the bell tinkling upstairs, signalling that someone was coming into the shop. She turned carefully on the middle step of the ladder and saw Kwesi, the doctor, hovering in the doorway.

'I am sorry, Fran. I am disturbing you. I will come back another day.'

'Not at all, I'm only doing the decorations for Halloween. It can wait a few minutes.'

He came in as if entering a private home, wiping his shoes on the non-existent door mat and looking round politely. They smiled at each other, Fran remembering again how he had come to her aid while others had stood by and then slunk away from the scene.

'How are you, Kwesi? Are you still at the library – and what about your asylum papers? Has there been any progress?'

'Unfortunately, I am waiting for my appeal to be considered. It takes a long time because there are many people asking for refugee status and I don't have an answer yet, or a date. I have to be patient but it is difficult.'

He spoke quietly, even though there were no customers or other staff in the shop. She stepped down off the ladder.

'I am still sleeping in the library but I may have to leave, as they are planning to close down the area where I have a space. Are you questioning why I have come to see you?'

'Well, no. I thought maybe you were passing by the shop and you noticed me in the window with my coven of witches!'

He looked shocked, just for a moment. It was a crass, thoughtless comment.

'Fran, my friend, I have come to ask you for a favour.'

'Okay, go ahead.'

'I have drums, traditional drums that I played at home, when things were normal in my life. I was in a band

and we played at weddings and local festivities and often for fun, out on the square where the old people rested on benches and children played football.'

'I can imagine it, you paint a good picture.'

'Yes, and there are four drums, different sizes. I brought them with me and I asked a friend, someone I met here in London and who lives in a big house with other people, I asked him to keep them until I have a place to live. Now he has to leave because the landlady cheated with her tax and she wants to sell the house. I thought, *Fran is a kind person and perhaps she will know a friend who can keep my drums.*'

She was quiet for a moment while her mind speeded through any likely pitfalls.

'Well, I have three bedrooms and both my children are living abroad. Anyway, they've left home now and will find their own places when they come back in two or three years. I'd be happy to find a space for your drums; it shouldn't be any problem.'

As she spoke, she became aware of the discordance in this: he had no home to go to and here she was, offering a bedroom for his drums. 'I mean, as well, maybe you'd like to stay with me, just for a week or two…?'

He jumped in quickly. 'No, Fran, thank you but that would not be a good thing. I want to be friends, if you wish it too, and it would not be right to stay in your house.'

'Oh, okay then, yes of course.' She was relieved at his firm position. 'When do you want to bring them over? I haven't got a car at the moment, so I can't collect them.'

'This evening, is that too soon? Or when will it be a good time?'

'Yes, this evening is fine, say between seven and eight?'

The small van arrived soon after seven and Kwesi and his friend unloaded the drums onto the pavement. Fran could see Marcus peering out over his front window blind and the poster of Marmalade, the missing cat. Then he disappeared from the window, opened his front door and waved at them.

'Oh, hi, Marcus, my friend Kwesi here is leaving his drums with me for a while. Don't be too alarmed – I don't know how to play them!'

Marcus came down the path to check out the drums, which were similar to the small one on Fran's hearth, Guacamole's seat, except cone-shaped and taller. She introduced the guys and they each picked up a drum and carried them into the house and up to her second bedroom. Marcus had lots of questions for Kwesi and their chat turned into a conversation about musical influences and their experiences of performing in bands.

'I haven't played the sax publicly for years now,' said Marcus, 'not since my twenties, but everyone assumes I do. I remember once going to a professional conference on health and care at a hotel, and as I was entering the front door, the doorman said, "Musicians round the back, mate!"'

Fran sensed that Kwesi was reluctant to leave the comfort of her kitchen. How did he obtain access to the library at this time of night? Was it warm enough to sleep in there? Is that where he kept the suitcase full of gifts for the Londoners he believed would invite him to their homes? As if on cue, he pulled something out of his tote bag and handed it across the table. It was wrapped in soft tissue paper, through which she could see a pair of spiral horns. She pulled off the paper to reveal a carved wooden antelope about eight inches high, excluding the majestic horns, very graceful and with its nose raised to sniff the air.

'Oh, thank you! It's beautiful, so natural and lifelike. I'll put it on the mantelpiece, near to my mole, Guacamole. He'll enjoy that.'

After Kwesi had left, Fran returned to Marcus at the kitchen table and picked up the carved animal, trailing her fingertip around the long coil of its horn.

'Do you remember, Marcus? I told you I'm drawing wild animals; it's an effect of the Junoco truffles. Well, this carving that Kwesi has given me has such an amazingly strong likeness to one of my sketches. Can I show you?'

She went to the chest in the front room and took out a folder of drawings. Marcus followed, and as she looked through the sketches for the one she wanted, he was picking them up at random.

'They're lovely, Fran. You should turn them into paintings, breathe colour into them. Yes, that one you've got there. It's so vibrant and full of spirit.'

'This is the one I mean. Look at it next to the carving! They are nearly identical.'

'Yeah, that's extraordinary. It's a classic pose for a deer but the horns are the same, and you're right, it looks like the same creature.'

'Is that what you think, Marcus, that my drawings are full of spirit? What do you mean by that?'

'It just came to me, as I skimmed through. Why, have I said the wrong thing?'

'No, it's just that I feel a spirit near me sometimes, a

presence following me around. It takes different forms and sometimes it's just a feeling. My best friend died a few months ago and one of the last things she said to me was that she wanted to be a spirit, not a ghost. I wonder if I am expressing it in some way, through all this drawing. I started sketching again on the day she died. She was like a gazelle, Judi. She had those soft, lustrous eyes.'

She raised her face from the carving and looked up at him, expecting him to be embarrassed or perplexed. He took his time before replying.

'Putting it like that, maybe she meant that a ghost is restless and comes back to haunt us, while a spirit is carefree and stays around to inspire us. A ghost is indifferent and cold, while a spirit is kind and compassionate. Does that make any sense?'

'Not entirely, I'm not sure. Maybe it's a bit harsh on ghosts; maybe they're just sad.'

She picked up the antelope and stroked its smooth surface from head to tail and back again, ending up at the tip of each horn. She felt too wobbly, had taken it too far. Now wasn't the moment to cry.

'I mean, Kirsty has come back to haunt you and it's not exactly indifferent of her to chuck a lump of brick through your window.'

'That's true, but she's certainly restless, so that part holds good. Anyway, I thought we were discussing non-earthly spirits and ghosts, not living people.'

Fran's phone buzzed at that point and she went over to check it. It was a text message from Andy, confirming the date for his overnight visit. Ned had also sent a text, asking, *Are you okay – dinner soon?* She hadn't been in contact with him since the night of the film premiere and she was intending to wait until the Junoco launch party to judge the lie of the land. Given the nature of their relationship, there were merits and perils in both her options – disclosing that she had seen him in Leicester Square or keeping quiet about it.

Marcus broke into her thoughts with a new question. 'Will he come over to play, do you think? Is that the plan?'

'What? Who do you mean?' Ned didn't come to her place; that wasn't part of the deal, or not yet anyway.

'Kwesi, your drummer friend, will he come over here and play? If he does, I'd like to join him sometime and see if we can get it together with the sax and drums. I think we'd get away with some light jamming at this distance without upsetting our dear friends Eric and Delia. What about you, would you mind if we did that?'

'Yes, that sounds good, it could be fun. Oddly enough, I hadn't thought about him coming over to play the drums until you suggested it just now. I'll ask him.'

'Great. And, by the way, it's too late to talk about it now but I've got more to tell you about that government research programme I mentioned, Bright Minds. Also, I don't know if you've seen her, but Lily was hanging around outside your house today. She wanted us to know that two more cats have gone missing.'

'Oh dear; if that's true, it is very strange, I have to say. I'll watch out for Lily. And yes—'

'I must go home now. Can I sneak out the back door and over the fence? I've a feeling Kirsty may be spying tonight, and she mustn't find out I'm here, as she gets jealous at the slightest thing.'

As soon as he had gone, Fran sat down to Skype Chaddy. There was an eight-hour time difference between London and Hong Kong, so she might catch her with a few minutes to spare before she set off to work. When Chaddy responded, it was lovely to hear the excitement in her voice as she offered snippets about what she had been up to and the people she had met so far.

'And what about you, Mum – are you doing okay? Not too lonely without us? How's life in London?'

'Yes, I'm fine, settling in. I haven't had time to be lonely. It's been a bit manic.'

'I can imagine, with all the unpacking and getting to know your way round and starting the new job. What about the weird couple that gave us that flak over the removal van?'

'Oh, that's Eric and Delia. They're the original neighbours from hell. The only good thing is that people bond well when they have common hate figures, so I'm getting on beautifully with the rest of the street.'

That was it, short, sweet and not very revealing on Fran's part. She went up to her bedroom and closed the curtains without turning on the light, then pulled the two edges open so she could put her face through the gap. There was no one under the big chestnut tree and no sign of cats, just a man in a long dark coat who slowed down to light a cigarette as he walked by.

Chapter 10

The plan was to launch the Junoco website on the same day as Daniela's party. Daniela had directed Fran to lead on communication with their individual customers and look after the social media side, while she took charge of the corporate customers herself. Vicky's IT role was to deal with the inevitable technical hitches and add features and capability as the business evolved. Following the idea to create the feel of a select club with an edge of mystery, Daniela had sent out the party invitations with a handwritten note, saying the venue would be in Central London and would be disclosed at twelve noon on the day.

It was a misty November morning and Fran headed to the office early to do the final trial run with Vicky. The minor glitches were sorted and at eleven o'clock they went live and began to get their first hits. The tone and language of the site were carefully measured and unsensational, as they aimed to attract the genuine curiosity seekers, rather than people wanting to chase the novelty of the latest mind-altering product. At the same time, there had to be an emphasis on fun and sensuality and they had put in a lot of effort to get the balance right.

'Do you know who they are, Vicky?'

'Who do you mean – Infrared and his gang?'

'No, not them; I'm thinking of the corporate clients, the party guests. Daniela doesn't want to tell me their names, but if it's so confidential, why is she having a party where they will meet each other and know who everyone else is?'

'It's a kind of private members' club, that's why. They love secrets. She didn't tell me who's coming either, but I found the list quite easily.'

She quickly brought up the party guest list on her other screen and they ran through it together. Most of the invitees were in high-level positions in businesses such as hotels, restaurants, property development companies, estate agencies, fashion retail, events management and accountancy and law firms. Two university professors had made it onto the list, along with three directors of online dating sites and other people that they weren't able to categorise from the company name.

'Accountancy and law firms – they seem a bit out of place, don't you think?'

'No, not at all; you absolutely need friends like that to smooth the way and help with major transactions and deals.' Vicky glanced back at the computer screen. 'Hey, look here – we've already made ten sales!'

At twelve o'clock, they received a copy of Daniela's promised email. However, instead of letting the guests know the party venue, it told them the event was unavoidably postponed due to sudden family illness. She would let them know the rearranged date as soon as possible and sent her sincere apologies for the inconvenience.

'*Sudden family illness*,' said Vicky. 'Maybe it's cousin Osvaldo or another of her relatives in South America. Do we know if her parents are still alive? It has to be serious for her to stop the party, surely?'

Before they had time to speculate any further, the shop bell tinkled and they heard Daniela's voice greeting the sales assistant. She came leaping up the stairs two at a time and burst into the office.

'Did you get my email? The party's off, I've postponed it. There's been a fire.'

'There's been a fire? It's not family illness, then, like you said?'

'No, it's a fire at the factory. The manager called me an hour ago and I'm going out there now, when I've picked up a few things. I've ordered a taxi.'

This was peculiar. A UK factory hadn't been mentioned before, except as a future possibility. The chocolates were produced in South America – that was what Fran had been told. It couldn't be Ned's warehouse unit, the distribution centre? She glanced at Vicky, who usually had more inside knowledge by virtue of her IT role, but Vicky was focused on observing Daniela as she scattered stationery and papers around the desk in a frenetic search for whatever it was she was missing. Fran was anxious not to aggravate Daniela further, but she had to find out if it was Ned's place that had been attacked.

'Which factory is it, Daniela? Where are you going? Tell us.'

Daniela looked up and swept back her thick hair with both hands, realising she wasn't going to get away with the minimal explanation she had so far offered.

'We opened a factory three weeks ago, on farmland north-east of London. You didn't need to know, but it made sense to move some of our production to the UK. Now it's been set alight. The building hasn't burnt down but there's smoke and water damage and at least one of the machines is ruined. It is arson, the manager is saying, he's convinced of it. It has to be Infrared and his cronies, almost definitely. Was that a car horn outside?' She went to the window. 'My taxi – I'll contact you later, when I've had time to assess the scale of it. You know nothing about this, remember. Don't answer any questions.'

As Daniela flew off down the stairs, Fran and Vicky looked at each other, stunned by the whirlwind visit. Then Vicky's face relaxed into an impish smile.

'I know it's serious, not funny at all, but it sounds like a bit of a meltdown, don't you think – Junoco melt?'

'That's a terrible joke, Vicky, extremely bad taste. It's like the newspaper story – this is true – about the migrant who hid in a lorry full of hot liquid chocolate and when it got unbearable, he had to climb out the top and walk back to the camp, dripping with chocolate from head to toe. That's not funny either.'

Vicky giggled and lifted her feet onto the edge of her chair so she could clasp her knees like a ten-year-old. 'Honestly, I don't know how we ever survived without each other.'

'Me neither. You're like Judi, in many ways, but with you and me, it's more even, it's mutual. I've taken on some of Judi's spirit and you and I will lead each other astray, that's the difference. In fact, we already have!'

'Very true, we have and we will. Whatever happens,

even if we don't... even if...' Her voice tailed off mid-sentence and she lowered her feet from the chair, swinging it back to face the desk.

Fran leapt straight in again. 'Seriously though, Vicky, it is alarming, isn't it, arson? Would a commercial rival go that far? And if it is Infrared, is he trying to get Daniela's cooperation or drive her out of business?'

'I can't say, but I've come to the conclusion, from all my experience, that the dividing line between risk-taking and criminality is perilously thin. The legitimate economy, the one we hear about, is the tip of the iceberg. It's even more the case now, with globalisation and the volume of trade and business carried out online. There's always been a crossover between the legal economy, the borderline legal economy and the black market. The bottom line is that everyone involved is interested in making money. It's the number-one global addiction, outrunning and driving everything. It's not altogether true but it seems as if every legal activity has its dark side, to a greater or lesser extent. It applies to chocolate as much as anything else, but with Junoco, we have to stay the right side of the line, and I still believe that's what we do.'

'Christ, Vicky, how the hell do you work all that out? It hangs together when you think of the people Daniela chose to invite to the party, the lawyers and accountants, but it's a pretty bleak assessment of humanity, isn't it?'

It was also an eloquent expression of what she had been thinking about lately: the blurring of the legitimate and illegitimate worlds.

'Don't get me wrong, Fran. I'm not saying that people don't have other motives, ideals even. Like with Junoco, we think of more imagination and curiosity as a good thing for the world, although we know it can easily be misused. And the researchers in South America hope to make their reputation as respected scientists. But we all want to make money from it, and hopefully good money, quickly. We can't wait around until Junoco's been officially tested and declared safe, ethical and effective because it will be too late. We'll have lost our edge.'

Vicky peered forward to study the information on the computer screen, which was full of numbers and fizzing with activity. 'Hey, someone's just bought a hundred boxes, twelve hundred truffles, and we haven't any idea who it is. It could be a student planning to sell them in a college or hall of residence. This new site will spawn plenty of new small businesses like that, believe me, and the entrepreneurs behind them will make money and feel oh so cool and clever.'

'Or it could be someone sorting out their Christmas presents all in one go, with a box of Junoco for Santa next to his mince pie!' Fran paused. 'I need to ask you something else, Vicky, it's bothering me. Do you trust Daniela? Is she being straight with us?'

'I think she's a talented businesswoman. I've always admired her for that and I wouldn't be working for her otherwise. She's also tough, which goes with it, and the people who think they can mess around with her should watch out. I don't believe she's dishonest and I'm reasonably sure she wouldn't cheat us, but she thinks about what she is and isn't going to disclose. What I can say, which might help to reassure you, is that I did some more in-depth investigation, going back through the email trail and checking out facts on the South American side, and I'm happy that it's all pukka. It is only the berry seed and not some iffy unknown concoction.'

'Okay, thanks, that does help. I've read lots of different things and they've got mixed up in my mind – the performance-enhancing drugs and the legal highs and the brain-boosting food and drink. It all crosses over, like you were saying.'

'Well, it does to an extent but it's up to us to keep clear of the bad guys and maintain a good image.' She stopped and tilted her head, listening. 'Who's this now, coming up the stairs?'

Fran froze momentarily and then relaxed when she saw Ned's face peering round the door. Vicky had met him for the first time in the past week, and she gestured for him to come in.

'Ned, it's you, you startled us. We're jumpy enough as it is, what with Daniela flying in and out like an angry bluebottle.'

'Hi, good, you're both here. You've heard about the fire at the factory, then? Daniela sent a message but now I can't get hold of her to find out what's going on.'

They filled him in on the little news they had. He didn't betray any obvious anxiety, but Fran knew his behaviour well enough to note small signs. At least, she reminded herself, she hoped she knew him well enough; that she could still have confidence in him.

'What about your premises, Ned, the distribution centre? Is it okay?'

'Yes, I've phoned to check and there's been no unusual activity. Daniela won't call the police and she'll make her own decisions about how to deal with it. If we have to relocate the distribution centre, I've a couple of other options in my back pocket. To tell the truth, I am concerned but not that surprised.'

Fran looked from Ned to Vicky and back again. They were so self-assured and knew things that were foreign to her, things she had missed all these years, despite her own sporadic questionable behaviour. Suddenly a random memory surfaced: that time she visited a show home where her company had provided the furniture. She was inspecting it with a young man from the property company and they walked round the house together, room to room, being unprofessionally flirtatious. She had even bounced on a bed to test the springs.

As they were driving back to his office he had said, in a confiding tone,

'When we walked into that house, I was terrified you would try and seduce me. And when we came out, I was mortified that you hadn't.'

Vicky was flicking her fingers to get Fran's attention. 'Hey, you're miles away! I was saying I'm going to go now and leave you two to talk. The website is running beautifully and I've been called to fix a problem with one of my other tech projects. I'll call you tomorrow, Fran, and we'll organise our own private launch celebration.'

Ned watched her leave and then looked up at the wall clock. 'What have you got me into, Fran? It's your fault and you owe me a lunch. You must know the pubs round here by now.'

This was plainly the wrong way round; he owed her lunch, but she decided to go along with it for now.

They walked over to the Green Duck, now her favourite pub, which maintained a display of unseasonably abundant flowers in its winter hanging baskets. As they entered, she was still unsure if she would challenge Ned about that night in town. She wanted to hear his account, but she feared it could kill off their evenings together. Then again, was it wise to carry on without knowing what he was up to, now she had inadvertently stumbled on it?

'Ned, there's something I want to ask you. It might be awkward.'

He looked curious, as well as taken aback at her serious tone. 'Okay, go ahead, shoot.'

'Well, the thing is, it was completely random, this, but... I was out with Vicky in Leicester Square, not this Saturday, the one before, and—'

'Ooh, you saw me there, strutting in all my finery. So much for discretion! Were you at the premiere too, you and Vicky?'

'No, we were on our way to a party.'

She suddenly had a vivid recollection of the cute army officer and the passionate kiss they exchanged before she left the party. Was that Paul, who had written on her arm? Why had she erased his number so quickly? Why hadn't he called her; did he have her number?

'Well, I don't mind telling you, Fran, and you've probably guessed anyway. I was on hire that night, working for an agency. I signed up a year ago and I've done two or three jobs a month, that's all. I've had a few fun jobs, like that night at the film, but it can be dull and hard going.'

'I can well imagine.'

'No, really, I mean it – and often it's a goodbye peck

on the cheek and that's it. I think you and I could do a whole lot better; we would attract a different clientele and make it far more interesting, if we set up our male escort business. We talked about it, remember, the first time we tried Junoco?'

'I certainly do remember the conversation and I wondered at the time how come you knew so much about it.'

'Well anyway, it doesn't interfere, does it? I mean, I love our twosome dinner parties and I'm still thinking we'd make good business partners, in the escort field or in something else, something that spins off from Junoco, perhaps...'

Fran was happier now, relieved that she had come out with it and that he had been direct in his answer. It could be a clever ruse, of course. He might still turn out to be a secret agent.

'I love our private dinner parties too, Ned, really I do. I don't want to spoil it.'

She smiled back at him sweetly, thinking, *have I gone stark raving mad?*

***

Andy drove up to London in his builder's van, as he was going on the next day to install a new bathroom at a friend's house in Essex. Fran was watching from the window and when she saw the van turning the corner, she went out to make sure he found a nearby parking space. Lily was dawdling along the street on her way home from school, trailing her hand over the untidy front hedges.

'Hello, Fran, did Marcus tell you two more cats have gone missing? I don't believe they've been run over or moved to live somewhere else. I think someone's stealing them, to sell them or do horrible things to them, like experiments.'

By this time, Andy had parked the van down the street and was crossing over towards them.

'Oh, Lily, they don't do that to pet cats, but it is strange, I agree. Look, my friend's just arrived. Do you want to come over after school tomorrow? I'm at home all afternoon.'

Andy was standing close to her now, playing with his keys and smiling in that self-conscious way of his. Lily gave him one of the dubious looks she specialised in when it came to first encounters with Fran's friends.

'Okay then. See you tomorrow. I'll bring Sahara with me.'

Fran hoped that seeing Andy at her place would be more relaxed than at the cottage. Not the sex but the conversation, which was often stilted and broken by uneasy silences. Maybe their love of Judi had other feelings mixed in with it, of course it did, or his grief made him emotionally detached from everything else. She was conscious that Judi had wanted them to go on holiday together. She should suggest a city break, after which they would part and go their own separate ways, or just see each other occasionally on a friendship basis. Falling in love with him wasn't an option, and neither was it what she wanted. Their lifestyles and circumstances were poles apart and anyway, it would be disloyal to Judi, to put it mildly.

She shut the door and they exchanged a coy look, pretending to be embarrassed rather than emboldened by the fierce passion of the time in the cottage and their enthusiasm for more. He waited, content to let her eyes slide up and down his body, undressing him already.

'Would sir like to go straight to the boudoir? I have sent up wine and chocolates.'

She took his hand and led him upstairs. It was different from her sense of anticipation with Ned, more single-mindedly lustful and less all-round sensual. She didn't want it to go too fast, this time. She had placed the wrapped Junoco truffles on the pillows and the sparkling wine was in a metal ice bucket on the bedside table.

'We only offer these chocolates to our elite guests. They're ultra-special and we don't want the rest of the world to know about it.'

Andy smiled but wasn't inclined to get into role as a fawned-over hotel guest. He picked up a truffle and held it to the light. 'Is it an aphrodisiac?'

'Yes. The formula is based on a wholly natural—'

'I'll try it, Fran – your word's good enough. I can't tell you how many mystery white powders and other stuff I've taken, especially since Judi got ill and was ordering pills and potions online, but before that too, long before. It's probably mad not to know what they've put in it but if it helps us all survive and get through, that's fine with me.'

They lounged half-dressed on the bed and ate the two blue-wrapped truffles.

'It's very sharp,' said Andy. 'I wouldn't choose it, too bitter for me.'

'I know, it is really strong, first time. It's an acquired taste, that's what I've found. Now I like it better than the normal types in the shops – and they're getting richer too, the expensive varieties for aficionados, true chocolate lovers.'

'Is that what I am – your chocolate lover?'

'Yes, that's exactly what you are, pure and unadulterated.'

An hour or two later, she emerged from her trancelike state and wriggled her toes. Sex was so absurd, the ultimate confection of the sublime and the ridiculous. She untwined her legs from Andy's and he shifted towards the edge of the bed.

'Are you awake, Andy? Shall we go down and think about dinner?'

He rolled over towards her and stroked her arm. 'I'm seeing shapes whirling in green space, extraordinary bright colours.'

When they entered the living room, Guacamole appeared to wink at Fran over his glasses. Any day now, she expected him to engage in conversation, to reply to her like Dad used to do. And it wasn't only Guacamole. Other creatures were responding too, including Kwesi's carved antelope, which had pride of place on the mantelpiece. As she stared at it now, the spiral antlers dipped and it bowed its head a fraction, too subtly for anyone to notice. She looked across at Andy, who was oblivious. He was still experiencing cascading shapes and vibrant colours but didn't report any other effects as they spent the evening listening to a selection of Judi's best-loved music.

In her dream that night, she was in a forest, watching a tiger stalking a stag with huge antlers. The tiger had to wait until the stag stopped moving towards it and turned away. As it did so, the tiger crouched down and crept forward. The stag lifted and turned its head, lowered its antlers and charged into the undergrowth, goring the tiger fatally down one side. Fran backed away, trying not to draw the stag's attention, and fell over a pile of branches into a sun-filled glade, which was set up as a laboratory. The scientists were in protective suits and goggles and she immediately knew it was a brain lab, with each group of scientists experimenting on a different method of brain enhancement. In one corner was a wicker basket full of wailing cats, and above it, a hanging cage of mice and rats with long wires stuck in their heads. *That's not right*, she said to herself. *Those are pet cats; they wouldn't experiment on them.*

With that thought, she became alert to the noise of a real cat yowling in the street. She got up to see if it was the missing Marmalade and if not, to scare it away. It was an unknown cat crouched on her wall, head up to yowl again, while its antagonist was hidden under a car or might have run off.

Andy stirred and asked the time.

'It's shortly after six. Sorry if I woke you but it was the cats fighting outside, they got into my dream. Maybe we have a rogue cat on the loose, scaring them all, and that's why they are disappearing one by one.'

She wanted to draw the dramatic scene of the tiger and the stag straight away, to try and catch the spirit of it.

Andy reached over the side of the bed to pick up two pillows from the floor.

'It looks like you've been having your own catfight, Andy, with those pillows.'

'Mine was a bad dream, a nightmare,' he replied. 'I thought I was awake, but I couldn't move a muscle and there was a horrible thing bearing down on me. It was standing at the end of the bed, a black-cloaked figure but I knew it wasn't human. Next it was on my chest, forcing me to lie petrified, threatening me and making it almost impossible to breathe.'

This was the classic description of a night terror, which Fran had come across in her reading but had never experienced directly. It happened when the mind and body were out of sync and didn't wake up at the same time. The creepiness of it was the consistent features: the downward force on the chest and the overpowering presence of a supernatural and hostile creature. She wondered if Andy had experienced it before, like Cerise and her sleepwalking.

'Never, and I don't want to experience it again, ever. It was terrifying, honestly. I'll have to stay clear of your fabulous magic chocolates, if that's what they do to me.'

Fran nodded sympathetically, not wanting to show too much concern about this reaction to Junoco. She suggested going to the café on the corner for breakfast, before he set off for Essex and the bathroom job. He wasn't keen to do it now, but it was a promise and the friend wanted the work carried out while she was on holiday. She had ordered everything ready for his arrival and he was expecting it to take three or four days, as the space was very cramped.

It was past eight when they arrived at the café, and Fran had to be in the shop before nine. Vicky was ensconced in her favourite corner with her laptop, as Fran had half-expected, and she soon came across to join them. It felt good to introduce them properly and show Andy something of her life in London, especially today when he was more animated than usual, despite the night terror. At first they talked about Junoco and then Andy moved on to asking questions: what they liked about the city, and why neither of them would prefer to live in a village by the sea.

After they had parted with Andy and he went back to Fran's for his van, she and Vicky walked the short distance to the shop.

'He's lovely, Fran. You can see the sadness in his eyes, but he seemed quite lively just now – obviously your influence.'

'Yes, and we had a Junoco session as well, which probably helped him lose his shyness with you. But what news on the arson attack, Vicky? Have you seen Daniela, got any more scraps of information? Are we still set to have a launch party?'

'Nothing on the fire itself, what or who caused it, that's clearly off limits. Apparently, she's found another farm building that's more or less ready to move into and that will work as the new factory. As for the party, the word is that it's going to be a smaller event now and we probably won't be invited.'

'It's a big trend, isn't it, these old barns and outbuildings around the countryside being taken over as new-style manufacturing plants and warehouses?'

'And making the products in the UK gets round the import issues, if you've got something to hide or you're operating on the margins. The problem is, as we've seen with Junoco, it can also be an easy target for commercial enemies or ordinary criminal types; too unprotected.'

They were almost at the shop now. Fran stopped walking and turned to Vicky, touching her arm to slow her down and allow the conversation to continue.

'It's ironic, don't you think, that Daniela aims to encourage greater curiosity and imagination, but she doesn't want or expect us to be curious about what's going on with the business and who's trying to scupper it? I mean, we don't know what danger we might get into, being involved in this.'

'It's a fair point, but she always said she would inform us on a need-to-know basis and we have to trust her judgement, to some extent. If we ask too many questions, she'll get shot of us in the blink of an eye.'

Fran wanted to defer to Vicky's view, as she always had up to now, but she felt dissatisfied and unnerved by her response. She had come close to admitting that the Junoco business might be operating illicitly, while Daniela herself always used carefully nuanced phrases. Fran wanted to pursue it, but they had arrived at Frocks and Chocs, so she just murmured in agreement and aimed her key fob at the door entry panel.

It was the quiet period between Halloween and Bonfire Night parties and the build-up to Christmas festivities. Fran ordered a wider range of accessories to maximise the stock of small gifts, as well as a supply of the leather items and embroidered evening bags that had sold so well since she introduced them back in the spring.

Busy with unpacking, she sensed she was being watched and looked up. It was Kirsty again, staring in the window. Fran turned away and started to open another box of display items, wondering if she was checking her out or just window shopping. She didn't appear to have recognised her, but it was impossible to tell. In any event, she was back in town and Marcus would no doubt know about it soon enough, if he didn't already.

She finished her shift in the early afternoon and paused for a moment in the shop doorway, wanting to verify that Kirsty had gone. This was what happened when you allowed yourself to be lured in. There was the street girl, whom she still spied every now and again, and Kwesi, and now Kirsty. Not that Kwesi was any problem. Actually, she was getting fond of him and he had come round twice for drumming sessions, along with Marcus on the saxophone.

The coast was clear both ways. She would stop to buy bananas and grapes for Sahara on the way home, and four strawberry tartlets for Lily and herself.

As she predicted, Lily was at her door within a few minutes of running past to change out of her school uniform and pick up Sahara.

'Is she hungry?' asked Fran. 'The choice is bananas or grapes, special treat.'

Lily put Sahara in her box and held a grape above her head, making her stretch upwards to reach it. Fran sat on the floor beside her and they took it in turns to feed Sahara the grapes. The legendary hamster cheeks filled out again and again as yet another fruit was greedily accepted and quickly shoved or sucked to one side or the other.

'Now, tell me about the missing cats, Lily. What's happened?'

'Okay, I will. There's Marmalade, you know about her and there have been no sightings. Then there's one called Leonie and another one called Sooty. I know they have gone missing from putting up the Marmalade posters.

They all disappeared late in the evening. The Sooty people found a dead mouse on the path, which means he'd come back in the night, but that's the only trace. I'm making a new poster, with all of them on it. I'm waiting for a photo of Leonie and then I'll print it out. I wanted to call the police but it's the same as the pigeon in your chimney; my mum says they're not interested.'

'The posters are a good plan. Otherwise, you just have to keep your eyes open for any sign of the cats or any suspicious activity. Don't get into trouble, though, and let me know as soon as you have a new lead in the investigation. We'll plan it together, okay?'

'And we won't have anyone in charge. We'll both be the boss.'

Fran brought out the strawberry tarts and Lily was quiet as she munched her way through three of them, along with a glass of milk.

'My brother Ferdi is coming home for Christmas, with Dad, but Dad's staying with Gran.'

'That's great. You'll have fun together.'

'You know your little sister, Marina. What did she die of?'

No one had ever asked her this question, as the subject was closed when she was so young and she had mentioned Marina to almost nobody before arriving in London. Even Judi had never asked her directly about it, all down the years.

'It was an accident, a road accident.'

Suddenly she saw herself carrying a big, multicoloured plastic ball in her arms as she walked beside her father, running after it as it rolled onto the road.

'I think I dropped a ball. Marina's pushchair tipped over the kerb. There was a motorbike. I think she fell out, I don't know. My dad picked me up and someone took me into a shop.'

She sat back on her knees with a hand clasped over her mouth and breathed out in a whistle between her fingers. She had eaten the Junoco truffles with Andy last night and it had made her come out with this account of the ball and the pushchair – but was it true? Was this how it happened: the motorbike, the black figure flying through the air, the terrible noise?

'Oh, Fran. I didn't want to make you cry. That was mean of me.'

'It's all right, Lily, it's not mean. It's probably a good thing to cry about it.'

She sniffed, stood up shakily to find a tissue and stared with blurred vision at Guacamole, who shifted his gaze towards her, nodding sagely and so discreetly that it eluded even Lily's razor-sharp observation.

Chapter 11

'I'm sorry, Fran, but I had to call someone. This is doing my head in.'

'Andy, what is it? What's the problem? Where are you calling from?'

'I'm stuck at my friend's place. I'm working on her bathroom and getting it done, bit by bit, but there's something creepy about this house; I don't like it, it's spooky. When I'm in the bathroom, I'm stripping the tiles and it feels like the walls are closing in on me, and the shower fitments and taps are behaving strangely, coming on and off, as if there's an evil force trying to get rid of me. And the guy next door doesn't help, either. He's complaining about me doing the cutting out front because his wife is ill and can't cope with the noise, but there's nowhere else to do it.'

'Oh God, it sounds weird and horrible. You said the bathroom's tiny. Maybe it's making you claustrophobic and you're getting paranoid as well, being there on your own.'

'There's not enough room to swing a flipping cat, that's true. It is oppressive, but that sort of thing doesn't usually bother me, and never like this. I'm losing things too, tools and so on, and then finding them somewhere else in the house. Tell you what, it's like a bad trip; everything's distorted and my mind's playing tricks on me – either that or a poltergeist. I think it's your chocolates, Junoco. I know it was a couple of days ago, but it began almost as soon as I got here and I'm prone to strong reactions with drugs, as Judi may have told you.'

Fran had been so well drilled by Daniela that she was tempted to correct him about using the word 'drugs', but it was the wrong moment and anyway, she was starting to wonder herself what the distinction was, given that people had used natural foodstuffs as psychoactive drugs for thousands of years.

'No, Judi never told me. I imagined the two of you were immune to bad side effects, like you'd built up resistance over time, although that's simplistic and probably unscientific. If it is Junoco, I'm sorry and I hope you won't hold it against me.'

'Don't be daft. I took it voluntarily and didn't wait for you to explain what was in it. It didn't do the trick for me this time, that's all, what with that night terror and now this bizarre experience. Actually, I feel a lot better now I'm talking to you, so I'll crack on with it and call you again this evening, if that's okay?'

After ending the call, Fran drummed her phone lightly against the palm of her hand, thinking hard. She had been meaning to contact Alice, the psychology lecturer, and this was the time to do it. With luck, she would agree to meet up and Fran could pick her brains, as well as discover more about her.

She told Vicky about Andy's reaction when they met in the office later to look through the customer comments and diary entries on the forum area of the website.

'We can't be sure, but I'd say it was a Junoco effect, given that his imagination has run wild, except it took him over and he hasn't been able to harness it or take control. He sounded really freaked.'

'Maybe it was too soon, after Judi died, I mean. His emotions are in turmoil. Did he take both chocolates, by the way?'

Fran considered the question. She had eaten her second truffle on the way to the kitchen to get them some nibbles, so she hadn't noticed.

'I didn't see him have it, but it wasn't there when I tidied up, so yes, I think so. Why do you ask that?'

'Well, it's the second one that's supposed to give you focus and concentration, while the first one unleashes the imagination. I'm right, aren't I?'

Had she missed this crucial piece of information or never been given it? It made sense and was glaringly obvious, now she thought about it. Daniela explained the Junoco effects in terms of 'releasing and harnessing' and said they were most effective if you took the blue-wrapped truffle before the gold. Up to now, however, it hadn't occurred to Fran that the first and second truffle might have different proportions of chocolate and berry seeds.

Vicky had returned to trawling through the customer comments on the site. 'The feedback is mostly very positive – people reporting insightful dreams and rediscovering their talents, that's a big one. The word "creative" comes up a lot and some of them say they feel more empathic and interested in other people, as well as wanting to learn stuff. Then there's a group, the neutrals I call them, who are disappointed because they haven't felt any effect, and a small number who've had a negative experience like your friend Andy. I'd say the bad reactions are in line with what we expected. They're similar to well-recognised sleep disturbances – nightmares, sleepwalking, anxiety and night terrors. We've had no reports of more outlandish or dangerous side effects.'

They left the shop at five, by which time it was dark outside and the Christmas lights and decorations were twinkling in most of the shop windows along the parade. Fran pulled up her coat collar against the biting wind and made her way straight home, as Vicky didn't have time to stop for a drink.

When she turned into her street, she raised her head as it was more sheltered here and saw Marcus walking home in front of her. His loping gait was easy to recognise in the darkness and she quickened her pace to catch up with him.

'Hi, Marcus, I haven't seen you for a while. Where have you been hiding?'

It was less than a week since they last spoke, but she had the impression he had hurried into the house to avoid her when she had almost bumped into him on the garden path.

'Fran, hi, I'm trying to keep out of Kirsty's way, that's my main objective at the moment. She's being a nuisance, but she's lost her job at the nursery because she missed too many days, so I'm hoping she'll soon magically disappear. How about you; is everything okay?'

She ought to mention that she had spied Kirsty earlier on, but she didn't want to put him off balance and lose the opportunity to talk about the other subject on her mind.

'Yes, I'm fine. Actually, I wanted to ask you about that Bright Minds research project. You said you'd found out more about it, but every time I've seen you, we've been with Kwesi or Lily, so I haven't had a chance to ask. And I've also been preoccupied with the Junoco launch and things going on at the office.'

They had arrived at their front paths and she paused, waiting for a response and wondering whether to invite him in for a beer or glass of wine. Marcus put his hand on the latch of his gate and turned towards her.

'I'm sorry but I shouldn't have said anything. I didn't know a thing about it and it was stupid of me to speculate, very irresponsible. I can't say any more.'

'Oh, okay. It's just that it came out of the discussion we had about Junoco, the legal side of it, and I'm still trying to get that straight in my mind. I shouldn't have pushed it just now.' She took a step towards him and tried to read his expression. 'I hope you haven't got into any trouble over it, Marcus.'

He looked embarrassed, irritated or shifty, she couldn't tell which.

'It's not a case of getting into trouble, don't think that. Please can we not mention it again?'

'Okay, if that's what you want. Well, have a good evening and I'll let you know when Kwesi is next coming round.'

He smiled, clearly relieved to be back on safe ground. 'Please do that, or when our intrepid detective Lily makes a decisive breakthrough in the case of the missing cats.'

***

Alice's office in the psychology department was in one of the older university buildings, which were now surrounded by soulless office blocks thrown up in response to the rapid expansion in student numbers over the years. She came along the corridor to greet Fran at the top of the stairs and seemed genuinely pleased to see her again.

Fran had prepared her introduction but didn't know how far she was going to take it after that. She might have to disregard Daniela's strict instructions on what information could be divulged, if she was to gain Alice's confidence. And then there was the Bright Minds research that Marcus had clammed up about. It was none of her business and probably irrelevant to the Junoco venture, but she was curious about it and intrigued by the little she had heard.

'I'd like your expert opinion on something, Alice. Well, perhaps two things, which may or may not be connected. Thank you for making time for me.'

'No problem, I've got forty-five minutes or so before meeting my PhD student. I enjoyed the interesting conversation we had after the lecture, which I seem to recall was interrupted by Professor Fred and his flailing wine glass.'

Fran smiled at the suggestion that the professor was something of a buffoon, as well as a world-renowned neuroscientist. She had enjoyed his lecture and felt a bit let down when he came up to them afterwards in that arrogant and mildly lecherous way. Still, she remained determined not to judge him on the initial encounter, when it was his big occasion and he'd had a few too many.

She gave Alice a quick rundown of how she had become involved with Junoco the previous spring, what Daniela had told her about the mystery ingredient, and how Vicky and Ned came into the picture. By this stage, Alice was leaning over her desk and nodding encouragingly, so she went on to describe her personal experience of the Junoco effects, the customer comments and the peculiar effect on Andy, whose hallucinations and extreme paranoia had continued on a sporadic basis for three days until he managed to finish fitting the bathroom ('but not to my usual standard or anything like it') and fled back home.

'What I want to know, Alice, is the composition of the Junoco truffles, what's in them. I'm not sure I believe Daniela any more, that it's just the chocolate and the forest berry seeds. I haven't mentioned the fire to you, or the business rival called Infrared who's hounding Daniela and might have deliberately started the fire, because I've already overstepped the mark, but I have to say I'm worried about the risks, about where it's going and if I'm getting too far out of my comfort zone.'

'That's understandable, from what you've told me. I'm a psychologist, so I'm not into that kind of lab analysis. However, my research spans various disciplines and it shouldn't be hard to arrange for an analysis to be carried out here at the university, informally of course. Anyway, it's quite a story – fascinating! If you leave it with me – and the chocolates of course – I'll get a test done as soon as possible. It will probably be early in the New Year, realistically, with the Christmas vacation almost upon us.'

Send the truffles off to the lab for analysis, as easy as that. Crikey, what had she done? What if the results showed something dubious? Or worse, much worse, if Daniela found out?

'Oh, thank you so much, Alice. I really appreciate it, especially when you hardly know me. I'll pay for the test if you let me know how much.'

'Well, I want to know too, it's my business to be nosy. I'll try and get it done for free. What's the second thing you wanted to talk about, that might be linked?'

Fran took two Junoco boxes out of her bag and handed them to Alice. Then she relayed the sketchy details she had gleaned from her exchange with Marcus about the government's planned research project on schoolchildren using natural brain supplements, vitamins and nutrients. Alice listened for barely a minute before holding up her hand to halt the flow.

'I know about this. Professor Fred is a leading advisor on the programme and his team are carrying out the initial selection of the products. I'm involved too, or I will be when it gets underway. I'm devising the interview questions and doing that side of the analysis. It's quite exciting and I'm looking forward to it.'

'What, are you really involved in it, this actual research programme, Bright Minds? What an amazing coincidence!'

'Yes, and now I'm the one who's said more than I should, because it's highly confidential and there won't be a public announcement for some months yet. I'm surprised you know the project name, as it's very hush-hush. You're right that it kind of relates to your work with Junoco, but there's nothing irregular or fishy about it, it's all above board.'

'Don't worry, Alice. It's safe with me.'

Fran raised her left forefinger to her lips and Alice

replied in kind before sitting back and mussing up her streaked, multicoloured hair, which was styled to go off in all directions.

'And now I do have to throw you out or I'll be late for my student and he's anxious enough already.'

At that moment, Fred Henson-Morris popped his head around the half-open door. Alice flinched, fearful that he might have caught some of their conversation.

'Hey, Fred, we were just... I'm just dashing off to a supervision session. This is Fran – you met each other briefly at the Esther Simmons lecture.'

Fred looked sideways at Fran and she couldn't decide if his expression was one of mild interest or suspicion. Maybe he simply didn't remember her.

'Yes, that's it, hello again. I knew we'd spoken recently but I couldn't quite place you.' He stepped forward to shake her hand. 'As Alice is about to abandon us, would you like to go over to the staff club for lunch with me instead?'

Her first impulse to reject his invitation quickly collided with the enticing prospect of finding out about the new research project, and perhaps about progress on cognitive enhancement more generally.

'Okay, why not?' This had come out too abruptly. 'That would be nice, thank you.' Nice and unthreatening, this was the way to go about it.

On the way to the staff club, she decided to reveal nothing about Junoco or her involvement in it. She would talk about her amusing times at Frocks and Chocs if he asked about her job but would try and keep to the subject of his research, which she imagined wouldn't be too difficult.

In the event, she didn't have to try at all, as he was so keen to impress her with all his major studies, academic awards and membership of committees that she had never heard of. He really was arrogant, in his eager and blustering way. The issue of whether he fancied her was less clear, as his whole look and approach was so completely unsexy, but she had the wearying feeling that he probably did.

'What about future work, Fred? Have you any interesting big projects starting up soon?'

He fell right into it, saying that he had been appointed as an academic director of the Bright Minds programme and it was expected to break new ground in its neuroscientific aspects. She had to choose her words carefully, not wanting to ring alarm bells, but as he seemed unguarded she threw in her prime question quickly and innocently.

'What do these brain supplements and nutrients consist of, the ones you'll be using in the research? Are they wholly natural or are they synthetic?'

'Ah, there's a question. These days, it's difficult to define "natural". The synthetic products can be so close as to be indistinguishable and, don't forget, natural doesn't mean harmless, by any stretch. Think about those mushrooms we used to hear so much about – but you're far too young to remember that.'

He had downed a glass of wine by now and was beginning to lean towards her. Five more minutes and she would have to make her escape.

'So what is in the supplements and nutrients, then? Are they safe?'

'You're asking me if we do our testing and recommending properly and to high standards, to which the answer is yes. We are stringent about safety. It's the primary concern in this type of research, whether it's children or adults.'

Fran looked at her watch and started to gather up her things. 'Well, it's been fascinating talking to you but I have to get off now, Fred.'

'Yes, I've got another public lecture to write this afternoon. It's never-ending. I've enjoyed our little chat, thank you. And...'

'Yes?'

'Well, you know how it is with these things. We have to be careful not to give the wrong idea and I've just been talking generally to you; not about the actual project, what it entails.'

'Yes, that's my understanding. The details would probably go over my head anyway, and I don't know anyone in your field – I sell frocks. Thank you, I enjoyed the chat too.'

He didn't ask for her number, which again provoked mixed feelings. She was sure she could extract more valuable information from him, but not at the cost of possibly offending him by a personal rejection. At least she had Alice on side as a result of today's outing, which was a fantastic coup.

She decided to walk home. It was a week before Christmas and darkness was falling by the time she got to Waterloo Bridge. She stayed there for several minutes, looking first upriver to the Houses of Parliament and then across the bridge to St Paul's Cathedral and beyond. She had expected some signs of the approaching festive season, but the river was a swirl of muddy brown and the views were wintry in a bleak and colourless way. The piers were deserted and the passing river cruisers almost empty of passengers, their lights looking more straggly than decorative. A few tourists were taking photos of each other against the iconic skyline, and near to the parapet of the bridge she noticed a couple in a close embrace. They were dressed in smart office clothes and the woman's feet had lifted out of her high heels, she was held so tightly by the tall man. She couldn't see their faces but could tell at a glance that they belonged to the privileged and beautiful set, Ned's circle and the future elite Junoco customers.

She lowered her gaze to a patch of water shimmering in a dancing white light. Perhaps Professor Fred was right and there was very little difference between natural and synthetic, in terms of possible harm. The issue was the ease with which manufacturers and suppliers could avoid regulation and sell dangerous substances, without even having to reveal who they were or where they were trading from. She had to know what was in the chocolates now, although in a way she wished she hadn't read so assiduously on the topic. Perhaps it was part of the Junoco effect? She was too curious for her own good. Would Judi worry about this, or indeed were Vicky and Ned losing a moment's sleep? Not a bit of it. And it was them she wanted to associate with, be friends with, now she was free and had no serious responsibilities to hold her back. It would be madness to jack it in, whatever the lab result.

She looked up and saw the young couple still in their embrace but loosening it now and staring at each other with an air of finality. The woman was the one to break away, turning and weaving at speed through the growing crowd of late-afternoon walkers until she was lost to view. The man watched her to the last second and then half-slumped, his back against the cold bridge rails, before collecting himself and walking closely past Fran, virtually touching her but unaware, his handsome features racked with emotion.

***

She arrived at the family home on the morning of Christmas Eve, as she had done for the past five Christmases during and following the split with her husband, Tim. The difference this year was the absence of Chaddy and Max, both of whom had previously joined them for at least part of the time. She had already had video calls with them, although she hoped to talk to them again on Christmas Day, if the mood was festive enough and the old folk were still speaking to each other. On the train journey she had wondered, yet again, if this would be the last year before the domestic situation fell apart through death, discord or disease. The prospect of flying to Hong Kong or San Francisco next year, or even both, was appealing but highly unrealistic under any likely scenario.

The annual tradition was now well established. Cerise ordered the tree from a local farm and their regular handyman came round with his daughter to set it up and help Cerise to decorate it. The daughter had to use every ball, bauble and ornament in the box, as 'they all mean something to someone'. It was true that many of them dated from Fran's childhood and brought back memories of her almost uncontainable excitement on Christmas Day.

The parcels, a dwindling pile now, were usually arranged under the tree but this year they were heaped on a side table, presumably to avoid anyone having to bend down to the floor.

The four of them had a light lunch of Cerise's home-made soup and soft bread rolls with a selection of cheeses. The mood was light too, much to Fran's relief, and even Eleanor was refraining from negative comments. This gave George a chance to talk to Fran about the scientific concept behind his computer design, why it was important and how it would revolutionise space technology and interplanetary travel. As he had worked in radar and been a keen amateur astronomer all his life, she was aware there could be a genuine nugget in it. Somebody ought to write it down, collect the torn-out pages of scribbled notes and line drawings lying round his room and put them in order. Or maybe George ought to try the Junoco truffles; it might give him the necessary focus.

Cerise saw that Eleanor was getting twitchy and suggested they retire to the sitting room. Fran had brought a Junoco box with her, hoping there might be an opportune moment to offer it to at least one of her unsuspecting relatives. Although this time she would give them the usual spiel about it first, so they could make an informed choice.

Cerise opened the lid of the piano stool and took out some sheets of music. 'Come on, George, it's time for our recital. You go first with your ragtime and the crooners and divas repertoire and I'll play a couple of pieces at the end.'

George set to with gusto, while his appreciative audience tapped their feet and clapped enthusiastically at the end of each popular ragtime tune. Then he took requests for the crooners and divas session and they all sang along and hummed through the bits they didn't know the words to. It was a pleasure to see her mother in a party mood, a timely reminder that her parents had thrown lively parties in their day and Eleanor's growing tetchiness was at least partly down to sheer boredom and frustration.

When it came to her turn, Cerise gave a beautiful rendering of three favourite classical pieces. Her playing was flawless and full of feeling, to the point that Fran was on the edge of tears. This was something to savour and to imprint on her memory. The concerts would soon be over and they would all be gone. She would get to keep the sheet music and the beautiful old piano, although she didn't have any place for it in her new home.

'That was wonderful, Cerise. Have you been playing again since the last time I was here, when you suddenly went back to it, do you remember?'

'Yes, I've told George and Eleanor I was sleepwalking and it was the chocolates that did it, the ones you brought with you. I have to say my playing is better than it was and I can remember these pieces perfectly, which makes all the difference as I can't read the music these days.'

Fran was encouraged by her directness and the simple and unquestioning way she had attributed her reawakened skill to the chocolates. She had to dive in quickly before the opportunity passed.

'Well, as it happens I've brought some more chocolates today, in case any of you want to try them. They're special because they make you more curious and imaginative and bring out your natural abilities, as you can see with Cerise and what she said about her piano-playing. It's because the chocolate is almost pure and has berry seeds added, similar to blueberries.'

'Ooh, blueberry jam, I love it. I'll have one but I'm not sure you should, George. You're too imaginative as it is,' said Eleanor, teasing him affectionately for once.

'It doesn't actually taste of blueberries but it is delicious, an ordinary chocolate truffle but darker chocolate and more interesting. What about it, Uncle George?'

'I'll try anything once, especially if it's an experiment. What have we got to lose anyway, at our age? No point in fading away quietly, lingering on.'

'Okay then. We'll have the first one now and the second one in an hour or so.'

It occurred to Fran that their collective willingness to take part was due not only to the liberation of old age and the love of blueberry jam but also to their trust in her. She was their rock now, and she'd better not have called it wrong.

After they had eaten the first chocolate with their coffee, they watched the big Christmas Eve film and had the second truffle halfway through it. Eleanor then went upstairs for her afternoon nap, while George fell asleep in his chair. Fran and Cerise chatted comfortably and Cerise began to reminisce about her life with Lawrence and, soon enough, her previous love life. It turned out she had been single up to her late forties and, contrary to everyone's impression at the time, she'd had a series of discreet love affairs over a twenty-year period.

'They weren't married, either, not the ones that lasted. I didn't get involved in that sort of situation, not with married men. You might think it was impossible in those days for a woman like me to have a string of love affairs and survive it but, as my mother used to say, where there's a will, there's a way. And I didn't want to marry them either. I was much too independent for that, before I met your father. I still don't know how he managed to win me over, creep up on me like he did, but I never regretted it. And Pansy has been the other constant companion in my life. She's been with me fifteen years and I've got used to her, even though by rights she should have been flying around in the treetops all this time. I'll miss her if she goes first.'

Fran was listening while enjoying a display of colourful, iridescent bubbles, from minuscule to enormous. And behind the bubbles, the ancient wooden ornaments and silver reindeer were starting to bob and swirl around the Christmas tree.

'I wanted to ask you about something, Cerise. It's personal and I haven't talked to Eleanor about it, but I will, I do want to.' Cerise was smiling at her fondly and Fran forced herself to continue. 'Did Dad ever mention Marina to you, my little sister? She died when she was about two and I was three, in a road accident.'

Cerise sat upright and put both hands over her mouth, evidently shocked by the question.

'No – he never mentioned it, not a daughter called Marina, an accident. It's not something I'd forget. He told me other things but not that. How strange. I'm awfully sorry.'

Fran felt confused, although it was conceivable that her father would have kept it to himself, given that he'd never spoken to her about Marina either. It was Eleanor who had mentioned her, always fleetingly and in a way that permitted no questions. She heard her mother's footsteps on the stairs now, and she entered the room, holding a box in both hands. It was a family game they hadn't played since Max and Chaddy were small. George was stirring in his armchair, Cerise stood up and the mood shifted, leaving Marina stranded again in Fran's fragmented memory.

'Did you have a good rest, Eleanor?' asked Cerise. 'I'll go and make some tea, shall I?'

'It was lovely, full of nice dreams. And when I woke up, I thought we should all play this quiz game. Let's see if those chocolates really make us cleverer!'

They played the quiz and then a new version of charades that they invented on the spot, before finally retiring to bed much later than usual.

Fran fell asleep quickly and woke at five, thinking she heard a sound from down the hall. It was perhaps Cerise again, going to play the piano in her sleep. She propped herself on her elbows and listened hard, but all was quiet. Something had happened, she could sense it. She got up and reached for her big jumper, pulling it over her head and down almost to the hem of her short nightie.

As she padded softly past Pansy's curtained cage towards the sitting room, she knew she would find the place disturbed, that there was a strange presence in the room. She slowed her step as she approached the doorway and peered in, switching on the main light as she did so. At first sight, nothing seemed out of place, but scanning the room and moving gingerly forward, she took in more detail and noticed that the spare pair of Junoco truffles she had left on the side table had been torn open; the blue and gold wrappers were in shreds and both chocolates were gone.

She stared blankly at the shiny pieces of wrapper, not knowing what to make of them, and then saw that one of the Christmas gifts was no longer on the table but lying on the carpet in the middle of the room, also ripped open. In fact, there was only the wrapping paper. The present was missing and there was a trail of paper, apparently from other gifts, leading to the corner of the fireplace. There she discovered a pile of soft fabrics, which on closer inspection consisted of a silk scarf, a single patterned sock and a pair of suede gloves. She reached down to touch the pile and then sharply withdrew her hand when she recognised animal fur and saw a mouse lying among the clothes, stretched out and perfectly still, the light in its eye extinguished.

She stepped backwards across the room, feeling off balance and frightened by the intrusion, what it might signify. At the same time, her mind was busy piecing together the clues and coming to the inevitable conclusion. Aided by Junoco, the mouse had taken its natural curiosity, its sense of mischief and its love of chocolates and soft material to an exceptional and fatal extreme. It was a heroic failure and a cautionary tale. That was all.

Chapter 12

Alice was standing inside the gates to Hyde Park, close to the Albert Memorial where she had suggested they meet. It was a frosty January day and she had pulled down her white beanie hat and wrapped her long scarf around so many times that it obscured most of her face. Despite her nervousness, or maybe to quell it, Fran took in the stylish lace-up boots, the tailored coat and the small lines around Alice's blue-grey eyes that were noticeable in the bright daylight. It was too cold to find the proverbial park bench where no one would be able to hear their conversation, so they walked and talked for over an hour, sharing the wide paths with joggers and young families with their balls, buggies and shiny Christmas scooters.

'What did they find in the lab tests, Alice? I've been dying to know.'

'Well, they did a first-level analysis and identified the presence of the berry seeds, although not the precise plant they come from. It could be an unknown variety of fruit bush, but the tests confirmed it was similar to the blueberry, as you said. And your suspicion about the truffles not only containing the magic seeds and chocolate seems to be correct as well. A significant amount of a synthetic drug has been added to the second chocolate, the gold-wrapped one. The gold one has more of the drug and less of the seed than the blue one, although the blue one also has small traces of the drug.'

'Ooh, ouch, that's not great news. I didn't want my intuition to be right, although I kind of knew it would be. Did they identify what it is, the synthetic drug?'

'No, it appears to be something new. It has some similarity to the drugs people are currently taking to enhance cognitive ability but it's a novel combination, which is the way the system works. Each new product has its own unique mix of substances and the components are constantly altered to evade and keep ahead of regulation. Even if we found out exactly what it consists of, the make-up of the Junoco formula could change again in the coming weeks or months.'

'I get it; that all figures with what I've unearthed myself and what I've learnt from you and Fred. I was fumbling forward but at some level I understood it had to be a double act to make it unique – one thing to release the imagination and another element to focus it and make it purposeful.'

'Yes, it mirrors the psychological studies of creative individuals, when they tackle a problem. They begin by letting their mind wander, allowing spontaneous association that encourages new and unusual thoughts. They play around with the concepts and then switch to analytic mode, focusing in on the most promising idea and starting to refine it.'

Fran watched the excited children as she walked, realising they had chosen the best possible setting and activity for their conversation: strolling side by side without any particular destination, surrounded by nature, water and human activity and not constrained by directly observing the other person's mood and reactions. She sensed Alice wanted to add something else and waited until she was ready.

'When I woke in the early hours last night, I was thinking about the research project we're carrying out for the government, the one led by Professor Fred, Bright Minds. I'm taking it on trust that the brain nutrients and supplements we're planning to use in the study are safe for the children and their effects, if any, will be beneficial. I've left this to Fred and his team of neuroscientists, but after this lab analysis on Junoco I'm wondering if I should ask some questions, or even do an investigation of my own – not at the university, obviously, but I have other contacts with access to lab equipment.'

Fran's mind was racing. She had been hoping for reassurance about Junoco, that it was as wholly natural as she'd been told. The idea that it might not be true had deeply unsettled her, because it made her question her trust in Daniela and the whole venture. However, now that Alice was giving the facts in her measured, academic way, she felt excited, elated even. Okay, she knew she was naive but as it turned out, not completely gullible. And what was the problem, anyway? Was it a deal-breaker, a reason to cut and run?

She thought of her powerful bond with Judi and Andy, her friendship with Vicky that grew closer by the week, the other promising relationships. And now here she was, walking along beside Alice and forging another new attachment over Junoco and the Bright Minds project.

Daniela had good reasons for holding back on information, as Vicky had often reminded her. The customer feedback was strongly favourable. Junoco could turn out to be a magnificent gift to the world.

They were distinctly chilly by now and decided to head to the Science Museum for a coffee. In the museum café, Alice broadened their conversation by talking about recent discoveries relating to the networks of genes that might lie behind the inherited aspects of human intelligence and cognitive ability.

'Once the genes are identified and their various roles understood, it may be possible to modify them to help people who have learning disabilities, schizophrenia or epilepsy. The spin-off, as usual, will be potential cognitive enhancement for people without any health problems and conditions. It's a long way off but I suspect the work on gene editing and stem cell research is more significant and will ultimately reduce demand for cognitive-enhancing substances. There's a world of difference between using drugs to stimulate or inhibit natural brain processes and making fundamental alterations to our genes and cells. Having said that, unregulated substances and modified food and drink will still be easier to get hold of and self-administer, for someone who doesn't have any recognised medical need, so maybe there will be a long-term future for them on the black market and in the dark recesses of the internet, or whatever may replace it in the future.'

Fran responded by gesturing towards the museum shop, with its high stacks of toys, books, games and gadgets. 'Then what about artificial intelligence, the onward march of the robots? Today's one-trick toy robot will be tomorrow's captain of industry. Maybe we won't need to enhance our brains because intelligent machines with advanced learning systems can do it all for us. Stuff like Junoco will be old hat, surplus to requirements. It's a horrible thought but we might not even need chocolate any more, it will all be about pills or patches.'

'Not quite yet, thankfully, but things are moving so fast in robotics, we can't predict very far ahead. It's all too much to think about and I have to concentrate on my work with Fred and his team…' Alice paused and looked directly at Fran. 'If you're up for it, we can put our heads together and tackle both dilemmas, if that's what they are – Bright Minds and Junoco.'

'I'd love to, Alice. I have to think about my position and who I can trust, besides you. There's Ned and Vicky… Yes, let's go away and think about it. Would you like to try the chocolates? I have a box in my bag and I can brief you in a couple of minutes on how to take them.'

'I've already tried them, remember: you handed me two boxes for testing. I slayed dragons all night and the next morning I wrote a brilliant paper on the appeal and value of cognitive-enhancing substances, except it was more of a polemic than a reasoned argument, far too biased and spacey!'

They parted outside the museum and Fran made her way back to the tube station, her mind brimming with new connections. The second chocolate, the gold one, contained more of the synthetic drug. However, the natural berry seeds were possibly the more dangerous part, being hallucinogenic and unstable if taken on their own. It was like with the CIA programme Alice had mentioned, where they experimented with LSD as a mind-control weapon and eventually decided they couldn't control the drug or rely on it to behave as they wanted. Perhaps they had solved the issue now, because hadn't she heard on the radio recently that new research was going on into using LSD for medicinal purposes – for depression, was it?

The streets were full of shoppers and day trippers streaming in and out of the galleries and museums. A gathering crowd waited to cross at the traffic lights, which turned green for pedestrians while she was still some distance away. She speeded up and reached the edge of the pavement with the green man flashing and the bleeping sign warning of three seconds to get to the other side, now two. People were still crossing beside her and she stepped forward, her mind elsewhere. When she was halfway across, with the cars, taxis and motorbikes revving up to race through the lights, her feet got entangled and she tripped up, one foot catching on the bottom of her other trouser leg.

She fell in slow motion, throwing both hands out to protect herself and hitting the tarmac of the road with her open palms, inside wrists and the end of her chin. She heard the squeal of brakes but was temporarily stunned and didn't react, simply failed to move. Then she was aware of loud voices, shouting and waving. A young woman was helping her up, half-dragging her to the kerb and out of danger. Others had clustered around now, asking if she was all right, but she could see only the fair-haired young woman who was about to turn and melt into the crowd. It was Marina, exactly as she had drawn her in her early twenties: the flowing curls; the kind, open face; the same nice physique as their mother Eleanor had in the photos from her youth, as Fran had herself. It matched perfectly, no shred of doubt.

'Marina!' she screamed. 'Come back!'

A middle-aged woman bustled forward with an air of self-importance. 'Keep calm, it's all right, I'm a nurse. Let's see; look up for a moment. You're going to need a couple of stitches under your chin. Can I examine your hands?'

Fran held out her hands, still looking ahead through the crowd but yielding in her sudden and mortifying helplessness to the nearest undisputed authority.

***

She had to rest at home for a few days after her fall. Her shins were grazed and bruised from her forward slide across the road and both wrists hurt, as they had taken the force of the jolt. The three small stitches under her chin were minor and would be taken out next week. She felt grateful to have got off so lightly, remembering the noise of the motorbike – she was sure there had been a motorbike – revving up at the lights as she lay directly in its path. That young woman had been her guardian angel, whether she was actually there or was a figment conjured up in the shock of the moment.

The enforced pause and time alone gave her space to reflect on her experience in London so far and to mull over the issues and decisions that confronted her. There was Andy, for a start. She had hoped to drop in on him after her family visit at Christmas, but he had failed to return her first two calls and then said he had Judi's daughter Zoe to stay for several days and it didn't feel right for Fran to come at the same time. It could be the emotional blow of his first Christmas without Judi, but if that were so, she felt he should want to share it with her, either in spending time together or at least talking to her rather than stalling any attempt at conversation, as he seemed to be doing. Judi had been her best friend forever and Andy was so wrapped up in himself that he wasn't acknowledging her feelings at all.

Then there was Ned; less complicated emotionally, in fact not at all in that respect. He was ridiculously attractive, both physically and in the mystique and aura of intrigue surrounding him. Ned, Judi and Vicky all had it, in their different ways. In Ned's case, it was magnified by his material success and the easy way he carried it – his offbeat humour, madcap schemes and readiness to make fun of himself at every turn. She loved falling into bed with him and she adored him for his attention to her as a prospective partner, not in life but in all kinds of unlikely enterprises.

And as for Vicky, she was to Alice what Andy was to Ned: more complex, more likely to stir unsettling emotions. It was a premature judgement, as she hardly knew Alice yet, but despite what she had said to Vicky about their friendship being 'more even, mutual', she had recognised early on that Vicky had the same captivating quality as Judi and was dangerous, in terms of the balance of power in the relationship. Her manner was generally mild and reassuring but there was steeliness behind it, an assumption that other people would go along with her and she would get her way, always win her case.

These trains of thought were fuelled by her regular use of Junoco, she was convinced about that. She was so much more curious about human nature now, what made people tick and especially what qualities and traits drew her to them. She had worried about being lonely in London but here she was after ten months, reflecting on her new friends. There were the neighbours too. Lily was definitely a friend, despite being eleven years old. She felt she could talk to her about her experience with the animals, Guacamole and so on, although she wasn't ready to do so yet. And Marcus next door, he was an artist and a free spirit who was never going to judge her. She hadn't been able to push him on why he had shut down their conversation about the Bright Minds project, but she hoped the right occasion might soon arise. And then Kwesi, who was courteous and kind and loved to come over and make music, despite his desperate situation as an asylum seeker awaiting a decision on his appeal.

This was all fine, very affirming, but she had to confront the urgent issue of how to handle the knowledge Alice had passed on about Junoco, the added element in the form of a synthetic drug. Should she keep it to herself? Or if she told someone, who would it be? Was it wise to confide in either Vicky or Ned, both of whom were intricately tied up with the business? Which of them would help to clarify her position? And if they were too risky, would any of her other friends be useful as a sounding board, perhaps one of her long-term girlfriends that she had been neglecting completely since her move? This idea was quickly dismissed, as she simply couldn't imagine any of her old friends coping very well with the information. They were more likely to think she was going round the bend.

No, the first port of call had to be Vicky, who would reinforce and justify her desire to stay with Junoco, to enjoy the roller-coaster ride and reap her share of the potential rewards. And anyway, she was missing Vicky as they had exchanged Christmas greetings but hadn't got together socially for weeks, due to one thing and another.

The response to her invitation was immediate and positive. Vicky was free and turned up at Fran's house at seven on the dot. They spent the first few minutes making their choices for a Thai takeaway and then moved on to Fran's accident.

'For heaven's sake, Fran, why did you make light of it in your last message? I'd have been right over to look after you, you know that.'

'No, I was fine, really, just bumps and scrapes and I felt embarrassed about it, I suppose. I needed to hibernate for a while, stay out of sight.'

She wanted to mention Marina, her guardian angel, but the hesitation persisted too long and her cautious side won out. Perhaps a day would come when this was unlocked, when she was allowed to talk about Marina. Maybe when her mother opened up and explicitly or tacitly gave her permission, or when she died and left Fran as the only witness, inadequate as she was.

They talked instead about their respective Christmases and Fran recounted the tale of Junoco and the excessively inquisitive mouse. This led Vicky to ask if she had been in touch with Andy and found out any more about his Junoco experience.

'No, he's said nothing, except that he doesn't blame me for it. I wanted to visit him on my way back, or possibly spend New Year with him, but he put me off. He's not picking up my calls and I think he's being evasive, cooling off. Honestly, Vicky, he's not what I want. I don't want to be with him, it's not meant to be, but still, he doesn't half turn me on and I can't get him out of my head. It's all mixed up with my feelings for Judi, loving and losing her, and the cocktail of emotions and my naked lust for Andy have unbalanced me, made me obsessive about what he's up to. It's not in the deal, feeling jealous like this, but that's the way it is. I should get out now, while I can still do it with a modicum of grace and dignity. Advise me, Vicky, please!'

She raised her hands to her cheeks, pulled an ugly face and wiggled her fingers in imitation of a monster. Vicky waved it away, laughing.

'Okay, let's look at the options. Judi hoped you two would go on holiday together. Those were her exact words, I believe. So, you can propose a little trip, say, a quick winter break in Austria or Switzerland, and resolve to draw the line after that. Or you can decide that the holiday has happened, it was her way of saying it should be a brief, passionate fling, and find the strength to end it now, before you get hurt.' She looked fondly at Fran. 'You have a hell of a lot going for you, a lot to be excited about, including your gorgeous London lover, Ned, I might add, and you need to preserve the wild and wonderful memories of your time with Andy. It's for Judi too, for her sake and her memory.'

Fran stood up, walked to the window, opened and closed the blind and turned round. Her words came out with a resigned sigh. 'Yes, you're right, Vicky, always the cool thinker. Whether I can actually find the willpower and hold to it is another matter, but you've helped me to put it in perspective, so thank you. Now, where's that takeaway? It won't be nearly as good as Ned's fragrant Thai curry, but that's too much of a tall order.'

When the food arrived, they moved through to the kitchen for dinner. She owed it to Vicky to tell her about Alice and the result of the Junoco lab analysis, but she was nervous and unable to gauge how Vicky would respond. Ned was different. He managed to turn everything into an adventure or, more specifically, a business prospect. She began to wish she had talked to him first, but Vicky was here now and she had to go ahead with it.

'I went to see someone, Vicky, about Junoco, the truffles. You know I've been a bit concerned and I met someone at a lecture, she's a psychologist and, to cut a long story short, she had the Junoco formula analysed for me. It contains a synthetic drug, as well as the chocolate and the berry seeds. It's not any of the ones that people are already using to improve attention, alertness and intellectual performance. It's a new compound, a mix of natural and synthetic.'

The words had tumbled out in a breathless rush. She leant back and wiped her mouth with her paper napkin, watching Vicky's fast-changing expression as she stopped eating and laid down her fork.

'You did what? I don't believe it, that you would spill the beans like that, with someone we don't know. It's an incredibly stupid thing to do, can't you see?'

Fran's stomach was tightening into a knot. It was true; she had gone right off-piste. She was so fixated with the truth of the 'wholly natural' claim that she had forgotten the big picture: the betrayal of Daniela and the risk to the whole operation. And in wondering how Vicky would respond, her mind had been hooked on Daniela's deception, the lies she had told them about the magic formula. She thought Vicky would understand, even share her concern.

'I'm sorry, Vicky, please don't get angry. I didn't see it like that. Alice won't say anything to anyone, I promise you. We made a pact.'

'I'm trying not to be angry, believe me, but does it matter what's in it, that's what I'm trying to get across to you. The business is taking off, people love it and it's going to soar to great heights this year, I'm sure of it. Plus, you keep saying how much you're enjoying Junoco and getting a benefit from it, with your drawing and insightful daydreaming and your awakened interest in people. Who is this psychologist anyway? What made you go to her?'

Did Vicky know already, about what was really in the truffles? It fitted with all that she had said before and with her clear lack of surprise now. Fran realised that the loss of Vicky's friendship, their intimacy, would mean more to her than anything else if she had to leave Junoco, if she got thrown out for her disloyalty and breach of trust. And it was true that the truffles themselves were affecting her life in many ways, all of them positive.

'Please don't say anything to Daniela, will you? I've made a terrible mistake, but it won't go any further. I'll put it right, Vicky, honest I will.'

Vicky remained grim-faced and wasn't going to let her off that lightly. She took out a notebook and noted the details of Alice's name, job title, university and connection with Professor Henson-Morris. Thankfully, she didn't ask the probing questions that could have compromised Fran's promise to Alice that she wouldn't pass on any information about the government project or their joint plan to investigate 'both dilemmas': Bright Minds and Junoco. Despite Vicky's angry reaction, Fran wasn't in the mood to drop that commitment.

Vicky closed her notebook and clipped the pen back onto it. 'It's a matter of damage limitation now, I'm afraid. I'll handle it from here – and I won't say anything to Daniela, this time. You're too valuable to lose and anyway, you're still my friend. Just don't take it any further, okay? What you haven't taken on board, or not enough, is that there are seriously ruthless people out there and we can't afford to trust anyone.'

She saw the dismay on Fran's face and her expression suddenly softened. 'Hey, come over here, silly old thing.'

They stood up and had an extended hug until Vicky slowly pulled away and said she had to go home. By this time it was late, and Fran wandered into the living room to switch off the lights and say goodnight to Guacamole.

'I've been a blundering idiot, Mr Mole, but hopefully all is not lost. Does she know more than she's letting on, do you think? Is she protecting me or fooling me, or what?'

Guacamole raised his right eyebrow as a sign of his scepticism, but exactly what aspect he was sceptical about was wide open to interpretation.

'I wish you would talk to me, Guacamole, rather than giving me all these hints and cryptic signs. You're wise and I think you want to help, underneath it all. I can't walk away from Junoco, can I? There's too much to lose. I'm like that poor little Christmas mouse. My curiosity has got the better of me.'

She had intended to go straight up to bed, but this one-sided conversation made her want to have her next Junoco chocolates now, rather than wait until the following evening, as she had planned. She had mouse-proofed her supply by moving all the packets from the kitchen to the top drawer of the chest. She took out the first truffle, unwrapped it, held it between her finger and thumb, shut one eye and squinted at it before popping it into her mouth and drawing in her cheeks until it began to dissolve.

That night, she woke around four into a typically seductive Junoco dream. She was kneeling on the floor in a kind of gallery. The floor tiles were elaborately patterned with a design of pink swirls intertwined with blue, gold and black petal shapes, and the paintings on the walls appeared to be alive. Her sketches were laid out across the floor: the wild animals, the set of Marina, the set of Judi as a child, and the three she had managed to produce of her father. She reached forward to pick up one of her favourites, the close-up of the tiger, and as she held the paper out in front of her to study it, the animal moved into a crouching position. She sat transfixed as the background started to move too. The grasses in front of the tiger swayed as it crept forward, and a bird hopped about on an overhanging branch.

She heard the sound of footsteps entering the room and dragged her gaze away to see Ned leaning against the wall, in his fedora and stone-coloured trench coat. He smiled, raised his hat in a mock-traditional greeting and strolled out the door, while Marcus walked in and looked around with satisfaction, as if he were the curator or owned the gallery.

As she floated to the surface, she had a strong impulse to follow this up; work out what kind of message it was giving her. She went to the bottom drawer of the chest, where she kept her sketches, and took out the now-bulging folder with the wild animal drawings. She found the tiger and held the sheet between her hands, half-anticipating that the Junoco effect would stretch to animating the actual picture. The tiger remained still, its head lifted to the sky as she had drawn it, while the bird sat motionless on the branch above.

***

She was right about Ned's response to the lab test results. It was in that brief, usually silent interlude between lovemaking and cooking dinner. She lay with her head on his chest while he stroked her arm with his fingertips, varying the length and pressure of each stroke.

'I'm not surprised, and I'm not bothered in the slightest. If it turns out to be a "legal smart"-type drug and people enjoy it, it's good enough for me. Come on now, we have to make hay while the sun shines. The online customers are giving it fantastic reviews and that side of the business is growing steadily, as we hoped, while at the upmarket end it's progressing even faster, if anything, after the select little launch party I filled you in on. I've introduced Daniela to several new contacts and she has real skills in forging relationships and closing deals. I don't know if her cousin Osvaldo even exists or what parts of the story are true, but I'm judging her on her performance as a business associate and I have to say it's first-rate.'

Fran was running her hand through his chest hairs, wondering if this might be the evening they would break with tradition and make love twice. She could see from the lifting duvet that he was becoming aroused and she slid her hand underneath it, following the contour of his right hip. It was about prolonging the anticipation towards a slow-paced and, in her wider experience, often more inventive second round. Ned hadn't finished talking and he playfully took her hand away and put it back on his chest, so it had to start its journey down his body again.

'I still think you and I would make a first-class team and we should consider breaking away at some point. I've kept back some of the best prospects, in case we decide to pursue it once Junoco is established. We've focused on luxury hotels and restaurants and haven't touched any of the top property developers or high-end dating sites and escort agencies yet. It mixes so well: mega-rich chocolate truffles and transgression, secrets and sex. The market in London must be almost infinite, and I can't wait to see you in those serious, black-rimmed specs.'

'I'll wear the specs when you parade your collection of hats, Ned. Can we please do another bit of business first?'

Her hand was curled lightly over his cock, which lay hard and straight up the line of his taut stomach, waiting.

'Okay, you win.'

They moved simultaneously to dive under the covers, banging heads and making Ned fall back on the pillow, mimicking pain while she released her hand and rolled on top of him.

Chapter 13

The drum and sax sessions in her back bedroom were growing longer and increasingly lively, as Marcus and Kwesi tuned into each other's skills and the music that inspired them. They listened to a new tune and chose their moment to join in, quietly at first and then with more volume and confidence as the piece progressed and they took up the repetition and rhythm. Some of their individual favourites worked beautifully as a two-piece, while others were abandoned as not right for their combination. There was plenty of improvisation too; their distinct brand of world music with an African beat and strands of reggae, soul and jazz.

Fran expected the session to last over two hours, but on this Saturday night all went quiet after the first hour. She stayed in her curled position on the sofa, waiting for them to pick up again or to come down and join her for a drink and chat around the kitchen table. Nothing happened and after twenty minutes she went upstairs to investigate. Kwesi was still sitting with a drum between his knees and Marcus was holding the sax, but they were deep in conversation, which they continued while acknowledging her presence in the doorway.

Kwesi had been evicted from the library, not because of the planned changes to the building as he had feared, but because someone had informed the head librarian and she said she had no choice. A relative or contact of one of his asylum-seeker workmates at the packaging warehouse had offered him a room, but it was in Leeds and he wasn't keen to leave London.

'My friends are here, you are here, and I am making a little money for food and what I need, although it is not legal and I could lose my jobs tomorrow. Also, I know it is better in London, quicker for me to have my appeal considered. If I move, it will take longer.'

'Could you stay with one of your friends in London again, just until—?'

'You can stay with me,' interrupted Marcus. 'I'm on my own with two spare rooms. You can stay for a few months if you need to, rent-free, and cook us some of those dishes you've been talking about. Then we'll see if your food is as good as your music. What do you think, Fran, good idea?'

'It's great, perfect. The drums can stay here, of course. I've got the space and we seem to be getting away with it, not aggravating the neighbours from hell, no names mentioned.'

Kwesi looked astonished, and then his face broke into a wide grin. He raised his arms and brought the drumsticks down to produce a dramatic roll and boom. Then, serious again, he stood up as if to address an appreciative audience.

'My friends, I am deeply thankful. I cannot express it. I will repay you for your kindness.'

'We know you will, Kwesi, one way or another. And now, let's all go down and have a celebratory drink.'

Kwesi moved in with Marcus the next day, bringing the same friend with the van and the pair of them carrying his worldly goods in two big suitcases, one of which Fran knew contained the gifts. Watching this operation, she wondered if Marcus would receive a similar wood carving to her own, and she thought back to their conversation about the uncanny similarity between her Junoco-inspired drawing and the antelope Kwesi had given her. Marcus had admired her work and said she should take up painting, breathe colour and spirit into it, in his words. One day, she might feel comfortable enough to tell him that she seemed to have the power to breathe life and motion into inanimate creatures too.

***

She was making her usual Friday café stop before going into the shop when she spied Delia and Eric walking by. She quickly averted her gaze as they looked in the window, stopped, came to a mutual decision and walked in. She wasn't sure if they had spied her sitting there, but sensed she was their target. She had never seen them in the café before and it was clear they didn't know Jean-Claude, as they rudely ignored his welcoming '*Bonjour*, Madame, Monsieur' from behind the counter.

They didn't approach her straight away, but Delia smiled and Eric nodded almost genially as they passed her table. Fran considered making a quick escape but felt mildly intrigued, not to mention disinclined to have her pleasant Friday routine disturbed by them. She would wait, enjoy her coffee and baguette and go on to Frocks and Chocs at her normal time.

It was Delia who came over to her first, while Eric fussed around gathering up their shopping bags.

'Excuse me, it's Fran, isn't it, from Number 26? I'm Delia, from Number 30, and that's my husband, Eric. We spoke briefly when you moved in.'

Fran gave her a weak smile. *Yes, and instead of being neighbourly, you welcomed me by telling me off about the removal van being parked outside your house. It's not something you forget, don't you realise?*

Both of them were standing beside her table now, inspecting her while doing their best to appear friendly. It would be safer to have them on her level, so she gestured for them to sit down. They didn't waste time asking how she was settling in or any such small talk but went directly to the issue they were perturbed about – or two issues, as it turned out.

They had registered Kwesi's arrival at Marcus' house with his luggage and then his comings and goings over the following couple of weeks, although they didn't know, or didn't admit to knowing, that he had also been a visitor to Fran's house for the past while. Did Fran know who he was? Was he a relative of 'the occupant' at Number 28? It was clear they had been suspicious of Marcus since he moved in, and their doorstep encounter with Kirsty, the 'fracas' as they called it, had confirmed him to be a highly dubious character. This latest development had made them 'concerned for all our safety'. The phrase was given great emphasis by Delia and accompanied by a ferocious glare from Eric, who had forgotten he was meant to be in friendly mode and had gone off-message.

Fran thought fast and decided she had two options: either claim ignorance or invent a story to put them off the scent. Invention seemed the wiser choice, given that Kwesi was working illegally and was in a precarious position with regard to his asylum appeal.

Passing over the idiotic question about whether the two men were related, she said that Kwesi was a student lodger who was training to be a doctor and had won a top scholarship to come to the UK. This was quite close to his actual history from some time ago, so he should be able to talk about if he were put on the spot. Eric looked unconvinced, however, and wrinkled his nose in a kind of sneer. Clearly, being nice in public couldn't be sustained for very long. It was a shame really, a waste; without his set of invariably sour expressions, he might have been considered quite attractive.

'That's what he told you, is it, a student? He looks too old to be a student.'

'Well, you can't tell very easily, can you, with them? How old they are, I mean.'

This was Delia's attempt at a conciliatory intervention, as she had seen Fran tensing up in response to Eric's comment. She wanted to move on to the other issue, which was about Lily and her mission to find the missing cats.

'We've noticed that odd little girl next door going into your house, or waiting for you outside, and you've got one of those *Missing* posters in your window. We find it hurtful because we lost our cat last year, she died of cancer and we don't want to be constantly reminded of it. Cats go astray, they get run over or they move in somewhere else, that's it. Can you talk to her, please?'

'Well, she's passionate about it and I have already made those arguments, but I'm happy to try again, if it's upsetting you. I'll speak to her.'

Fran was well into the game now, trying to keep them on side while finding the notion that they were grieving for a pet cat somewhat laughable. Although, maybe it was indicative of the kind of people they were: devoted to a cat and horrible to their neighbours and the rest of the world. Looked at that way, there could be some truth in it, although she was fairly sure they had told Lily they hated cats.

She ran through the encounter in her mind during her afternoon shift at the shop. Eric and Delia were observing her more closely than she had imagined. Given the various activities she was involved in, she would have to take more care and watch her back.

Lily was sitting on her front wall when she arrived home, her legs swinging and heels bumping on the worn bricks. The weather was mild for early February, but it still seemed too cold to be wearing shorts and a light T-shirt. She was holding Sahara on her lap, looking down to talk to her and lifting her back each time the restless hamster made an effort to edge forwards. On the wall beside her was a pile of new *Missing* posters held down by a chunky grey pebble. Fran saw that there were now three full-colour photos, of Marmalade, Sooty and – what was the other one called? – Leonie. Lily scooped Sahara into her arms and jumped down to the pavement.

'Hi, Fran, I've got something to tell you, an important

development. And look at this – I've done new posters, got them properly printed and paid for it myself.'

'Come on in, then. They look great, well done.' Eric and Delia might want Lily to be diverted from her mission and detective work, but they had no inkling what a strong-minded, intelligent and spirited child she was.

The new development was startling. Lily had heard about it at school, in response to being allowed to put up a poster on the student noticeboard. A family living in the next street, running parallel to theirs, had moved out a few days previously. After the removal lorry had left, they had loaded their most precious belongings into their car, including a Siamese cat and a rabbit in travel cages. Both the animals and their cages had vanished. They had been taken from the back of the car in the space of a few minutes, while the family were in the house. They had searched in every direction and driven repeatedly around the local area, but there was no sign of the stolen pets and no one claimed to have witnessed the snatch.

Here was the evidence, as far as Lily was concerned, that all the lost animals were victims of crime and hadn't wandered off by choice or been run over. She had got her mum to call the police and they were expecting to be interviewed, as Lily had what she referred to as 'important information about other crimes'.

'Yes, they may want to talk to you and I'm sure the family will have reported it, but they might just write down what your mum has told them over the phone. It's even possible there is no connection between the cases. This could have been opportunistic, you know, a spur-of-the-moment thing, and we don't know what exactly happened in your other cases, just that the cats went out in the evening and didn't come back.'

Lily stared incredulously at her, while Sahara stopped nibbling her carrot, puffed out her cheeks and joined in, fixing Fran in that meaningful way that certain animals seemed to have now, since she started with Junoco.

'You don't really believe that. You're just saying it; I don't understand why.'

Fran hesitated. She wanted to protect Lily from any risk, danger even, and the possibility of actual danger had been heightened by this latest news. She also had to take account of Eric and Delia, who were both thoroughly wound up and had the potential to be extremely vindictive if crossed. And yet, here was Lily, adopting a cause she believed in and doing the planning, the painstaking investigation, the publicity, the analysis, doing it all brilliantly. She was eleven, the same age as Fran and Judi in the last childhood summer they had spent together. Lily was completely different from Judi, much shyer and less prettily confident, but wow, didn't she have her own brand of boldness and an unwavering will to succeed.

'Okay, you're right, Lily, there could be a link and maybe someone planned to target the family when they moved, knowing they had a cat and a rabbit. It's possible. Let's put the new poster up in the window, for a start, and then we can think about the next steps.'

Lily jumped up, almost dropping Sahara in her eagerness. 'And I have something else important to tell you. I don't want to be a vet any more. I want to be an astronomer instead, studying planets and asteroids, after we talked about it those times. They're so cool and amazing. What are they thinking about, up there in space?'

'Who do you mean, thinking up there in space – aliens? We haven't found out yet if aliens exist beyond our imagination.'

'I know that, silly.'

Lily stopped, thinking she may have gone too far, but Fran gestured for her to continue.

'I mean the asteroids, what are they thinking? Do they wish they were planets, that they could be smooth and round and big enough?'

'Perhaps they do, Lily. My favourite asteroid, Juno, was a planet when she was first discovered and later they downgraded her to an asteroid. It was in the 1800s this happened. I think she was the third asteroid to be discovered, when they were looking for a suspected planet in that area. Some other asteroids are named after goddesses too, like Juno; there's Ceres—'

'Maybe the asteroids are angry and that's why they collide with the planets, make dents and craters in them. They're angry and they want revenge.'

Fran laughed, shaking her head in amused disbelief, while Lily gave a satisfied smile, pleased to have articulated her wild theory.

'Lily, if you do study astronomy, I'm sure your ideas will be miles ahead of their time and everybody will think you're mad, like they've done with all the greatest scientists and adventurers! No, really, you have a truly original mind and I think it's a fantastic plan. What about your mum – what does she think about it, or your dad?'

'I haven't told them. I've only told you and no one else.

You're my best friend and you won't make fun of me. And Sahara, she knows.'

Fran wished once again that she could tell Lily about the Junoco effects, her animal drawings and how certain creatures responded to her and tried to convey their thoughts and emotions. Lily seemed the best person on earth to confide in, the one who would most easily understand, but the imperative of keeping it quiet was too great to impose on her.

They were interrupted by the doorbell. It was Petra looking for Lily, who should have been home half an hour ago.

'I thought I would find her with you, but she never takes her phone so I couldn't call to make sure. No, thank you but I won't come in now. I am cooking dinner and then we shall have a Skype call with Ferdi, but very quickly, I wanted to tell you something, confidentially.'

'Just come into the hall, then, and I can shut the door.' Fran had already made sure there was no one keeping watch from across the road or lurking nearby, but she felt more secure and at ease talking inside with the door closed. Lily had disappeared back into the living room and Fran could hear her chatting to Sahara. Petra listened too and decided it was safe to speak in a half-whisper.

'Do you remember, we talked about Lily being different and creative and you asked what the school was doing, if they were doing anything special for her? And you know too that I'm a teacher, at a different school?'

Fran nodded impatiently, eager to know what was coming next.

'My head teacher has told us about a project that will

be set up in our borough and in five other areas. They intend to test some new vitamins and supplements, to see if they improve concentration and can make the children learn better and faster. They will select children from the top and bottom five per cent academically, and a third group who are disruptive or have problems with attention. I expect Lily will be in the top group, because she comes first or second in all the tests.'

Lily put her head round the door at this point and Fran only had time to say she was very interested and would like to hear more. As she showed them out, Marcus was turning into his front path on his return from work. Lily gave him one of the new Missing posters, but Petra was hurrying her on and she had to pass by without explaining the latest twist in the drama of the missing pets. Marcus paused on his step, having checked out the chestnut tree just as Fran was now in the habit of doing. She leaned over the wall, her voice low.

'I'm glad I've caught you, Marcus. I met our neighbours in the café today, Eric and Delia. They approached me and came over all friendly, but it was obvious they only wanted information. They have clocked that Kwesi's living at your house and I told them he's a lodger, a medical student here on a scholarship. I don't trust them, not one jot, so I wanted to alert you both, because we mustn't let them find out he's working illegally.'

'Oh shit, sorry, thank you for that. We've got another problem as well: Kirsty. I should have warned Kwesi, but she came round when he was at home on his own and he let her in and gave her a coffee. He probably wouldn't have said he was a refugee, but I'm not sure what story he told her and she certainly got out of him that he's now staying here. Apparently, she was perfectly nice to him but she won't like it at all, you can bet on that. I'm expecting some kind of repercussion at any moment.'

'Okay, that could complicate matters too. I'll keep an eye out.' As she said goodbye and closed her front door, Fran realised she hadn't said anything to either Lily or Marcus about Eric and Delia's professed torment at being reminded about the missing cats.

***

In an unprecedented move, Ned, Vicky and Fran had been summoned to the office. Daniela spoke to them from behind her desk, as if to stress the formality and gravity of the occasion.

'These recent events are linked, and it's now crystal clear that we face a campaign to damage and destroy Junoco. If anyone in this room is passing on intelligence or is involved in double-dealing, I assure you they will regret it. I am not accusing any of you, but I have to consider every possibility. And if you think this may have resulted from an indiscretion or some kind of coercion that you have experienced, please speak up.'

Suddenly, Fran was ten years old again, sitting at the back of the class behind a double desk with Judi. Not one of the other children betrayed them by turning round, all of them looking instead at the irate teacher and, behind her, at the offending charcoal drawing stuck to the blackboard. The likeness to Miss Bell was unmistakable and far from flattering. Fran had drawn it, egged on by Judi, and everyone had giggled and fidgeted as they waited for their fierce and normally respected teacher to enter the classroom.

The vivid memory came and went in an instant, but the emotions lingered as she was brought back to the present by Vicky's assertive response.

'I accept you have to consider it, Daniela, but we need to work together against the threat and I think we've all shown how much we want Junoco to be a success and what it means to us personally. I agree that it looks like a concerted campaign, starting with the factory fire and now the break-in at the distribution centre and the hacking of the website. I don't yet know whose personal details have been stolen, but a number of our more savvy customers are already querying what's going on and asking if their information is safe. And what about the break-in at your place, Ned – can you give us any more details?'

'Several hundred boxes of truffles nicked; I'll have the exact number when Joe calls me from the warehouse. It was a very neat operation: no mess and only the door-opening mechanism damaged. They disabled the security system, but it was never going to be effective anyway because we can't have a functioning alarm, for obvious confidentiality reasons, and the new cameras we ordered aren't installed yet. It was dry last night too, so there's no sign of tyre tracks on the lane.'

Fran was aware of Daniela scrutinising them all, her eyes narrowing as they glided from one to the next and back again. Did she suspect someone in particular, or was she just using authority and threat to keep them loyal and on their toes? When she spoke again, her tone was less angry, more neutral.

'I don't believe it's a competitor this time; I've already handled that after the fire. It could be a police operation, but that doesn't make sense. I mention it because there's a journalist sniffing around. At least, he claims to be a journalist and he's hinted that the police might have an interest in Junoco, as part of a bigger exercise. I shall give you his description so you are on your guard.'

Fran wrote it down in her notebook – male, early thirties, Asian appearance, slim build, average height, cultured English accent. The meeting concluded immediately after that, as Daniela's phone rang and she gestured for them to leave the office.

As they went downstairs, Ned whispered to Fran and she arranged to follow Vicky to the café in five minutes. She and Ned walked a short distance in the opposite direction and down the side alley, where they could talk in private. The narrow passage was damp and chilly, and Fran pushed her hands deeper into her pockets.

'It's not you, is it, Ned, doing this?'

He smiled and gave a low chuckle. 'Me? What makes you think that? It was my place that got broken into, remember?'

'I know, but with all this talk of double-dealing – and Daniela isn't accusing Infrared, she said she's handled it, did you notice?'

'Yep, that was interesting. But never mind the double-dealing; I'd like to ask you over for dinner tonight. It's short notice but there's something I want to try out on you.'

Her heart and mind weren't in it, but she couldn't resist responding to his banter. 'What's that, then? Is it a beautiful ballgown for the next film premiere?'

'Yes, at least that's where it's all leading: to a spectacular ballgown.'

'But seriously though, Ned, what do you think about Daniela? I wouldn't like to see her in a full-blown rage. The controlled anger was scary enough. It reminded me of my primary teacher, Miss Bell, who humiliated me by ordering me to sit in kindergarten with the four-year-olds for a whole day and do their work.'

'Ha – I bet you deserved it too. Daniela needs to act fast and transfer the site to one of the parallel websites Vicky has prepared for this eventuality, that's the safest thing, and we'll move everything to a new distribution centre. I've got a few thoughts which I'll tell Daniela about later.'

It all sounded a bit glib, too easy and relaxed for the circumstances.

'What is it, Fran? Why are you frowning at me like that? It's you and your weird expression that's making me nervous, more than anything.'

'I don't know. I'm surprised you're not more anxious or freaked out by what's happening. I feel guilty about pulling you into this, Ned, but you almost seem to revel in the danger of it.'

'Well, it's better than me turning round and blaming you, isn't it? I knew all along it was going to be a risky business, and risky businesses tend to yield the highest rewards – that's the way I look at it. I'm quite good at picking my way through a minefield and coming out unscathed. If we stick close together, we can have a big win. But listen – you told Vicky five minutes and we're freezing in this alley, so if you're free and want to come over, I'll pick you up at seven.'

She found herself nodding and felt the familiar frisson flowing through her body, despite her head still spinning with thoughts of criminal intrigue and conspiracy. What a total pushover. Maybe it was this character flaw, this weakness that would ultimately be her downfall.

'Yes, I'd love that. Seven it is. I'll bring the chocolate; orange intense, not Junoco this time.'

They walked back to the pavement and parted with a simple wave. Fran walked in the direction of home to catch up with Vicky at the café, pulling up her collar and shaping her mouth into an 'O' to blow out steam with her warm breath. As she got close to Frocks and Chocs, she noticed a man standing by the door and lifting his sleeve to consult his watch. Peering more intently in the growing dusk, she confirmed that it was Professor Fred Henson-Morris from the university. She was almost level with him now and it was too late; he had recognised her and he looked equally uncomfortable. She decided not to stop but just to slow her pace a fraction as she went past, not enough to invite any genuine conversation.

'Hi there, Fred, how are you doing?'

'Fine, yes – much colder today, isn't it?' He stamped his feet for emphasis.

'Freezing – I can't wait to get home. See you later.'

What was he doing there? Did he know she lived near here and worked at the shop, or was it pure chance? Had he seen through her seemingly innocent questions over lunch? Or, worst of all, had Alice raised suspicions with her covert investigation into the products they were planning to use in the Bright Minds project?

She strode on quickly without a backward glance

and was relieved to reach the safe haven of the café and see Vicky's winsome smile as she approached. Fran was disconcerted but knew she mustn't let on to Vicky about seeing Professor Fred, as it would reawaken her righteous anger with her for confiding in Alice and allowing her to analyse the Junoco truffles. She would have to put the episode aside for now and call Alice when she got home.

Luckily, her lack of composure was readily explained by the dramatic scene in the office. Vicky knew how hopeless she was at handling conflict, and that she would have been shaken by Daniela's tone and direct threat of retribution. She was more resilient than before all this started, but not yet resilient enough.

Vicky had ordered two large slices of cake. 'Sit down and say which one you want – I'm easy. The coffee and walnut one looks particularly moist and squidgy today. I fancy a smoothie as well.'

She beckoned to Jean-Claude, who served at the tables when it wasn't too busy. Fran took a single deep breath, appreciating the enveloping warmth and familiar smells of the café as well as the close affinity she felt with Vicky, despite their contretemps over Alice. Maybe Vicky was a teeny bit put out by Alice, jealous even? It was a novel thought, which she didn't have time to explore now. Vicky had moved on to a new topic entirely.

'He's really dishy, is your Ned. I've got half a mind to book him for a night out on the town, go to a jazz club and then on somewhere to dance. What do you think? Would you mind?'

Fran blinked and jerked up straight, genuinely taken aback but making more of a play of it than she really felt.

'The trouble with you, Vicky, is that it's difficult to know when you're being serious. I have the same problem with Ned. The short answer is, I don't know. Yes, of course I'd mind, that's my immediate reaction, but then again, maybe I wouldn't if it was on that basis: a paid night out. But please don't throw a googly like that when I'm trying to work out what's going on with Junoco. It's quite tangled enough, don't you think?'

'Okay then, let's get the serious bit out of the way,' said Vicky. 'I have sadly come to the conclusion that Daniela is playing a fast game. She's making the insinuations, but I think she's the one who may be about to double-cross the rest of us.'

'Why, Vicky? What do you mean? You've always said we should be loyal to her and that she has good reasons for keeping us in the dark about certain things.'

'Yes, but the website hack was nothing to do with me, and she was showing a lot of interest in the privacy aspects of the site, the technicalities of how it all works.'

'And…?'

'I could be wrong here, but I've been looking into her associates, who she meets up with…'

Vicky paused, as if about to make a major revelation, and Fran picked up on the cue.

'Well then, who are her associates and who does she meet up with? Tell me.'

'She has met your university professor, Fred Henson-Morris, several times in the past month, and they've had lengthy huddled conversations with a lot of gesturing and animated discussion.'

Fran jolted backwards, tipping her chair almost to the

point of instability. 'Who, Fred – what on earth…? Do you think she's…? What about Alice, Dr Stevens – was she there?'

'Alice? I don't know what Alice looks like, but no; it's always just the two of them.'

Fran was trying to make sense of this extraordinary turn of events. Fred must have been waiting for Daniela outside the shop. It wasn't anything to do with her, Fran; she just happened to walk past at that moment. He may not even have made any connection between her and Daniela. But why were they meeting for 'huddled conversations'? Had Alice let something slip and inadvertently shown him a path to Junoco and Daniela?

Vicky was studying her, waiting for a response but also pensive, as if turning something over in her mind. Fran sat silently, her thoughts whirling.

'Before you ask,' said Vicky, 'I'm still investigating and I don't know what the nature of the link is or if the relationship is fundamentally friendly or hostile, although the body language suggests friendly. Either way, I think you should consider backing out of Junoco now. It's getting dicey, too hot to handle.'

This was even more alarming: Vicky changing her firm and much-repeated opinion so fast. And who was she to decide what Fran should do, just like that?

'Why should I back out? Why me? What about you, and Ned for that matter?'

'I'm advising you, as a friend and someone who's been in this kind of business longer. I don't want to patronise you, I'd never do that, but it's getting messy. I might quit soon as well, but I have to take things a little further. It's something I can't explain; I haven't got any choice.'

Fran gawped at her friend, overwhelmed by surprise and a sudden hollow feeling of abandonment. Vicky maintained a steady stare, her evident concern laced with a different quality: a kind of detachment. Fran's eyes began to well up, but she resolved not to allow herself to shed tears, or be stared out.

'Okay, Vicky, that's your opinion. I don't agree but... I'm finding this hard, on top of... everything else. Like, it's difficult with Andy now – he's avoiding me and he won't talk about it. I don't know what to do, or I know what to do but I can't do it, I'm too weak. I don't want to end it with him because... it's partly about Judi and partly desire, or lust if you like; he's so seductive without even trying, and it's special because of Judi and...'

There – she had blurted it out now, all wrong and at precisely the wrong moment; she had exposed her weakness. Vicky reached for her hand and squeezed it.

'I understand. You've been saying that for a few weeks: he's acting differently. You need to end that too, find the strength to do it. It will only get worse if you don't, and deep down you don't want to be with him, you've said that.'

'I know, and it's plain ridiculous. *I'm* ridiculous, and I'm being very shallow.'

'No, I'm not going to accept that. You are an A1 gorgeous woman, strong and kind and one of the best I've ever met.'

'I'm sorry, Vicky, it's these waves of sadness, the grief, it just comes over me. It magnifies everything...'

'I do understand, and I don't want to be hard on you. It's all part of the process, Fran, the stages of grieving, and you're dealing with a lot of changes and stress in your life right now. It's bound to get on top of you sometimes.'

'Tell you what, I can't see Ned tonight. Whatever wacky proposition he wants to put to me, it'll have to wait.'

They sat in silence while Jean-Claude, in his long blue apron, discreetly tidied up around them, their hands gripped tightly at first but steadily loosening until Vicky slid hers gently out of Fran's grasp.

Chapter 14

She had switched her Saturday shift at the shop so that she could visit her relatives, now a welcome prospect as she needed to get out of London and gain some perspective on the Junoco situation. There was also the car to be picked up, the family car that Cerise was passing on to Fran after a minor bump at some traffic lights that had shaken her already declining confidence. The condition was that Fran would regularly take them out to their favourite haunts and events.

On the train journey, she sat near a family with three young kids, all immersed in their electronic games. She thought of the schoolboy she had half-minded on that final journey to visit Judi. Gazing out the window, she visualised the rabbits and foxes in which the boy had showed zero interest. The fields and the railway embankment were wintry now, but the greenery, flowers and wildlife would take over again within the next few weeks; perhaps sooner if there was an early warm spell.

He was an unusual child, that boy, not like these kids, and the most peculiar thing was how he transformed when he leapt off the train, switched to a completely different persona for his school friends, who seemed to idolise him. Judi had possessed that chameleon-like quality, as well as her natural charisma, and Ned and Vicky had something of it too, which might be why Fran found them so hard to read. Why did Vicky advise her, almost order her, to leave Junoco; change tack so sharply? What was it that she couldn't explain, that she still had to do?

Arriving at the family house, Fran stopped to examine the copper-coloured Mini on the drive. There was no sign of any damage to the front bumper and the car was in good condition, consistent with its light use over the past five years. Cerise stepped out of the front door and swept across the grass with her arms outstretched to give her a generous embrace.

'Will it do for you, this nice little car? I'm very fond of her, but she's just sitting there most of the time. It will be a much more exciting life for her in London.'

'It's fantastic, Cerise. I really appreciate it and look forward to our outings too. Is everything okay? Anything you need to warn me about before we go in?'

'Just one thing – we're all keen to try your chocolates again, so I hope you got the message about bringing a box down for the old folk. It did perk us up at Christmas.'

'Yes, I got that, and I have it here in my bag. I'm glad you weren't too put off by what happened to that poor little mouse.'

As they crossed the hall, Pansy paused in scrabbling around for seeds and nuts on the floor of her cage and produced one of her prolonged and indignant shrieks.

They all gathered for lunch, a beef stew with dumplings followed by Cerise's lemon meringue pie with its high and well-burnt peaks. George was keen to accompany Fran and Cerise on a drive, but Eleanor declined the invitation, saying bluntly that she didn't want to squash in the back with George and his funny smells. Fran drove the two of them to the coast, where they walked slowly along the beach and had vanilla ice cream cones, sitting on the sea wall surrounded by voracious seagulls.

After a light supper round the television, Cerise announced it was time for a party.

'A Junoco party, that's the name, isn't it? We can have the chocolates and play that game of charades we invented at Christmas, unless we're inspired to come up with something else. Is everyone in favour?'

Fran looked at her mother, expecting her to dismiss this jollity and retreat with a barbed comment. Instead, though, Eleanor seemed positively keen.

'Well, come on then, Cerise. What are we all waiting for?'

Fran fetched the Junoco box and handed out the blue-wrapped truffles, then suggested that Cerise light some candles to enhance the visual effects and accentuate the shift of mood. For Fran, the vivid geometric shapes appeared more quickly each time, perhaps because her brain was anticipating them, but there was always something unique: new objects spiralling into her vision, or unfamiliar sounds and scents. This evening, the tumbling shapes were tactile. She could reach out and feel them, finding the jagged-looking ones soft and the smoothly rounded ones hard and dangerously spiky to the touch.

She looked down at her hands lying placidly on the arms of the chair, reaching out only in spirit. The falling shapes joined to form a stunning kaleidoscope of symmetrical patterns that instantly collapsed, breaking into a thousand tiny fragments of coloured glass. At the perimeter of her vision, the pieces appeared to transmute into minuscule hummingbirds, lightning flashes of feathers.

The long silence was broken by George, who spoke loudly and formally, as if talking to base station. 'Are you hearing me, loud and clear? We are maintaining velocity and direction through a shower of heavy particles, comprising large chunks of ice, metal and rock along the visible spectrum from red to violet. No white and no black. The target is off-screen, repeat, target is off-screen. Do you have it, please confirm?'

Fran caught Eleanor's eye. Her mother was clearly enjoying this and responded in good humour.

'We are receiving you, loud and clear. You should have been a sci-fi actor, George, one of the ones who get permanently lost in space.'

After a while, during which time Cerise leaned back with a serene expression and George continued his reports from outer space, Fran picked up the gold-wrapped truffles and handed them round. The initial effects on the old folk were more dramatic this time, and it would be fascinating to see how the gold truffles performed. She felt like an experimental film director, a little unhinged herself but responsible for not letting the plot or the cast get out of hand.

'I have something to say to you all, before we play any games.' Eleanor also spoke loudly, commanding their attention. 'I've kept it to myself up to now, but I think you should know.'

Fran held her breath. Was this going to be it: the truth about Marina, the accident, what really happened that day and how her mother saw it, who she blamed for it?

'Fine, do tell us, Eleanor', said Cerise calmly.

Eleanor cleared her throat. 'I have met a new boyfriend. He's called John and he works up at the hospital. He's not an important doctor like Lawrence was, he's more of a dogsbody, but he is very gentlemanly and he drives a swanky red Alfa Romeo.'

This announcement struck Fran as very odd. Firstly, the use of the term 'dogsbody' to describe a new boyfriend, and secondly, the naming of a car as an Alfa Romeo when Eleanor disdained all interest in cars and claimed she couldn't tell one end from the other. It certainly wasn't a case of Junoco reawakening old interests and talents.

'Well, that's a turn-up for the books,' said Cerise. 'And if he's still working at the hospital, he must be a lot younger than you.'

'Yes, he's nearly sixty. It's his birthday coming up soon.'

'Did you hear that, George? Eleanor has a new boyfriend called John. He's nearly sixty.'

George rubbed his eyes, looking more than a touch bewildered. Cerise clapped her hands, seemingly delighted at the new turn of events.

'And now, everyone, shall we celebrate with that game of charades?'

Fran wondered if Eleanor's new relationship would stick with them and become one of those legendary family stories, known to be false but accepted as a shared truth and important to their acceptance of each other. She smiled and said nothing.

After a few remarkably well-acted turns of charades, Eleanor said she wanted to call John to say goodnight and went up to her room. George quickly fell asleep in his chair, leaving Fran and Cerise to enjoy one of their intimate chats.

'I don't ever want to leave this house, you know,' said Cerise. 'I don't see how we're going to manage like this forever, but I hope we all leave in a box, when it comes to it. And you will make sure they play the right music at my funeral, won't you – the crooners and divas and ragtime – and the same for George?'

'Yes, I promise. And one of those lovely classical pieces you played after eating the Junoco truffles. I hope we'll hear some of that later tonight.'

'If I get too old and doddery, I don't want to be shunted off to a quiet place in the country where nothing happens. I want to have a nice little corner flat in an accident black spot in the middle of a red-light district!'

Fran laughed. 'Okay, I'll do my best. I don't know where that scene bubbled up from, but you realise you'll have to move to a bigger town to get all that.'

Cerise was in full flow now; veering between emotional reminiscences of her youth, wild aspirations for her old age, which in her eyes hadn't yet begun, and the happy times she had spent living with Lawrence. Fran waited for the right moment to reopen the conversation they had begun on her last visit.

'Do you remember, Cerise, you said you hadn't been told about my little sister Marina, but Dad had told you other things? I'm curious to know what the other things were, if you are able to tell me.'

'Other things… I'm not sure…'

'Anything from when he was with Eleanor?'

'Well, perhaps… I don't know if I should say this, but

he told me they had a baby who didn't live, a stillborn girl.'

Fran was silent. It was no good – she had to go on with it, had to finish. 'Do you know when this was – the date? Was it before or after me?'

'I don't know, I'm sorry; that's all I can remember, or it's all he told me.' Cerise suddenly looked anxious, bordering on defensive.

'It's really okay, Cerise; I'm glad you told me. I'll ask Eleanor about it tomorrow.'

George was stirring in his chair and Fran took the opportunity to say goodnight to Cerise and escort him up to his bedroom. It was a slow climb and when they got there, George swayed badly and put his hands on the door frame to keep his balance.

'This is the hedgehog's room – that's how I think of it. Tomorrow morning I'm going to tidy up all these papers and magazines and fold my clothes. I've had enough of this muddle and I'm not going to get anywhere with my work until I've got it all in order.'

'You're right, Uncle George, but will you actually do it? Would you like me to come down one day soon and help you get it organised?'

He sat down clumsily on the side of the bed and leaned forward to take her hand. 'Yes, please. And I need a scientific expert, someone who can turn my theories into reality. I haven't much time and it will soon be too late.'

That felt like more than enough of astonishing conversations for one evening, and Fran was grateful to crawl into bed and stare at the ceiling until she drifted off.

***

When she woke, it was to a Junoco dream set in the asteroid belt between Mars and Jupiter. The asteroids were chocolate truffles, the two Junoco varieties of rocky and smooth, but vastly differing sizes. Fran was on a silver space-motorbike with the widest imaginable mirrors, and it was her job to prevent the asteroid truffles from being drawn down towards the earth. Her plan was to keep on the outside of them, circle with them so they didn't fall or push each other out of orbit. It all seemed perfectly manageable.

As she emerged, she became aware of movement and music in the house. She reached for her sketch pad, the original one with the early sketches of Marina. She pulled her jumper on and tucked the pad under her arm. Passing through the hall, she was drawn to the cage, where Pansy sat on her highest perch.

'Hello, Pansy. You're a pretty bird, aren't you? Tell me something.'

The parrot fluffed up a little and rearranged her feet on the perch, then cocked her head so it was close to horizontal. 'Pretty bird, my pretty blue and gold...'

Fran stepped back, startled. It was so long since she'd heard Pansy talk. 'Blue and gold, that's right. You're a blue-and-gold macaw.'

'Lovely flowers – come again soon. Box of chocs,' trilled Pansy.

The parrot had adopted her own version of the meaningful look that Fran now recognised in her animal encounters. She emitted a rasping screech, then turned away and began to preen herself, conversation over. There was only one likely explanation – Cerise or one of the others had offered their captive exotic bird a taste of Junoco; a taste of home.

George was in the kitchen setting the table for breakfast while Cerise sat at the piano, fingers poised for her next piece, and Eleanor was on the sofa listening. Fran checked to confirm that Cerise was awake and then sat next to her mother, who touched her on the shoulder.

'Good morning, dear. We're having an early recital today. Cerise is such a wonderful pianist.'

As the music began again, softly, Fran moved closer to her mother so she would hear her words. 'Eleanor, Mum, there's something I need to ask you; that I've wanted to ask you for a long time.'

'A long time – is it about the baby, about Marina?'

Had she known all along how important this was to Fran, or had Cerise said something already this morning? It didn't matter. What mattered was her mother's tone of voice, her acceptance that the secret would come out now. Cerise's playing was quiet and low but also strangely intense, the accompaniment to an historic family moment.

'Yes, it is. I need to know what happened to her. I remember the accident. It's my earliest memory, with the motorcyclist flying through the air and—'

'There was no motorbike. I don't know what you're saying. That must have been another time, maybe when you were with your father. I have no memory of it.'

'What, then? What did happen to Marina?'

Her mother stood up and went to gaze out the window, then turned and came back to sit beside her daughter again.

249

Cerise had stopped playing and swivelled round on the piano stool, while George was coming in with four mugs of tea on a tray, which he placed carefully on the coffee table.

'We called the baby Marina, but she didn't survive. She was deprived of oxygen at birth and she didn't survive; she died while she was being born. I wasn't able to tell you, to talk about it. I imagined it would upset you, but if I'm honest, it just upset me too much.'

Fran pushed her sketch pad under the cushion. There might be another time to tell Eleanor she had done all the drawings, imagined her little sister's looks, her personality and her life right through to now, to her early fifties.

After a quiet interval while they sipped their tea, Cerise suggested breakfast. As they stood up, Fran and Eleanor turned to each other for a quick but sincere hug, which avoided any need for further explanation or comment.

Fran went to have a shower and get ready to drive home. Cerise handed her the car key fob with a ceremonial flourish and all three of them came to the front door to see her off. As she walked to the car, she made out a figure near the gate, half-hidden by the overgrown hedge. It was Tom Harrison, the man who had been bothering George and attempting to exploit him. She called out to him, loudly enough for the group gathered on the doorstep to hear her.

'I can see you, Tom Harrison. Come out from behind that hedge. George has got something to say to you.'

Tom came out, his face contorted and defiant, and walked past Fran across the grass, trying to ignore her. When his expression tightened and he raised his fist as if preparing for a punch, George stepped forward and put up his hand.

'Stop right there, hold it. I've had enough of you, Tom. I'm running out of time and I've got important things to do, for the future, for science. You're standing in the way of progress. I've tried to help you, but you have to sort out your own life, so go away and do it.'

'And don't ever come back here,' added Eleanor. 'We have far more power than you can possibly imagine, and we'll give you short shrift if you try anything on us. I wouldn't dare come near us again, if I were you.'

Cerise had the last word as Tom simply stared at them, all three standing close together, before turning down the path and stumbling off.

'Good luck to you, Tom. No hard feelings.'

Fran opened the car door, threw her bag onto the back seat and waved to the exultant and formidable trio as she drove away.

A few minutes later, she was out of town and softly humming that last piano tune to herself as she tested the windscreen wipers and checked out the horn and light controls. She had ten miles before she came to the main road; ten miles to decide whether to go straight back to London or drop in on Andy. If she did go, she would stop and text him on the way and if he didn't reply, well, maybe she would turn up anyway. Her mood was light, still influenced by the Junoco party and the amazingly good effects the truffles seemed to be having on her relatives. She would keep her promise to help Uncle George organise his ideas so he could discuss them with a current expert. And she would go along with Eleanor's imaginary boyfriend, as long as it didn't get too loopy.

Then Marina, the subject her mind left until last,

too busy absorbing the fact that she wasn't a toddler in a pushchair and she never grew into the mop-haired, mischievous little girl or the young woman with flowing curls of Fran's imagination. It was a hefty shock, but beyond that she felt enormous relief, unburdened of the lifelong guilt at having caused or contributed to her sister's death.

She pulled into a lay-by to send the message. If she had the will and courage to ask Eleanor about Marina and then provoke the final departure, she hoped, of Tom Harrison, she could surely have a grown-up conversation with Andy about their relationship and whether it was going to continue, change or simply end. Maybe she could draw a line by luring him into bed one final time, before or after a bracing walk with Winnie on the beach? No, that would never work. She had to summon up the strength of will to end it today, gently and affectionately, with no hard feelings or disappointment.

She waited for a few minutes after sending the text, walking around the car to inspect the bodywork for minor scrapes and finding a couple of tiny scratches and a small dent at the rear. Jumping back in, she started the engine and decided she was going to visit Andy right now, whether he answered or not.

***

The short lane leading to the cottages was bumpier than she had noticed when walking from the taxi drop-off point. Seeing the pony standing near the fence, she found a widening in the lane opposite the paddock where she could park. A car was sitting in front of Andy's house, which made her nervous enough to pull up some rough winter grass from the verge and offer it to the pony while stroking her nose. The animal nuzzled into her hand as if she recognised her, and Fran wondered how much she missed Judi's loving attention. It was typical of Judi to tease Fran and Andy by suggesting, decreeing almost, that they go on holiday together. Had she suspected how electrifying it would be, how madly Fran would anticipate falling into bed with him each time, the sheer physical thrill that coursed through her body when she heard him coming upstairs to the bedroom or watched him undress?

The pony flicked her tail and began to turn her head away. Fran played for time by checking her car doors were locked and nothing valuable was in sight. Then she walked along the row of cottages towards Andy's front gate and the silver Volkswagen. It looked familiar, the registration number was familiar; she had been driven in this car last summer, to Judi's funeral. It belonged to Vicky.

She ducked back, out of sight. Probably no one had spotted her and she could flee now, drive straight home. But why would she do that? She could feel the rising adrenaline, the strange excitement of something wholly unexpected that might turn out to be terrible – and the absence of fear that made it possible to act.

There was an overgrown path between two of the cottages, leading to a small gate into the field behind the back gardens. She brushed her way through and kept close to the hedge as she crept along until she could peer into the garden and through the glass patio doors. Vicky was there, in the room, in Judi's lilac dressing gown, gesturing and talking to somebody, although Fran couldn't see Andy. She watched, a plan forming in her mind even as she reeled in disbelief. The side door was left unlocked in the daytime and she just had to wait until Vicky moved out of view, then run across and catch them by surprise. She was acting in a film now; part of her had detached from the reality of the scene she was witnessing, and all the more so as she was still under the influence of Junoco.

Vicky walked forward, out of the room, and Fran darted to gain the side door. Straightening up, she smoothed her hair and took three deep breaths before turning the handle and entering the kitchen. There was a smell of burnt toast and Andy was at the hob, spatula in hand, jiggling the frying pan to stop the eggs sticking. He turned towards the sound of the opening door, as if in slow motion, then screwed up his eyes and took several uncertain steps backwards, dropping the spatula to the floor.

'Hey, it's you, Frankie! Where did you come from?'

That was it. He turned and bolted out of the kitchen and through the front porch before Winnie could do more than stand up and wag her tail in expectation of a good walk. Vicky wandered through to the kitchen, perplexed. The dressing gown was too big for her and she had rolled up the sleeves.

'Hello, Vicky. Excuse me a moment.'

Fran turned off the gas beneath the shrivelling fried eggs. A slew of emotions skimmed over Vicky's face, too fast for Fran to take in. She was curious now, waiting for a reaction.

'Frankie, what are you doing, what the fuck? Why did you burst in like that?'

'I could ask you the same question, Vicky. And don't you dare call me Frankie, just don't dare. You've no right.' She had the advantage of surprise and was going to make the most of it; ensure Vicky didn't have the chance to disarm her and gain the upper hand.

'Okay, so I stayed here last night. It was the only time. It's not such a big deal, is it?'

'Not a big deal? You've only destroyed two beautiful friendships in one fell swoop.' Fran was amazed at the deadly calm and certainty in her own voice.

'Oh, come on now, girl, you can talk. We both know how you carry on.' Vicky attempted to muster her conspiratorial smile, but her voice was trembling. 'What about Ned – he's your lover as well, isn't he, your London one? And you insisted it wasn't what you wanted with Andy; you wanted out, it was just a holiday fling. You told me that, I'm not making it up.'

'It's irrelevant. Lots of different and contradictory things can be true, all at once. I thought you understood that, understood me and knew my feelings, how complicated they were. I thought you were a special kind of person, someone I could trust and believe in.'

This was straying into perilous emotional territory, giving Vicky a handle to manipulate her emotions again. Before Vicky could reply, Fran jabbed a finger towards her waist.

'Take it off. It's too big for you.'

Vicky undid the towelling belt and slipped the soft gown off her shoulders, letting it fall. She stood naked, her arms at her sides, waiting for the next move. Fran stepped forward and swept up the gown, then continued with it out the front door, closing it behind her. As she reached the gate, she stopped to look over the fields towards the coast. Andy would be halfway to the headland by now, and anyway she had no desire to see him; not today or ever again.

She gave the waiting pony one final stroke on the nose and decided to reverse down the lane, rather than driving forward and having to turn in front of the cottage. This demanded concentration and as she backed out carefully into the village high street, she was assessing her emotional fitness to drive. It was fine. She was in full control and just had to avoid speeding and pay attention to the task, in effect letting Junoco take her back safely before its influence wore off.

What she hadn't bargained for was the feathered missile that descended from the sky and landed splat in the centre of her windscreen, detaching the rear-view mirror from the glass and leaving a trail of blood and gore that obscured half the view in front as well. Luckily, there was no other traffic on the immediate stretch of road and she was able to pull into the side without any further jolt. This was a replay of that dream, not a Junoco dream but the one where the car had been hit by a bird or bat and she had died and been led to heaven by a friendly robot-like being flashing blue and white lights. Or was it a different dream, the one with Judi ignoring her and the terrifying line of nannies? There was a child in the car too, who in the dream had survived unhurt. Now it was Lily in the passenger seat, but only for an instant before the ghostly image vanished.

She needed fresh air. Her mind was playing tricks and she had to stay grounded and deal with the practicalities of the situation. Clambering out of the car and walking round the front to inspect the damage, she saw that that the crushed pile of feathers with stalk-like legs was a pigeon. That glistening black eye again; maybe it was the same one that dropped into her chimney, taking its suicidal revenge. The deranged idea made her smile at the absurdity and futility of everything. She would clear this mess up as best she could and stop at the next service station for a jet wash and a strong coffee.

***

Afterwards, she wished she had stayed in for the rest of the weekend and kept her feelings to herself, but she was too restless to be confined and anyway, she had failed to buy any food and there was nothing left in the house. She opened the fridge and surveyed the near-empty shelves. The cream cheese was going mouldy and the cheddar was as hard as a rock. She shut the fridge door, too forcefully.

'You know what, your days are numbered. I'm going to junk you and replace you with the latest, smartest fridge on the market, one that will tell me what's running out, what's out of date and what I can put together for a sensational dinner – or better still, one that can order and stock up by itself. It will be one better than Ned's fridge, a few notches up on that.'

She went into the living room and spoke to Guacamole.

'Hello, Mr Mole. Did you miss me? Are you ever going to start speaking to me? At least you would never betray me – or maybe you would, I don't know.'

Guacamole stared at her squinting face over his glasses. He looked crestfallen.

She picked up the shopping bags and left the house, but had barely reached the pavement when Lily bounced off her front wall and came running towards her.

'Fran, I've been waiting for you!' She was close to tears.

'I'm sorry, Lily, but I can't talk to you right now. I'm busy – later, perhaps.'

She started walking away quickly, but Lily persisted and ran along beside her.

'But I have to tell you, something terrible has happened. My mum found a cat on our path, dead.'

Fran's step faltered, but she didn't stop or look down at Lily. 'That's terrible, I'm sorry. It's just that it's none of my business; you've drawn me into this and I can't cope with it, on top of everything else. I need my own space, Lily, and you should be playing with your friends, not doing this stuff.'

'But you are my... I thought...'

Lily stopped running and pulled at the loose sleeve of Fran's shirt. Fran looked down at her with a mix of extreme irritation and guilt, causing Lily to release her grip, stand up straight and put her hands down by her sides before making a solemn and heartfelt pronouncement.

'This is the worst day of my life so far.'

Fran watched her walk off with a stiff little stride, proud and upright.

Her next encounter was with Kwesi, who was in the patisserie sitting at a table with the street girl, the one they had tried to help when she was out for the count that day. It was too late to turn and leave without being seen. He waved and beckoned her across.

'Fran, will you sit with us? This is Charley.'

Fran closed her eyes and looked pained. It was all too much. The girl gave her a hostile stare and stood up, pulling her oversize parka tightly around her.

'Okay, I know when I'm not wanted. Thanks for the trainers, they're ace. See you around.'

Kwesi opened his hands in a gesture of mild exasperation as Charley scowled once more at Fran and left, giving the glass door a careless shove as she went. Her worn-out pink canvas trainers lay under the table and an empty shoebox was on the chair. Kwesi shook his head and turned back to Fran.

'I want to tell you, Fran, I heard something.'

What was it with everyone? They had all heard or seen something or they wanted something from her; it was exhausting. She'd had enough.

What Kwesi had heard was a cat wailing through the adjoining wall, in Eric and Delia's upstairs back room, and another time what sounded like a cat fight. Normally, Fran would have treated this as a possible breakthrough in the investigation, but today it seemed trivial and irrelevant. She replied that she and Lily would 'take it on board' and perched on the corner of the chair for a minute or two longer, then made a mumbled excuse and left the café without buying the bread she had come in for. At least she had avoided being overtly rude or mean to Kwesi, even if her dark mood had been picked up by the savvy street girl.

As she approached her house, Petra was parking her car outside. She opened the window to talk. Couldn't she sense either that Fran needed to be left alone?

'Hi, Fran, I'm glad I caught you. Lily is very upset; did she tell you about the cat on the path? Now she's shut herself in her bedroom and she's refusing to talk to me. It is not like her.'

'I don't know anything about it, Petra. I have other issues at the moment.'

Petra was clearly confused by the sharp change of tone, but after a momentary hesitation she responded sympathetically. 'Yes, she's disturbing you, I understand. She is not an easy child, my daughter.'

'No, Petra – well, yes actually… I just need some space, I'm sorry.'

Petra nodded and left Fran on the pavement, cursing her crass insensitivity but incapable of giving any other response right now. And to make matters worse, she had a pair of ladies' leather gloves in her bag, fuchsia pink, which she had deftly slipped off a table and up her sleeve while she was leaving the café.

'Look at these ridiculous pink gloves, Guacamole; look what your idiot friend has gone and done. I'll have to ignore Daniela's instructions and have more Junoco truffles tonight. It's the only way to stay sane.'

Guacamole raised his paw, only slightly but there was no mistaking it this time. Whether it was a sign of agreement or disapproval was impossible to say.

Someone was knocking on the back door; it could only be Marcus. She waited until he had knocked three times before going through to the kitchen to let him in. Despite the evident risk of upsetting more people she cared about, the thought of being on her own throughout the rest of the afternoon and evening was now just too depressing. It could also lead to even more regrettable behaviour, either online or on the phone.

'Hi, I'm sorry to be a nuisance but Kirsty is loitering out front again, under the tree. Can I shelter with you, just for an hour or two? And we haven't seen each other for a while, so if you're not busy...'

She put the kettle on while he told her that Eric and Delia had stopped Kwesi in the street, in a neighbourly way of course, and asked how he was settling in and enjoying his studies.

'Fortunately, I had filled him in about being a medical student on a scholarship and it seems he did a decent job of expanding on it, telling them he was training to be a paediatrician. When they heard that, they got onto the subject of Lily and her 'abnormal and obsessive carrying-on', as they put it. Anyway, it seems like they were put off the scent.'

'Ah, that's why he was alerted by a cat wailing; they must have mentioned—'

'What's that about?'

'Oh, it's probably nothing. Just that they told me their beloved cat had died, and Kwesi said this afternoon he'd heard a cat fight through the wall of his bedroom. It could have been a telly programme or anything. To tell you the truth, I've had a peculiar couple of days, really up and down, and I didn't absorb what he was saying.'

'Oh, sorry, am I intruding? Do you want to talk about it?'

'No, it's fine, good to see you in fact. It's been like a bombardment, too much coming at me at once. I don't feel ready to talk about it rationally.'

She sounded a lot saner than she felt. She had kept it at bay while driving back, but since she got home she had experienced a series of visual flashes, graphic scenes of Andy and Vicky making passionate love on the beach, on top of the cliffs, in bed. It was physically painful; the proverbial kick in the stomach. And mentally even more so, although there was still that internal voice questioning why it mattered so much, why she didn't just shrug and let it go.

'I think I should leave.' Marcus was uncomfortable with the prolonged silence.

'No, please stay. I want you to. Let's see if Kirsty is still outside. I'll go into the room first and shut the blinds, so she doesn't see you.'

Kirsty was still there, and was moving out from under the tree. She came across the road and stood on the pavement, legs planted slightly apart. The large sports bag was at her side, an ominous sign that she might invite herself to stay the night again, and Fran saw she had hold of something in her hand.

'She's got a brick again, Marcus, a half-brick!'

She turned back to peer through the slit in the blinds that she was keeping open a little with two fingers. Kirsty started to shout.

'Come out, you coward, Marcus! Man up and talk to me, let me in. You know we're fated to be together. I love you, man, for God's sake.'

This was the familiar first volley, usually followed by much more belligerent fire.

'I know you're in there, I followed you. I'm going to follow you for the rest of your life, and if you don't get it, this brick here is coming straight through your window, smash! And you have to get rid of that fucking lodger, end of.'

Fran shifted her position slightly so she had a view of Eric and Delia, who were turning out of their path towards Kirsty, marching side by side. Eric spoke first.

'I've told you before, young woman, and I'm not going to tell you again. Put that brick down at once and go away, leave us alone. We don't want to know about your wretched love life and we won't have that kind of language in this street.'

He fingered his phone, ready to make a call, while Delia took over.

'Aren't you ashamed of yourself? He's finished with you; don't you understand that? In my day, we accepted these things and had to pull ourselves together, get on with it.'

Fran couldn't help feeling a grudging admiration for their willingness to confront a torrid and potentially violent situation. Or, more likely, they just thrived on conflict. Marcus was hiding behind her, showing no inclination to go out and join in, so she took her own decision.

'I'm going to talk to her, Marcus. Don't worry, I won't let on that you're here.'

She opened the front door and Kirsty fixed on her immediately.

'Look, it's the prima-fucking-donna, thinks she knows everything. Where is he then, you old slapper?'

Eric rode in again, with a vestige of old-fashioned chivalry. 'How dare you speak to the lady like that? Apologise at once.'

'You're not my fucking dad, you know. You're just a pair of old tossers.'

'Come on, Eric. We're not putting up with any more of this, it's disgraceful. Call the police and let's go home.'

The couple moved away while Eric keyed in the number and held his phone to his ear, both of them walking half-backwards so they could monitor Kirsty's movements. Fran tried to keep her voice soft and authentic.

'Kirsty, listen to me. You are just making things worse for yourself. It won't help. You can't win someone back like this, and sometimes not at all, believe me.'

'Believe you – why should I? You're old. What do you know about it?'

Her tone had changed, however, and Kirsty put the half-brick down on the wall. She looked about to burst into tears, and her final words were in a low mumble directed to no one in particular.

'I hate people. They don't fucking get it and they never will.'

Fran walked back into the house and Marcus came through to the hall, anxious as ever.

'It's okay now, Marcus. She's run off. If they're quick, the police will catch up with her. Are you happy to talk to them this time, if they turn up?'

'I'll think about it. Thank you for defusing the situation. I always manage to reignite her fury, but maybe that's just my excuse for keeping out of the way.'

The police didn't arrive, and Fran wondered if Eric had actually called them. She opened a bottle of wine and was soon telling Marcus what she had found out from Cerise and Eleanor about Marina. Then she showed him her sketches of Marina, which she hadn't unveiled to anyone before. Marcus was intrigued at her imagining of her sister and the poignancy of the drawings.

'They would make a beautiful series in an exhibition – not that you would want to exhibit them publicly, but you're extremely gifted, that's what I'm saying.'

'I don't know, maybe one day I might exhibit them.'

It was early evening now and getting dark. As usual, Marcus showed no sign of wanting to leave. As they pored over the drawings, Fran eyed his slim, muscled thighs in his tight black jeans and felt a definite stirring. Bad idea – it would be madness to dive down on the sofa with him right now, complete and utter madness. She was still thinking this when he turned towards her and gave her shoulder a firm but playful push, his inconceivably dark eyes lit up with desire.

Chapter 15

When she had arrived home on Sunday, resigning from everything had seemed the only self-respecting option. Daniela was in league with Professor Fred, although how or why was still unclear, and what Vicky had done was too painfully awful to think about. Vicky *and* Andy, Fran reminded herself, but the thrust of her anger was directed at Vicky, who had been destined to be her new best friend and clearly didn't have a clue what that signified or how much of a privilege it would have been to sit alongside Judi in Fran's affections. And at a more primitive level, the pangs of jealousy and the flash visions of their lovemaking were gut-wrenching. The impromptu Sunday sex on the sofa with Marcus had stemmed her feelings temporarily, she had to admit, but that had created another difficult issue with its own potential fallout.

Here she was, trying to work out whether to stay with Junoco and her job at the shop and allowing herself to be taken over by such negative emotions. Surely as a seasoned Junoco consumer, not to mention a mature woman who should have known better in the first place, she should override this tosh and focus instead on enjoying the memories of the wild times that she and Andy had enjoyed and, more importantly, on their shared love for Judi?

Luckily, Monday was her day off so she could put her hundred favourite songs on shuffle, turn the music up to full volume and throw herself into a flurry of housework. It wasn't a calculated decision, but it fell in with what she now knew about the workings of the brain: that carrying out routine tasks while allowing the mind to meander was an effective way to promote insight and come up with useful ideas.

By lunchtime, when the shelves, tables and mirrors were gleaming and the carpets thoroughly hoovered, she had reached the conclusion that resigning would be defeatist and unjust to herself. It was what Vicky wanted her to do, she had said as much, so why give in and let her have the satisfaction? She would face up to her instead, act calm and dignified in any further exchange about her treachery and, if it came to the crunch, put Vicky in a position where it was she, not Fran, who was compelled to walk away from Junoco.

On top of that, now was the wrong time to leave, when she felt on the brink of discovering the truth about what was going on. No, she would turn up at the shop as normal and play it by ear when Vicky came in for her usual Wednesday afternoon shift.

This train of thought led her to revise her first plan for handling the aftershock of her fling with Marcus. They were still high on it when he had left by the back door and she pushed his bum and dangling legs up over the fence. However, she fully expected him to be cringing with embarrassment by the morning and she had resolved to avoid him for a few days, to let it settle. Now she realised the best action was to talk to him and acknowledge their frivolous bit of fun.

This was how she happened to open the front door just as he arrived home from work. She was right, he was highly embarrassed, but as he began his apology, she waved it away and whispered to him across the low dividing wall.

'It was lovely, Marcus, thank you. It was just a sweet moment and we were free to do it. I don't want it to change anything in our friendship.'

'I'm sorry, I thought you might—'

'No, Marcus, that's not me at all. I think it was me who started it anyway, but there's no need to have an argument about that. The important thing is not to let it prevent us from remaining friends – and not to give any hint to Kirsty or she'll have my guts. She thinks I'm way past it anyway.'

'Please don't remind me – it's excruciating. I'm trying to avoid Eric and Delia but I'm bound to bump into them soon; they'll make sure of it so they can put in their latest complaint about Kirsty. It's a relief, anyway, knowing I don't have to avoid both my neighbours!'

'No, you certainly don't, and I hope you and Kwesi will keep coming round for our music sessions. I listened to all my favourite tracks today and I'd love to have a request session and be the lead singer.'

It seemed to have done the trick, got them over the hump. Fran chuckled at her unwitting thought-pun as she closed the door. There was still the Lily hump to smooth over, but that shouldn't be too difficult.

**

The next day, she began to sort through the new spring collection in between attending to customers. Neither

Vicky nor Daniela showed up. After closing the shop, she popped into the café to buy two of her favourite little cakes, now her regular habit on a Tuesday. The waitress called to Jean-Claude as she boxed up the cakes and he came out from the kitchen, wiping his floury hands down his long apron.

'*Bonjour*, Fran. How are you? I have a message for you. A man came in and asked when you were coming to the café next time. I said I don't know and he wrote you this message.'

'A man, that's mysterious. What did he look like, Jean-Claude?' She was fiddling with the white envelope he had handed to her, but she didn't want to open it until she was out on the pavement. The possibilities flashed through her mind. She had met various people here and introduced several to the café. Then there was Professor Fred, he had spied her near here; and the man from the dance class that Daniela had warned them about...

'He was Indian, maybe – a young man.'

'Did he ask for me by name?'

'Yes, he said your name, Fran, and he said you worked in the boutique.'

'All right, thank you so much, Jean-Claude. See you soon.'

She picked up the paper bag holding her box of cakes and left. It had to be the journalist, the one Daniela had described last week when she threatened them with dire consequences if they double-crossed her. She had said he was poking around, and something else about him suggesting the police were shadowing them, Fran couldn't remember exactly.

The note was typewritten in red:

Fran, you don't know me but I would like to talk to
you. I have information that you may be interested
in and could be important to you. Please keep this
communication confidential until we have spoken.
Meet me at 7.30pm tonight at the Green Duck pub
or, if you can't be there, please call...

Then there was a phone number, but no name or signature.

She walked home by the pond route, feeling bemused. How did he know she would come into the café today – had he been tracking her? Why did he bother to contact her, a very small cog in the Junoco wheel? And what could be important to her, in particular? What would he expect in return? It was unnerving, but at the same time, she couldn't resist it. She had to know what it was about, at the least.

***

She dressed casually in jeans and a long sweater and arrived at the Green Duck at seven, so she could choose her position and watch him coming in. In fact, he was already there, sitting at a corner table some distance from the bar, and he stood up to announce his presence with a subtle wave. It felt a little like a first date, but with less of the eagerness to make a scintillating initial impression. They shook hands and he introduced himself as Ravi, thanking her for coming and adding that he had ordered some snacks.

As they settled down, she half-expected him to lean forward and glance to both sides, in true spy style. Instead of which, he assumed an upright pose with both hands folded over the edge of the table, his elegant fingers flat on the surface so that she could see he wore a wedding ring and a signet ring on the opposite little finger. She fought the impulse to fiddle with her wine glass and kept her gaze on his face, as she had planned. It was up to him to open the conversation and she wasn't going to make any attempt at small talk.

They stayed silent for what seemed like an age, while Ravi scanned her once, helped himself from the bowls of snacks and contemplated her again, nodding his head with what seemed like confirmation or approval. If this was a deliberate tactic to unsettle her, it wasn't going to succeed. She had come here freely and she could leave at any time, as she had abruptly done on more than one misfiring first date.

Finally, he was ready. 'So, let's start. You were curious enough to come tonight, which I fully expected. That's a compliment, as I'm sure you'll appreciate. I'm a freelance reporter and I am researching a story about mind-altering drugs, and specifically drugs that claim to increase intelligence. It's for a review article initially but it could turn into a book, if there's enough material. I don't have an angle as yet. I'm looking into who is involved, the suppliers and customers, the size and operation of the market, and the effects of course, individual experiences. Your Junoco website is in the lead in terms of feedback from users.'

She mustn't let down her guard. He might genuinely be a journalist, but even if he was, and perhaps especially if he was, she had to tread carefully and only reveal publicly available information.

'It's not my website; you have to understand that, Ravi. I work on the promotion and social media side. It's our director you need to talk to and I'm not at liberty to say who that is. And as for the effects, the Junoco chocolate contains a wholly natural element that enhances the imagination, uniquely we believe.'

'I know – I've seen that on your website. What I haven't seen or read about is the other kind of drug, the manufactured one. I know how this is being done and who is behind it.'

His fingers had loosened and were drumming almost soundlessly on the table. Fran did her best to look inscrutable, knowing that a true poker face was next to impossible for her. He had her attention now and she couldn't walk off.

'So, your director Daniela is in league with a supposed business adversary, a rival operating in the same market. In fact, they were adversaries to begin with but it suited both of them to come to an accommodation and work in a complementary way. Effectively, he has access to her natural secret ingredient in return for Junoco's use of his synthetic drug, which is more refined than the one Daniela was purchasing previously. It's a mutually advantageous arrangement that improves their products and offers more cover and flexibility if things go wrong. There's still some mistrust, but they are close associates.'

An avalanche of questions cascaded through Fran's mind as she tried and dismally failed to show no hint of surprise. She had to ask for more, although it seemed as if she were caving in to an unwanted seduction. It was crucial to choose her words with care and not to reveal anything Ravi hadn't yet discovered.

'How do you know all this? Who is it, then, this associate character, Mr Big?'

'Within your inner circle, I believe you refer to him as Infrared. However, Infrared is only a bogeyman and you should be informed of his real identity. You won't like me for this, but I want to show you some photos.'

He pulled a tablet computer out of the bag lying beside him, set it up and turned it round so that the screen faced Fran. The photo was close-up and clear, showing Daniela, Vicky and Fred Henson-Morris at an outdoor café table, engrossed in conversation. Ravi watched her expression.

'There are another four pictures – here, look at them.'

Fran swiped her finger across the screen, sitting back to distance herself from the evidence in front of her. The first two photographs were of the three of them at the outdoor café and the other two, clearly taken at a different time as they wore different clothes, showed Daniela and Fred together in a park, smiling and chatting on a bench in relaxed fashion. Fran pushed the tablet away from her and turned it round so that it faced her companion once more.

'I don't get this – I don't get it at all. It doesn't make any sense.'

'I know – and I'm sorry.' For the first time, he seemed a bit sympathetic. 'They're misleading you, Daniela and Vicky. This man here, he's the famous Infrared.'

He turned the tablet again and touched the screen to point at Professor Fred. Fran winced with revulsion. As before, Ravi was observing her reactions closely.

'You're upset, Fran, naturally, but you mustn't forget, you are going behind their backs too, making your own private contacts at the university and in the government, and investigating the constituents of the chocolate.'

So Marcus *had* been warned off at work and told not to ask any more questions about the Bright Minds research, as she suspected. Or else he had picked up on a certain atmosphere around it and made his own decision to shut up. And she hadn't heard back from Alice, her other 'contact', who had wanted to arrange an analysis of the vitamins, nutrients and brain supplements to be used in the new research, Fred's ground-breaking study. Fran felt a cold shiver and pulled her jacket tightly around her. It was awful to believe what this stranger was saying, about Vicky especially, but clearly she now had a track record when it came to betrayal. Ravi had offered plausible motives for Daniela and Fred, but what did Vicky get out of it?

'Why are you telling me this, Ravi? You don't know me from Eve and have no reason to trust me. What do you want?'

'I'm a journalist and we feed on useful and interesting information, it's our lifeblood. I'd like you to give me some inside intelligence about Junoco over the next few weeks or months. Granted, I am taking a risk with you but you're perfect for the part and something tells me you'd relish it as well. Also, you would be involved with my venture after that, helping me write the book, if you fancy it. I'm offering to pay you an advance fee and something for the information too. We can negotiate the details later.'

On the surface, this was presented as a straight business offer, fees and all, but implicitly he was threatening to expose her involvement in Junoco if she didn't go along with it. At least she had come some way since getting tied up in all this and gained a more sophisticated understanding of the scheming and manipulation.

They left the pub soon afterwards and parted with another handshake. He gave her a small white card with *Ravi* and a mobile number printed across it; no indication of his occupation or location. It was important to stay cool and businesslike, make him wait for an answer.

'Thank you, Ravi. I'll let you know by the end of the week. I need time to think about it. You can trust me not to say anything to anyone, whatever I decide.'

It was satisfying to tell such a blatant lie, in response to the mounting layers of deception piling up around her.

As she walked home and sat up late with Guacamole, she tried to fit the pieces together and identify what was missing. If Daniela and Infrared were working together, then who had carried out the latest vandalism, the break-in and the hacking? Had it perhaps been staged or not happened at all? And if Professor Fred doubled as Infrared and his covert enterprise was friendly to Junoco, did it mean that Junoco was also linked to his university research project and the Bright Minds programme? And was it credible that Ravi, an investigative reporter, hadn't yet tumbled to the fact that Fred Henson-Morris and Infrared were one and the same – or was he keeping it from her for a reason?

She went to Guacamole and carried him to the sofa to whisper into his non-existent ear.

'They're on to us, Guacamole. They need a mole, or they want to unmask one, I can't decide which. There could be a bug-bot in this room, listening to us right now – maybe one of those cute little insect ones with cameras that can perch anywhere and fly around, get into every corner.'

She looked over to her computer sitting on the dining table and remembered the time she had invited Vicky over to fix her software glitches, when Lily and Sahara were here so she let Vicky get on with it. The hidden bug could be wirelessly connected to the computer right now. She scanned the room in the semi-darkness, particularly the picture rail and curtain rail. If there was a bug, it would be too small to see in this light and too well concealed. She went to the table to lift the lid of the computer and sat staring at the blank screen. It would be a silly distraction to start it up and at this time of night, in her current frame of mind, it would lead her inexorably to the dating sites.

She could try a Skype call to Max – it was still late afternoon in the US – and have a chat with him to calm her down. No, impossible; he would sense her mood, which had nosedived beyond the familiar evening dip into a frightening place where she felt trapped and alone.

She had to warn Alice urgently about Fred's dual identity and Ravi's claim about the use of manufactured drugs. Could she trust her, though – was Alice also capable of double-crossing a friend? And was it possible that Ned was in on it? Surely he wouldn't hang Fran out to dry, make her look an idiot? Even if he wasn't in cahoots with Daniela and the others, Fran was even more convinced now that he was holding something back, something that explained why he had stayed so cool and unruffled in the face of the attacks on Junoco and on his own property.

She walked over to the glass-fronted cabinet where she kept bottles of spirits and her stash of chocolate. There was a large bar, eighty-five per cent cocoa with pieces of ginger, luxuriously intense. It was very tempting, but she passed over it, going to the chest of drawers and taking out the Junoco truffles. Why wait for her mood to lift hours later, as it usually did between five and seven in the morning, when she could shift it quickly with these mighty little asteroids, and perhaps also find the insight to work out what was now destroyed and what, if anything, she could still have faith in?

It was past dawn when she awoke to a Junoco dream, or trance, as she now sometimes thought of them. She had fallen asleep on the sofa with Guacamole squashed beside her, his wire spectacles now decidedly bent. In the dream, she was among a group of children, all playing with kites in a field of long, spiky grass. Except that they weren't kites, they were miniature drones, insect toys, and the children controlled them remotely, making them rise and dive and make complicated formations. Among the group were Judi and her brother Jeremy, Fran and Marina, Lily and Ferdi – siblings and friends together, adventurous, free and gloriously unafraid.

When the scene finally faded, she got up and left a voicemail for Daniela to say she was unwell and couldn't come into work today. Then she sent text messages to Alice and Ned. She had a responsibility to warn them, to maintain her own integrity at least. If her instincts about them were wrong and they were also duping her, then so be it.

***

That evening she was in Ned's bed, sitting up against the silky pillows. He had departed from their usual ritual by bringing a bottle of bubbly into the bedroom before they put on their twin crimson robes for dinner. As he walked in, fully naked, with the tray, Fran began to hum a tune. Thank God for Junoco and its power to make her think better of the world. Ned came round the bed and planted a light kiss on her head.

'Francesca, my girl, that's not *The Stripper*, it's *The Pink Panther*!'

'I know it is. I've muddled them up this evening; I can't think why.'

'I shall ignore that insinuation, which isn't worthy of you.'

'Oh, you know you're wonderfully sexy, Ned, but—'

'I shall ignore everything before the "but" – that's a golden rule an old girlfriend taught me when I was trying to dump her as tactfully as possible.'

He poured the champagne, put on his robe, smoothed the striped duvet and pulled up the pillows before sitting beside her on the bed. 'Okay, you go first. Your piece of news sounds more serious, judging from the hints you've already dropped.'

Having turned down his last dinner invitation, she hadn't passed on Vicky's revelation that Daniela was meeting up with Professor Fred, so she dealt with that first. Then she told him about the mysterious message in the café and her encounter with Ravi in the pub – was it really only last night?

She had turned to study Ned's reaction, but his face was largely hidden by the pillow. He wiggled and stretched his toes, then bent both feet towards him, pushing his heels out and lifting them into the air.

'So they're all up to something, Ned, and Vicky has blatantly lied to me. She led me to think it was just Fred and Daniela in a conspiracy and that Daniela was playing a fast game, as she put it. Now I've seen the photos and it's all three of them meeting up. I still don't know why she's pushing me to leave Junoco, but I feel I'm getting closer to the answer.'

She would never confide in him about Vicky's more heinous betrayal with Andy, as it would violate the tacit understanding between them. He knew that a close friend of hers had died soon after they met, that was all. He didn't know Judi's name or anything about Andy, or how and why it all mattered, or what a strong legacy it had left, although in a convoluted way he was part of it.

'And Ravi, the journalist, he knows I've been talking to Alice and Marcus and trying to fit all the pieces together. I don't know who to trust any more, or even if I can trust you.'

Ned stopped exercising his feet and toes and took her hand between his. 'I have been keeping something from you, Fran, I admit it, but it's only because I don't want to put you in a dangerous position. I've been hinting all along that I'd like to go into business with you, and that's all I can say about it yet. If you agree to my immediate plan, then all will become clear, I promise.'

'Okay,' she said with deliberate wariness, noting how he had neatly avoided a response to her dramatic revelations. 'What's the immediate plan?'

'The plan is to go away; go on holiday to a mystery

destination. I've checked the flights and just need your passport number. We can get a flight on Friday and fly back overnight next Thursday. I think it's high time for some tropical sunshine and romantic evenings under the stars, don't you?'

Chapter 16

It was vital to see Alice before she went away. At first, she sounded hesitant on the phone, but when Fran suggested they take a boat cruise upriver to Kew, she accepted and they arranged it for Thursday afternoon.

It was a bright day and the late-February sun lent a touch of warmth as Fran waited on Embankment Pier. She scanned the riverbank and Waterloo Bridge for Alice or anyone who might be following her, who might have one or both of them under surveillance. There was Alice now, in a red beret and scarf this time, stepping onto the wooden walkway.

They were joined by a group of Chinese tourists, an elderly man, a couple with a baby and two backpacks, and three middle-aged couples, who appeared to be acquainted but chose to sit in different areas of the boat. None of them looked in the least suspicious.

As the engine leapt into life and they began to chug away from the bank, Fran sensed that Alice was as jumpy as herself. She had to alert her to the latest developments while offering some degree of reassurance. It was she who had got Alice into this quagmire by asking her to test the Junoco truffles and leading her to investigate the substances they intended to use in the Bright Minds project.

'How have you been, Alice? I was concerned when I didn't hear back from you after we met that time in Hyde Park. It was freezing cold, I remember, and I was so buzzing with ideas that I managed to trip myself up and fall flat crossing the traffic lights – no, don't worry, no serious injury, but it was mortifying.'

'It sounds horrendous.' Alice paused. 'I'm sorry I didn't get in touch, but it's all become more delicate and dicey. I haven't managed to obtain any new info on the brain supplements and nutrients, and I don't know where the laboratory is. It's definitely not part of the university. I don't have the evidence to back this up, but my strong feeling is that at least one element in the Bright Minds formula is novel and untested, which means they'll do everything they can to hide it. I even went so far as to rummage in Fred's office when he was overseas last week, but these days you don't find anything significant in piles of paper and unlocked cabinets.'

Should she speak up now, tell Alice about the incriminating photos and the possibility that the formulas for Junoco and Bright Minds could be identical or very similar? No, she decided to let her finish.

'And there's another reason for not contacting you before, Fran. I'm not having a good time at work generally. I've been told that the university isn't going to support a major study that I've been working on for the past twelve months, in fact leading on the proposal. It's not unusual for this to happen but my hunch is that it's connected, that I've been asking too many questions and I'm getting a warning not to step out of line.'

Fran half-snorted and couldn't resist a sardonic reply. 'That's rich, isn't it – you're penalised for asking too many questions, being too curious about a programme that aims to boost curiosity and creativity!'

Alice turned towards her, her expression anxious rather than amused. 'Yes, but is it a correct presumption, about the programme's aims? It says it in the project documents but can we be sure of its benign intentions? We know governments are capable of unethical activities and sophisticated ploys to disguise their real motives. And ambitious scientists will fall in with it and come up with their own justifications for taking part.'

Fran thought about what Petra had told her about the three sample groups in the schools research – the top five per cent on academic achievement, the bottom five per cent and the kids with attention and hyperactivity disorders. Were the groups equally important or was it actually about one of the groups, perhaps, with the rest receiving a placebo – and if so, which group would they go for and why?

'Do you have your own theory, then, Alice, about the aims of the schools trial?'

'No, I don't, and I can't afford to speculate on it right now. I have to ensure that I don't get dislodged, forced out of the research team. It shouldn't be difficult as they need my skills, but no one is indispensable and the political drivers may be more important than the scientific or academic ones. Anyway, I'm determined to hang in there long enough to suss out if there's anything nefarious going on. It is intriguing, up to a point, but I'm a sensible girl on the whole and I don't want to lose my job or be whacked over the head in a back alley.'

There it was, the quality Fran loved in all her close friends: the readiness to take a humorous turn and lighten the mood. Did she have a sixth sense for it when she first met them? Or, more prosaically, was it just something that happened when you reached a certain stage in life and were lucky enough, and perhaps wise enough, not to take everything too seriously?

'I've got news for you too, Alice, some information I found out this week from a new contact who claims to be a journalist. He showed me a set of photographs that definitively link your Professor Fred to my boss Daniela and my ex-friend Vicky. The evidence suggests they are collaborating – or colluding, whatever you want to call it. Daniela has got Junoco and Fred has an online enterprise selling cognitive-enhancing drugs, according to my informant—'

'What, Professor Fred, selling drugs on the internet? Jesus, that's not right, it can't be. Are you joking?'

The couple sitting in the bow of the boat turned round at Alice's loud exclamation. Fran looked around and moved closer to Alice, so she could speak almost under her breath.

'No, I'm not joking. He even has a code name, Infrared, but let me finish, there's more. My informant claims they're meeting up because they've done a deal, some kind of exchange between the Junoco berry seeds and the synthetic drug that Fred uses in his cognitive products. It suggests that the government's research on schoolchildren could involve a variant of Junoco, the magic seeds blended with an unregulated new drug. It's a strong theory, at least, not yet proven.'

'Wow, that's dynamite, if it's true – sheer bloody dynamite!'

They continued their whispered conversation until the boat drew up alongside Kew Pier, where they disembarked and walked over the bridge to a riverside pub. As they went in and found window seats overlooking the towpath, Alice was still shaking her head.

'I'm gobsmacked and yet, at the same time… It's you, Fran, bringing out my subversive streak. I shouldn't find it remotely exciting, but at one level, I do!'

'Yep, hands up, I have lured you in, but you were involved anyway and it's probably better to know than not, that's my reasoning. Look, Alice, this isn't great timing but I'm going away on Friday for a week, so we'll have to stay in touch by text, if anything urgent comes up. I can call you back if there's a decent phone signal.'

'Okay, hopefully nothing drastic will happen in that time and I'll only call you if I have to. I'll keep my head down, or look as if I am, anyway. Are you going anywhere nice?'

'I imagine so, but actually I don't know where. It's a surprise trip sprung on me by a friend, a man I've been seeing since I came to London.'

'Ooh, one of the last true romantics, is he?'

Fran tipped her head sideways with a mischievous smile as Alice glanced at her.

'Not exactly – possibly a new variety… but you'll have to wait till I get back.'

***

Their eco-lodge hotel on the edge of the rainforest was only accessible by boat or small plane. The tiny airstrip was the other side of a wide waterway, and beyond the airstrip was a long sandy beach with its fringe of upright, leaning and near-horizontal coconut palms. Their room was more stunning than any Fran had ever stayed in before, with its curved walls, undulating ceiling, vibrant primary colours, beautiful stained-glass windows, and artwork in the form of abstract paintings and wooden or metal sculptures. They had their own private terrace with a small plunge pool and a low pink wall separating it from the main garden, its tall trees hung with drooping birds' nests, and the dark wall of foliage marking the edge of the forest.

On the first morning, they were woken by the howler monkeys but managed to sleep again in the lull that followed the noisy dawn chorus. It was nearly ten when they arrived at the wood-framed open-air restaurant for breakfast.

'This pineapple is so delicious, so much juicier than the ones at home. I'm going to live on pineapple smoothies and these scrummy pastries while I'm here.'

'Hang on a bit. You haven't tried lunch and dinner yet – or the cocktails.'

'This is wonderful, Ned. What a fabulous place. What shall we do today – just explore round and about, go across to the beach and maybe venture into the forest to see what wildlife we find along the trail?'

'That sounds about right for day one, as well as an afternoon siesta, naturally. We can also book one or two tours for later on. I thought maybe the boat trip and a visit to the local history museum, which has indigenous art and a collection of gold pieces dating back to pre-Columbus… and we have to do the chocolate tour, don't you think?'

Her eyes lit up and she replied, through a mouthful of fruit and cream, 'Chocolate tour – it's one hundred per cent unmissable.'

'It will be too, one hundred per cent cocoa, and they show you how it's traditionally made. We'll book it for a couple of days' time, if that suits. Tomorrow morning, I've got something else planned, something just as fascinating.'

Fran narrowed her gaze, immediately alerted to the change in his voice and, she realised now, primed for the possibility that there might be more to this spontaneous holiday than he had so far revealed.

'What's that then, Ned? I know you well enough to be deeply suspicious when you get all cryptic.' She was racking her brain, trying to reimagine what was happening and make a new set of connections. The solution felt close, tantalisingly out of reach.

'It's a little mystery. Let's have a great day today and I'll tell you this evening – how about that?'

'It's rubbish. It's not going to work on me and you know it. Come on, Ned, you have to tell me now, it's too late to keep it secret.'

'Okay then, I'll come clean. I did want to come on holiday with you, I'm so happy to be here with you, but...'

Fran giggled despite herself. 'If this weren't such a truly enchanting place to end up, I'd be inclined to ignore everything before the "but".'

'Well, I'm hoping it might even add to the enchantment, you never know. The truth is that I've set up a meeting with Osvaldo, Daniela's cousin. He comes to Central America regularly and he's flying up here tomorrow with one of the scientific boffins, Rick, he's an American. I don't want you

287

to be mad at me, Fran, so please hear me out. It's because we'd make great business partners, I've always said that.'

Fran set down her spoon, put one elbow on the table and scratched her head, messing up her hair so it stuck out at all angles. Then she brought both curled fists to her cheeks and fixed him with a stare, which he unblinkingly returned. After a minute of this, she turned and nodded to the hovering waiter, who refilled their coffee cups and brought fresh glasses of orange juice and another plate of pastries that they couldn't possibly eat. Eventually, she smiled at Ned and spoke in a flat, mock-resigned tone.

'Okay, we're here now, let's talk. We can take the hotel boat to the other side and wander along the beach.'

It was impossible to be angry, especially here and especially as she believed he was sincere in all the positive guff about enjoying her company and admiring her supposed brilliance. Also, the prospect of meeting the enigmatic Osvaldo, although clearly risky, was undeniably exciting. And the other guy, Rick, was the academic she was regularly communicating with over the customer feedback on the site and the diary entries that many users were sending in by email.

As they walked, picking up stray coconuts and watching the antics of small red crabs along the way, Ned outlined his idea, the idea that had been on his mind since the start: that they could set up a rival business to Junoco with a different clientele, more 'luxury end' as he put it. The aim of meeting with Osvaldo was to explore and hopefully begin to negotiate a deal on the production and supply of the new chocolate, which would have its own form, look and brand name. Fran listened and asked questions, many of which were unanswerable at this stage. After an hour of talking, they clambered into a pair of hammocks strung at the back of the beach, lay back in the welcome shade of the swaying palms and agreed not to say any more about it until breakfast the following day, before Osvaldo and Rick arrived at eleven.

***

They sat beside the swimming pool and watched the distant speck in the sky turn into a recognisable tiny aeroplane coming in to land across the water. What was Osvaldo going to look like: one of the tough loggers in Fran's daydream during Daniela's chocolate briefing; an urbane businessman; a shady character; or someone else entirely, defying any stereotype? When the plane passengers stepped off the ferry boat, she identified him easily as the burly, bearded man in a creased, light blue suit. Standing beside him on the wooden quay, next to a gigantic, motionless iguana that seemed quite unfazed, was a slim, younger man in a red-checked shirt and dark jeans. Fran and Ned walked forward to greet their guests.

They stayed beside the pool to talk, as there were few people about. Osvaldo's command of English wasn't much better than their Spanish, but Rick was able to act as interpreter. It was unclear how Ned was going to deal with the sensitive issue of their double-crossing Daniela, but Fran soon understood that this part of the conversation had already taken place. Osvaldo knew of their relationship to his cousin and was willing to talk openly about her activities, although he possibly didn't realise that he and his companion were imparting new and startling information. Rick confirmed that Fred Henson-Morris was one of their business partners and was known to them as Infrared. He also said they had cleared a new area of rainforest to grow more fruit bushes under cover of the logging work. This was to meet the anticipated demand for the berry seeds arising from Infrared's private business and a planned research trial in British schools.

Fran was dying to ask about Vicky, her role in it, but when she managed to get the question in, both of them looked blank and claimed they hadn't heard of her. This wasn't altogether surprising, given Daniela's insistence on minimal contact between the different parts of her business. However, it provoked a diverting train of thought. Why hadn't Vicky attempted to make contact with Fran, if only to say sorry? Had the shock of the breakfast confrontation in his kitchen frightened Andy off the affair, or were the pair of them still bonking like there was no tomorrow? Seeking visual distraction, she spotted a gecko on the side of the wall behind Osvaldo, then several more, well camouflaged against the sun-drenched stone but alert and poised to vanish into a crevice at any sign of danger.

Tuning back into the conversation, she picked up on Osvaldo's references to his 'number-one contact' in the British government, the senior civil servant who had commissioned the Bright Minds research. Despite this person's obvious high position, Osvaldo claimed she was still in the dark about the addition of the synthetic drug. This was the confirmation that Fran was looking for, and from a rock-solid source. The government's schools research project, like Junoco, involved the use of a synthetic drug mixed with the berry seeds. Alice would be knocked sideways when she gave her the news.

She didn't take out her notebook but memorised the name of the civil servant. She was playing catch-up and Ned should have given her a much more thorough briefing, at the least, if he wanted to enlist her as a business partner. She would make this point forcefully, but for now she needed to concentrate on what was being said.

Osvaldo was proposing to manufacture their chocolate product in South America, importing the synthetic substance from one of the laboratories he used in Vietnam or Cambodia. This would involve smuggling the final merchandise into the UK along with legitimate produce. In Osvaldo's view, importing the drug and seeds separately and producing the chocolate in the UK was too risky, especially now that Daniela's business had been targeted for sabotage. Ned responded by saying he was undecided and that he and Fran would have to consider it.

Osvaldo inspected her once more, trying to size her up and no doubt thinking she was an unlikely associate for this kind of scheme. Rick smiled but she couldn't see his eyes either, as despite the big sun umbrella they had all kept their shades on against the midday glare. Two of the geckos had disappeared from the side of the wall but another bright green lizard was on top now, posing for a life drawing, one of her Junoco sketches. The waiter came across carrying lunch menus, a tray of tall glasses with ice and lemon and two complimentary bottles of water, fizzy and still.

After they had put in their order, Fran was able to turn the conversation to the aspects of the enterprise that most interested her: the cognitive effects of Junoco and how safe it actually was; if it was dangerous to health. She addressed her question to Rick.

'You've been analysing the data from the Junoco site and maybe other sources. What's your view of the evidence to date?'

'Yes, Junoco and a couple of other operations in the US that use the same basic compound, but with different products and different presentation. All in all, it looks highly favourable. The customers have reported various effects but with significant common features, such as the development of talents and aptitudes that comes over strongly in your Junoco diaries. Also, users are aware of a deepening curiosity, in terms of wanting to gain knowledge, pursue ideas and understand other people better. We're not sure of the extent to which these mind-shifts lead to the acquisition of skills and more creative approaches as the work is still in its early stages, but some users believe it does and have given some interesting examples.'

'Are you saying the effects go beyond the twenty-four hours that it's noticeably active in the system?'

'Yes, there may be a cumulative effect and actual changes in the neural networks, the way in which the neurons connect and interact. This happens when someone develops a new skill; learns to play an instrument or speak a new language, for example. It's still far from being confirmed but Junoco may turn out to have a long-term physical effect on the brain.'

'Thanks, that's all great – but what about the negatives, the side effects?'

'Well, the first thing is that you need to take both doses – eat both chocolates in the case of Junoco. We've had few reports of bad side effects and we think most of them are due to taking the first dose alone or leaving too much time between the doses. This can result in hallucinations and a frightening dislocation of reality. It's the second dose that provides the focus, as you know, so you have a freer imagination that is tamed enough to actually be put to use. The second negative effect, also rare to date, is a tendency to become obsessive and unduly perfectionist, for example in pursuing an activity or skill. Speculatively, we are wondering if this is due to having too much of the second dose, although it may be linked to existing character traits.'

This was riveting, but Fran was aware that Osvaldo was getting fidgety and overtly consulting his watch. She had to wrap it up for now.

'I could go on all afternoon, but you need to catch your plane. I have just one final question, Rick. Have there been any reports of extraordinary communication with animals, or even inanimate objects? I suppose this would be a minor form of hallucination due to the berry seeds, do you think? Is it too far-fetched to think that Junoco can take us to another level, where we not only make new connections within the brain, but also in the world, with other animals?'

'Jeez, that would be kind of momentous and I don't know, is the short answer. We have had a number of people reporting higher-level kinds of communication with animals and we've tended to put them in the box marked hallucinatory effects. You're suggesting a hypothesis that seems unlikely, but who knows? It may prove to be right. Also, the birds that we went to study in the first place are acquiring more sophisticated skills in nest-building and hunting for food, including the novel use of sticks and wires as tools. Birds may have physically tiny brains but they have a phenomenal number of neurons packed in there, more than many primates, and eating the berry seeds is adding to their cognitive power, no question.'

'It's a compliment, then, isn't it, calling someone a birdbrain?'

'You bet – and there's much more to come. We don't know the half of it.'

'And on that fascinating note,' said Ned, 'we'll have to end it. I'll find the boatman to take you back over the water.'

***

They hadn't brought any Junoco with them on holiday, partly because of the risk of being searched at customs, but also because they wanted to enjoy the sunshine and local cuisine in a direct and unfiltered way. In line with the plan, they spent a good part of the afternoons in bed, or rather on top of the bed as it was too hot for sex under the covers, even with the fast-circling fan directly above them. Ned had turned a pre-brown pink and Fran could see he tanned easily, like herself. He was super gorgeous and defenceless, spread out on his back across the crumpled whiteness of the bedclothes, eyes closed and with a light top sheet partly covering his feet and calves. It was an odd thing, perhaps, but it was this luscious afterglow with

Ned that she wouldn't forget, while with Andy it was the intensity of anticipation.

Ned stirred and turned on his side, unfurling his legs from the loose sheet and crooking his knees to bring his feet together. He propped himself up on his elbow and ran his fingers lightly over her stomach.

'You know the theft at my warehouse, the Junoco distribution centre?'

She shifted to mirror his position, propped up on her side. 'Yes – do you know who did it, why they did it? Was it Infrared, or do you share Daniela's suspicion about a police operation?'

'It was me; it was a set-up. I arranged it to give Daniela a scare and see how she would respond, see if we'd get more of the low-down when she was cornered and needed to rally morale. I didn't expect her to react as aggressively as she did, but then it coincided with the hacking of the website. Also, I wanted to give out some of the truffles informally among my circle of contacts, without you all knowing about it, so I decided to nick them. But back to Daniela – I don't feel I've got the measure of her yet. Osvaldo says she's a distant cousin and that he grew up not knowing her, as she was living in England. He doesn't seem bothered about being disloyal, doing a deal with us behind her back.'

'Well, Ned, I must say I half-expected it was down to you, all along. I would have been angry if you'd told me at the time, but now we know she and Vicky are both hand in glove with Professor Fred, although I'm not sure we'll ever get to the bottom of it. She's mystifying; it's her persona, brand Daniela. Vicky, now, that's different altogether. I stupidly imagined I was getting close to her, as a genuine friend.'

'Yep, it's all deeply murky, what they're up to. But hey, girl, don't forget we're on holiday now. Shall we take a plunge in the pool and then wander along to the bar to check out the cocktail menu? I think we've got just about enough energy left for that. And it's a busy day tomorrow – early walk followed by our private chocolate tour.'

'Sounds idyllic – let's spend the next five days relaxing and having fun and leave the business stuff till we get back home.'

'Done, agreed – that's perfect.' He leaned over and planted his butterfly kiss.

'Oh, and one last thing, Ned…' She pointed to the floppy straw hat that he had bought at the airport.

'I think I know what's coming.'

'We hold the first of the naked hat parades before we depart from this sexy paradise. And don't tell me you have to talk to your agent. Your agent isn't here to protect you this time.'

On the chocolate plantation the next day, they were shown the cocoa bean pods on the trees, the process of fermentation and how the beans were dried and flavoured. This was presumably when the berry seeds and the synthetic drug were blended in, instead of the flavouring or along with it. As Fran expected, the one hundred per cent chocolate was too fiercely bitter for her taste, although Ned loved it.

They also took in the museum of early artefacts, where she learned a little about the beliefs of the indigenous people, their connection with animal spirits and the spirits of the forest. Was it possible for this gift to be transferred through Junoco? Might there be a link to her new-found affinity with animals? It was the kind of far-out theory Lily would dream up. Fran touched one of the golden iguanas in the shop display and knew she had to buy it for Lily, despite the eye-watering price tag.

In the middle of the night, she was woken by loud hissing and growling on the small terrace. She crept warily to the glass door and peeped through the light curtain and mesh netting, stepping back in fear when she saw the group of bandit-eyed raccoons prowling on the table and edging round the corner of the wall. It must be the nuts that had drawn them in, the large half-eaten packet that had spilled over the paving. She tried to shoo them away without opening the mesh door, but they retreated only to return in seconds, so she decided to shut the glass door and ensure they at least stayed outside. She had a vague recollection that raccoons had the ability to pick locks, but surely that would have been anticipated in a place like this?

She padded back to bed, wondering how Ned could sleep through the racket, but she knew the simple answer – he was a man. How men had lost the ability to be instantly alert to danger, while women woke up at the slightest sound, was one of the great mysteries of modern life. She lay listening to the squabbling raccoons until the last few appeared to have slunk off. Creeping back to the door and lifting the curtain, she locked eyes with the one remaining animal, a young one that gazed openly at her with a soft expression, more curious than ferocious. The two of them held it like that for what seemed like an age, until the raccoon turned with a whisk of its long tail and walked away.

As she loosened her grip on the curtain and began to turn into the room, a larger raccoon came into the periphery of her vision, rounding the corner of the terrace and stalking towards her. Despite the firmly locked door between them, she stood petrified as it bared its teeth and snarled at her, its eyes hostile and its whole body pumped with aggression. She jumped back, dropping the curtain so she could only see the creature as a dim shape, and then pressed herself into the wall, well out of its line of sight. She waited for several minutes, heart racing, knowing she could call out to wake Ned but not wanting to do it, preferring to remain spellbound in the dark until she heard the slight shuffling noises of the raccoon moving off. Then she was able to return to bed and sleep for an hour before the raucous howler monkeys started up.

Chapter 17

Walking past the green towards Frocks and Chocs, Fran noticed how quickly the daffodils, crocuses and dandelions had come on in the short week she had been away. Spring was in the air, she was invigorated by her holiday and flying at thirty-three thousand feet had provided the ideal perspective to take stock and make some significant decisions. Plus, she had enjoyed her regular Junoco fix the night before and completed satisfying sketches of a raccoon and an iguana before breakfast.

The main thing was to act naturally with Daniela. Vicky was never around on a Saturday and so she wouldn't have to deal with them both at once.

While she was away, someone had rearranged the stock, moving groups of items from one rail to another and draping scarves and necklaces over the dress hangers. Fran was surprised at the extent of her irritation, at how she had appropriated the shop as her own little fiefdom. As she set about putting the clothes and accessories back in their usual places, she heard Daniela's light footsteps descending from the office. She turned round, still holding the blue-and-yellow day dress she had been coveting for some time now.

'Those gorgeous colours really suit you, Fran,

especially that blue with your new golden tan. You should buy it today with your discount – go on, treat yourself.'

'I know – it's lovely. I might do that. How has it been – busy?'

'Yes, the new season range is going well and the sale items slowly, but that's to be expected. Those leather handbags you ordered, they've been flying off the shelves.'

It was a perfectly natural conversation to be having, but it felt like they were going through the motions. Daniela looked tired and strained. What was it leading up to – had something else upset her? Fran wasn't prepared for yet another bombshell, if that was what it was.

'This isn't the best moment as we could be disturbed by a customer, but there is something I need to tell you, Fran, while it's quiet. You won't believe it.'

Fran mentally ran through all the things Daniela thought she didn't know, or she thought Daniela didn't know. It was a long, convoluted list: the Junoco formula was a mix of berry seeds and a synthetic drug; Daniela and Vicky were conspiring with Infrared, also known as Professor Fred Henson-Morris; Fred was leading a research project that was planning to trial a version of the Junoco formula on schoolchildren; Ravi had secretly approached Fran to spy on Daniela; Ned had staged the latest break-in and was setting up a rival concern using a new variant of Junoco; and she and Ned had met Osvaldo on holiday and were close to agreeing a double-crossing business deal.

Daniela was staring hard at her over her wide-winged glasses, apparently happy to prolong the suspense despite the high probability of someone coming into the shop at any minute.

'Okay,' said Fran, 'I've had a few big surprises lately but hopefully I can take another one.'

There was a further long pause. When Daniela finally spoke, her voice sounded mechanical, full of steel-cold rage. 'Vicky has disappeared, gone. It was Vicky who hacked into our website. Vicky doesn't even exist, she's not real. She was an undercover police officer.'

Fran instinctively recoiled and had to stabilise herself by clutching the counter. 'No!'

It was just the single word that came out, shrill and shaky. All the intimacy, the banter, the fun, all the things she had given up on after the traumatic encounter in Andy's kitchen came surging back and disintegrated once again. Her vision blurred and a sudden pain spread across her head, making her dizzy. She held fast to the counter edge, gripping its solidity and trying to regain control.

'I'm sorry, Fran. She's betrayed our trust, deceived us all.' Daniela was speaking normally now, but very fast. 'She's been working for a special unit that the police set up to infiltrate the supply chain at all levels and gather intelligence on the online drugs market.'

Fran nodded dumbly but her brain was whirring, trying to fit the pieces together. That night of the singles party, being let off so easily for stealing the leopard-print jacket. It hadn't just been her lucky night, or not in the way she had imagined. Someone had taken care of it.

Meanwhile, Daniela was continuing her explanation. 'We got swept up in it because they were interested in so-called "smart drugs", as well as the banned Class A and B and the legal highs. It's quite outrageous. We are trading openly with Junoco, not in some immoral corner of the dark web.'

It was true, everything Daniela was saying and the buyers were mostly delighted, but the awkward fact remained that they didn't know what it was they were consuming; the added ingredient was not wholly natural, as advertised. It hadn't been banned but it hadn't been approved either and it was definitely a psychoactive substance, so...

'How did you find out, Daniela, about Vicky? What happened?'

'Someone contacted me, an informant. He's a journalist, the one I warned you about. He had a tip-off and he tracked her identity, proved it was false and showed me the evidence. She's been spying on our competitors as well, so the police can crack down on the trade as a whole, but in our case it's not going to work. Junoco is too well connected. We have friends in high places.'

Well connected, with friends in high places – that was the essence. Daniela and her band of associates were protected by their link to the government and its plans to test an unknown and unregulated drug on children, under false pretences.

'Did she just vanish or was there a confrontation – did you challenge her?' Fran needed to find out how Vicky had left; what justification she had given, if any.

'There was no confrontation. I communicated with her through the journalist and then she disappeared, as undercover agents are trained to do. They may have our data but they can't do anything; they'll find their hands are tied. However, I have decided to close down the Junoco website and move the business overseas, somewhere there won't be the same level of surveillance. I told Ned when we met last night. We won't carry out any more deliveries from within the UK.'

No message then, nothing. How idiotic to think there might have been. Vicky had had access to Fran's personal data too, if she had taken her chance to acquire it. Thankfully, it was no more than mildly embarrassing, nothing worth the smallest blackmail sting.

An old saying came back to her; something a former lover had written in a note telling her he didn't want an explanation for her decision to end the relationship: *Silence speaks harsh words in whispers*. It just wasn't true; silence wasn't always so kind. Too often, it spoke of indifference – and indifference was cold and ghostly, worse than hatred. Unlike hatred, it couldn't be explained as the flip side of love or friendship, intimacy turned inside out.

'So, Fran, you've done a great job but I can no longer employ you on Junoco. I am going away for a few months. I would like you to continue in the shop and I value and trust you so highly that I want to offer you the position of shop manager, to oversee the business while I am away. Will you accept?'

'I think... well, I'm honoured but it's too much to take in; I'm all over the place. It's too early in the day but I think what I need right now is a gin and tonic!'

It was the kind of jokey thing she would have said to Vicky, to break the tension. Daniela responded as she wanted her to, smiling widely to reveal the dimples Fran had noticed on their first encounter.

'Well, I'll let you think about it. I know you and Vicky had become good friends. Maybe she genuinely wanted to be a close friend, if the situation had been different.'

'She came to my friend Judi's funeral, Daniela. She drove me there in her car, sat beside me and listened to what I was feeling. She comforted me. That's what I'll never forgive.'

Daniela spread her arms out wide and Fran almost fell into her enfolding embrace.

***

She phoned Ravi as soon as she left the shop that afternoon, stopping on the corner and waving at Jean-Claude through the café window. A plan had come into her head ready-made while she was serving customers, reorganising the stock and trying to suppress her cynical thoughts. Not the plan she might have expected but a different idea altogether, an opportunity to help a friend. She needed to get onto a positive track.

'Is that Ravi? It's Fran, calling you back... Hello?'

'Did you say Fran? Ah yes, bad connection, sorry; I was waiting for your call but I heard you'd been away.'

'Can we meet, now if possible? I can wait in the Green Duck again, if you can get there within the next hour.'

'I'll be there, give me thirty minutes.'

He hung up immediately, like any good spy. She was even less convinced by his journalist persona now but recognised it could be her overheated imagination.

He was dressed in a light grey suit, with an open-necked shirt revealing the top of a hairy chest. Once more, they greeted each other formally and he placed his hands in his signature fold-over position on the table, as if preparing to tip it over. She was determined to take charge of the conversation and make it brief.

'Okay, Ravi, here's the thing. I assume you already know that Daniela is about to shut down the Junoco site and open a new business outside the UK. She has also told me that Vicky, our so-called IT consultant, was working undercover for the police. I believe this information came from you but in any case, I presume you're no longer interested in me acting as your mole, as I'm no longer involved in Junoco. Daniela has stood me down, as they say.'

She watched his face, then looked at his hands but couldn't fathom how much he already knew of Daniela's plans. He gave a non-committal shrug.

'Circumstances change. I could still be interested in coming to some arrangement with you. Why did you ask to see me urgently, if you thought I wasn't?'

She had to tread carefully, reveal just enough and keep the best cards close to her chest. 'Daniela is in a business partnership with Infrared, as you already told me. Infrared runs his own online enterprise in cognitive-enhancing drugs, so it's possible he has been targeted by the police operation. That's kind of beside the point. The point is that there's a bigger story behind all this.'

He nodded as she spoke and gestured for her to carry on. She wasn't going to be rushed and this was the judgement call. She needed Ravi and his influential contacts to get access to the senior civil servant mentioned by Osvaldo, her plan depended on it, but she didn't know if Ravi was aware of Fred's dual identity and the link between Junoco and the schools research programme. In other words, she didn't know if she had any power to exploit the situation. And despite picking up handy tips from Daniela, she was feeling her lack of tactical training.

'Infrared is not only a dodgy businessman. He's an eminent neuroscience professor working here in London and the lead academic on a research project to test, quote, "brain supplements, vitamins and nutrients" on schoolchildren. It's a government initiative. My information is that the substance will be similar to Junoco – an officially unlicensed drug.'

Ravi took his slim hands off the table again and clasped them tightly, cracking a knuckle, while his face betrayed no reaction. 'That's interesting. It fits with the story so far. Do you know who's managing it from the government side?'

'Yes, I have the individual's name but I'm not going to divulge it yet. I think that this person has been misled on the so-called vitamins and supplements and believes them to be harmless natural products. We have to get the truth of it confirmed or denied at the top and then we can expose what's going on.'

'Hold on, that may not be the best approach, to expose it. We need to do more investigation first. It will take a little time to build up the picture, develop it into a full story.'

'I'm sorry, Ravi, but I have reasons to be impatient and no time to waste. Either you agree to use your high-level contacts to arrange an early meeting with this civil servant person or I'll keep silent on their identity and call the other journalist who's approached me. I'll do it tomorrow if I haven't heard from you by 4pm.'

He grimaced, probably to show he hadn't fallen for this obvious ploy. 'All right then, okay, hold your horses. I'll work out how to contrive a meeting with the civil servant, as long as I can come with you. And for your part, you must agree to say nothing to Ultraviolet.'

'Who's that, Ultraviolet? Sorry, I don't get it.'

'Your boss, Daniela; it's the code name used by the Infrared associates.'

Ultraviolet; it was perfect. Vicky would have adored playing with that, in the days when they were fooling around together.

'Are we agreed on the way forward then, Fran? I'll get back to you as soon as.'

It was a massive gamble and she may have overplayed her hand by handing Ravi the end of a new thread to follow. For all that, it felt like a risk she had to take.

∗∗∗

'Can I help you? Are you looking for something in particular, a gift?'

The young man had been wandering round the shop, pausing in front of the display of lacy lingerie, peering into the jewellery cabinet and fingering the velvet and beaded evening bags. It was lunchtime, which usually saw a small surge in customers, especially since Fran had suggested they made room for a stand of greeting cards. Today was no exception, and it was only now that she had found an opportunity to respond to the man's frequent glances, which indicated he might like some advice.

'Yes, it's for my girlfriend's birthday. I thought maybe one of these bags but I'm not sure about the colours, whether they'll go – this red and gold, she wears a lot of red...' He gazed across to the other side of the shop. 'Or earrings, I was thinking, or a silk scarf, but it's the same problem. I don't know, maybe I'll have to bring her in to choose.'

'It's always difficult but I'm sure she'll like it that you took the time to look for something special. We have a returns and exchange policy, twenty-eight days to bring it back.'

As she was speaking, Fran saw Kirsty out of the corner of her eye, first passing the window and then coming into the shop. She didn't look in Fran's direction but turned to the far clothes rail near the fitting room and started picking out items on their hangers and folding them over her arm. The lunchtime crowd was thinning out and with any other customer Fran would normally walk over or call across to encourage her into the fitting room. Instead, she half-watched Kirsty moving along the rail, unsure whether she knew Fran worked here and aware that any suspicions Kirsty might harbour about her neighbourly relationship with Marcus were now at least partially justified.

There was a crash and she turned back to see that the cards stand had toppled over, sending its contents sliding across the floor. The young man gripped the left side of his head, looking dazed.

'Oh, I'm so sorry, what happened? Are you hurt?'

'Yes, the fucking thing hit me, didn't it? I just reached across to look at a card and it tipped right over, just like that. It can't have been fixed down properly.'

'I'm sorry, sir. It's meant to stand alone like that, inside or outside, so I thought it was safe. Would you like to sit down? Can I get you a cup of tea or anything? How's your head now?'

'It's okay, I'll live. But I'm not buying anything from your stupid shop after that.'

As he stomped out, she righted the stand, tested its balance and bent down to gather the cards and put them in piles on the counter, ready to restack them later. Kirsty had turned to observe the scene but showed no sign of recognising Fran.

Would you like some help? Can I put those in the fitting room for you?'

'No, I tried them on the other day and said I'd come back to buy some stuff.'

Kirsty approached the counter with her chosen items, which came from the new spring range. Fran laid them out on top of each other, preparing to process them for payment. There was a short lemon-and-black dress, a dandelion-yellow cardigan with large pockets, and a pair of loose-fitting, cool white-and-grey trousers. When she came to these, she looked up at Kirsty, standing there with an air of assumed nonchalance, now laced with defiance.

'These trousers are beautiful, they're new in. They'll go well with the white jacket – a good choice.'

Kirsty stared blankly at her.

'The white faux fur jacket – the one you put into your sports bag a few minutes ago, when you thought I was preoccupied with picking up the cards.'

Kirsty had set the sports bag on the floor beside her. Now she kicked out her left foot to pull it in close and hold it tight between her ankles.

'And the bra and panties set, the silk blouse and the red dress. I know something about shoplifting, Kirsty, because I used to do it myself. I also know how to cause a distraction – I've tried that too, more than once. Now, open your bag or I'll call the police.'

Kirsty glared at her, but underneath the hostility Fran could tell she was unsure what to do: whether to fight, flee or cave in.

'I'll tell you what, Kirsty. You give back those things right now and nothing will happen. Hand them over and go, move on with your life and don't come anywhere near this part of the world again.'

'I am moving on. I'm going to Australia with my boyfriend, if you must know. That stupid old fucker Marcus said I'd find someone better than him and you can tell him I have.'

She knew perfectly well, then, who Fran was, although she had pretended otherwise. She had called her an old slapper, after all, so Fran must have made some kind of impression.

'That sounds great, Kirsty. I wish you well and I hope your boyfriend hasn't got too big a headache from his clash with my card stand. Now put it all on the counter and scram, before I change my mind.'

Fran smiled to herself and couldn't help admiring Kirsty's long glossy braids falling over her shoulder as she bent down to unzip the bag.

Chapter 18

'Shall I slice the carrots and courgettes, or do you want them done in strips?'

'Whichever you like, Alice. I call it the chopper's prerogative. I've got a spiralizer as well, although I've never actually used it – in the top drawer over there.'

Fran got out her biggest wok and the dark soy sauce. Her cooking was nowhere near Ned's standard, but she enjoyed doing these tasty one-pot dishes. One day she would have Ned over for dinner, but tonight it was Alice in her kitchen and she had invited Marcus and Kwesi, who were upstairs practising for the request session featuring her favourite songs.

'How was your holiday with the mystery man, then? Did it live up to expectations?'

'It was great. A fascinating country – I'd go again like a shot. But, Alice, there are things I need to tell you quickly, before the guys come down. My mystery friend – Ned, that is – plans to set up a new venture selling mind-enhancing products, using a variant of Junoco and targeting the luxury London market – hotels, corporate events and the like. And for some reason, he's fixated on having me as his business partner. Oh yes, and he thinks we could run a high-class male escort agency on the side, through the same contacts.'

'Fran, you are such a dark horse! Have you said yes to any of these offers?'

'Not yet, but I'm inclined to go for the first one, for starters. I'd appreciate your thoughts but not now, there isn't time. There's something else, more significant to you.'

'Go on. Are these strips coming out right? I'm not sure I've got the hang of this whatsit.'

'They look fine. Anyway, when we were away, Ned arranged for us to meet Daniela's cousin and business associate, Osvaldo, at our hotel. Osvaldo and his companion confirmed what we already knew: that Professor Fred doubles as Infrared, the sinister business rival. I also found out that Osvaldo's logging company has cleared a larger area of forest to grow more berry bushes to supply the Bright Minds programme. And there *is* something else in the mix, as you suspected: a drug manufactured in Vietnam or Cambodia.'

Alice arranged the courgettes neatly on the plate, folding in the stray strips that had curled onto the counter. She picked up one of the stools to reposition it, so she could sit and look at Fran while she poured them another glass of wine.

'Yes, I did suspect,' said Alice, 'but still I can't get my head around it. Fred seems so wrong, miscast. I'm bitterly disappointed in him. How can he imagine they're going to get away with it? It's in the name of science, I suppose, and making his reputation. He has been helpful to me, to my career, I will give him that.'

'I know. I'm disappointed too but I don't want to go into it, it's such a tangled web. The last thing I must tell you is that Junoco has been under police surveillance from

312

the start. That's how the site got hacked. Daniela has now decided it's too difficult to trade from here and she's going to relocate abroad under a new brand name, close down Junoco. It's what we were told at the beginning: be light-footed, ready to cut and run.'

She hadn't planned to avoid naming Vicky, but when it came to it she felt some kind of misplaced loyalty, or perhaps it was just her distress and loss of pride.

'Oh God, really, this is insane! It does figure though; I can see they're getting jumpy at the university and Fred has muttered about deferring the project. He's rattled, that's obvious. Maybe it's more naivety on his part, I'd like to think.'

'I hardly know him, so I can't begin to second-guess his motives but from what you say, the university team can sense the approaching tsunami, if it hasn't already crashed over the beach. But shush now, I can hear the others on their way down.'

Marcus and Kwesi were stepping down the stairs with the drums, which they planned to set up in the front room. Alice followed Fran into the hall to be introduced and pick up her guitar case. She liked to sing and had promised she would play some of her own numbers at the end, as well as joining in with the others if it felt right.

The music lasted two hours and included several of the songs Fran had on her playlist, an eclectic mix of classic rock, '80s pop, blues and country. She knew the duo had put in many hours of practice, but she was amazed by their versatility, their ability to adapt tunes to their instruments while staying faithful to the original tracks. Within half an hour, Alice was strumming along and joining in with the smiles and nods passing between them as they experimented with small improvisations and modified the tempo, volume and emotional tone. Her singing voice was lower than Fran's and they harmonised so naturally that at several points the men stopped playing to listen to the women's duet. Following the main session, Alice played some of her own numbers, with Marcus and Fran joining in the singing and Kwesi tapping his foot, blissfully happy.

'It is the best evening I have enjoyed in England. Thank you, my wonderful friends.'

Fran smiled at him, marvelling at how they had all tuned in so well, and not just in terms of the music. She looked round, including everyone in her gaze.

'And thank you all too, from me. You should get out there and perform together, the three of you. It's a great sound, and you could add in the jazz that we haven't heard tonight yet.'

Marcus adopted a lounging position on the sofa, his long legs stretched out under the coffee table, perfectly at home. It was a good thing Alice was staying the night, as Fran couldn't risk a recurrence of what had happened the last time he stayed late. She looked across to Kwesi, who placed Guacamole on the floor, picked up the mole's drum seat and put it between his knees to stroke and tap it.

'I wanted to ask you, Kwesi. How's your asylum appeal going? Have you heard anything?'

'No, there is no word. They don't answer my emails and they are not helpful on the phone; they don't answer.'

'That's just wrong. They're leaving you in limbo when you could be working as a doctor in one of our hospitals. It doesn't make sense.'

'You must not be anxious for me. You and Marcus and Lily have been very kind, and I hope I can repay you one day, invite you to my home.'

'Hey, man, we love you!' Marcus interjected.

'Speaking of Lily, how's she doing, Marcus?' asked Fran. 'I haven't seen her for ages, what with being on holiday and everything.'

'She's been round a few times, still wound up about the missing cats. I daren't take the poster down and I see yours is still in the window too.'

'I must get to see her soon, tomorrow.'

She felt another pang of guilt about the way she had spoken to Lily after she came back from confronting Vicky in Andy's kitchen; how she had brushed her off like an annoying little gnat. She hoped Lily hadn't said anything to Marcus, hadn't shown she was upset. Now, however, Fran needed to take advantage of her friends all being here together.

'I know it's late, but I need some advice, if you don't mind.'

Marcus pulled a cushion towards him, shoved it behind his back and sat up to listen. Fran gave them the summary she had mentally prepared while hoovering that afternoon. Marcus and Alice already knew certain parts of the story, but Kwesi needed to be filled in on how she had met Daniela and been persuaded to join her Junoco business. Then there was Ned, how he had been brought into it and his ambition to start a similar venture with a different client base. This was pretty much the bare bones, leaving out most of the machinations and betrayals, as well as the entire account of the schools research programme.

'So this is my question: should I accept Ned's invitation and become his business partner?'

She didn't mention Daniela's parallel offer of promotion to manager at Frocks and Chocs, as it was the ethical issues, the morality she was confused about. She had wanted to include Kwesi in this as she imagined, rightly as it turned out, that as a doctor he would be sceptical. His initial contribution, however, came as a shock.

'I must tell you that the sick young girl we found on the grass – that was the day I met you, Fran – she has died of a drug overdose. It wasn't heroin. It was a cheaper drug, what they call a legal high. It is impossible to stop people selling them on the internet and on the street.'

'I'm so sorry. I know you were trying to help her – Charley, wasn't it?'

'Yes, that's right. It was difficult to talk to her but she wanted to stop, to change her life. She had chances but she didn't take them, or she fell back each time. She was lost – no family, her friends were addicts. It is easy to become addicted to drugs and be destroyed by them.'

Marcus leaned forward. 'You're right, but it's different with Junoco, the curiosity chocolates we're talking about, isn't it? It's true that people can often be irresponsible or desperate, but the Junoco effects are positive and it could be good for society as well. Just like penicillin or any new drug, except it hasn't been officially approved. Look at Fran. She's pursuing her artistic flair and her drawings are just getting better all the time. And while we're talking business partners, I'd love to work with you too, Fran, turning your sketches into paintings, maybe try digital animation – they'd be perfect for it.'

She blinked in surprise. Wow, that was a bolt from the blue, digital animation.

They talked late into the night and it was well after two when the men left. By this time, Alice was curled up on one end of the sofa, fast asleep. Fran fetched a blanket and laid it over her before leaning down and kissing her on the cheek. Then she restored Guacamole to his customary place on the hearth.

'Goodnight, Alice. Goodnight, Mr Mole – one day, I'll get you truly animated.'

'Goodnight, Frankie. Sweet dreams.'

She stared at Guacamole, and then turned to Alice, who sighed but didn't wake.

Fran turned off the light in the hallway and stepped onto the bottom stair, then stopped and looked upwards. The moonlight was brighter than she had ever seen it from this position, shining through the back-bedroom window and illuminating the landing. She continued up and into the bedroom, noting the scent of the purple and yellow freesias she had arranged in the decorated glass vase for Alice's overnight stay. The orb of the moon was immense and seemed very close. It was spellbinding; normally familiar and reassuring, but tonight majestic and full of mythic power.

She cast her gaze across the night sky, her eyes adjusting to follow the pattern of the stars. Out there beyond the moon was Mars, and way beyond Mars was mighty Jupiter, with its mysterious red spot and its captured circling asteroids, among them Juno, unearthly rock and space goddess.

Drawn by the magnetic lure of the giant moon, she began to discern faint outlines forming on its surface and blending into a sequence of faces, faces she recognised: first Marina as a tiny girl, the elfin child; then her dad Lawrence in old age, older than he ever was in life, the ancient sage; and finally Judi, best friend and good spirit, indistinct and transforming into a classic profile of Juno, as if stamped on a coin.

Forced to blink twice, she brought her eyes down to her garden, which had been landscaped by the previous owner as far as the small wild patch at the end. Opening the window, she heard voices; not ordinary conversation or the drunken shouting matches or agitated night phone calls of the city street, but the sound of chanting, low and rhythmic.

She stepped back into the dark room and tried to work out what direction the sound was coming from. It was from the left, one of the neighbouring gardens or the path that ran along the back of the terrace. Moving stealthily forward, but not to the point of making herself visible, she trained her eyes on the unlit area at the bottom of Marcus' garden and then across the next fence to Delia and Eric's. Through the tall hedge that ran across their garden halfway down, she could see moving pinpoints of light, and attached to the lights were the shadowy figures of several people. She pulled the bedroom chair towards her so she could stand on it to see over the hedge. The chanting figures were dressed in monk-like robes with loose hoods and they were swinging long light-wands as they followed each other round in a small circle.

Fran sat down heavily on the bed. There had been no Junoco session tonight, and anyway this was no Junoco dream; it was too creepy. She stood up again and peeped around the curtain, knowing the figures were real but hoping they might dissolve and fade away. Did the full moon explain it, or make it into something more than what it was: an unusual but harmless ritual, or even a game? No, this was Eric and Delia; they weren't harmless. She had no choice but to call Marcus, force him to come with her and discover what was going on.

Within two minutes, she had clambered over the front wall close to the door and Marcus let her in. Luckily, he and Kwesi had stayed up 'to put the world to rights' and were still awake and alert. She briefed them quickly and, to her relief and surprise, Marcus was immediately up for it and concocting a plan.

'You and I, Fran, go out the front and round your house to the side path. We creep down there and along the back path, then we crouch behind their fence and earwig on what they're saying and doing. Kwesi, you stay inside and if we need you to do anything, we'll call you, okay? You mustn't come with us. It will be too risky for you, especially if we've got it all wrong and the operation goes pear-shaped.'

Kwesi nodded. 'This happens often in my country. It is religion; religious perversion, not true religion.'

Fran shuddered. 'Maybe – we don't know that yet.'

It felt quite exposed on the back path, which in parts was bathed in moonlight. The chanting had speeded up and become more impassioned. Reaching the wooden gate in the high fence at the back of Eric and Delia's garden, Fran pointed out a small hole created by a lost knot in the wood. They looked through it in turn and exchanged grim expressions.

'Did you see – it's a cat, isn't it? They're passing it round the circle and lifting it above their heads,' Marcus whispered, miming the actions as he spoke.

'There are animal bodies too, two or three dead ones I think, lying on the table to the side. The lights are flickering; it's hard to make out but I'm almost certain of it.'

They slipped down to a sitting position with their backs to the fence. Marcus was in battle mode now, wanting to create an opportunity to charge or slip in and get the evidence, while Fran favoured calling the police straight away.

'We'll have to call them anyway. We can still stay here and grab our chance if we get one, although we'll need to climb over as this gate is bound to be locked, unless they've left it open as an escape route. We'll hear the police car when it arrives and I'll dash round to the front before Kwesi has to answer the door.'

'Just five more minutes, let's see what happens. I think it's ending now; they're sloping off back to the house, listen.'

She stood up again and looked through the peephole. He was right. The whole group was gliding away in their robes, leaving the scene of carnage.

'Now, Marcus!' She tried the gate and it swung open. The table was very close. He ran in, keeping low, and snatched one of the limp and bloodied corpses.

As they came down the side path, she let him run ahead while she called the police. It was almost comically macabre, seeing the silhouette of his lanky figure lolloping along with the lifeless creature held out to one side by its tail.

The police call-handler would be used to bizarre calls at this time of the night, both genuine and hoax. Thankfully she registered Fran's voice and decided to treat it as genuine.

'We'll send a car over. Call again if anyone leaves the house. Don't approach them, but if you can get a vehicle registration number, that will be helpful.'

***

The moon was pale but still dominant in the lightening sky as Fran gazed at it from her near-horizontal position on the bed. The police had arrived in two cars, one pair of officers running round the back as the other two walked up the path to Eric and Delia's front door. The couple had been taken off to the station along with three or four others, all back in normal clothes. Eric had looked old and dishevelled as a female officer pushed his head down sharply and eased him into the back of the car. They had also come to Fran's door and arranged to take witness statements from her and Marcus the next afternoon.

Eventually, she dozed off and found herself in a strange hotel lobby, where she was asking for a room number but getting no information from the blank-faced receptionists. Then she was joined by a group of friends, all fired up but none of whom she knew in real life. They ran up long flights of stairs and along the corridors, knocking on doors and being shouted at by angry guests. Finally, they burst into a room to find Andy and Vicky sitting in bed side by side against soft, silky pillows, holding fizzing flutes of champagne and not at all perturbed by the interruption and Fran's triumphant shriek of 'Found you!' Her friends slunk off like the insubstantial ghosts they were, leaving her facing Vicky's pixie smile and Andy's innocent expression, which said, *What did I tell you, Frankie? I'm easily led.*

She awoke abruptly, disturbed by the humiliating dream episode but knowing it held an important message, something she had to consider later. Now she needed to think about the night's actual events: the sacrificial animals, and what she was going to say to Lily. The main thing was to catch Petra as she left for work. Petra had to decide how to play it with Lily; it was her responsibility.

Fran went downstairs to find Alice, who had slept through the whole drama. She was incredulous and horrified by the tale of ritual sacrifice but allowed herself a little amusement at Fran's pivotal role in the arrests.

'What is it about you? Have you always created mayhem wherever you go?'

'That's unfair. I'm just a naive country girl who's ridden into town.'

'Yes, and on a frisky little horse!'

'A runaway pony, more like.'

The long-ago picnic scene in the field resurfaced in Fran's memory: how she had hung back and watched, huddled in her thin towel, while Judi leapt through the thistles and spiky grass after Jambo, naked and fearless.

When Alice left for work, Fran positioned herself at the front window and was able to run out and catch Petra as she had planned. To begin with, Petra was decidedly cool, but this changed as she heard the account of the night before, and especially when Fran ended by saying she would love Lily to come round after school. As she walked back to her door, Marcus also emerged.

'Hi, Marcus, how are you this morning? How do you feel?'

'How do I feel – sick and angry, but glad we went in there and did what we had to do. The grisly sight of the animals, I can't get over it. I hope they get banged up for a long time. The cruelty – what the hell drives them? Were they on something, do you think – spaced out?

'I don't know – it has to be some kind of cult. Perhaps we'll never be told.'

'And they found a couple of pet snakes in there too, don't know what type; did the police tell you? They must have—'

Fran raised her hand. 'Stop now – I don't want to hear it! It just doesn't bear thinking about. But, Marcus, can I talk to you after work, about something else? It's important.'

'Now is okay, if it's important. I'm on flexitime and I've got half an hour to spare.'

He stood in the hall while she reported in summary on what Osvaldo had said about the link between Junoco and Bright Minds, her pub encounters with Ravi and her plan to contrive a meeting with the senior civil servant.

'You can't do it like that, Fran, go along with a journalist. It won't work. She'll never open up if you're with him. And as you say, he might not even be a journalist. Have you any proof?'

'What then? How should I do it? Who should I go with?'

'Go by yourself, as yourself, the small, ordinary person who has been unwittingly drawn in and now wants to pass on a vital piece of information to the authorities.'

'But Ravi is going to arrange access, set up the meeting through his contacts.'

'It's a complete no-no, I'm telling you. I work with civil service types every day, remember; I know what they're like. If she's pressured by a journalist, if she feels in danger of being exposed for incompetence or worse, she'll be on the defensive and you won't get the right response. She'll be less guarded with you on your own – especially you, you can look like butter wouldn't melt in your mouth.'

'Okay, I take your point and you're not the first or last person to say it. What do you suggest?'

She presented the question as a form of challenge. This was Marcus' issue too, something that mattered to him, but he was miles too timid, it wasn't going to happen – although to be fair he hadn't been timid last night; far from it.

'I'll do it for you. I'll get you in to see her by the end of the week, promise.'

'Oh, Marcus, thank you so much. I realise you're going out on a limb.'

'If you win, if you manage to bring it off, it'll be more than worth it.'

'Another thing, quickly – that idea you mentioned of bringing my sketches to life, digital animation; it sounds fantastic, pure genius. It all fits with Junoco too.'

'Then we'll go ahead and do it after this is over – what's to stop us? We'll try it first with one of your favourites and see if it catches on.'

***

All week, Lily had marched past on her way home from school without turning her head. Today, for the first time, Fran saw she was with another child, a boy, and engrossed in a lively conversation. She went to the window and removed the *Missing* poster with the now-distressing cat photos, then waited.

Petra had said she would get home early to try and prevent Lily picking up any information or rumours about the fate of the animals from the local kids. Fran felt nervous, although less about that than about whether Lily would turn up and allow her to restore their friendship. Kids moved on, as adults did, they blanked things out and bounced back in unpredictable ways. Had she left it too late?

When the bell rang, she opened the door to see Lily cradling Sahara against her chest with one hand and struggling to hold a large hardback book under the other arm.

'Hello, Fran. You told Mum I could come round here again.'

'I did, and I've missed you lots, you wouldn't believe. And Sahara too; I bought some juicy grapes today, her favourites.'

'Do you still have her special box?'

'Of course I do, silly. We're still good friends. I was upset about something and I was mean and thoughtless; I shouldn't have spoken to you like that. I never wanted to hurt you, not in a million years. Come on in now and let's have some grapes and strawberry tarts.'

Lily gestured for her to lift the book out from under her arm and repositioned Sahara safely before stepping inside. She began on the subject of the dead animals straight away, her voice initially flat and emotionless.

'Mum told me that our nasty neighbours stole the cats and rabbits, kidnapped them so they could sell them. The police say they killed them, if they were too old or sick.'

Fran nodded, waiting for the questions or the ideas and speculation, but they didn't come. Lily just stood there, looking miserable and holding Sahara tight.

'Yes, it's horrible but at least now they've been arrested.' The local paper was bound to make a huge splash of this, complete with all the gory details. It was inescapable.

'I hope they never come back. I hate them and I never want to see them again.'

Lily's lip was trembling as she tried to hold back the tears. Fran moved forward to put her arm around her and guide her to the sofa.

'Hey, come on, let's talk about something else.'

She reached for the big book, which was a new one about the solar system that Lily's dad had ordered for her. Lily leaned towards her so they could turn the pages together.

'I'm still going to be an astronomer. Jack is too. I gave him the idea, but I'm going to study asteroids like Juno, your favourite, and he's into planets. Have you heard about the space probe *Juno* circling round Jupiter, taking photos and investigating what it's made of?'

'Yes, it's exciting. And there's a mission to intercept an asteroid and pick up material from it. By the time you're grown up, we could be mining asteroids. They're packed with valuable minerals, some of them, things like platinum worth trillions and trillions.'

Lily frowned. 'It's not good. If that happens, I hope they break away and crash-land on the earth in a storm of meteorites.'

'Your imagination, Lily, it's extraordinary. There is one out there that's going to come pretty close to earth in 2079, might even hit us. But tell me – is Jack your new friend, the boy you were walking home with today?'

'Yes, that's him. He told me *Juno* was a space probe as well as an asteroid.'

'Maybe you'll make great discoveries together, you and Jack.'

'And did you know Ferdi is coming home to live with us? Dad is going to America and Ferdi will stay with me and Mum for two years or even longer. How brilliant is that?'

'It's fantastic news – great! I can't wait to meet Ferdi and Jack.'

'Yes, but you're my special friend, aren't you? I like talking to you on my own.'

'We'll leave plenty of time for that. In fact, I've just had an idea. We could go and visit my Uncle George, who is designing a computer system to transform future space travel. I've promised to sort out his stuff with him, and he'd love to explain his invention to you. He's eccentric, mind you, a bit mad.'

Lily squatted down to put Sahara into her box. 'That's okay. I like the sound of Uncle George. My uncles and aunties are boring, and I've only got one interesting cousin. Sometimes it's good to be a bit mad, don't you think?'

'I think so, and look at Guacamole over there, smiling at us. He can change his expression and sometimes he turns his head. I'm sure he thinks the same.'

'How does he do it? Can I see?'

'He's not ready yet, but it's not far off. You'll be first to see it, I promise. And that reminds me – I brought a special present back for you, from my holiday. Do you want to know what it is, or shall I go and fetch it first?'

'Oh yes, please tell me now!'

'It's a golden iguana.'

'A golden iguana – I never had anything like that. Will it talk to me, I wonder?'

'You never know, Lily – being you, it just might.'

Chapter 19

Someone was standing under the chestnut tree; a man, she couldn't see any details from this distance. Now mistrustful of anyone who might be stopping to watch her house, Fran swung round and retraced her steps so she was out of sight beyond the street corner. She counted to twenty and then peered round the end house. The man had disappeared, or at least she could no longer see him under the tree or walking in either direction. She had to be careful, not get paranoid, but it felt difficult to maintain the balance, as it was entirely possible she was being spied on.

Her front door was locked as usual but there was a draught of cool air coming through the house, which could only mean the back door was open. She stood stock-still in the hall, heart pounding and listening for any sounds – nothing. Marcus would be out at work and Kwesi needed to stay hidden as much as possible, especially as Eric and Delia might try to save themselves from their own predicament by pointing the finger at him. Anyway, Fran's sense was that the intruder had gone, probably in a hurry as the back door was wide open. An attempt had been made to break the lock, presumably without success as one of the long door panes had been smashed in with her large wooden mallet, which lay on the ground on top of the broken glass. She picked it up, feeling more than ready to use it on anyone she might encounter in the house.

The kitchen looked intact and the living room just as she had left it, except for one glaring gap – her laptop computer was missing from the dining table. Thinking fast, her eyes darted to the large chest, where all the drawers were firmly closed. She would check in a minute, once she had searched the bedrooms. Running upstairs, she looked under the two beds, where the spaces were crammed with stuff, and opened every cupboard where someone could possibly hide. It didn't feel as if they had been up here, which was no surprise as she knew this wasn't an ordinary burglar.

Back in the living room, she went to the top right drawer of the chest, easing it open slowly as if expecting something might jump out at her. She could see immediately that the current Junoco box, which still contained four chocolates, had been touched. The truffles were out of order; there were two blue and two gold ones next to each other. They still had their wrappers on and didn't appear to have been opened.

She perched on the edge of the sofa to think. She had got home half an hour earlier than usual and had possibly disturbed them, almost caught them in the act. The man under the tree could have been the lookout, ready to raise the alarm in time for the guy inside to escape through the side gate and down the back path.

'Holy moly, Guacamole – who was it, what did you see? Talk to me, mole, won't you? It's important.'

Guacamole looked ruffled and disconcerted, not his usual easy-going self.

Should she call Ned, or Alice? Definitely Alice, as Fran felt most worried about the chocolates and why they had been changed about. Alice would take it seriously, be over-cautious if anything. Thankfully, she picked up the call straight away and Fran gave a quick rundown of the scene she had come home to and what she had found when she opened the drawer.

'They're still wrapped up and I don't think they've been opened.'

'You don't know that, Fran; there are ways and means. They could have been replaced, for a start. Don't touch them, whatever you do. I'm cancelling my next meeting and coming over. And don't call the police, not yet anyway.'

'Don't worry, I've no intention of calling the police – it would be a disaster.'

She heard the anger in her response and reminded herself that Alice knew nothing about Vicky's betrayals and her unmasking as an undercover officer. She didn't want Alice to know. She had told her that Junoco had been under police surveillance from the beginning; that was enough to justify not bringing the police into it. Suddenly, she felt a different fear: the fear that she could lose Alice as well through this, have her back off because she had to hang on to her career or because it was simply too frightening. She had been enchanted by Alice, by her look and ideas, and then her music, her easy way with Marcus and Kwesi, and her open-minded attitude. It was very odd, she realised, that in this perilous situation her mind should be occupied by thoughts of their friendship, but there it was.

They agreed not to resort to subterfuge but to have Alice arrive as normal by the front door. This was on the assumption that the burglars knew about the side path entrance to the house, and also knew their connection to each other. It was a risk, but they reckoned no more so than meeting elsewhere, if Fran was being watched.

She waited by the window, even waving at Lily as she passed by with Jack on her way home from school. When she arrived, Alice immediately slipped on her gloves and lifted both the open box of truffles and the one remaining unopened box out of the drawer. She picked up a chocolate, turned it round under the light of the table lamp and then held it up to the daylight, being careful to remain invisible from the street.

'What are you thinking, Alice? Who the hell would do this?'

'That's the second question, although the questions are linked – how and who? The "why" is easy – someone wanted to find out what's on your laptop and scare you off by meddling with the truffles. How they've meddled with them is what we need to find out. I'm going to take these boxes straight to the lab to have the contents analysed. My suspicion is that something else has been added or the balance altered. It could be done through the wrapper, simple as anything. I'll get off now, so there's a chance of a result this evening, if I can charm the lab assistants and persuade them to work late.'

It was all said so matter-of-factly, but the implications were frightening and Fran had the rest of the afternoon to dwell on them. It seemed incredible that someone might try to harm her like that. Was it possible that Fred Henson-Morris would do such a thing, in his guise as Infrared; or maybe Ravi, if his journalist identity was just a front; or even Daniela, if she had found out from Osvaldo that Ned and Fran were planning to break away and set up their own rival company? She was fiery, but could she be so callous?

'It's starting to freak me out, this whole thing. Is it possible… could you perhaps stay over tonight, Alice, just for reassurance? Or maybe you've got other—?'

'No, I can do that, no worry; I wouldn't leave you here on your own.'

When Alice left, Fran felt guilty about not having mentioned the showdown with Andy and Vicky; not acknowledging or sharing her feelings about it. It was just too soon to disclose her vulnerability again, to trust anyone with the story of her loss. She was missing Judi so much, missing all of them, all gone. It would be hours yet before she heard back from Alice and she felt restless, scared and unable to concentrate on anything.

Then her phone pinged – a text from Ravi. Could she meet him at the Green Duck in half an hour? She sat looking at it, wondering if he perhaps wanted to discuss a new plan, now that she had changed her mind about him setting up the meeting with the civil servant. That would be tricky, given that Marcus had now fixed the meeting for Friday, just two days away, but it was less alarming than the alternative idea that Ravi was involved in the break-in and his call was connected to that.

She looked over to Guacamole and then to the spiral-horned antelope, which stood above him on the mantelpiece. There was no sign, no indication of what she should do. She shook her head and sighed in exasperation.

'Tell you what – I'm feeling hemmed in, with you two for company. I don't know if you're smart and pretending to be dumb, or dumb and pretending to be smart. I've got to get out of here before I go stir-crazy, have a walk, and yes, I will drop into the pub, just for five minutes, see what it's about.'

She should really call a glazier, but she couldn't face the hassle of tracking one down right now. Also, she had to find out why Ravi needed to see her at such short notice, even if it might be some kind of trap.

This time she got there before him and was able to order a glass of wine at the bar and choose a comfortable corner. Today, his behaviour contrasted strongly with the way he had presented himself before. His hands were moving around instead of pressing on the table, and he kept touching his face and smoothing down his already-sleek hair as he spoke.

'So, I've decided I don't want to work on this story any more, Fran, I can't. Our house was broken into last night while we were asleep and they stole my laptop and camera, nothing else. Then I was accosted in the street and warned to stop digging around, as the guy put it. He made it clear that they know where my children go to school; that they're prepared to go to extreme lengths. So I'm backing off, it's not worth it. I can't stay here with you now either and we shouldn't be seen together again, but I wanted to tip you off in person. It's not a kids' adventure story, believe me. There's too much money and too many reputations at stake.'

'I'm well aware of that, Ravi, and it's awful that they violated your home and made threats against your family, unforgivable. Thanks for the warning, I appreciate it. It's coming to an end for me now anyway, with Daniela closing down Junoco and going abroad. The other thing, the research in schools, is too big an affair for me to get mixed up in, so don't worry, I'm going to stick to my safe little boutique from now on.'

After Ravi left the pub, she stayed for another half-hour and then set off on a long route home, not heading towards the river as she usually did on her solitary walks but in the other direction, through the maze of residential streets and garden squares with their myriad architectural styles and stark contrasts in housing design and quality. The deck-access blocks of flats reared up behind elegant Georgian and neo-Georgian terraces, and a number of the modern gated developments with their soft-yellow town houses and low-rise apartments had thick coils of barbed wire over the iron gates and high walls.

She didn't believe Ravi's version of events for a moment, but she believed he was genuinely afraid and he hadn't met her willingly. Someone had twisted his arm, thought it important enough to add the verbal warning to her burglary and the interference with the truffles. She couldn't claim to read anyone's mind, but since discovering Junoco she had become more astute at reading emotions, even when the clues seemed discordant. Except she had misjudged it badly with Vicky – unless Vicky's seemingly artless affection for her was still authentic, despite the extreme deception. That was the frustrating teaser, the puzzle and optimistic thought that would in all likelihood never be solved or tested.

As she got near to the high street, the sound of wailing police and ambulance sirens turned into a continuous background din and the street environment became noticeably more dirty and dilapidated. Many of the shops on the main street were closed up, their metal shutters decorated in graffiti, and knots of young men took up the pavement space at almost every street corner. Nobody took any notice of Fran, but they eventually stood aside as she weaved her way through, determined to keep walking straight on and not be forced to step onto the road.

She wasn't aiming for anywhere specific and had no goal, other than to arrive home before Alice returned from the lab. When the main road branched off into a large paved area that would once have been a thriving shopping square but was now full of fast-food joints and sad market stalls, she turned in that direction and wandered towards the disused fountain in the centre. There were a few people milling about and a group was gathered by the fountain, some sitting on its low concrete walls. She stopped to watch, suddenly thinking of Charley, the street girl who had panicked her all those months ago and Kwesi had tried to befriend. What if she had been hooked on Junoco, instead of filthy, toxic drugs and endless cheap alcohol?

'C'mon, sweetheart, come over 'ere and join us!' a man shouted to her, noticing the attention she was paying to the group. He held up a cigarette as if to invite her to have a drag.

Fran emerged from her reverie, acknowledged him with a friendly wave and walked on. She quickened her pace now, suddenly anxious that Alice would be early, although she hadn't had any text alert from her.

As she turned into her street, approaching home from the far end for a change, she saw a sign in Eric and Delia's front garden; their house was up for sale. They hadn't been seen since their arrest, although Marcus said they had been charged with serial animal cruelty and bailed. Now they were leaving for good, which was a tremendous result whatever the eventual outcome of the trial.

Marcus came out of his door and waited on his front path. She pointed at the 'for sale' sign as she approached, and he gave her a thumbs-up.

'Hi, that's fantastic, isn't it, and I was hoping to catch you. Are you still okay for this Friday afternoon at the department? It's at 3.45 but you need to get there a bit early to go through security. And remember – less is more, keep it brief and to the point.'

'Yes, definitely, I will – thank you, Marcus, I really appreciate it.'

She was surprised at her lack of hesitation, her willingness to see this through. Was it irresponsible to push ahead with the meeting, given that it was not only her safety that was at risk? Marcus, Alice, and Ned too, they were all involved. She should ask Marcus if he had seen or heard anything, obviously, but not yet. She didn't want to make him anxious.

She went into the house and straight into the living room, scanning it swiftly. Her eyes alighted on Guacamole, who had shifted his gaze up to the mantelpiece. The antelope had changed its stance and lowered its head, so the spiral horns were facing forwards and its front legs were positioned further apart. Fran stepped backwards, startled by the definitive nature of it, the message that she should stay strong and follow her passion and intuition.

When Alice arrived, Fran had their one-pot dinner ready and had made up the spare bed. She was already convinced by Alice's initial hunch that the truffles had been doctored and, sure enough, the lab tests had confirmed it. There was a second synthetic drug in the mix, an unlicensed hallucinogenic substance that had been injected through a fine needle.

'It wasn't close to a fatal dose, but it would have given you a bad trip at the least and you could have reacted more strongly than they intended.'

'Who was it then, Alice – your Professor Fred, our top villain, Infrared?'

'It's looking that way, although we don't have the proof. This isn't a common substance and Fred would know where to get hold of it. He has a clear motive for wanting to stop you spilling the beans to his precious government contact, assuming that he's controlling her and not the other way round. And another thing – I went along his departmental corridor this afternoon, while waiting for the results, and the porters were clearing out his office, piling stuff onto trolleys. They were getting it ready for someone else to move into on Monday. I asked the secretary what was happening and although she was tight-lipped to start off with, she finally confided that Fred has taken up an offer of a sabbatical visit to another university and she hasn't been told where or for how long.'

'Well, it sounds like someone or something's put the frighteners on him, don't you think? But I'm not backing down now, that's for sure. I'm even more resolute. Are you with me?'

'Are you not scared witless, Fran? This is heavy stuff.'

'I am scared, don't get me wrong, and I'm upset that someone has it in for me. I wouldn't have asked you to stay over otherwise. But honestly, I feel angry more than intimidated and I'm not going to be shot down or knocked out of orbit by this, I'm just not.' She paused. 'But you can distance yourself from it, Alice; I'd quite understand if you wanted to back out.'

'Me? I'm embroiled in it just as much as you, there's no wimping out now. And anyway, I like you too much, I won't abandon you. I can at least promise that.'

'Thank you, Alice – it's a fantastic promise, more than enough.' She raised her hand and they brought their palms together with a grand flourish.

***

The security level was severe, according to the green wall screens in the foyer of the government building; that was probably normal these days. Her photo had been taken, her bags checked, and she was waiting nervously, practising her opening lines and wishing it was all over. What on earth had compelled her into this, driven her to stick her neck out instead of running a mile? What if she dried up, or much worse, if she had got it all wrong and her evidence collapsed like a pack of cards, was reduced to weak conjecture? They were clever, these civil servants, whatever anyone said. And they had power, which of course answered her question about why she was here.

Each time a young official came through the barriers to collect a waiting visitor, Fran jerked forward or half-stood up, she was so on edge. After what seemed an age, but was only fifteen minutes according to the clock, a young man let himself through and picked her out as his likely prospect.

She followed him into the lift and then along a corridor with glass-fronted offices all down one side. Turning the corner, the offices were closed in with proper walls and each had a nameplate on the door; they were obviously for the senior members of staff who didn't have to work in the open-plan area. The young man stopped at one of the doors, knocked lightly and led her into the room. Inside, there were two people: a short, dumpy woman in a loose black trouser suit, very unstylish, and someone Fran had expected and hoped not to see again: Ravi.

The woman introduced herself as Amanda and acknowledged with a throwaway gesture that she knew Ravi and Fran had already met. She dismissed the other young man, who seemed taken aback as he was already opening his tablet to take notes, and the three of them sat down at one end of the table.

'So here we are; we won't stand on ceremony or waste any of our time. There's a jug of water if you need it. You requested to see me, and I believe it's about a research project we are planning – you have a concern about it, something we may be able to clarify.'

Fran's well-prepared opening lines had gone right out of her head. Her strategy was derailed by Ravi's presence, what it meant and whether she should change tack as a consequence. It was too complicated to decide now; she just had to take a deep breath and dive in.

'First of all, thank you for agreeing to see me, Amanda. It's about the Bright Minds project, which I've come across because I work for a company that sells a specialist type of chocolate with unique cognitive-enhancing properties. What I'm concerned about, as you put it, is that the formula to be used within the Bright Minds project contains a new and unlicensed drug. I believed you were unaware of this, although seeing Ravi here I'm not sure of that now. In any event, my own interest in this is very specific. I have no wish to challenge or undermine the project as a whole.'

That was rather good – no wish to challenge or undermine the project. But she was skating on thin ice. Ravi could point out at any moment that the make-up of Junoco and the Bright Minds formula was similar, if not indistinguishable. Amanda's expression was unreadable and Ravi looked impassive, his fingers outstretched on the table again in his characteristic pose. Amanda picked up a pen and made a note on the small pad in front of her, then laid it down again and put her hands together.

'A quite specific interest, you say? What is it, this specific interest?'

Amanda looked and sounded aggressive as she asked the question, or maybe more defensive, it was impossible to tell. Anyway, it felt discomforting and the sooner Fran was able to say her piece and get out, the better.

'My interest is this. I have a doctor friend who has applied for asylum in the UK, been turned down and is waiting to hear the result of his appeal. Put simply, and this is my only demand, I want his appeal to be fast-tracked with a positive result, so he can live and work here.'

Amanda was doodling on the notepad, producing overlapping circular squiggles as Fran set out her demand. Then the doodling stopped, pen in the air, and the two women were locked in an unwavering gaze until Amanda dropped her eyes and spoke again.

'All right, if that's it, I'll arrange it. If there's anything else, let's hear it now.'

'No, there's nothing else. I don't want to be involved any further and I'll keep quiet.'

'Yes, you will keep quiet because if you don't, if you speak to anyone or the story gets out in a damaging and uncontrolled way and it's traced back to you, your friend's refugee status will be revoked overnight and he will face immediate deportation.'

'I understand that, and I accept your terms.'

Surprisingly, Ravi decided to accompany her back down in the lift and see her out through the barriers. This gave her the chance to ask her burning question.

'Why did you approach me, Ravi – such a minor player?'

'I don't work for this department. I got pulled in to investigate what was going on, once suspicions were aroused about information leaks and misinformation being spread about the programme. We thought you were the weakest link, but I have to say, and I sincerely mean this, we were wrong. And I got hammered for letting you turn the tables on us. What you did today, that was a quiet master stroke. It takes a lot to topple Amanda.'

And for the first time, he actually smiled.

Chapter 20

Standing in front of the bedroom mirror, she remembered how indecisive she had been when choosing what to wear to the public lecture on brainpower. Today was different. It was her birthday and Alice had invited her to lunch at a restaurant near her home in North London. Putting together her outfit was easy – the close-fitting blue-and-yellow dress that Daniela had encouraged her to buy, together with a twisted gold belt, short jacket, dangly earrings and ankle boots. She spun round, examining all angles in the mirror. It looked chic and a tad sophisticated, altogether very Vicky. It felt liberating to recognise her inspiration. And another thought, a distinctly odd one – would Vicky look any different in her true identity?

The doorbell rang. It could be Lily, who had gone on a special trip with Petra to choose a birthday present for Fran. It wasn't Lily, though. It was a delivery boy with a bumper bouquet of spring flowers and ferns. The fragrance of the ferns came through strongly as she lifted it to her face, inducing a sudden flashback to the days with her teenage boyfriend, romping in the ferns on the pretext of taking the family dog for a walk.

She carried the bouquet into the kitchen, laying it on the counter while she opened the little envelope with the card, which bore no personal greeting or signature. She turned it over to check it was blank on the back and then filled the vase with water, stuck in the flowers and ferns all at once and stood back to view the result, which was untidy and lopsided. Had she let slip to anyone why she loved ferns so much? It was unlikely, but she couldn't remember.

It might be Vicky; surely anyone else would have included a birthday message, a few words. She wasn't allowed to do that, though; it would be forbidden once she had cut and run. Did that mean she had also disappeared from Andy's life? Yes, it had to; Vicky couldn't maintain any contacts from her undercover existence and Andy must be wondering why, or thinking it was the confrontation with Fran that put paid to it. Did he even think he was doing anything wrong, behaving like that? Was she presuming too much, turning it into something that it was never meant to be?

And Vicky, sitting in bed with him in that dream scene, her foxy smile, who was she? Was she a nice person who had been promoted to the wrong job or was she in the job precisely because she enjoyed the deception and lies, leading people on, winding them in? Did she believe Fran was a legitimate quarry or had she truly been fond of her and overstepped her role because she wanted to be close to her? If she had sent the flowers, what was behind it – what kind of emotion? What was it Fran had said to Vicky in Andy's kitchen? Many contradictory things can be true, all at once. She shouldn't expect consistency. The feeling and the words, they didn't always fit.

She turned on the tap to wash up her breakfast mug and small plate. It was a long, knotty string of questions, with no real answers.

Before leaving the house, she took a peek at the drawing of the sloth she had done before breakfast, following last night's Junoco session. It was the perfect sketch to animate, a languorous pole dance down the tree trunk, limbs and paws slowly extended one after the other.

She looked out for Lily on the street but there was no sign of her, only a young tabby cat padding up to purr round her ankles. A new generation, maybe even a replacement for one of the stolen pets. She decided on the pond route past the green and, as she had hoped, the lines of fluffy yellow ducklings had now appeared, paddling fast to keep up with their aloof but watchful parents.

'*Bonjour*, Jean-Claude,' she said, as he stepped out of the café with a stack of chairs for the few small tables he managed to fit along the inner edge of the pavement. She also had to stop off at the shop to check that all was okay and remind the young sales assistant to unpack the new chocolates, the richer ones she had ordered to keep up with the trend in all the premier chocolate stores. It was fun, having the authority as manager to make these decisions now Daniela was away.

Her direct tube journey to North London took thirty-five minutes. When she arrived at the restaurant, Alice was sitting there with a large, gift-wrapped box on the table.

'Hey, is this for me? You shouldn't have. Can I open it straight away?'

'Yes, get on with it, I can't wait any longer.'

Fran untied the ribbon and tore off the paper, opening the box with a mystified expression before extricating the object from its packaging. It was a black-and-silver robot standing about ten inches high.

'Oh wow, it's beautiful! What does it do?'

She pressed a couple of buttons and lights started flashing, blue, red and white. She had a sudden sense of déjà vu. She knew this robot creature, had met it before and followed it, perhaps in a dream?

'It's one of the most advanced bots,' said Alice, 'or so I've been told. It has speech recognition and learns to anticipate requests and instructions. It's a reader as well, and will fetch and carry, pick things up, do a spot of housework, feed the cat, organise your love life, who knows? You can read the booklet.'

'It's mind-boggling – thank you, Alice, you're so sweet, such a perfect present. I think I'll start a collection, buy one every year to track how they evolve.'

'Lovely idea – history, as it happens. I want to come over and play with it too, if you let me. Now, let's have a bottle of birthday bubbly to get us going.'

As they raised their wine glasses, Fran was reminded of her first meeting with Alice and Professor Fred, after the lecture when he was so tipsy.

'I must ask you about Fred, what's happened to him, but before I do, I've had a thought about robots, how we're all in danger of falling in love with machines, inanimate objects. Ned claims to be in love with his smart fridge and he'll make anything it suggests. I'm in love with my mole friend Guacamole, if you can call him inanimate. He's somewhere in between. What about you, Alice? What thing are you most in love with?'

'That's a good question, I've no idea. I expect for most people now, it has to be their phone because it is their gateway to other worlds. For me, being rather old-fashioned, it's probably the radio. Anyway, just for you, Fran, I do have an update on our Professor Fred. He's supposedly on sabbatical for twelve months and we haven't been given any contact details. The research project is on hold for the time being, although I think they might be reshaping it; that's the rumour.'

'Reshaping it?'

'Well, it might be retargeted at a narrower group, not the cleverest children but the least academic ones. They're making a calculated judgement, I think, about how parents will react, how curious they'll be about what's going on. And cognitive-enhancing drugs tend to have a bigger effect on the bottom thirty per cent, the people who struggle most intellectually. I shouldn't be saying any of this, but I trust you and I have to talk to someone.'

'I feel the same way, Alice, about you and Junoco. My trust has taken a bashing in the last while, but it's still intact and I've learnt some lessons about how to respond when it does break down. Without Junoco, I'd be spinning like a top.'

'There are whispers that the Home Office is interested, thinking about how to get prisoners off legal highs and give them a curiosity boost instead.'

'Really – that's fascinating! They'd have to offer outlets for creativity too, of the non-criminal kind I mean. But going back to children and the Bright Minds study, I may have played a part in the reshaping you just mentioned.'

'What do you mean? Is this to do with your assignation on holiday?'

'Yes, it is, indirectly. Osvaldo gave me the name of the senior civil servant involved in the project and let on that she was based in the Home Office, not in education or health as I'd assumed. This fits with what you said just now – maybe the Home Office has taken charge. Osvaldo also let slip that the civil servant didn't know that the compound they're planning to use, a variant of Junoco, contains an unlicensed synthetic drug. When I got home, I saw my chance and managed to contrive a meeting with her. Marcus next door set it up for me.'

'What chance – your chance to do what? I'm not following you.'

'I know – it's a sideways leap. It's for Kwesi, who's been waiting forever to hear the outcome of his asylum appeal. I went to the Home Office and struck a deal with the woman, to get his appeal through.' She stopped talking to top up their glasses with the remaining champagne.

'What did you say?' Alice affected a husky drawl. '"Give me the money or I'll shoot"?'

'Yes, in so many words. I said his appeal had to be fast-tracked with a positive result, so he can stay in London and work as a doctor.'

'Smart move – how did she respond?'

'She was quietly fuming, but she agreed to do it. And she said if the story gets out through me, she'll have his refugee status revoked and he'll be deported. That's her hold over me.'

'Yikes, that's some deal! Does Kwesi know yet?'

'Yes, he's had confirmation by letter and he's over the moon, as you can imagine; says he always had faith in British justice.'

'Nice one – and was that it? Or did you intend to stop the whole project in its tracks, make the government row back or change course on Bright Minds? I guess it's going to make them think, anyway, now they know the cat's out of the bag.'

'Well, maybe it will but my only aim was to win it for Kwesi, take advantage of the information I had and use it to his benefit. Bright Minds is too big for me to go into battle with and I'd only get crushed. I'm not prepared to put my life on the line, and the burglary and near-poisoning did unnerve me, I won't deny it. And anyway, it would be hypocritical of me to rail against Bright Minds while developing a new enterprise using a similar product.'

'So you are going into business with Ned, then – you've accepted his offer?'

'It's irresistible, yes. Junoco has done wonders for me personally, it's made me stronger in so many ways and by the time Daniela closed the site down, we had umpteen inspirational stories about its effects, how it enriches people's lives.'

'Reinvention by chocolate, then – everyone's wildest dream.'

'Alice, I love you!' Fran blew her a kiss. 'Still, I do believe it's wrong to push it onto kids because of their immature brains and lack of choice. And I can't support an experiment in social engineering where the participants are ignorant of what's going on.'

'But surely the Junoco customers are ignorant of key facts and being hoodwinked, aren't they? I presume it will still be marketed as wholly natural, whatever that means.'

'Exactly, whatever it means. Look, we've talked loads about this and we both know the moral compass spins all over the place. Like, there's an asthma treatment now, it's selling legally on the open market with an advertised "secret ingredient". Who knows what is in it, whether it's harmless? Anyway, I'm insisting we don't make any such claim about being "wholly natural" in our new business and Ned has agreed. He has no qualms either way. As you said in your public lecture, humans have taken mind-altering drugs down the ages, deciding the rewards outweigh the risks or just because it's the thing to do and they enjoy it.'

Alice unfolded her arms and sat back, her posture relaxed again. 'Okay, you're right. I'm not sure if I included in the lecture that dope dealers emerged in the Bronze Age, when nomadic herders got into horse riding and began to transport cannabis along with their other trading goods. It goes back a hell of a long way.'

They chatted on about other things and it was after three o'clock when they left the near-empty restaurant and parted to go home. Feeling a little light-headed, Fran sauntered to the tube station and didn't run for the first train because she knew she might easily misjudge the closing doors.

When she stepped onto the next one and placed the robot box on the seat beside her, a man appeared at the far end of the carriage. He was swaying down the aisle as the train moved off and she noticed he too was carrying an unwieldy package, now revealed to be a box of wine bottles. He half-threw himself across the seats opposite her, barely managing to keep the box from dropping to the floor. Then he looked up, rearranged his slipped spectacles and beamed openly at her. She smiled back, indulging his gaucheness while taking in his distinguished features, kind eyes and razor-short grey hair.

'*Bonjour*, Madame. You like Chardonnay?'

'No, no I don't, not at all. *Toujours* Sauvignon.'

'*Fantastique* – I have Sauvignon also.' He opened the box, pulled out a bottle and handed it across to her.

'What's this – a surprise birthday present?' She held back from taking it.

'It is your birthday? It is my birthday tomorrow – we will celebrate. This is why I have the wine with me today, for your birthday. I import wine from France, it is my business. I am Sebastien, and you?'

She hesitated, turning over this simple question as he leant forward to shake hands.

'Francesca. It's nice to meet you, Sebastien, but I can't take your wine, just like that. You need it for your own birthday, if that's tomorrow.'

'I insist; please accept it, Francesca – my surprise gift, as you say.'

'Thank you then, I will. It's very generous of you. I have another ten stops to go.'

That was odd, telling him. Sebastien didn't miss a beat.

'*Moi aussi* – perhaps we are living near each other. Will you have a drink with me before we go home?'

She laughed and nodded her agreement. It was mid-afternoon on her birthday. She was planning a quiet evening in, but that could still happen later. There was nothing to stop her from being spontaneous, if she felt so inclined.

By the time they got off the train and up to pavement level, they were flirting madly and she suggested he wait outside the café while she bought cakes and then he might like to come home for tea with her.

'Ah yes, you English, always your tea and cakes. That will be *superbe!*'

'They're French cakes, actually, from my favourite French café.' It was obvious he didn't live round here.

They walked slowly past the green towards her street, with Fran pointing out various landmarks as if she had lived here all her life. That was exactly how it felt – her familiar home territory with its favourite haunts and hang-outs.

She was pleased not to bump into Lily this time, as she didn't want to put her off again and Lily always had a wary response to Fran's new friends. As she and Sebastien came nearer, she saw a cluster of balloons hanging beside her front door. She found her key, but before she could insert it in the lock, the door opened and Marcus was standing there.

'What, Marcus? Has something happened?'

Despite the swinging balloons, her first thought was of disaster, some dreadful consequence of the Eric and Delia horror story or the burglary, although she had kept that last episode from Marcus and Kwesi.

'Yes, it's your birthday and we're having a big party!' This was Lily, coming up from behind Marcus and pushing herself into the door frame beside him.

Fran turned round to Sebastien, who seemed amused and not in the least fazed or put out. She dismissed her half-formulated apology and put an arm around his shoulder, still holding her robot box in the other.

'Hey, Sebastien, the party's already begun. We're late.'

'Come on in,' said Marcus. 'Hi, Sebastien, Marcus – and this is Lily. Thank you for having the foresight to bring the wine!'

'And this is Sahara!' added Lily, thrusting the long-suffering creature forward.

Fran could hear the buzz of conversation and, as they got close to the living-room door, a long drum roll and a jumbled start to *Happy Birthday*. She put down the box before turning into the room and extending her arms in a gesture of welcome and appreciation. It was too much to take in at once. She had to scan the room for several seconds while the guests finished their singing and came forward to greet her and Sebastien. There was Ned in his sexy pink shirt, and Alice, who must have leapt into a taxi to arrive ahead of her, then Petra and Kwesi and, most surprising and gratifying of all, Eleanor, Cerise and Uncle George.

Marcus came in with a tray of champagne to toast the birthday girl, and the next two hours passed in a haze of headiness. It was delightful to see the new connections being made; the ones that Fran might have predicted but had never imagined would actually be forged. Lily was talking earnestly to Uncle George; that one she had pre-imagined. Kwesi was deep in conversation with Cerise, who was wearing a crazily elaborate hat, while Eleanor chatted on the sofa with Alice and Marcus. Ned stood by the door with Petra and Sebastien, speaking in a fluid mix of English, French and German. Even Fran's mole-mate Guacamole was in on the party, observing everything from his perch on the largest of Kwesi's drums.

When the doorbell went, Ned waved across to her and disappeared to answer it. Fran followed, but stopped transfixed in the hall when she heard the voices and then saw the two figures on the doorstep, large rucksacks at their feet.

'Mum! We're home!'

Ned leant back against the wall and then picked up the rucksacks while Max and Chaddy rushed in and overwhelmed Fran with a double hug. She dissolved into tears as she held them tight and heard their enthusiastic explanations.

'We wanted to give you a surprise. It's so brill that you're at home.'

'At first we thought maybe we ought to warn you, but it seemed more fun just to show up. We met at the airport. Hey, and this is cool, all these people.'

Fran looked past them to Ned, who was trapped by the door and visibly moved by the family scene in front of him. When the threesome's huddle finally broke up, Fran said it was the best birthday surprise ever and ushered them into the living room to say hello to everyone. Ned walked forward as she wiped her eyes, ready to make her entrance again.

'Hold on. Are you okay? No need to rush, they're having a whale of a time.'

She almost fell against him, put her hands on his shoulders and reached up on tiptoe for a proper kiss.

'Oh, Ned, it's all gone mad.'

'Today, beautiful Francesca, you are the luckiest woman on the planet and you deserve it, every bit. But what's with this French guy, the dashing Sebastien? I have to ask – does he have any idea what he's getting into?'

'I met him on the train, on the way back from having lunch with Alice.'

'That's no answer.' He smiled, teasing and almost wistful.

At that moment, Chaddy and Max reappeared from the living room.

'Mum, come on! Everyone's waiting. It's champagne-and-birthday-cake time!'

She put her arms around them and they squeezed along the hallway, with Ned following close behind. Just before they went in to join the party, she half-turned to give an answer to his question, but amidst the rising swell of music and laughter, he didn't catch what it was.